Pride of Eagles

Part IV of the
Autobiography of Empress Alexandra

by

Kathleen McKenna Hewtson

ISBN-10:   1546671706

ISBN-13:   978-1546671701

'Pride of Eagles: *Part IV of The Autobiography of Empress Alexandra*' is published by Taylor Street Books.

Chapter 1

Anya looked so young and innocent, and confused and dreadful, on her wedding day.

Nicky and I had decided to pay for both the wedding and Anya's dress, as Anya's father, although a court official, was not a wealthy man. Also, I suppose, to be wholly truthful, since the marriage itself had been brought about almost solely through my own efforts, I felt some responsibility for the affair.

In fact, the entire winter just past had been overtaken by Anya and her dramas, so much so that there had been many times when I had thought of simply nodding my head, throwing up my hands, and saying, "Yes, Anya, end the engagement and have it your way."

That I did not do so, I think, reflects how completely fond I was of Anya and how much I needed her, my only real friend in this strange land I had come to as a bride. I had missed her terribly the preceding year and had planned to have her back at court, but then I was informed by Count Fredericks of the most vile gossip imaginable circulating about us. He said that 'people' – and by that I knew he meant the social flotsam and jetsam of Saint Petersburg – were accusing Anya and me of prosecuting the most unnatural sort of relationship that can occur between two women.

I had feared gossip and judgment since my first days in Russia, and as Job once said, "The thing you have feared has come upon you," by which I mean that none of the terror and resentment I felt against Nicky's family and his court was unwarranted. I was not, as my mother-in-law frequently put it, paranoid. They hated me. They had judged me and found me wanting.

It had started when I was just a young girl of seventeen, when the sweet little childish love that Nicky and I had formed when I was a mere twelve and he a handsome sixteen year old, became apparent. There has always been something about me that has repelled some people rather than drawn them toward me, and while I was never unaware of this fact, I had not felt it forcibly until I came to Russia.

Before that, I had just been a girl living in Hesse-Darmstadt, where my little family had always made me feel loved and wanted, and in England with my dearest Grandmamma, where I had felt the same.

When Russian society, the court and Nicky's family had first rejected me, I used bravely to tell myself, 'It is not really me they do not like. It's that I am new to them and I cannot speak Russian at all or French [the court language] very well,' but you can only tell yourself a thing so many times before you stop believing it in the face of contrary evidence.

The reality was that all the Romanov brides over the previous century had been foreigners, and probably could not speak the language much either, and had dressed differently, and maybe, like me, enjoyed Wagner's music, and did not know how to dance the Mazurka, but they had been accepted and even loved, as Nicky's mother was.

My sister Ella had arrived in Russia a decade earlier to marry Nicky's Uncle Sergei. She and I were not too distinct from one another in appearance, clothing, mannerisms and taste, and yet she had been greatly loved almost from Day One, and this despite having rejected conversion to the Russian Orthodox faith for years and years. I had converted right away, and more, I had embraced my new country's religion with true fervor, but in Russia, when it came to me, all was wrong and twisted.

Nicky's mother loved clothes and ordered them by the trunk-load from Paris and Petersburg. The people said she was gay and charming, and that you could recognize her by her carriage a mile away. She loved to dance and they said she was Russia's brightest light. My sister was so vain about her beauty that she would not wear a dress twice, and they said she was luminous. *My* fashion choices, on the other hand, were called frumpy and fussy, and either too extravagant or too plain.

My grandmamma was the very name of the age we lived in, and I had spent a great deal of my youth in England and considered it to be my second home. In consequence of this, I had decorated our rooms at the Winter Palace, and then at our dear Alexander Palace here at Tsarskoe Selo, in the fashions that had always surrounded me, whereupon the sharpest voices of Russian society piped up as one, claiming to be scandalized by my bourgeois taste, this despite their having identically crowded Victorian drawing rooms of their own.

Minnie was called an exemplary mother, as was her sister, England's Queen Alexandra. They both obviously enjoyed and adored their children and they were praised for that. I adored each of my babies, and even nursed them myself, but for that I was called "the old woman in the shoe." Oh, I knew – or I thought I knew – why

7

nobody really liked me: I had not had a son yet; ten years, four beautiful little girls, all healthy and wonderful, but no heir, no precious boy.

I prayed, I tried, I turned to men of God, and at last I had what I wanted, what I thought everyone had wanted – Alexei, my beautiful, beautiful boy. However, he had been born with the disease I gave him, that my grandmamma had given to my mama, and that I, in my darkest moments, feared I had given in my turn to my girls. I used to lose myself in prayers that turned to tears, and sometimes to hysterics, and eventually to the breaking of my own heart over what I might have passed down to my children, but no one knew about this besides Nicky and his ghastly mother, and even she would not have told anyone about that.

No, Minnie, much as I knew she despised me, would never let the world know that the Romanovs now carried tainted blood. That she blamed and hated me for it, I even at times understood; not that it made it easier, but sometimes I knew why. What I did not know was why everyone else did. My giving them what they thought was a perfect boy, the exquisite boy portrayed on every postcard in Russia, should have made them like me, should have led them to forgive me for crimes I did not know I had committed, but it didn't, and so at last I understood all.

It was actually just me, for myself, that everyone hated ... and it truly was everyone. Nicky's family despised me – well, primarily his mother, but as the whole Romanov clan lay firmly under her tiny thumb, that was sufficient. Those who did not actually find me repellent said and acted as though they did, so if somewhere in their secret hearts they might have liked me, or at least pitied me, I certainly was unaware of it. Nicky's sister Xenia was a dear, and ironically the only one of his family whom I thought was really fond of me, but she had six sons, six perfect sons, so ruddy with health and Romanov height, and good looks and high spirits, that the very mention of their names, let alone the sight of them, turned me to stone.

Then there was her husband Sandro, so handsome, with the usual towering height and booming voice that came with the Romanov pedigree. He was considered within the family to be intelligent and ambitious, so he was disliked for the former and hypocritically gossiped about for the latter.

Once upon a time, when I had come to Russia as a young bride some thirteen years earlier, this couple had been Nicky's and my closest companions. Xenia had ignored her mother's dislike of me, and Sandro and I had been united by it, as Minnie, a truly jealous mother, had not wanted anyone to come before her in her daughter's affections. Xenia and I had shared our first pregnancies together. We had had our little girls – my Olga and her Irinia – a month apart, and it had all been such fun, but then it had started to go wrong.

I suppose at first it was Minnie saying how much prettier Irinia was than Olga, and Xenia not disagreeing with her. Then there had been the disaster during our coronation week at Khodynka Field with its thousands of dead. Sandro had told Nicky to blame Sergei, my sister Ella's husband and one of my few defenders in the family. I had taken Sergei's side. Nicky had not punished Sergei and Sandro had never really thought much of me since then.

Still, Xenia had remained my friend. It was I who chose to pull away from her when the birth of my third daughter coincided with the birth of her third son in as many years. Each subsequent birth only caused me to become more envious of her, an envy that somehow turned into an aversion. When she responded to my increasing coldness toward her by acting puzzled and hurt, I dismissed her yet further from my thoughts as lacking the necessary intelligence and common sense to deserve my society.

Nicky's younger siblings had not much counted with me when I had first come to Russia as a bride because they were so young. Well, not Georgie, Nicky's nearest in age and favorite brother, but poor Georgie had become sick with consumption and had gone to live far away, and then had died, and I had never truly got to know him before he was gone forever. Nicky's other brother Michael – "Misha," as they called him in the family, or more pathetically "Flopsy" – had been a dear boy, a sweet boy, whom I had loved immediately. Michael-Misha-Flopsy had returned my affection, as he did everyone's, with the cheerful nature of an indulged puppy, which is what he was in truth. But then I hadn't had a son, and I had continued not having a son, and Georgie was dead, and suddenly good old Flopsy was Nicky's heir because not one of my four girls could inherit the throne according to the dictates of Salic Law. After that I never called him "Misha" again. Nicky did, of course, he adored him, but to me he was both a threat and a reproach, and he was always the Grand Duke and Tsarevich Michael to me.

Even someone who is congenitally dimwitted and unaware of all but himself is going to notice eventually that he is not liked, and so it came to be with Michael, but he was such a silly, spoiled young man that he seemed to shrug this off with the attitude that if I didn't like him, it must be because there was something wrong with me, not him. After all, people were always telling him that I was not quite right, and after a bit he seemed to agree with them. None of this touched his life of playing soldiers in the elite Cuirassier Blues regiment of his mother and the endless rounds of mindless enjoyment that made up his life; he simply did not waste his time coming to visit his brother at Tsarskoe Selo, even though Nicky loved him so, and this too I was blamed for, mostly by Nicky's youngest sister, awkward little Olga.

Olga had been a wee child when I had come to Russia. Fourteen years younger than Nicky, she had been such a sweet, lively little girl ... a funny-looking little one too, as she had inherited none of the good looks of her awful mother, or of any of her outstanding Romanov ancestors. She, in fact looked like a miniature version of her ungainly, potato-nosed giant of a father, who all whispered was a throwback to some distant mating of a lecherous former tsar and a bear. Well, to be fair, he truly had resembled a peasant in every sense, his habits included. Olga looked as though she should have been born in a hut somewhere, not in the palace of Gatchina.

Minnie was so obviously appalled by her youngest child's lack of beauty, and by her open, boisterous ways, that I had made a special attempt to be kind to her from the first. She had responded eagerly to my interest in her, and after Nicky and I had married and started living at Anichkov with her and Minnie and Michael, she had followed us about until I had begun to find her a little tiresome, but I remained fond of her.

Given the wide differences in our ages, though, we lost touch after Nicky and I moved to Tsarskoe Selo. She was far too young to come and visit us on her own and I did not like to visit Minnie, and then my babies began to come, so little Olga was only a presence at whatever Romanov gathering I could not avoid. When she was barely eighteen, the odious Minnie married her off to a much older, openly homosexual man, Peter Oldenburg.

I have reflected a great deal upon Olga's marriage to a man she neither loved nor knew. Minnie had cynically imposed this particular marriage on her daughter only because she wanted to keep her in town as a sort of glorified handmaiden. Minnie had a history of trying to hold onto her daughters, and had previously acted as though her elder daughter, Xenia, was being kidnapped and sent away to some faraway land when she and Sandro had fallen in love. Selfishly, she had even gone so far as to delay their wedding as long as possible, and although Sandro and Xenia would have been perfectly happy to live in their palace in Petersburg, Minnie had so monopolized Xenia's time that Sandro had taken her off to live most of the year on his estate in the Crimea, Ai Todor, where they could carve out some semblance of privacy for themselves. Minnie had apparently vowed not to make the same mistake again, so she married off her younger daughter early to a man old enough to be her father, a dissolute and unnatural man besides, who was known to like men in an ungodly way, doing all this so that she could keep her near her and under her thumb.

At the time, shocked and dismayed by the horror I was witnessing, I had asked Nicky to refuse Peter Oldenburg's suit on his young sister's behalf, but predictably he did no such thing – Nicky never went against his mother's decisions – so poor Olga had married and vanished into the palace next to her mother's, her bright spirits dimming by the day.

I still saw Olga occasionally. She and Nicky had remained very close and she liked to come to Tsarskoe Selo of a Sunday to see him and the girlies and Baby, and to have lunch *en famille*, but I was usually too ill to attend these lunches, and so mostly we communicated through friendly little notes. I suspected, though, that when she was not visiting us, she amused her mother by passing on gossip about me, as everyone did. It was nearly *de rigeur* to do so.

My own sister and I had never been close, or not since I had been a little girl myself and she the glamorous, beautiful older sister who had, I thought, adored and cosseted me, but once I came to Russia and became the Empress, I realized she had only been patronizing me. Her husband had been an odd man and yet a true friend to me, but after his violent death Ella and I had little left to say to each other.

I had made friends with the eccentric, dark Montenegrin Sisters mostly because they were the sole members of Russian society who had ever bothered to be nice to me or to show an interest in what I thought or did, and they probably only went this far because Nicky's prickly mother, who ran her own court, did not like them and therefore drove them to turn to me for social advancement.

I liked them, though; at least I think I did. Who can really know what or whom one likes or loves if one never gets to meet anyone? They asked me over to teas and dinners, and I went.

Nicky enjoyed these outings, for he was naturally sociable, and after a very few years the Montenegrins became our only friends, although it is questionable whether Nicky liked Mitsia or Stana's husbands much as they were somewhat unprepossessing, but at least they shot billiards with him and never spoke of politics, something he hated.

Mitsia and Stana were truly different from other people I had met in Russia and interesting to me because of their fascination with all things occult and spiritual. My darling mama had believed completely in this and had indeed spent the few years I shared with her on earth communicating with her dead papa, Prince Albert, and later with my lost little brother, Frittie. So I had long known that there was great truth and power in the unseen.

Although my relationship with the Montenegrins eventually became strained, I will remain forever grateful to them, for it was through them that I met my first great friend in Russia, Philippe Vachot, my Msgr. Philippe, the man whose prayers and directions brought my son to me. His holy presence, and Mitsia and Stana's belief in him, had kept us close, and then Stana fell in love with Nicky's favorite cousin, Grand Duke Nicholas Nikolaevich, a man I at times admired and at other times feared and detested, but his relationship with Stana brought us all closer still as Nicky adored the company of the Grand Duke. Then Msgr. Philippe died and Alexei was born, and it became nearly impossible for me to see anyone at all except Anya.

Anya had come to me as a lady-in-waiting, or as they called them here, a *"freilina."* Freilinas were a perpetually annoying feature of court life, at least of *my* court life. If I had been a stupid, frivolous woman like my mother-in-law, or my sister-in-law Xenia, I could have made use out of the silly young creatures that were sent to me, to learn, I suppose, how to be a lady of the court. If one were like Minnie and Xenia and the other ladies whose custom it was to parade from palace to palace calling on the same women they had seen the night before at dinner, then one's freilina could come in quite handy as someone who could hold one's wrap or leave one's calling card if the person called upon were not at home. At balls, she could hold one's flowers and the rest of the time she could occupy herself by sitting in whichever room her Empress or Grand Duchess was in and stare at her adoringly until something terribly exciting arose, such as her being called upon to do something.

Given this, my freilinas were a great nuisance to me, for I was either pregnant and very sick, or nursing my babies and wanted to be alone with them and Nicky, or really I just simply could not think of what to do with them, and they made it no easier for me by staring at me non-stop and inquiring what seemed to be every other minute, "Is there something I can do for Your Majesty?"

If I had been able to answer them truthfully, I would have said, 'Yes, go away, that is what you can do for me." However, given my low standing within society and the muttering that had started up against me from the day of my arrival in Russia, this I could not afford to do.

Then I had been sent Anya who was quite a different kettle of fish from the first, making an utter spectacle of herself and getting every single thing wrong, prompting the other young freilinas to view her in the same vaguely disgusted and suspicious way that society eyed me. Naturally I was enchanted by her. In addition, she turned out to be a born, if accidental, comic and Nicky, to my delight, enjoyed her as much as I did. Thinking that I had the same rights as any other woman, I made her my friend, part member of our family, part daughter, part court jester, and my dearest companion.

That was too much for the court and Petersburg society who demanded indignantly what this "ordinary, vacant-faced, fat girl of limited intelligence" had that they, massively cultured, beautiful, and amazingly gifted as they were, had not. How could this be natural and above board? And if it wasn't "natural," then it must be … stifled gasp, averted eyes, whispered utterances … "unnatural."

Yes, of course, any true and lasting friendship that I made could only be wrong and twisted in some way. It was not, though. It was lovely between Anya and me. All the things I liked, she liked too. She played four-handed on my pianos with me. She cheerfully sat embroidering beside me for hours, and when I would

16

criticize her stitching and say she needed to unpick it all, she would nod and giggle and stuff a cake in her mouth and speak around it, and make me happy – happy with myself and happy with her. She agreed with me on every subject and took my side in every dispute, and although I suspected she did not understand a great deal of what I said, she never let on by a word or an expression that she wasn't entirely content simply to be with me.

If that is not what another person would consider innocent friendship, then I pity them, for if there is a shred of honesty in a person's soul, they will admit that all of us are the same, no matter how exalted or humble our status. We all want to be liked and agreed with, but that sadly seems to be the very rarest of things to find, in humanity at least.

My situation as the wife and mother of our own dear family verged on perfection. I did have this, and I was never ungrateful for it, but saying a thing verges on the perfect is also a way of avoiding what one does not like to look at too closely. It means we have tried, and it can mean we have failed, and in many ways I had failed – we had failed, I should better say.

I had just turned thirty-five. This seemed a great age to me and there were moments that I felt older than time itself. I wasn't that old, of course. Thirty-five is not old by any standard, but it did mean that Nicky and I had now known each other – and at least for my own part, loved each other – for twenty-three of those years. My love for Nicky had changed over time, though. I had been a little girl who had fallen deeply, hopelessly in love with a handsome young prince, and in those years after I first met him, I was filled with every sort of girlish musing, sketching a thousand pictures of brides and of castles, and imagining our entire fairytale life together. Then, when I was seventeen, we fell in love most truly, or so I thought. He asked me to be his bride and I oh-so-happily assented.

He was handsome and appeared to be the very epitome of what a prince should be. He was just twenty-one then and was universally adored. Everyone who looked at him, me included, saw limitless possibilities in him, all that was and could be for the best for Russia and its tens of millions of peoples. I was well then and he twirled me through dances, and drove me in sledges over the snowy roads and under the most star-filled winter skies imaginable. Basking in what seemed the whole world's approval of him, even I began to shine a little bit, or so I thought

But I was wrong for no one approved of me. Young and in love, and terribly innocent, and so filled with love for Nicky and certain of our glorious future together, I did not see the smirks behind the smiles nor the disdain and gossiping behind the courtly pleasantries.

Even then they whispered that I was stiff and unfriendly, and that I danced and walked as though I had a rod stuck up inside my dresses, dresses which, they were only all too quick to point out, were frumpy and unflattering. Maybe that was why Nicky had pretended our engagement had not happened. He never mentioned it in his letters, and if he spoke to his parents about it, he did not say anything to me. Nor did I ask him why he had done that because a girl cannot really ask. How could I say, 'Have you rejected me? Do you not love me any longer?' No, if a girl has any pride, and I will admit to having a great deal of it, she holds her head up and pretends none of it is happening, that nothing ever did happen.

Which is what I did, and soon I began to receive sweet, chatty letters from my "dear friend Nicky." I was also in correspondence with Xenia, with whom I had made friends, and she regularly used to allude to Nicky's being "lovesick" for me, but his letters never said as much. In the meantime, Ella and Sergei had decided, for whatever their reasons were, that it would be a good idea for Nicky to marry me. To this end, they spoke of my many virtues to Nicky each time they saw him to counter those who suggested otherwise. They encouraged him to write to me, and convinced me during their visits to Hesse-Darmstadt and through their letters that I should write back to him, that he did indeed love me, and that it was just that he was facing so much opposition to his suit for my hand. As Sergei pointed out, Nicky was unused to going up against people and it would take time for him to learn to stiffen his resolve, but I was never to forget that he loved me deeply and wanted me for his wife.

I was torn in half. I loved him, and if it was true that he loved me too but was simply afraid of opposition, was it not my duty to hold firm?

We began to write to each other in a funny little code. I called him "Pelly One" and he called me "Pelly Two." When Ella and Sergei invited me back the next summer, my eighteenth, I said yes, this visit would decide things. Nicky and I would be together in the summer fields at Sergei and Ella's beautiful dacha in Illinskoe, but he never came, not once that summer. Instead he sent me one – *one* – note of regret for his absence and this was addressed to Sergei and Ella with a postscript of, "best love to Alix. Tell her I so regret being unable to visit but I am all under it with Guards duty this summer."

Ella tried, unsuccessfully, not to gloat, which I found maddening as the whole idea of renewing my romance with Nicky had been her idea. Sergei remained quiet and I counted the days until I could return to Hesse-Darmstadt. This time I would not think of, speak of, or write to Nicky again.

This was easier than I had initially thought. I went to Grandmamma and became involved in avoiding my strange Cousin Eddie's advances, then those of Max of Baden, these having been Grandmamma's ideas of mates for me. Then my papa, my dearest one, died abruptly and I was plunged into the deepest mourning of my life. When Ella and Sergei came to Hesse-Darmstadt for the funeral, and dared to raise Nicky's name at such a time, telling me that he pined for me again, I turned my face to the wall.

My darling Ernie, my sweet brother, supported my desire to remain at home, mourn Papa, not marry anyone, and be his best friend and companion. Ernie was as lost as I at Papa's passing and nearly bent double under the weight of his new responsibilities as Hesse-Darmstadt's Grand Duke, and we shared three years of perfect healing amity together.

Not that I wasn't asked about my intentions because I was, by Grandmamma, by Xenia, and by Nicky – all the time by Nicky – inquiring as to whom I might choose to marry when my mourning period was over. Nicky, it was now said, had fallen terribly, irrevocably in love with me again, or as he put it, "My entire life will be spoilt if you say no, my dearest little girly."

Did I still love him? Well, it seemed that I did; I was somewhat sure that I did. No, I knew. I did know, yes. I loved him. He was the only person I had ever wanted to marry, so that meant I did indeed love him, but...

... I was happy with Ernie in Hesse-Darmstadt; I was happy in my Lutheran faith; and no one at all, it seemed, cared if I were never to marry at all by then, least of all my dearest Ernie who needed me so very much, and I do love to be needed. I was his constant companion and his hostess, and in the latter role I felt comfortable, even joyful, presiding over our little dinner parties when other Landgraves and other members of our family came to see us.

This, of course, puzzled seemingly everyone – besides Grandmamma. She and I were kindred spirits. She knew that a great throne meant nothing without love, which was why I had turned down Eddie and England, the country of my heart. She might have been called the "Grandmother of Europe" for arranging marriages, but, great position or not, she did not want Russia for me and she strengthened my resolve by reversing everything she had ever told me about the importance of love.

"Yes, Alicky, mine was the greatest love story of our times, possibly of all times. My dearest, dearest Albert and I were matched by God and there has been no love to compare with ours. You tell me that your little heart longs for Nicky, and I am sure he is a good young man, but it can never be. You must see that."

I was not sure that I did, so she reminded me of the undeniable fact that neither Sasha nor Minnie – Nicky's parents – seemed to like or want me much.

"What happiness can come from a non-united family, and you so young and innocent. You would be all alone there, with only poor Nicky, who, I hear, is not one to contradict his parents, and nor should he," she added strongly, Grandmamma being a great believer in obedience. "But this does mean, Alicky, that you cannot expect him to stand up for you."

It was odd. I did not like her saying that at all, but I was not in the habit of disagreeing with Grandmamma; no one who wished to remain in her good graces ever did. And then, too, I thought she was right.

I loved Nicky because I was in the habit of loving him by then, I think. I had met a charming young prince as a little girl, and his gentle sweetness had made any other gentleman after that seem crude, and when I looked at Ella's marriage to Sergei, I saw a once-happy young woman who lived under the complete domination of her husband. She said she could not wish it any other way, it was as God willed, she loved him and she proved it through her obedience to him, it could be no different ... but I thought it could.

I thought if one was going to marry at all, one should have love and happiness, and I knew myself enough to know that having no will of my own would create the opposite of that.

I did not mind Nicky's easy ways, nor did I think they mattered. His parents were young. They were also, excepting Grandmamma, the most powerful people on earth. If I did decide to marry Nicky, and if his parents did decide to approve of the marriage – and I did not truly think either would happen – but if it did, then not much would be expected of Nicky and me for years and years. We might even be very old, like my Uncle Bertie and Aunt Alexandra, before we were called upon. People in England said jokingly behind their backs that Grandmamma might even outlive everyone and that there would never be a King Edward at all.

Young women, no matter what their station in life, can never inquire about their future daily lives when a young man proposes. I did not like to do so either, so when it came to pass that Grandmamma rather abruptly decided that my brother Ernie must be married, and to my detestable cousin Ducky of all people, I was aghast at the prospective change in my circumstances and my future prospects.

Providence or fate intervened there, and then again when Nicky's rudely healthy papa became suddenly ill. Now his parents said he must marry, to help to mature him, to help prepare him to rule, should the worst happen, whereupon Nicky, having rather rewritten his memories, stated that he had never loved anyone but me and that I was the only one he would have – it would be Alix or no one at all. Apparently I was better than no one at all, so his parents graciously consented to his proposing to me.

I really did not want to marry Nicky by that time. I was twenty-two and somewhat settled in my ways, a devout Lutheran, and maybe, yes, a devout spinster. The entire world knows how I continued to refuse him, until my defenses were broken down by his impassioned pleas

23

and tireless professions of his love for me, but that is not the whole story, for feeling I had little to lose in this matter, I did indeed ask him what our lives together would be like if we were to marry. The question confused him, clearly, but after a while he said that he supposed we could live exactly as we wished.

He did not think at the time that his father was terminally ill. He could not imagine it, and so nor did I. However, his father did die, and Nicky became Emperor, and made me the Empress of the largest stretch of land on God's earth, and from that day forward I had to struggle with all my might to do as Nicky had said we might, to live how we wanted, and yet it had never truly happened.

Yes, after a perfectly punishing year of living under his mother's roof at Anichkov, we moved to our dear Alexander Palace, but for several years in the beginning we were forced to spend a large part of the year at the vast, forbidding Winter Palace in the capital, where I was hated and where I hated to be. Only a near revolution freed us to live at Tsarskoe Selo. If I always got my own way, as people claimed, if I ruled the roost, then I certainly did not see it that way.

All of this I explained to Anya when she shared her girlish doubts and fears with me about getting married herself, although she did not put it quite like that. Rather she said, "I won't do it. I won't marry him. I'd like to marry Dmitri, but if you won't allow me to do that, then I don't see why I should have to have that sad sap who always looks as though he's damp. You tell me that you married the Emperor, who I think is lovely, and that you didn't get everything you wanted, so isn't it a bit much to ask me to marry that creature and expect to be happy?"

Oh she was exasperating.

I tried to explain to her the vast difference in our cases. "But don't you see, Anya, it is completely the opposite, because I am nothing like Minnie. I am going to see to it that you have all sorts of nice things that you must want when you get married so that you will be happy."

"How is it different?" she asked, bottom lip protruding mutinously. "I feel just like poor Grand Duchess Olga, except that I probably won't get a big palace and I wouldn't care a fig if Alexander likes men better than me. When he tries to kiss me, he leaves slobber all over my chin, and I can't even eat when he's nearby because he stares so, and I haven't the faintest idea what he will expect of me if we do get married, and I'm not planning to find out."

"Anya, pull yourself together and never dare again to compare me with Minnie. Of course you will not be getting a palace. How ridiculous! Now that you have said that, I hardly even want to tell you what Nicky and I have been planning for you."

She eyed me with much less anticipation than I would have expected.

"Well, tell me, then, but I'm not going to promise anything," and then stuffed not one but two seedcakes into her mouth simultaneously.

I looked away in disgust. Really, it seemed to me that Anya had no idea how fortunate she was to have my friendship, and then the unkind thought entered my head that I could not believe that even the evil-tongued gossips of Petersburg could accuse me of having an unnatural relationship with someone like Anya. At least when the French said the same ugly things about Marie Antoinette and her favorite, the Duchesse De Polignac, the Duchesse had been a slender and beautiful woman, not a fat, sulky lump covered in spilt crumbs. Truly it was disheartening that so little was thought of me.

Gathering up the shreds of my rapidly thinning patience, I smiled in her general direction and said, "His Majesty and I are gifting you and Lieutenant Vyroubov with a nice little house right here in the park, the darling yellow house in fact by the gates."

She smiled at last. "Oh, ach, that is a pretty house. I'll like having my very own house, but if it's all the same to you and His Majesty, I'll just live there alone. I don't want to marry Lieutenant Vyroubov, and since you won't let me marry Dmitri, I think I'd rather not marry at all."

I put a hand to my aching back and sighed as I answered.

"Anya, the very reason that I have confided to you the stories of my own difficulties was to make you realize two things: One, a woman's duty is to marry, and to make the best of it, no matter her situation –" I shook my head as she began to interrupt me. "No, you must listen. It is a woman's duty to marry, it is your duty to marry, but you could never marry Dmitri. He is far too young for you."

"Only by four years," she declared rebelliously. "That's the same as you and His Majesty."

"Anya, that is a completely different case. The man must be older so as to be in charge of his wife. And Anya, I will only say this once more: I do not wish … no, I will not accept … ever hearing another word from you about your desire to marry His Imperial Highness the Grand Duke Dmitri. His Highness will marry a princess of another sovereign state, or possibly one of my own girls, when he is old enough," I raised one finger to count out my points, "and when His Majesty sanctions the match," I said, raising a second finger. "Now that is that, and if you will not marry Lieutenant Vyroubov, then you are an unnatural woman and it will look like it is true what the gossips say, and …" I broke off horrified. I had never meant to repeat that to another living soul, least of all to someone as indiscreet as Anya. She returned my appalled gaze unperturbed. "You knew, then? You knew what people were saying, what they had accused you of?"

She shrugged.

"Well, everybody says it. It was bound to get back to me. And they don't just accuse me, they accuse you too."

"You are a past mistress at stating the obvious, Anya dear, but then, if you know all about it, why are you being so difficult about getting married. Don't you want to be my friend, to live near our family?"

She nodded vehemently. "I do, oh so much. I love Your Majesties and your dear children, but –"

I seized on the former. "Then that is what it is best to do Anya, to live near us and be a part of our family. Why, you are like a daughter to Nicky and me –"

27

"Although I can't marry Dmitri," she said maddeningly.

I ignored her, as I had promised I would, instead saying cunningly, "You can have children of your own, though, and that is a woman's greatest satisfaction and fulfillment this side of heaven."

Anya, who was never totally as one expected her to be, sat her tea cup down and looked at me with what appeared to be true curiosity.

"Is that true? Do you mean that? Will I like it, having children? Do you like it really?"

"I … of course, I … Anya, my children are everything to me. How can you even ask that of me? Well, you don't have children, of course. You'll see when –"

"Yes, well, I know, that's what everyone says, 'You'll see when you have your own,' and mostly I think, 'Well, that will be nice,' but then all the people who do have children don't seem to like them much. My own parents act as though they have a headache every time I'm near them, and you said that Empress Minnie is always so disappointed in His Majesty and tells him that he gets everything wrong all the time. That's what Mama and Papa say to me, and you…"

She broke off in confusion.

I drew myself up and beckoned to a footman to pour me more tea. When he had finished, I waved him out of the room and took a sip before saying coolly, "Are you implying in any way, Anya, that I do not love my children, because if so –"

Her plump body trembled with agitation and her face blushed red.

"No, no. Oh, I'm sorry. I never say anything right. I never get anything right. No wonder my parents don't like me, no wonder ..."

She burst into noisy sobs and her obvious misery moved me. Poor Anya, she really was so impossibly clumsy. She hadn't meant what she had said.

I set down my cup and reached out a forgiving hand, which, after wiping her nose, she grasped as I tried not to flinch.

"I only meant ... well ... that is, I meant to say ... Oh, I'll never say it right ..."

I squeezed her hand reassuringly and let it go, resisting the urge to wipe my own hand on a napkin.

Speaking gently, for now I was curious, I said, "No, it is all right, Anya, tell me. I shall not be angry."

She sniffled loudly and pawed at her runny nose again.

"All I meant to say ... that is ... is that you seem sad much of the time, and it has made me wonder, because you're so beautiful and His Majesty loves you, and you are the Empress ...So I've wondered, what is it that makes you sad, and all I could think of was that maybe being a mother isn't so delightful, because my own mama –"

I held up a hand for silence, but as soon as she stopped talking, instead of my speaking to disabuse her of these stupid notions, I found myself pondering the question myself. Did I truly enjoy motherhood?

What a terrible question to even entertain, and one that is not so easily answered. It is one that every woman would be quick to affirm, if asked. Yes, of course it is all to us. It was what we were created for, but did we mean it …? Did I?

In the beginning there had been Olga. She was twelve now, thirteen this coming winter, my first baby. When I gave birth to her I was twenty-three and Nicky only twenty-seven. Our rule had just begun.

Her appearance in our lives brought us unalloyed happiness. She had practically been a honeymoon baby and the mere fact of her, my pregnancy, had spurred Nicky to move us away from his awful mother and into our dear Tsarskoe Selo so that I would have a happy and comfortable confinement.

I was not terribly ill with her, but I was ill enough to avoid many appointments. My first year as Empress had also been one of mourning for Nicky's papa, and so any expectations for me as a future leader of society had been put off anyway. They didn't yet know how badly I would perform as Tsarina, and nor did I.

Olga's sweet baby self made me a mama, made Nicky and me a family, and reassured the watching world that I was fertile. Her being a wee girlie did not make anyone question the possibility of a boy coming soon, and as Nicky said at the time, "I'm glad she's a girl. A boy would have belonged to the nation, but she is all ours."

She was, too – a fat little girl, my sweet darling, our darling. We gloried in her. She had made us parents, and put a sacred seal on the touches and kisses we shared at night. She had even had the great kindness to come late. Because of that I was able to miss my first Winter Season in Petersburg. She gave me time, approved time, to avoid the world stage and its coming judgments. Maybe that was my only time of unexamined happiness as a mother and as a woman. I don't know.

I suffered a miscarriage shortly after the ghastly tragedy that marred forever our coronation. I was certain then, and have remained so, that the baby I lost was our first son. I think it took the shine off our marriage, the shine off me.

I got pregnant again almost immediately after that, which should have been reassuring, but I wasn't reassured somehow, partly, I suppose, because I became so very, very ill. My old leg troubles reasserted themselves, I could barely stand, and I was violently nauseated from the moment I woke up until the time when I could persuade myself to fall into a light, pain-filled sleep. Plagued by my weak legs, a throbbing back, and fearsome migraines, I was a complete physical wreck of a human being. I even aroused Minnie's pity.

She came bustling out to Tsarskoe Selo to see me and to advise that I should keep my feet warm and eat raw bacon as a sop against nausea. I adopted neither of these habits but I was touched by her interest in my welfare, which, as it turned out, would represent the last real kindness or pity she was ever to show me.

I did not think I was carrying a boy – I had already lost my boy – and I sensed somehow that this terribly difficult pregnancy was not destined to end as everyone so obviously hoped it would, Nicky included. They were sure the baby would be the heir. I was equally sure it wouldn't be, but I did not like to say so as I feared that I would be blamed for wishing ill on myself and on the

31

country, Russians being among the most superstitious people on earth.

The closest I ever came to voicing my concern was to tell Maria that I hated making plans because they never came out the way people thought they should. She smiled sweetly and reassuringly, no doubt dismissing my concerns as pregnancy fancies, the megrims of a sick young woman confined to her bed for nearly a whole year. Of course it was a boy!

So, when Tatiana was born, all acted as though this could never have happened. "The Empress has had a second daughter. What a shocking disappointment."

Nicky said that he was pleased, that she looked just like me, and that we were doubly blessed in our two cherubs, but I knew he did not truly mean it, and this time, although I did love my new little girlie – I did, even if I didn't feel the innocent joy I had in her sister – I was already beginning to worry.

I nursed Tatiana as I had Olga, but I didn't feel such a pang of loss when she went up to the nursery to join her sister at a month old. I had kept Olga in her cradle beside me for six months and had been utterly bereft when she had been removed to her nursery. I told myself that it was natural for me to feel less, that I had been so ill, and that in time she would mean as much to me as Olga did. After all, she was a truly beautiful baby and seemed to have been born knowing that I was a troubled soul, for she gave us no troubles of her own, and has since spent every year of her life trying to please me in so many pretty little ways. I did love this daughter too.

Anya shuffled uncomfortably in her seat, waiting for me to speak, but as was happening more and more to me these days, my thoughts distanced me from time and place. I could not seem to help this. When it happened, I was aware of my surroundings, but less so than one who is not as governed by the oppression of their circumstances as I have been. Once a feeling or thought occurred to me, I was at its mercy. This actually began at the time of Maria's birth, after Nicky nearly died.

I became pregnant again when Tatiana was a year old and Olga was three, my fourth pregnancy in as many years. My body had already begun to wear down, but the desperation for a son was upon me because members of the court, with nothing better to occupy their time, had begun whispering to each other that I could not give Russia a son, and court gossip inevitably reaches the masses. They said I had been brought from Germany, as my predecessors had been, to do one thing and only one thing – to breed a son. German women were not beloved by Russians, but it had been thought that we could at least produce children as we always had managed to do so. I had too, but it seemed that my daughters were not *real* children, not male children.

My fourth pregnancy started off better than with Tatiana and so I suppose I let myself hope, let Nicky hope. This time, I thought, it might indeed be a boy. It was a question of the law of averages. I had had a girl, miscarried a boy, and had another girl, so why should there not be a boy this time?

Then Nicky fell ill with typhoid during our visit to the Crimea that fall. Witte had been Finance Minister then and it had fallen upon him to inform me that if

33

Nicky died, Grand Duke Michael would be named the Tsar. I gestured angrily to my protruding stomach and proclaimed, "My son is in here. If, God forbid, Nicky dies, then Michael will be Regent until my son comes of age, unless I, your Empress, am appointed Regent, which would make the most sense as I am your Tsaritsa and the next Emperor will be my son."

Witte, a grand old man whom I was supposed to dislike because Nicky hated him, but I didn't really, replied with what appeared to be genuine sadness, saying, "No, Your Majesty. I am sorry to be the one to burden you with more bad news and at such a time, but Russian law does not allow for a waiting period. The throne must never be vacant. And once a Tsar has ascended the throne, he is Emperor until his death. I'm sorry."

I think he was, too, although I knew he had no respect or genuine liking for Nicky. Later, of course, I learned that he did not like me either, and yet I always felt there existed a certain sympathy between us. Maybe I was wrong. I am not particularly successful at gauging what the elite of Petersburg feel about me as it turns out.

In the end, these emotionally fraught discussions proved to be of no consequence. I nursed Nicky back to health – putting my own at risk – we returned home, and I gave birth after an excruciating back labor to a twelve pound baby girl, my third living child and my third daughter, while my suite tried to hide from me the fact that Nicky, unable to face me with his customary stoicism, had left the birthing chamber to take a long solitary walk to calm himself.

Nicky and I loved Maria every bit as much as we did our elder two daughters and I only sent her up to the nursery from the beginning as I was too sick following her birth to care for her.

"Msgr. Philippe," I muttered.

Anya started, having fallen asleep during my reverie. "What? What?" she exclaimed, kicking out her feet in surprise and sending her cup clattering down from the tea table.

"No, Anya, leave it," I said as she began floundering about in the direction of the bell pull. "They can clean up after we are done."

"But what did you say about that Frenchman. I'm sorry, I was thinking of other things."

I laughed. "You were sleeping, Anya, but it is all right, I don't mind. I said the name of Msgr. Philippe. He was my first friend, before you, before Father Grigory. He gave us Alexei, you know."

She looked down at the mess at her feet with distaste and nodded at me.

"Yes, well, that's what you have always said. So, I was thinking, if I marry Lieutenant Vyroubov, and –"

"Anya, you are interrupting me again. You know you must not do that."

She colored – whether in embarrassment or anger I could not say – and started thumping her ample thighs with both hands.

"What *are* you doing?"

"You said I wasn't to interrupt you unless I let you know I wanted to by doing this." She thumped her leg again for emphasis. "So I did it, and now can I talk?"

I shrugged. She had broken my train of thought, or better to say derailed it.

"Yes, go ahead, Anya."

I yawned to show that I was already bored.

"Good, I shall. After all, this was supposed to be about me and Lieutenant Vyroubov. I wouldn't have asked about children if I'd known ... I mean to say, thank you for telling me ... Now, if I do marry the Lieutenant and I don't like it, what will happen to me? I mean, can I have a divorce and marry a grand duke, say Grand Duke Dmitri? You let Stana divorce her husband and then marry Grand Duke Nicholas, so I thought that perhaps –" I reached down and picked up my own bell and rang it, cutting her off. "But you said not to ring, that we were talking and –"

I shook my head.

"I am suddenly quite tired, Anya, and need to go and rest. And no, you may not even think of divorce, nor could you ever marry a grand duke. Stana is a princess, the daughter of a king, you are not. I am horribly weary of listening to you on this matter. I shall tell you what I shall do: I will summon Father Grigory to luncheon here tomorrow. He will consider the matter and give us his thoughts upon it," although, unbeknown to me, Father Grigory had already given Anya the benefit of his foresight on the matter in front of Mitsia and Stana.

Chapter 2

In the little time I had known him, I had already begun to venerate Father Grigory, but I was still nervous of him. One never knew quite what to expect of him, and then there was Nicky's attitude toward him.

Nicky had not yet warmed to Father Grigory, which was painful as it was so clear that, despite Father Grigory's obvious devotion to me, it was Nicky he felt he had been sent especially to help and guide.

This was not the first time that Nicky had shown a certain distance toward a messenger from God. When I had become pregnant after Maria, I had already begun seeking the care and counsel of my first friend, Msgr. Philippe. Among Philippe's many gifts, the greatest was his ability to change the sex of a child already in the womb. I have never said it aloud to Nicky, but I think he knows that I blame him for Anastasia being a girl. Philippe as much as said so.

"I regret this for Your Majesty. Your faith was strong and you followed my every directive, but His Majesty hardly ever saw me and I fear his lack of faith may have blocked my intercessions on your behalf."

I believed that this was indeed true, but I did not reproach Nicky, and funnily I did not resent my fourth living baby for being a wee girly.

My dearest grandmamma had died during my pregnancy with Anastasia, and from the moment she was born it was as though she had felt compelled to bring in sunshine where there had been darkness. A merry, smiling little baby, she no sooner gained her fat tiny feet than she began toddling into mischief, always the comedian. She joined Nicky and me together in laughter and was so marvelous a small person in her own right that neither of us felt it possible to regret her.

After Anastasia, our "Nastinka," was born, Nicky did seem to be willing to listen to Philippe, at least for a time, following, if reluctantly, Philippe's instructions to have Saint Serafim of Sarov, that most alliterative of gentlemen, canonized, and I quickly became pregnant again with a baby created in real joy.

My baby vanished, though. He was there; I felt him; I saw him grow; my breasts became fuller; my stomach grew; I was pregnant with the blessed boy that had been promised us; and then he was gone, as though he had never been. The doctors said I had never been pregnant at all, and my terrible mother-in-law judged me to be mad and Nicky's sisters Xenia and Olga pitied me, but Nicky himself only said, "It doesn't matter, darling."

Of course it mattered; it mattered more than anything in the world. I did not know then, because I was too ill with grief, that Nicky used this great embarrassment to banish my friend, packing Philippe back off to France without a word to me, or any thanks to him for his care of me. I never saw Philippe again for he died soon after this.

Almost immediately I was pregnant again, a pregnancy confirmed by the doctors this time. I did not plan, I did not let myself hope, and anyway Nicky and I, along with Russia, had entered a dark season. My final pregnancy, although I had made no decision to that effect at the time, was marked by assassinations, war, and a near-revolution, all poisoned yet further by family acrimony.

Then, one terrible day, while Maria was doing my hair, a mirror nearly jumped from the wall and fell and broke, and that on a thickly carpeted floor. Did I think this startling, ominous event boded ill for my baby? No, I do not think it did. At that particular moment I feared more for Nicky losing his crown or his life, and was otherwise as placid as one in my precarious position could have been. I no longer let myself hope much for a son.

I picked out the name 'Victoria' for my baby, not caring that it wasn't a Russian name. I missed Grandmamma, so in those dangerous days I wished to honor her.

Then he was born, when I had stopped hoping, when I had nearly stopped caring, he came – my baby, my boy, the crowning of my marriage.

Maybe it was too late by then for the Russian people to forgive me for my years of infertility as they saw it. Maybe the war we were fighting and losing – and then lost – devalued his arrival in their eyes, although we did try to make it as joyous a time for all of Russia as it was for us. Nicky even appointed every Russian soldier in the army to be Alexei's godfather. Maybe they were pleased about this, but surely their dying far from home placed a shadow across their happiness for us.

Even within the Romanov family everyone acted more relieved than overjoyed, saying in unison something to the effect that, "Oh, finally that hopeless girl got something right," but Nicky and I were living in joy, our love flowered again, Nicky's hopes for the future returned, a constitution to save us from anarchy was drafted, and for a moment life was as golden as that little girl from faraway, long ago in Hesse-Darmstadt, had dreamed it could be.

Then my baby, my savior, began to bleed, and this was no temporary affliction. I had given him bad blood – literally – and cursed his new life with the so-called "English disease" of hemophilia. We vowed to keep his illness forever a secret from the Russian people, but I knew, and Nicky knew, and, worst of all, his mother knew its savage consequences – no, that wasn't the worst of it; the worst of it was that our baby knew that I was responsible for his disease.

No one would credit me saying this out loud, so I never did, but so often when Alexei bled, suffered, screamed, and writhed about wildly in agony, he would suddenly open his large eyes, ringed black by pain, and stare directly into mine, and in those moments I knew that he somehow understood that his misery had been passed on to him by the one he loved and trusted the most. I saw reproach there. That was why it was my name he sobbed out when he was in his worst agonies and why it was my arms he sought. I have found that is so often the way: We seek comfort from the one who has injured us the most, as though we think that only they have the power to fix what they broke in the first place. It is true with the heart of a woman and in my situation it was true in the heart of my little boy.

I could not fix him, though, and I think my relentless despair might have turned to madness if God had not finally answered my desperate prayers by sending me help and solace in the form of Father Grigory, and that

Nicky did not understand this was driving a wedge between us where none need ever have been.

On his very first visit, Father Grigory stopped Baby's pain completely with a single prayer when no doctor had ever managed even to mitigate his pain before. They were useless men of supposed science in their black merchants' frock coats and with their self-important expressions, shaking their heads, telling Nicky it was all my fault.

"Science teaches us, Your Majesty, that the disease is incurable. Few live to adulthood. The Tsarevich's case appears to be particularly severe."

Bah, what did they know? What were their paltry qualifications compared with those of a man chosen by God Himself to help us?

That is what I told Nicky. "Look what Father Grigory has accomplished. Isn't he the answer to my prayers, to our prayers? Isn't he the friend promised to us by Msgr. Philippe to come when he was needed?"

I asked all of this of Nicky as he tried to brush off his lack of appreciation of Father Grigory. It wasn't in Nicky's nature to openly defy me, so he fell back on mumbled comments to pacify me instead.

"Yes, darling, he is most interesting. I am glad you feel better when you see him. I am glad Baby is better too."

However, when pressed, he turned away from me or invented a pressing matter he had to address urgently elsewhere. Once, he stopped my rapturous talk about Father Grigory by telling me he had an urgent late-night meeting with his Interior Minister, but I found out later

that the meeting had been a game of billiards with
Dmitri.

Chapter 3

These matters were what I was concerned with when I informed Nicky that night in bed that Father Grigory was coming to lunch at the palace the following day to discuss the matter of Anya's marriage, and, as I had expected, a trapped look came over his face before he could disguise it.

I exulted inwardly. I hardly ever joined Nicky and whomever of the suite was about for luncheon, but I knew that my having announced that I was proposing to attend this particular luncheon in honor of our guest, it would be impossible for him to choose to be elsewhere.

Nevertheless, he attempted to do so anyway.

"Oh, Sunny darling, I am afraid I shall be unable to join you. You see –"

"Nicky, you are in for luncheon every single day, and unless you can give me an extremely compelling reason for not being there tomorrow, I will consider it a personal slight."

"But darling, how do you know you will be well enough to attend the luncheon tomorrow? You have been ill for so long and the trouble with your heart rarely gives you a moment's warning before it strikes."

I sat up outraged.

"Nicky, are you suggesting that I am in some way manipulating my illness?" Involuntarily, I clutched at my chest, which had begun to palpitate dangerously as my upset grew.

Nicky saw this and blanched visibly.

"Darling Alicky, my wee girly, please don't upset yourself," he said, his hand stroking my shoulder. "Don't let stupid old hubby upset you either. Of course I don't think that. I know how ill you have been, dearest. That is all I meant by asking if you were up to luncheon. Most of my suite attends, and I often have the older girls join me too, and I know you don't enjoy large gatherings at mealtimes, even when you are feeling well, so I merely thought —"

"Nicky, isn't it enough to run an empire? Don't those responsibilities weigh on you?"

My tone startled him as much as any words I used.

"What? Well, yes, of course they do. You know that, Alicky."

I nodded.

"I do too, and so you must not interfere with my responsibilities, hubby dear. As a wife and a mother, I wish — no, I need — Father Grigory's counsel to fulfill them, just as you seem to need Mr. Stolypin's and your mother's counsel to fulfill yours. If you interfere with my running of our little household, you leave me with little, Nicky, and little incentive to try to get better either."

He sighed, took a puff from his cigarette, looked away, crushed out his cigarette, and turned off his bedside lamp.

"It is impossible to fight such logic, Alix, but what I don't understand is why I have to involve myself with Father Grigory. If he is, as you say, to become your … household Prime Minister, then what does that have to do with me?"

44

"He wants to see you, Nicky. He is, I know, hurt by your lack of interest in his mission from God. You may find that he has much to impart to you from his talks with God about the empire."

I felt the bed shake. Was he laughing? To my horror I heard a chuckle escape.

"How marvelous, Sunny. He wants to help with the empire … Did he tell you this?"

I felt my heart spasm a bit.

"No, of course not … well, not in those words. He is here to guide us, and –"

"And you sense that is why he wishes to forge a closer relationship with me, to guide, us … to guide me?" Before I could answer, he went on, the laughter ebbing from his voice, "Is that what you want, Alix, for him to help me rule my empire?"

I shifted irritably.

"No, Nicky. Please let us not be ridiculous or blow this whole situation up into something it is not. Let us not act like your mother does about things. Father Grigory is simply a kind, plain-spoken man of God, whose humble presence comforts me."

"That you find him either plain-spoken or humble is worrying to me, Sunny."

Wanting, no needing, to make him understand, I held my temper and swatted him playfully three times on his hip. He laughed in spite of himself.

"Now you've taken to beating the Tsar to make your points, darling," he said cheerfully.

"Only if the Tsar is a naughty boy who interrupts. That is what I have taught Anya, or tried to anyway," I said ruefully, "to hit her lap three times before interrupting me. Since you did not hit your own lap before interrupting wify, I did it for you."

I heard him chuckle and felt better. Nicky amused was Nicky ready to fall into line.

"Forgive me, Your Majesty. I shall now quietly proceed to hang upon your every word and promise, on my honor as a Tsar, not to interrupt you."

I swatted him again in mock annoyance.

"Oh you! But really, Nicky, this matters to me. I know that because I am ill all the time, well, you probably simply forget about me." I pinched his arm. "You promised not to interrupt me." His shoulder was tight under my hand but he remained silent. "I didn't mean to say that you deliberately neglect me, Nicky, or are even that you are aware that you are doing it, but I do feel it. I am alone and isolated from all of you up here in my rooms, worrying ceaselessly about Baby." He rolled toward me and clasped me against him. I continued speaking with my face against his chest. "I thought it would all be so different. Didn't you?" I felt him nod against the top of my head and that arrested me. I didn't like him feeling that way too. It was somehow a black mark.

"Nicky?"

"Ah, I am allowed to speak now?" His words were light, his tone less so.

"Yes, of course. I was only joking before. So you are ... you are disappointed with our lives and with me?"

His arms tightened about me.

"Oh Sunny, you know how I feel about you."

"Then what is it?" Suddenly I desperately wished that I had never said I was dissatisfied with our lives. Now

46

the single most important thing in the world seemed to be that he convince me that he was happy with me, terribly happy with me in our small world.

"I don't know. I suppose it is exactly as you have just expressed it. I mean, I think about it all sometimes, you and I, so young and with it all ahead of us, the way we were in Wolfsgarten and when we stayed with your grandmamma in England. I thought, I suppose, that it would all be easier. That is all I meant."

I was not satisfied.

"You mean 'easier' because you did not expect to be Tsar so early on?"

He nodded against me, but then said, "Well, that certainly. Losing dearest Papa so early was a terrible blow, but that is not precisely it. I suppose like all young men, when I looked ahead, I couldn't see so many changes and –"

Desperate to make him stop what I had accidentally started, I interrupted him.

"All young people think that. I mean, if we were to ask any young person what they thought would happen to them in the future, they would be certain to look at us as though we had run mad. No one can imagine something they do not know about."

He shrugged.

"Except people who claim oracular powers like Msgr. Philippe and now your Father Grigory. And yes, it is true what you say, but I don't think I am explaining myself well. I am certain I never do. It is why I often find myself being so terribly misunderstood."

I chose not to address this momentary bout of self-pity which is one of the few characteristics of my adored husband that I truly despise.

"Nicky, what you say only underlines our luck in having found, or having been found by, Father Grigory, and Philippe before him."

"What?"

I pulled away from him and sat up, feeling wide awake and determined to make him see my point of view. Unusually, I also asked him for one of his cigarettes, which pleased him enormously. He lit both cigarettes and handed me one of them as he leaned back against our headboard to listen attentively to what I had to say. It was nearly black in the room, but I could see the whites of his eyes gleaming. Sleep, it seemed, was far away from us both.

"Don't you see that everyone, even those of us chosen by God to occupy exalted places here, suffers disappointment and wonders occasionally at their circumstances, even if they live amid great love and happiness, as you and I do, dearest. They pray, they hope, but often it seems no one hears them. They worry about the future, what is the best thing to be done. *If we do this, what will happen? Will we make things better or worse?* It is the one true universal human condition, Nicky. Father Grigory made me see that and he says that, while God is indeed everywhere, He cannot truly be everywhere and help all of us. Can you see that?" I saw him nod. Encouraged, I continued. "But God knows that those set above others on His earth must be heard, no matter how preoccupied He is with other matters. It is just like ..." I groped about for a comparison and then came up with the perfect one, "… it is just like when you give an audience to Grand Duke Nicholas whenever he asks for one."

"He is the Commander-in-Chief of the Saint Petersburg military district, so one might tend to."

"Oh no, don't mistake me, Nicky, I am not criticizing you. I am simply saying you have to give priority to people."

"Naturally I do, but –"

"No, dearest, there is no 'but' here, there is only that shining truth that explains why we are sent these special friends."

I heard his yawn and saw his head shake.

"Sunny, I haven't a clue what you are talking about, but if you will just finish saying it, I shall agree with whatever you say, and then we can both get some sleep, which is much needed in both our cases, I think."

I hated his bored tone. People are always bored when they cannot grasp a thing, I find. Nevertheless, I tried to make him see.

"God hears our prayers before He can attend to those of others. It has to be so – you can see that, can't you? He placed you in a position to care for millions of His people and He knows that, despite your great intelligence and sensitivity, you are still just one man, albeit a very special one, and obviously He cannot just appear in your study one afternoon and sit down for a chat."

"Helpful as I might find that," Nicky said laconically.

I ignored him and plunged onward.

"So He sent us Father Grigory, one of His chosen ones, to help and guide us specifically."

"Clearly, Sunny, I will never cease to be surprised by the rare privileges of my position, and I find it miraculous too that he, Father Grigory, God's messenger, stoops to come to luncheon to advise poor, lowly Anya upon her nuptial confusions. I wonder how she came to be chosen for this honor."

I gritted my teeth.

"Please, Nicky, if you can manage not a single kindness to me for the remainder of our lives together, if I mean so little to you as that, then at least I ask in memory of what we have been to each other —"

"Stop it, Alix."

I continued. "In memory of your dead love for me, I ask you to appear at least to be polite to Father Grigory and to my one friend," my voice broke, "poor Anya, who is of interest to Father Grigory only because she is of interest to me."

There was a long silence. For a horrified moment I thought he had fallen asleep, but then at last there came a sigh and a rustle of the bedclothes, and he said. "I cannot fight you, Alix," he made a choking sound which could have been a wry laugh or maybe a sob, "and it is becoming increasingly noticeable to everyone that I cannot really manage to fight anyone at all, can I? No, don't answer, my dear. You and I perhaps need to learn more what not to say to each other than the converse. I cannot do it, you see, Sunny. I cannot sit behind that desk all day trying to avoid the looks in the eyes of those damned ministers. I cannot bear to read a single report from that cursed Duma, where day after day they say more and more unspeakable things. I cannot bear Stolypin's pity, for that is what he feels toward me, or rather I cannot bear it if I have to face yours at the end of my never-ending days as well. I know your heart hurts, darling, and your head, but do you ever consider that you may not be alone in that?"

"Oh Nicky, forgive me, I –"

He shrugged off my questing hand, keeping his back to me.

"No, Sunny, there is nothing to forgive. It is what it is," He cleared his throat, his whole frame shuddering. I felt wretched. "If you want Father Grigory to join our family circle and for me to listen to him, then that is what I shall do, for I cannot fight you too. If I do that, what will I have left? So go to sleep, darling. I have a great deal of work to do in the morning and I imagine I will not see you until luncheon, whereupon I shall hang on his every word and follow each and every one of his directives, no matter how bizarre they may turn out to be, for at the end of the day it probably won't make much difference."

"Nicky?"

Only silence answered me back, and after a long time – long enough for the early dawn to break through the windows, for we were in the beginning season of Russia's endless days – I heard him rustle and tiredly begin to rise. It was my turn to pretend to be asleep now. I felt him lean over me and press a kiss to my forehead, and then waited immobile until I heard his dragging steps leave the room and his soft voice call for his valet Volkov.

All triumph was mine, then. I had won, but I wished that my winning felt less destructive.

51

Chapter 4

I feel I might not live long enough to be able to describe adequately my feelings about the strange luncheon party that finally convinced Anya to set a wedding date and that made Nicky regard Father Grigory with at least a vestige of respect. I suppose, given those positive outcomes, I should consider it to have been a triumph, but its memory has always left me feeling somewhat unsettled.

For me, the lead up to the luncheon began prosaically enough. I arose late that morning, leaden of limb and sore of heart and head, our terrible words from the night before still hanging in the air of our bedchamber like the scent of a spoiled perfume spilled years before onto a rug. For once I could hardly wait to bathe and dress and let the maids in to clean the room, although I felt that the room might possibly need to be blessed again before I could find in it the refuge it had once been.

I then proceeded to take no small amount of trouble over my toilette – not for Father Grigory's benefit, no matter what tiny-minded gossips might choose to say – but for Nicky.

My maid Maria was in a rather quiet mood that morning as she arranged for my bath, my gown and my hairdresser, possibly bowing before the effects of the weather, which was glowering and undecided as to whether summer should begin in earnest or whether there should be one last freeze. In any case, I was too preoccupied with my own thoughts to draw her out as she was so clearly hoping I would.

I therefore remained mostly silent, speaking only to tell the hairdresser to arrange some more small curls about my face to soften my tired appearance and to instruct two clumsy maids to add another row of lace to the hem of the pale pink silk afternoon dress I had chosen to wear.

Once dressed, primped and prepared, and with a final settling of fifteen strands of pink pearls about my neck and waist, I felt a little sprig of optimism in my breast when my cheval glass revealed me to be still a somewhat beautiful woman, leading me to fancy that when Nicky saw me he would not have to look too terribly hard to find traces of the girl he had fallen in love with so many years and pregancies ago.

While I had been dressing, I had been told by Maria that there was much rushing about in the rooms on the next floor, which made me smile. My oldest girls were evidently rather excited about the prospect of luncheon with their old mama and her new friend, sweet things, and I made a private vow to try to see more of all of them in the future if only I could regain my health.

I had hoped that Nicky might appear to escort me down to luncheon, but, as the clock struck one, I understood that he was not coming, so I sallied forth to make my entrance alone, dismissing Maria's suggestion that she wheel me downstairs in my chair, announcing proudly that I would walk, no matter the pain in my legs.

My heart lifted as I approached the Maple Room, where I had instructed the table to be set for luncheon, on hearing the noise of loud laughter coming from there, only for it to fall again as I asked myself whether my family and guests enjoyed themselves this much every day while I lay in a cold, darkened room in pain. That seemed intolerable to me, but all too possible. Nicky's family had a long tradition of treating meal times as if they were dining in a bear garden, throwing food around the room and at each other, much to the consternation of the suite and of the servants. When I first arrived in Russia it was as Nicky's papa lay dying, so it was nearly a year before I was forced to be a witness to this unruly behavior that I considered better suited to savages than to members of an imperial dynasty. Still, when I protested at all the unseemly activity and the noise, Nicky would explain, "We always behaved this way at Gatchina. Even Mama approved. She liked us to have fun."

That gave me pause – my censorious mother-in-law, who never ceased to criticize me for what she deemed to be legion transgressions, expected, and indeed encouraged, her family and friends to behave like zoo animals at meal times? I would never understand these people.

My steps faltered and I think I might have returned upstairs if I had not heard Father Grigory's unmistakable voice booming out, "Look, fellows, open the doors. Mama is out there. Just there. I feel her," startling the Abyssinians – who were always somewhat unnerved in his presence – by bounding out of the room at a considerable pace and falling joyously to his knees in front of me. He then followed up this piece of exuberant courtliness by grasping my hands and pulling them to his lips to kiss them loudly and to leave smears of gravy behind, before smiling up at me, whereupon I discovered that I could only smile back at him, despite the shock of sensing the traces of gravy on my hands, because I felt instantly so well and so at peace with everything.

He then jumped to his feet again and most improperly offered me his arm, which I accepted after a hesitation, allowing him to escort me to my empty chair opposite Nicky, who had the good grace to rise, bow, and throw a smile in my direction, although I remained disappointed that he had already ushered our guests into luncheon and seated himself before I arrived.

My irritation quickly turned to amusement at the sight of Anya. She was wearing what appeared to be a dress made of purple fur. Nicky caught the direction of my glance and winked at me, and it was all reconciled between us again.

Seated next to Anya and her imposing garment was a small man who appeared to be somewhat damp. There is an odd English expression that people use to describe someone they find rather pathetic, they say they are wet, but this young man appeared to be so literally. He had a large, drooping mustache and it looked as if he had soaked it in his water bowl for some inexplicable reason. He was also sweating profusely, although the room was not particularly warm, and this had caused his uniform to display unsightly dark patches at the rim of his collar and under his arms.

This I recognized as being Lieutenant Vyroubov, Anya's intended, who had definitely not improved since the last time I had seen him at the party I had thrown for their engagement.

Unfortunately, Father Grigory sensed my dismay and spoke my thoughts out loud. "Oh Mama, this is, as I believe you know, Lieutenant Vyroubov, your little

Anya's fiancé. He is a sorry-looking specimen, as I was remarking to Mitzia and Stana and her guests just the other night, but here he is, safe and sound, for lunch with us all."

The poor lieutenant looked extremely uncomfortable and upset at this pronouncement – as well he should have been – but said nothing, confining himself merely to staring down at his hands while Anya nodded in fervent agreement with the sentiment Father Grigory had expressed. This didn't surprise me but it did surprise me that they had met before.

Father Grigory's remark also angered Count Fredericks, who said, "I say, you, you, priest there. You cannot speak to one of Their Majesties' guests like that. Apologize immediately, sir."

Father Grigory, who had meantime placidly seated himself across from me and in between Olga and Tatiana, smiled, picked up a bread roll and threw it at Count Fredericks, then tilted his head back and roared with laughter at his astonished face. Olga began to giggle and Tatiana looked horrified, glancing over at me to see how I would react to this type of behavior which she knew her father encouraged and I greatly disliked.

Nicky half-rose from his seat. "Good Lord, Father Grigory, what has come over you?" It wasn't that Nicky objected to anyone throwing bread rolls around at table, it was that he resented 'just anyone,' such as a peasant, leading the charge.

Anya seized this moment of confusion to throw a bread roll at her hapless fiancé seated next to her, and Olga, emboldened by all the fun, picked up hers and threw it at Nicky. It landed in his soup and splashed him.

56

Father Grigory roared and slapped both his hands into the soup, soaking both girls badly. Tatiana shrieked in distress and burst into tears.

Father Grigory looked at her in surprise.

"Why the tears, Tanushka? It is only soup. You can still eat it, see?" He demonstrated this by dipping his spoon into it and downing it with great satisfaction.

Tatiana looked at him and then at me to see what to do. I was rather torn. It is true that I tended to have strict principles in relation to table manners and court etiquette, but in a Romanov court pelting each other with food was in compliance with this etiquette, not in defiance of it. It was one of the reasons, beyond the effects of my illness, why I preferred to avoid meal times, not being able to tolerate the ensuing noise and confusion. Equally, I did not wish to demean Father Grigory, who in this earthly life was a peasant, all said and done, and little versed in such things.

I looked at Nicky, hoping he would address the matter, but I could see immediately that no help would be forthcoming from that quarter. He was sitting there open-mouthed, still considering how to respond to Olga's volley with the bread roll, then he giggled, picked up the cutlet from his plate with his bare hands, and tossed it in her direction, catching poor Tatiana by mistake.

Utterly over-stimulated by all the fun, Anya joined in and overturned her entire plate onto the head of her hapless fiancé.

There was no saving anything after that. I began to laugh, and so did Nicky and Olga, our chortles nearly drowned out by Father Grigory's bellows of joy and Tatiana's rather theatrical protests.

Poor Count Fredericks could only repeat, "I say, I say, what is this, then?" and Anya shouted above it all, "This is good fun!" to which Nicky replied, "In the great tradition of Gatchina!"

Olga, who was clearly enjoying herself immensely, nodded enthusiastically and said, "I think so too, Anya. Wait until I tell Nastinka and Maria what they've missed. They'll be madly jealous, don't you think so too, Tati?"

Tatiana shook her head, eyes streaming with tears and some meat juices. "My dress is spoiled forever."

Father Grigory seemed somewhat nervous as to what he had started as he looked around furtively, but then I realized he was more concerned that one of the servants would snatch his plate away before he had finished eating.

Addressing no one in particular, his mouth still full of food, he commented, "It is good when friends come together to enjoy food. In my village we like to do that very much, but it is rare that we have food on our table, so we can only talk about the food we would like to have. That makes for an excellent conversation but this is more satisfying to the body." He nodded, satisfied with his statement, and turned to look at Anya with his piercing eyes. "You do not want to marry this fine fellow," he said as he smiled inclusively at poor Lieutenant Vyroubov who appeared to be on the point of fleeing the room. "Tell me," Father Grigory continued, "do you wish to marry young Anya, my poor friend?"

The table hushed, straining to hear Lieutenant Vyroubov's response, even Anya.

"I think so. I asked her to marry me and she said yes, so I suppose ..." His voice trailed off.

Father Grigory nodded as though this was just right and I found myself nodding as well. "And do you know why you wish to marry Anya?"

Lieutenant Vyroubov made an ineffectual swipe at the mess on his face - the poor man was simply dripping with food – and shook his head mutely whereupon Father Grigory sat up abruptly and smashed his hands down alongside his plate, startling us all.

"Of course you do not know. Why would you, my friend?" Then, without waiting for an answer from the utterly shaken Lieutenant, he bellowed out, "We are none of us allowed to know why we do anything. But then we must do something all the same, is that not right, Batushka?"

Nicky looked surprised to have Father Grigory turn the conversation toward him, but oddly also rather pleased to be consulted on the matter. Tilting his head and lighting a cigarette, he inhaled and then angled his head back for a moment to study the ceiling.

"Yes, Father Grigory you are quite correct. In fact, as you may or may not know, I was born on the Day of Job the Long-Suffering. You are no doubt familiar with the story."

Father Grigory nodded enthusiastically while I sighed inwardly. All roads led to Job with Nicky.

I heard Count Fredericks hiss slightly as though he were a balloon and Nicky's reference to Job had made him leak air.

Pleased at Father Grigory's response, Nicky continued.

"In common with Job, I have often found myself despairing of the trials that have come upon me, and so upon Russia." At that moment, I noted that the only people at the table who were looking at Nicky were Father Grigory, Anya and Lieutenant Vyroubov. The rest of the suite and of our family were studiously eyeing the tablecloth.

"Because you are the Tsar, Batushka, you must do something, no matter if it comes out right or wrong. Isn't that so, Papa?"

Nicky looked relieved to hear someone, I suppose anyone, say this and beamed at Father Grigory for the first time with genuine delight.

"Yes, it is exactly true what you say, Father Grigory. No Tsar, however much he loves and reveres Our Lord and Savior, has the luxury of waiting for Him to speak." At this Nicky made the sign of the cross and we all followed his example, except for Father Grigory who merely grinned approvingly at Nicky, who continued, "I am a man of faith and I pray a great deal, but things still must be done, ministers must be directed, orders must be signed, that sort of thing. Sometimes even wars must be fought."

I saw Lieutenant Vyroubov and several of the suite – including Count Fredericks – flinch at this final remark, but Father Grigory only nodded and then, after a moment's thought, put his hands together in a deafening clap.

"Yes, it is just so," he roared. "We all must do everything all of the time. We hope for the best but our

60

best is often very poor in the eyes of God. It doesn't matter, we go on, and it is like the day. In my village some days are very bad, but before a man can get too angry, look, it is already nighttime and the day is over. This is our life here, so there is no need to mind mistakes because soon it will be over." Turning to Anya he smiled widely. "Your marriage to this poor fellow," he threw a sympathetic look toward Lieutenant Vyroubov, "will be most unhappy, as I have already told you. I can see no good in it at all, so it is best to do it quickly and then it will be done." He looked at me warmly. "Mama and Papa will see to it. They will make it a good day for you, and I will come to see it too."

With this astounding pronouncement Father Grigory seemed to think the matter was settled.

I glanced at Nicky. He was nodding and then raised his glass to Lieutenant Vyroubov.

"Lieutenant Vyruubov, I wish to congratulate you again on your upcoming wedding. You too, Anya. And although Father Grigory appears to feel that it may not come to a completely happy resolution, he is certainly right when he says that, no matter what, we must all do something. In any case, for our own part, I feel I can safely speak for Her Majesty and I when I say that we hope you shall be as happy as we are. Is that not right, darling?"

It was easier to smile at Nicky and agree than to meet Anya's horrified expression. Unfortunately, Nicky decided that our mad luncheon, such as it was, needed to draw to a close, so he rose and addressed the men of the suite.

"Gentlemen, I hope you will join me briefly for a small brandy and a cigarette before we disperse for the afternoon. Not you, Lieutenant, you must be anxious to go and wash, but Fredericks and Father Grigory, please follow me if you will."

Count Fredericks rose, gave a half-bow and said apologetically, "Forgive me, Your Majesty, but I have several members of your family awaiting me in town this afternoon to discuss various outstanding matters. I am sorry, but I've already kept them waiting an interminably long time, so I should …" His voice trailed off.

Nicky looked dismayed but said, "Of course, Fredericks. Never a moment's peace, is there, as I know all too well. In that case I suppose I should just get back to it all as well. Gentlemen, darling, girls, Anya, thank you for a most fun and interesting luncheon."

However, Father Grigory was only too willing to continue their conversation, even if Nicky was visibly much less keen to do so.

"I will join you for a brandy, Papa," Father Grigory assured him. "I have many things to tell you. I do not smoke but I will keep you company while you do."

Father Grigory had risen while he spoke and moved next to Nicky, making it impossible for Nicky to leave the room without him. Nicky looked distinctly nonplussed by this maneuver yet increasingly resigned to the inevitability of having to spend time alone with Father Grigory, which pleased me no end.

I addressed the girls. "Darlings, let us retire to my boudoir. We all seem to have eaten very little this luncheon, so I shall order up some tea for us to keep the wolf from –"

Anya interrupted me. "I'm coming too. I hardly ate a thing and I am starving. Besides, I don't think I should be alone now. I'm very upset and confused."

"Oh, Anya, I really am quite tired. I don't usually come down for lunch and I feel quite drained."

Horribly interrupting me yet again, Anya continued, "You have just asked the girls to join you, and you'll only be lying on your chaise, so I can't see how my being there would be any more tiring for you."

There was no way to explain my feelings, so I merely nodded tiredly, and Tatiana, seeing this, came around to take one of my arms. Olga did too, but with a little grimace that I noted and disliked. In this manner the four of us inched through the doors and down the halls to my elevator.

I indicated that Olga and Anya should take the stairs, for the elevator was only designed for two at the most, and shooting each other looks of dislike, which dismayed me but which I did not have the resolve to address just then, Olga and Anya shuffled off.

In the elevator, during our moment of privacy, Tatiana spoke tentatively. "Mama, why do you want Anya to marry Lieutenant Vyroubov, whom she doesn't like? Will all of us have to marry people we don't like, too, one day?"

The door opened and I leaned heavily against my daughter as we walked. What a funny little girl to think of such things, but her small face was so serious that I didn't wish to laugh at her. Tatiana was my gravest child.

I stroked her little shoulder and delayed answering her until we had entered my boudoir. Lying down with a great sigh of relief, I motioned for her to come close to me. I put my arms around her and said to the top of her head, "Dearest, your wedding day is hardly something you need to worry about just yet. Why, you are only ten."

She nodded under my chin.

"I know I'm only ten, Mama, and it's ages away, but when it comes, will you and Papa make me marry someone against my will, Olga and Nastinka and Maria too? What about Baby? You wouldn't want him to marry someone horrid like Anya, would you?" Realizing what she had just said, she gave a little gasp of horror and put her hands over her mouth, tears already beginning to spill. "Oh mama, I'm so sorry. I didn't mean it. I love Anya, we all do, I –"

At that moment Anya and Olga bustled into the room.

"I am glad you do, Tatiana," Anya proclaimed, "and as you know, I love all of you with great devotion myself. On a day as terrible as this one, it is nice to hear such a thing."

I felt poor Tatiana stiffen in my arms and I gave her a squeeze to reassure her that Anya had only heard the last of her words.

Olga asked, "What were you talking about, Mama? Was it Anya's wedding?"

She seated herself at my feet and Anya went to her customary chair and pulled the bell pull without asking me. At my raised eyebrow she smiled and shrugged.

"I knew you wouldn't have ordered tea yet, and I'm sure the girls and I will perish if we don't have something, won't we, young ladies?"

Olga grinned and nodded, and Tatiana, still reeling from her fear of what Anya might have overheard, buried her face in my shoulder in shame.

I looked at Olga and Anya over her head and shrugged.

"Tati's tired. I think that our luncheon party was too much for her. And Olga, darling, Tatiana and I were indeed talking about Anya's wedding, discussing how all of my four girlies would have weddings, too, one day."

Olga's face lit up with interest. "I already know whom I'm going to marry."

Curious at this, Tatiana raised her head to look at her sister, while Anya focused her attention on my maid Maria, who had entered the room with two other maids pushing a trolley laden with a samovar and a tray of cakes.

"I'm going to marry Dmitri, and I'll do it when I turn sixteen," Olga continued. "That's only four years away. I'm sorry, Tati, but I'm the oldest, so I get to go first, and you'll have to try and find someone as good as him, not that anyone is. Oh good, tea!"

Maria giggled and both maids flushed, and I shot Olga a look to remind her that our family was not to discuss matters of importance in front of the servants, no matter how charming the topic. She smiled and raced Anya for the first of the pink cakes. She lost, which is why Anya was unable to voice her displeasure until she had managed to swallow it down.

"So, this is why I have to marry Lieutenant Wet Bottom!" Anya declared indignantly. Tatiana and Olga gasped in delighted laughter. "I don't want to do it, and you are making me, and it's all because you were afraid

I would steal Dmitri away before Olga was old enough to marry him."

Olga and Tatiana's expressions transformed from delighted to appalled at Anya's latest profession, and I waved Maria and the other maids toward the door, but Maria, seeming to misunderstand me, merely opened the door for the other maids and then busily began rearranging the flowers in my vases.

Drawing in a shaky breath, for I could feel my heart starting to pound erratically, I said sternly, "Anya, you know that is simply untrue. As I have said over and over again, His Majesty would never allow a member of the Imperial Family to marry a commoner, however beloved to us she might be. And as for my Olga marrying Dmitri, this is the first I have heard of it."

Tatiana burst in, "It might be the first you've heard of it, Mama, but we have had to attend a thousand of stupid Olga and Dmitri's pretend weddings. Even Baby has. He plays the groom. Olga told Nastinka that if she told Dmitri what we do, she'd tell Papa to send her to Siberia, and –"

She was silenced by Olga hitting her in the face and began to cry while I called for Maria to separate them.

"Girls, that is quite enough. You have both behaved abominably all day and I want Maria to take you upstairs right now. When you get there, I want you both to sit quietly and ask yourselves if this is how young grand duchesses should behave."

This prompted Tatiana to exclaim in outrage, "That's so unfair, Mama. I have behaved perfectly all day and I never said I wanted to marry Dmitri. If I do have to get married, I'll marry either Papa or Count Fredericks. Olga

66

hit me, so she should have to go and I should get to stay. I never see you and I miss you all the time."

While everyone argued, a headache of blinding proportions was building up inside of me. Tatiana was right, though – she didn't get to see me much; none of them did, except for Baby. My health was lamentable and it kept me from them. Poor little girl, I thought, and she out of all my children, Baby excepted, so obviously longed for my company.

I suppose that I had been lying to myself about how my enfeebled condition was affecting my girls. They all adored Nicky so much, and they had each other for company, and I liked to think that was enough for them – more than enough, more than I had had at their age as I had no mama at all since I was a wee childy – but while I was responding to their funny little daily letters, it had not occurred to me that they still felt deprived of a mother's care.

Looking at Tatiana's desperate tear-stained little face I saw that she was suffering badly.

I addressed Olga. "Darling, please go upstairs with Maria. I am going to let Tatiana stay for a bit," I raised my hand against her protests. "No, Olga, not now. Mama is not feeling well."

"You never feel well, but Anya's here, she's always here, and now you're letting Tatiana stay and not me. Why don't you like me as much as you like them?"

I thought my heart might jump out of my chest, so great was the pain caused by her words. Did they all think this, that I didn't *like* them? I loved all of them, but I simply wasn't well enough to try to explain it all then. I wished all of them, including Anya, who was watching

67

all of this with an avid expression, would go, but I had already told Tatiana that she could stay for a bit.

So, sighing, I smiled at Olga and said, "Dearest, don't be silly. Papa and I love all of you equally. Anya is not the same as you. She is my friend. Mama does not have a nice sister living here with her the way you do, so I like to talk with her about grown-up things. Now please, darling, go with Maria and be a nice girly for Mama."

Anna interjected unhelpfully, "Here, Olga, take some of these nice cakes with you for your little sisters. You can have as many as you wish. That way you'll be happy, even if you never get to marry Dmitri."

Olga looked scornfully at the cakes Anya was offering her and promptly left the room in aggrieved silence.

I heard Tatiana give a little gasp of pleasure at the thought of being included, just her, in one of Anya and my apparently fabled teatime tête-à-têtes. At least that is how my girls seemed to regard them.

Ignoring Tatiana's presence, Anya groaned and wiped at her eyes. "I see that I'll never be allowed to marry Dmitri, I do see, I do, but what if I don't marry anyone? Why would that be bad? I could stay near you and that's all I want anyway."

I could not repeat to her why that should be so with my innocent child in the room, and instead looked down and stroked Tatiana's little hand and mumbled that all brides were prone to an attack of the nerves at first.

"You weren't," they said in unison.

I looked at them, startled. Is that what they thought? Is that how everyone thought now, Nicky too?

That pleased me, oddly. All my uncertainty and tears and doubts had seemingly all been erased with our marriage, which, it appeared, was a golden success in the eyes of all.

I flushed with pleasure and smiled happily at them both, my headache and heart pains receding.

"That is not strictly true, my sweet ones. Even silly old Mama had her doubts, her girlish whims. All ridiculous of course, for see how happy I am with Papa. Yes, we are terribly happy, he and I."

Anya said doubtfully, "So you think I'll feel this way too, even after what Father Grigory said –"

I waved my hand and laughed in a manner I hoped was convincingly dismissive of her concerns.

"Oh, Anya, and you too, Tati, listen to an old married woman like me and I think I can explain that. You see, Father Grigory is a holy man and he has visions and receives messages from God, but I think he would be the first to tell you that the meanings of these visions are somewhat unclear at first. You see, as a priest and as a man he might have seen visions of Anya crying or looking sad because no one is happy all of the time – no one should be. You both know that I have suffered much and cried many tears, but I am most happy with my lot, as is your papa. So we cannot know what Father Grigory saw, but I do know this ..." I clasped my hands together and eyed them both seriously, "... God does not wish for a woman to be unmarried. In fact, to remain a spinster is to violate our sacred pact with Our Creator. We must marry and produce children, lots of children, is that not right, Anya?"

Tatiana looked rapt at my explanation – Anya less so – but after a moment when it appeared she might do herself serious mischief if she were required to think any harder, Anya nodded.

"I will, and I will try, and you and His Majesty will give us the nice house here at Tsarskoe Selo, as you promised, so that I can always be near you."

I nodded, too emotional to speak, and Tatiana impulsively moved over to Anya and kissed her, and then moved back to snuggle up against me.

"Mama, wouldn't it be nice if Anya and Lieutenant Vyroubov had four girls, like you and Papa?"

Anya giggled and turned tomato red.

"Maybe we'll have four boys, one for each of you to marry."

Tatiana looked puzzled at that and I decided not to bother trying to untangle all that was mistaken in that sentiment, but rather nodded in agreement. One can only educate people for so many hours in any one day and this had been an inhumanly long one.

Chapter 5

So, Anya married Lieutenant Vyroubov and they lived happily ever after ... for nearly a month.

Anya was found outside the doors of our private apartments in a state of utter hysteria early in the morning shortly after her wedding day. The footmen had let her pass as far as the doors that divided our rooms from the rest of the palace, but no further, and so my maid Maria was sent for. Exasperated, she refused Anya's entreaties to either allow her to see Nicky at his breakfast table or to have me awoken, plying her instead with much food and scarce sympathy, observing to me afterward that Anya's distress had in no way dimmed her appetite.

When Anya was finally allowed to see me, she reported many vague, if alarming, things about her new husband's attempts to "violate and injure" her. With many pats and stifled laughs, I did for poor Anya what I was shocked to find out that her own dear mama had not done, that is I explained to her the ways in which God has created for a husband and a wife to create children, and with many blushes even went so far as to tell her that it could provide other pleasures besides.

"I know I am a sinful, wicked woman to say this, Anya dear, but the great love that His Majesty and I share between us, and in this I address the way in which a wife and a husband may know each other ... well, it has brought me a happiness that I did not know existed here on this earth. It may well be that this is seldom spoken of, nor should it be, between an old married

71

woman like me and a young unmarried girl, but you are a wife now, Anya, so I feel that I can speak of it and say …" I suddenly felt overcome with confusion and broke off, for in very truth how could I say, give voice, to the astounding, nearly otherworldly, feeling that Nicky's caresses gave me?

Anya was gaping at me, her tongue nearly hanging from her mouth in astonishment.

I sighed. "Oh Anya, it is really impossible to speak of, but –"

"I saw his naked feet. They were horrible and I didn't want to see any more. And besides, I'm certain he's a sodomite … so I ran for my life."

On delivering this alarming statement, she burst into noisy sobs once again.

"Anya, no, it cannot be. What can you mean, 'a sodomite,' and how do you even know of such things?"

She sniffled and looked at me with indignant pride.

"Oh, I know all about sodomites. The soldiers talked of such things when Mama and I visited them in the hospitals during the last war. Besides –"

I raised my hand for silence.

"I am certain that you know no such things, and moreover, are you accusing Lieutenant Vyroubov of attempting to …? Oh, this is terrible! I hardly know what to ask. But how do you mean, Anya?"

She could not meet my eyes. Blushing furiously, she muttered, "After he came in naked but for his nightshirt, his ugly horned toes sticking straight out, he … he jumped at me … No, no, he leapt at me … and began pulling me about. I rolled over to my side to try and escape him, and that is when he put his hands on my, my

72

..." She broke off to blow her nose and gestured at her well-padded posterior with a look of despair.

I buried my face in my hands and, fortuitously, she mistook my stifled gasps of laughter for sobs and even rose to pat my shoulder in comfort.

"I know, it was a great shock, but what can I do with such a beast except to ask His Majesty to approve an immediate annulment?"

It was only with many encouragements to think over the matter more seriously, and finally a promise to speak of it with Nicky, that I managed to get Anya to return to the small house we had given her and the Lieutenant as a wedding gift. It was a lovely little place and located right next to the gates of our dear park. In that tense half hour of consoling Anya, I wondered if bringing her right into our home, so to speak, might have been a lapse of judgment on my part, but I dismissed the thought. Anya was good company and quite removed me from my daily worries with her funny little ways.

Later that night, Nicky and I were most naughty about her. After listening to my story, Nicky groaned and then laughed somewhat ruefully.

"Well, I really cannot just grant an annulment willy-nilly. Besides, this may be a bit out of my hands, darling. I think she will have to apply to the Church for one, and God help us if this story gets out. I say, why don't you ask them both to come with us next week when we take the old Standart out for our cruise? Maybe all the poor Lieutenant needs is some bracing sea air. And as for Anya, we could ask Botkin to give the fellow something he could use to calm his bride and all might work out for the best in the end."

I tried not to laugh and failed.

"Oh Nicky, you're too bad. Are you suggesting he chloroform her? Poor Anya! But truly, have you ever heard anything so ridiculous? Can you imagine that her mother never told her about such things in this day and age? And the Lieutenant, I do think he might have tried to be a bit more persuasive, and –"

"And pushed his way onward, Sunny, is that what you think?" Nicky said, pulling me closer. "Is that what I did on our bridal night, my darling, my angel? Was I persuasive?"

I closed my eyes in pleasure at his touch and only sighed in answer.

His hand, which had been caressing my neck, moved in small circles first to my shoulders, then to my back, and then lower still. He whispered in my ear, his breath nearly as hot as my skin was growing. "Did I touch you here? Were you afraid, too, my one darling?"

I shivered in delighted anticipation.

"Nicky …"

And for a night we became one again, and in that becoming all the troubles of the greater world and of the smaller one were lost.

Chapter 6

When I consider matters, I think I can speak for everyone in our little family when I say that our times aboard our dear Standart constituted the sole stretches of unclouded happiness we ever experienced together. Individually, we all had our favorite places and times, but they were not usually the same ones. I, for example, felt most safe and contented in my pretty rooms at our dear Alexander Palace, as did, I think, Baby, who in any case was most happy when with me.

I despised the cold immensity of the Winter Palace and its location in the middle of the dreadful, gossiping, artificial Saint Petersburg. Moscow was pleasant in its way, but strange and different, and I could never settle there comfortably. Peterhof was Nicky's favorite home, excepting The Standart, because he was such a fresh air man that the nearness of the sea made him feel free. I suppose our girls felt the same way, for they rather inexplicably hated Tsarskoe Selo to varying degrees.

I found their dislike painful but understandable. In my own girlhood we had lived at the new palace right in the middle of my dear bustling little Darmstadt and had grown up freely, able to wander where we chose. This was not the life of my girls, or, for that matter, of Nicky.

Due to the seemingly never-ending plots of the implacable revolutionaries who hunted the Romanovs like exotic trophy animals, our family – Nicky's family – had to live in what amounted to a series of prisons. Our Tsarskoe Selo prison was certainly a beautiful one with its parks, and palaces, and follies, and a zoo, and a lake, but it was also completely fenced in and guarded at every moment by Cossack patrols. My girls had never been out unaccompanied by guards and chaperones in their lives and the mere thought of their being able to pass outside the gates and step into a shop in the village of Tsarskoe Selo was one that sent them into raptures of excitement for days.

Nicky had grown up behind the fences of Gatchina and now lived behind the fences of Tsarskoe Selo, and although Peterhof was hugely guarded as well, he and the girls sensed a greater measure of freedom there – one cannot fence off a sea – although that sense of freedom was ultimately illusory. For my own part, since I had become so ill ... well, maybe before that too ... I needed the familiar and the small and the safe. My world was limited, and in my sickness I could not manage it in any other manner.

For these reasons The Standart suited us all wonderfully.

I had decorated it in such a way that, if one did not look out of the portholes, one might fancy oneself still at our dear old Alexander Palace. I was particularly proud of my boudoir and Nicky's green leather study, for they were near perfect replicas of the ones at home.

Dispiritingly, Nicky hadn't been quite as pleased as I had expected him to be, saying only, "It seems as though we haven't left Tsarskoe Selo at all," before beginning to settle in, as I knew he would, surrounded by such comfortable and familiar surroundings.

My girls' obvious joy at our trips abroad only increased my own enjoyment of the peace and rest I received. At home they could be rather restless and needy, sending me so many daily notes and questions that sometimes I was forced to spend hours doing nothing but answering them. Their tutors also tended to bother me more at home. However, on The Standart all that was changed.

Each girly had a sailor assigned to her. At first, when they were small, the sailors' primary duty was to keep them from falling overboard, and in the case of Anastasia – our mad Nastinka – the poor sailor, I fear, was kept permanently on his toes, for she was a very monkey for climbing and for mischief. My big pair, of course, Olga and Tatiana, were beyond that now and so their sailors played games of hoops and taught them how to roller-skate on deck. At night, before dinner, they would all dance in a ring together, and I think my Olga developed several little girl crushes upon our handsome sailors, which both Nicky and I found endearing in the extreme, although he was wont to tease her, which I disapproved of, reminding him that I had been only her age when my child's heart was handily won.

I can now admit that before Anya joined us on her first cruise, despite taking great pleasure in the evident joy of my family, I had felt a bit left out. Nicky liked The Standart to cruise the Finnish Fjords and to anchor there for swimming and daily excursions onto the islands, in which adventures he was almost always joined by the girls and our suite, whereas I could not for the life of me get the girls to accompany me for embroidery or quiet play as the lure of these adventures with their adored papa was too strong to resist. I had, therefore, been rather left to my own devices and made to feel, even on our lovely yacht, that I was an invalid – loved but not included.

All that changed when Anya accompanied us for the first time. Due to her size and clumsiness, Anya was not particularly interested in shore excursions as there was always the possibility that she would tip over the small landing boats or slip and fall out of one. And then, of course, she truly enjoyed my company. So we spent that cruise serenely chatting away, reading aloud to one another, and occasionally playing four-handed on the piano I had installed, and even singing. So gladdened was I by her grateful and at times unwittingly humorous presence, that I managed to regain enough health and vigor that even Nicky noticed the change in me. As he famously said to Anya at the end of our cruise, she must always accompany us from then on.

Then there was the war, a near-revolution and, even worse, a spate of vile rumors concerning Anya and me, so it was not until two years later that she joined us again.

I can selfishly admit that I initially feared that, due to the presence of her new husband, she would be less available to me, but I could not have been more wrong. Anya avoided Lieutenant Vyroubov with a fervor seldom seen in her excepting at teatimes, and she stuck so closely to my side that I even became a bit annoyed as it was left to Olga and Tatiana to try to entertain her poor abandoned husband by teaching him to roller-skate. I found him to be rather sweet, but sadly Nicky, like Anya, fully disliked the man, and, despite my exhortations, would not invite him to bathe or to go ashore.

"I'm sorry, Sunny darling, I do try to include him in conversations at dinner, but it is too much for you to ask me to drag the poor fellow along in whatever limited leisure time I have. He always looks as though he is about to cry, not that I blame him, given the way Anya treats him. And I was sorry that Nastinka bit him yesterday, but you do have to admit he is wholly pathetic and very poor company."

Personally I wasn't quite as convinced of his overall feebleness as Nicky was, as it seemed to me that if a person is repeatedly neglected and scorned, it will be difficult for him to perform at his best. So, having experienced this truth for myself, I made a considerable effort with Anya's despised husband and at the end concluded that while I might be able to find some virtues in the poor man – patience being one of them – I was destined to remain alone in my intuitions about him. In consequence, I concluded that upon our return I would ask Father Grigory to offer them both advice as to how to make the best of their unfortunate, if God-ordained, predicament. For my own part, I could only attempt to help them by trying to demonstrate to Anya the endless joys of motherhood by displaying Baby to her at every opportunity.

Baby had just turned three years old the previous month, and although I know that every mother finds her baby to be exceptional, our sunshine truly was, and I was often surprised and pleased, as was Nicky, to find that every person who beheld him said that he was the most beautiful child they had ever seen. Naturally, we had always thought so, but I will admit it was gratifying to have our opinion so widely confirmed.

Baby was quite tall for his age, having, to my distress, lost his baby plumpness. Worse, this year I had been obliged to put him out of short dresses and into his first little sailor suits. He adored them and had begun to strut all about The Standart in the same slightly martinet way that the officers did. Nicky had ordered a toy wooden gun for him and he carried it over his shoulder and at times looked such the tiny man that my eyes filled with silly mama tears for the sweet baby he had so recently been.

That Nicky and I loved him to distraction was something that surprised none of those nearest to us, and Nicky fancied that he saw much of his dear departed papa in him. Our Sunshine could be very stern, and even at the tender age of three he already understood that he was a personage of some importance, having early on noted that people immediately sprang to their feet and bowed upon seeing him. To our amusement, when they did not do so quickly enough for him, he would sometimes poke or kick them.

Nicky said, "I fear for our people, darling, under the coming reign of Alexei the Terrible."

He was, of course, speaking in jest, for although even I can acknowledge that our baby had a strong sense of himself – one which would certainly stand him in good stead as a future emperor – he also had a serious and reflective side that was striking in one so tiny. I had to conclude that this might have come more from his early sufferings than from a natural predisposition, for when he was well he lit our whole world with his sunshiny ways. He was quick to giggle at every pleasure, and as curious and monkey-like for a romp as his favorite sister Anastasia.

He was every inch a boy, and to our total delight during that fall aboard The Standart, it was as though he had never known a single day's illness. He awoke early, ravenous for his breakfast, and soon afterward he would treat us all to a raucous banging and crashing on his miniature soldier's toy drum. Then there was a deck march to lead. This involved his stamping at the head of all the deck hands and officers, regardless of rank, Nagorny on his heels, leading the entire party in a circle or ten around the deck, pounding his tiny drum and issuing orders.

"Look sharp, boys," he would shout out, creating helpless laughter in Nicky and me no matter how many times we heard it, although we would straighten our faces and solemnly salute back at him when he encountered us on his circuits.

Life aboard The Standart allowed me to rest on deck or in my boudoir and yet to be a full part of every day's proceedings, and with Anya by my side I no longer felt alone.

One afternoon, while watching Baby's antics, I impulsively reached for Anya's hand and said, "Look around you, Anya. Doesn't all of this make you want to try to reach an accommodation with your husband?"

She looked at me with stupefaction – Anya nearly always appeared to be surprised to some degree – and shook her head.

"Well, I don't suppose that my husband is going to buy me a yacht like The Standart. I'd be amazed if he could even buy me a rowboat. And if he did, it would be to no avail as I'd just fall out of it anyway, they rock so wildly."

She began to chortle at her own witticism and I was smiling back at her tolerantly while beginning to prepare to deliver a speech about a woman's highest glory being her children, when all the world suddenly turned upside down and I found myself being hurled to the ground and sliding toward the rear deck as screams and shouts erupted about me.

Panicked, I grasped at a rope that was flapping above me and held on to it for dear life. Shortly afterward I heard Nicky's concerned shouts and mercifully felt his arms thrown about me, drawing me against him.

Too shocked to do more than say his name, I looked about frantically for baby.

"Nicky, what ...? My God, my God, where is Baby?"

"Alicky, we have hit something, I think. The Standart is sinking. It is all right, darling, I think Nagorny has Baby, or maybe Derevenko has him, but look here, there is no time, I have to go and help the officers. You are all right, see, look ..."

He eased me to my feet although already the boat was sloping terribly toward the water and I had to lean against the wall to avoid falling. I felt very dizzy, but looking at Nicky I could see I was on my own.

His face was terribly white and two hectic spots of color had painted themselves onto his cheeks. He was twisting his hands and nearly jumping about in place, and would have, I think, but for the angle of the deck. Then, to add to all the horror, the ship's steam stacks began letting out terrible noises that sounded like screams.

"Nicky … Oh never mind, go!"

"I fear we'll go down quickly, Alix. I am needed, so I … Well, I … What do you want me to do?"

"Go, Nicky, go where you are needed. Anya, Olga, Tatiana – find Baby," I shouted into the melee, hoping someone would hear me.

I heard a nearby shout and grabbed Anastasia as she began gleefully to climb a railing, taking advantage of the fact that none of the nanny sailors were near her. Clutching her with one hand and holding on to the wall with the other, I screamed Anya's name at the top of my lungs.

I heard an answering hoarse shout.

"Your Majesty, Your Majesty, we're all going to drown."

I looked in the direction of her voice and saw her lying on her stomach, clawing ineffectually at the deck beneath her

Irritation at her stupidity straightened my spine.

"Anya, stand up this instant and come over here and watch Anastasia. Baby must be found and I haven't a second to spare for your nonsense."

My attitude was just what Anya needed to persuade her to pull herself together. She didn't get to her feet but she did crawl up the deck to Anastasia and me, the latter protesting loudly as I bent and tied her sash to Anya's wrist.

"Stay right here, the both of you, I have to find Baby and the other girls, and get them into boats. Right here! I mean it!" I said into Anya's stricken face and Nastinka's rebellious one. Assured that they were going to do what I said, I then moved cautiously forward, calling for Alexei.

"Here, Your Majesty. I have him safe and sound."

I looked at Nagorny, Baby's second sailor-nanny, with astonished gratitude.

"Nagorny, God will thank you for this service, as do His Majesty and I. Are they lowering the life boats yet? His Majesty was going to … Well he … I think is in charge of that. I want you and Baby to get into the first one. Are they being lowered?" I finished a little hysterically. I was trying very hard not to give way, my new relief at finding Baby being replaced by a growing fear for my girls and for the others on board.

Nagorny's broad smile was the best moment amid the chaos. Rubbing Baby's back, he said confidently, "All under control, Your Majesty. This fellow and I are off. The sailors have two boats ready. I can take Madame Vyroubova and Anastasia Nikolaevna with me right now, if you'd like."

Nearly kissing him in gratitude, but managing simply to kiss Baby's sweet face instead, I answered fervently. "Nagorny, you are a great servant. I will never forget this. And yes, please, please, take Nastinka too. Madame Vyroubova will remain with me. I have need of her help."

I ignored Anya's squawk of outrage behind me, and with Nagorny's strong free hand guiding me, made my way back to Nastinka who was clearly delighted with the great adventure of it all.

"Mama, Baby and I are going to swim to shore. Nagorny and Anya can stay here."

"Yes, darling, that is nice," I said absent-mindedly while urging Nagorny to hurry with my eyes.

Wordlessly he nodded, and in an instant had Nastinka under his free arm, and despite the by-now badly tilting deck, began carefully making his way to port and to the boats.

Over his shoulder he called out, "Your Majesty, the other girls – Maria has them. They're probably in the boats already."

"Thank God for that. Come on, Anya. For Pete's sake, pull yourself together."

She gawped at me.

"But we're going to drown and I don't want to. I'm going to the boats. Nagorny and Maria will need my help with the children. They'll be frightened."

I clamped my hand firmly onto her wrist and began tugging her toward the cabins.

"The children will be fine and Nicky is overseeing it all, I am sure. Come on, Anya. We will both drown if we don't get started and that will be too bad."

She tugged back stubbornly, trying to free her hand.

"My husband ... I should be with him now!"

I pulled harder. "Your concern is touching, Anya. Come on!"

"Where ... where are we going?" she asked in a shaking voice.

"To my rooms. There are things that I must save."

She looked at me in real horror.

"The cabins will be flooding."

I pulled her so hard that she was forced to follow me and said, "I do know that, Anya, which is why there is no time to waste."

Inside, though, I was trembling. She was right: there was water sloshing up the shallow steps that led down to our cabins.

Instantly deciding to forego the children's rooms to gather clothes, and still holding the shaking Anya by the wrist, I led us down the steps into a changed watery world. Nicky and my bedroom was flooded to the knees with objects washing all about. The electric lights were not working, and despite the bright sun outside, we were already nearly submerged.

Beginning to panic now myself, I released Anya and grabbed a wet sheet, hoping she would do the same.

To my eternal gratitude, and, yes, surprise, she did just that. Drawing down on a strength that I believe only women possess in times of great tempest, she suddenly knew what to do, and working hurriedly and silently we stuffed the soaking sheets with my jewelry and as many icons as we could take. Then, dragging the absurdly heavy things behind us, we struggled back up the steps. The slant was so severe by then that it was almost like climbing a ladder. Worse, we were soaked to our waists and severely hampered by this additional weight.

By the time we made it to the port side of the boat I could barely keep my legs. Some of the sailors rushed over to Anya and me and relieved us of our burdens. Anya abruptly dropped to the deck in a faint and slid ignominiously toward starboard and the water. It took four sailors to haul her back to our side and load her into a boat. I held my courage and my legs and looked about me in wonder. Our beautiful yacht was nearly on its side and almost abandoned. There were just myself and a few sailors.

Then I saw Nicky …

He was standing at the aft-most end of the boat where it was furthest off the water. He wasn't looking at me, or the sailors, or any of the life boats, he was staring at his watch, and with an odd movement of his head he peered at the water, glanced at his watch again, and repeated the exercise.

I looked over at Captain Sablin who had, naturally, remained onboard.

"Captain, do you know what His Majesty is doing?"

He stared at Nicky, avoiding my eyes as he answered me.

"Yes, Your Majesty. He is keeping the time of the sinking. He told me that he felt it would take twenty minutes and he wished to remain where he was to keep track of the time."

I turned away for a moment to gather myself.

"I see. Thank you, Captain. Please tell your remaining sailors to tell His Majesty that it is my express wish that he now enter a lifeboat with them. Tell them to say to him that I shall not depart The Standart until I see him safely inside one of them."

"Your Majesty, forgive me, but …" His voice trailed off.

"You may speak frankly, Captain, and speak hurriedly as well, for it appears we shall be swimming in a moment."

"Yes, Your Majesty. I only thought it might be better if you addressed His Majesty directly rather than … I could help you up the deck to him."

I shook my head and fixed my eyes on the growing closeness of the sea to my feet.

"No, I will not do that. See that I am obeyed on this, Captain, and tell your men to use force if necessary."

"Your Majesty, we cannot touch His Majesty without his permission. Please –"

"See it is done, Captain, and done now. If the Tsar of Russia dies holding his father's watch in his hand, I will see to it that you are held responsible."

His expression turned cold.

"Understood, Your majesty."

He stepped away from me with some difficulty and summoned his sailors, and after nervous looks were shot in my direction, they made their way hesitantly toward Nicky. I could not hear what was said over the screaming clarion of the ship's alarm and the general clatter, but I saw Nicky glance at me, startled. I met his look with an expression of cold fury and saw his shoulders slump as he allowed two sailors to help lower him into an empty boat.

Captain Sablin approached me once again, even managing to bow from the waist, which was no easy feat given our circumstances.

I smiled at him and he stared back curiously.

"Your Majesty, will you enter the boat with His Majesty? There is very little time left, but several naval boats are on the approach and you will not be stranded long in the lifeboat, if that is what concerns you. But truly, we must hurry now."

"Yes, Captain, you are right, but tell your sailors to get in the boat with His Majesty. I will leave the yacht, as you shall, when there is no one left aboard."

He looked at me for a long time and smiled.

"Yes, Your Majesty, I shall tell them. And may I say it will be my great honor to escort you into the last boat, my great honor indeed."

We did not languish in the small boats for more than a few minutes. At sea, as by land, guards always surrounded us. Nicky did not like to pay attention to them, wishing to pretend we were all to ourselves out on The Standart, but torpedo boats had been tracking us within a few miles at all times, and one of them, The Asia, promptly came to our aid and our poor crew and guests were made as comfortable as possible with blankets on the deck area. Fortunately the weather was mild. The captain of this modest vessel gave Baby and me his own sad cabin and the officers handed theirs to my four girls, who luckily were still infected with an air of excitement about it all.

I had not spoken to Nicky, or sent a message to him, and we boarded The Asia on different boats. I did not, in truth, know what to say to him, so I was a bit discomfited, when answering the humble knock at my cabin door, to see him standing there with a cup of tea in one hand and a washbasin spilling water in the other.

I tried to smile, failed, and gestured for him to set his burdens down upon the miniscule dresser. Baby crowed with delight, shouting "Papa!" loudly, and began scrambling off our bunk to reach him. The cabin was so tiny that Nicky was easily able to catch him up before he could reach the floor. Nicky buried his face in Alexei's neck and looked up at me, his eyes filling with tears.

"Thank God. God be praised. He is safe. We are all safe. The girls are safe, aren't they?"

I nodded and sat back down on the bunk, all my strength long since spent.

"They are fine – a little crowded but cheerful. They are right next door. You should go and say hello to them. They will be delighted. They asked about you when we came onboard. I told them you were busy. Were you, Nicky?"

He sat down heavily beside me, Baby on his lap. I shifted away from him as far as the tiny bed would allow. He didn't seem to notice.

"I was, darling. There was much to see to. I know this funny boat is terribly uncomfortable … You should see everybody up top. They look like the most desperate of castaways and you can hear Anya bellowing about saving all our possessions all the way to Denmark." He chuckled and looked at me hopefully to see if I would return his smile. I didn't. He shrugged and went on. "We have already telegraphed, and tomorrow morning, probably even before you wake up, darling, the nice Alexandria will be here and we can continue our cruise. I have sent for engineers to come from Yalta to oversee the repair of The Standart. Probably by next summer she will be as good as new, and –"

"Nicky, I do not want to continue our cruise. I want to go home as soon as we possibly can. This is ridiculous!"

He looked at me in such genuine puzzlement that if Baby had not been on his lap, I would have pushed him off the bunk.

"Alicky, why? We were all having such a fine time, weren't we? All of us – Anya, the children – and, you know, these cruises are my sole time of relaxation. I am

90

nearly crushed by it all the rest of the year. What can you possibly mean you want to go home? Surely you don't blame me for this, do you?"

"Nicky, of course I blame you for it. Captain Sablin as much as told me that you ordered The Standart right into the middle of the Skerries where he told you the water was far too shallow. Your stupidity could have killed us all. It is a clear miracle that Baby didn't sustain an injury and start bleeding. As it is, you have terrified everyone and destroyed our pretty yacht. And then you just stood there ... stood there ... like a stuffed dummy and did nothing to help. Oh God, do I blame you? What do you think I should feel?"

He didn't even have the good grace to look ashamed; in fact he looked outraged. He set Baby down carefully.

"I shall reassign that old gossip Sablin to a scow in Korea for daring to say that to you."

I jutted my chin toward him.

"And if you do, I shall never set foot at sea again, nor any of the children, and then you can sail our yacht onto every island and sandbar in Finland and do so without us, Nicky."

I pulled Baby into my lap and nuzzled his hair. He was sleepy; we were all so tired. I knew that Nicky must be as well, but I didn't care.

Nicky gestured at our tiny cabin.

"Given your feelings on the matter, Your Majesty, I suppose you would like me to sleep on the floor ..."

I nodded.

"Yes, on the upper deck, along with our displaced officers and poor Anya. You have always been a fresh air man, Nicky. It will be a great adventure for you.

91

Have someone, Anya or Maria, sent to me in the morning when this Alexandria of yours arrives, so that the children and I can switch ship and go home."

"If I don't send the Captain away, will you continue the cruise?"

"Are you negotiating with me, Nicky?"

"That is a strong choice of words, darling. No, I am merely asking."

I looked at him curiously. "Do you feel at all responsible for what occurred today, Nicky?"

He shrugged and spread out his hands.

"Not particularly, no, Alix ... Or yes, in that I am held responsible for everything, including every season in Russia. If there is no rain and the crops fail, it is my doing. If there is too much rain and the crops fail, it is my doing again. If there is disease, and hunger, and want, and anger; if there is war; if there is a peace that no one wants – all these are blamed on me." Not allowing me to interrupt this pointless and self-pitying speech, he closed his eyes, sighed heavily and continued. "There is no moment or time when all do not blame and judge me. Why should you be any different? But that isn't what I asked you, is it? I asked you if you would continue our trip if Captain Sablin, who has disloyally spoken out of turn, is allowed to retain his position?"

"Nicky?"

"Yes, Alix?"

"Do you ever tire of feeling sorry for yourself?"

He opened his eyes and smiled without any warmth into mine.

"Do you ever tire of feeling sorry for yourself, darling?"

Chapter 7

So our cruise resumed on The Alexandria, where Anya, in a burst of particular emotion, declared that she could not possibly share a cabin with her husband lest he attempt his "perverted tortures" of her again, and spent a fortnight sleeping in one of the bathrooms to avoid him. In some ways I envied her, but my marriage was a different case altogether. Divorce was not possible, or even thinkable. I did not want a separation, I just wanted … oh, I do not know what I wanted. I loved Nicky, I did, but after all these years I had begun to despair that he and I would ever reach a meeting of minds, although we did meet in our hearts. My Nicky was a good man, a wonderful husband and father, but I had begun to doubt in the deepest recesses of my soul whether God might have mistakenly placed him, and consequently me, where we were in the world.

I did not want to think this way as it was disloyal to my husband, a man who could not, as he himself said so many times, help being Tsar. God, he said, had called him to his position, placed him above all others. It was God's will, and if he failed at it – and I could not help knowing that others besides me saw that he often did – then that too was God's will. He was born on the Day of Job after all, and so what could he do? He considered himself to be the Sacrificial Lamb, the Golden Calf, set up for calumny. That was how Nicky saw things and it was consequently how I needed to see them as well, for if I did not, I was questioning not just Nicky but God Himself.

Yet, by the end of our ill-starred cruise, I saw dark omens all about me, and Anya's energetic protests at her state made me wonder whether it was always wrong to wish to back out of a mistake. Did everyone need to see everything as God's will? If so, why had He even bothered to give us free will?

Standing on the deck of The Polar Star, which had been sent to get us after numerous complaints had been made about the over-crowding on The Alexandria, I stood on our final day beside Nicky, who had demanded that the Captain sail The Polar Star right back to where The Standart had foundered so he could survey the scene, evidently oblivious to the very real chance that The Polar Star might hit a rock in the shallows as well.

We stood there, we three – Nicky, myself, and Baby in Nicky's arms – as he pointed out the sunken Standart which lay on its side in water no more than five or six feet deep.

"You see, Alexei? Do you see our ship down there?" Nicky asked him in seeming delight.

Alexei leaned so far over the railing that, despite Nicky's arms around him, I put out my own hand to clutch the back of his little jacket.

Nicky smiled at me.

"Don't worry, darling, I've got him. He is simply curious, that is all. It is not a bad trait in a future tsar. He simply likes to see how things are. It is hard to believe she is so close to the surface, isn't it, Sunny? See, Alexei, that is your very own cabin," he said, gesturing to one of the flooded and broken portholes. I couldn't look at it anymore.

Nicky was already cheerfully cabling ships architects with plans to have The Standart rebuilt and refitted, and naval ships were already massed to drag her from her place of temporary repose and haul her to Sebastopol for repairs, but I knew that, no matter how perfectly she was repaired – "better even than before," as Nicky said – I would always remember her like this, doleful and ruined on the bottom of the Finnish Skerries for no better reason than being the result of a stupid whim. The woeful condition of The Standart, at least, was clearly not the will of God, but merely the will of Nicky. I hoped fervently that he might learn to recognize the deep truth of the saying that God helps those who help themselves, but I didn't have much faith in that hope.

I was still in this frame of mind when we finally reached home for the winter, and it was my growing sympathy for the position of all women in unfortunate marriages that made me approach Nicky on Anya's behalf for her divorce.

I had spoken to Father Grigory at length on the matter before doing so and Father Grigory had said with his usual happy equanimity, "It makes no matter if poor, fat Anya is divorced or not, for God does not make marriages – man makes marriages and man makes mistakes. God forgives us them, and then we can make some more, and it is all good fun, and He does not mind. If He did, He would have made better ones out of all of us."

I was both shocked and delighted by such an unorthodox view of Christian marriage and felt obliged to respond, "But Father Grigory, surely you cannot be saying that what God has joined together we are allowed to tear asunder at will?"

He drank his tea and stuffed some cakes in his pockets; this was but one of his many endearing habits. The first time he had done so, I had asked him why, and he had replied solemnly that there were many people in need who came to him, and because he had no money, he liked to share food with them if there was any extra. Unsaid was that at Tsarskoe Selo there was always a great deal of extra, but he did not reproach me for that, and in return I had taken to ordering three times the number of tea cakes when he was coming.

Today, I waited patiently for him to arrange his cakes before answering me. When he was done, he shook his head and sighed.

"You will agree, Mamushka, that there are arguments and arguments."

I waited for him to explain his pronouncement, but when he said nothing else I tried to puzzle out what he meant. For the life of me, I couldn't, which was often the case. Father Grigory's observations were all too often as indecipherable as the advice given by the legendary Oracle at Delphi.

"Forgive me, Father Grigory, but I do not understand – arguments and arguments?"

"Yes, Mamushka. In my village, why, a man might say, 'I think you stole my turnips, you rascal.' Now, that is a serious thing to say to a man, whether it is true or not, for it accuses another of taking the food a man needs to feed his family. So there is a deep argument to ponder, and can it ever be healed?" He shrugged and raised his hands to heaven. "Only God knows."

"I … Forgive me, Father Grigory, but I do not see how this relates exactly to marriage."

"Everything relates to everything, Mamushka, but tell me," he fixed his penetrating gaze on me, "are these questions about funny Anya's marriage or about another's?"

"Father Grigory, you forget yourself."

He rose without permission, raising his shoulders dismissively.

"I suppose I do. Everyone should, for those who think too much about themselves think too little about God."

"Yes, Father, that is all well and good, but –"

"I am going home, Mamushka. You are cross with Grigory today and I do not like to be scowled at."

I arched my back imperiously. "You may not go, Father Gregory, until I say you may go. Sit back down and answer me about what is best to do about Anya."

He raised an eyebrow and remained standing.

"Anya? Who cares? She may stay married, she may be divorced, what does that matter to anyone? What does it matter to millions of Russians who fear that the coming winter might be a day too long, even an hour too long to save their starving children? Does it matter to the grand priests in Petersburg or to the poor teachers in the villages? Does it matter to the boyars wrapped in their furs and sleighs? Does it matter to the poor whore who does not know if she has enough life to earn one kopek before she dies under a boyar's carriage? Will she go to Hell? she wonders, as she lies dying in the street. But only God knows that and maybe He does not care either. I know that I, Grigory, do not care about Anya's marriage. Why do you, Mamushka? But now I must leave you."

Which is exactly what he did, without a bow or a by-your-leave, and I found myself suddenly alone in my boudoir. It had grown dark early, as it always did in the winter, and the snow was beginning to fall.

Father Grigory had been right to pose that question: Why did I care?

Nicky unsympathetically seemed to agree with Father Grigory, which both annoyed and pleased me at the same time, for I wanted Nicky to think highly of Father Grigory, but never at my expense.

Getting into bed and lighting a cigarette, he said, "I am glad that it was your friend who asked you that question, Sunny, for I would never have dared to. You are so touchy about Anya."

"I am not!" I spluttered back indignantly.

He looked away from me at the windows, seemingly contemplating the drifting snow.

"I have had a letter from Mama about it, actually. She asks that she be allowed to come to see you. I hope you will agree to her visiting us. You see her so little."

Nicky's request disturbed me horribly.

"A visit? I don't know why, Nicky. Christmas is only a short while away and she will be coming then, so –"

"No, she won't. She has decided to celebrate Christmas this year in town with Xenia and Sandro instead. So, may I tell her you will see her?"

"Oh Nicky, must I? You know I am completely exhausted after that cruise and the strain of all that happened, and I have so much to do getting us all ready for Christmas. There are the trees to order, and the gifts for the servants, and the children's stockings to organize ... Also, I was thinking that –"

Dismissing out of hand whatever I had been going to say, he interrupted me. "Sunny, I want you to say yes. I understand that you are not well, and," he extinguished his cigarette, "that you have to organize Christmas, and that you wish to plan for the children, and that you are tired, and that you need time to yourself, and that it is all a bit overwhelming for you, as it has been for a long while now, but you always have time for Anya and her myriad troubles, so I would like you to set aside an hour of that time and give it to my mother, Her Imperial Highness Empress Marie Feodorovna, your children's grandmother, your mother-in-law."

"My God, Nicky, you make me sound –"

He lit another cigarette and looked at it ruefully. "I do not know what I would do without these fellows." He inhaled deeply, turned his beautiful blue eyes soft with love to face me, and smiled. "I know you do not like her, darling, and I do not mean to make you sound like anything. I would very much like it if you agreed to see her, and if you were to call her personally to invite her to tea with you. I know she would be most pleased to receive your invitation, and so would I. If you cannot, well ..." he shrugged, "... you can't, but I hope you will."

Having no choice, I agreed and arranged for Count Fredericks to issue the invitation on my behalf, for Minnie and I were never going to have the sort of relationship where either of us could pick up the telephone and say casually, "Do come to Tsarskoe Selo and join me for tea."

Chapter 8

Before I could even gather the energy to face this coming nightmare, I was struck down with shocking news from Petersburg involving my dear friends, or so I had thought, the Montenegrin sisters Stana and Mitsia.

It seems that while I was away with my family and Anya on our cruise, they had spent the summer trying to destroy Father Grigory for no better reason than that I liked him and that he had paid me visits without their prior permission. That he had done so at my request and to help my poor baby endure the tortures of his disease apparently made no difference at all. He had offended them grievously by overstepping his boundaries, which is to say *their* boundaries.

I had considered them to be my true friends. I had stood by Stana when she had broken her marriage in order to become a grand duchess rather than a mere princess and I had argued with my mother-in-law on their behalf when she called them the 'Black Princesses." I had believed – and this was the worst realization of all – that they cared for me for myself and not because I was their Empress.

Why would I never learn? No one alive, save our tiny family and my dear Anya, truly liked me for myself alone.

It was poor Anya who was obliged to tell me about the entire sordid affair, rushing in without an invitation following a visit to town to see her parents and her family lawyers. She said that she had suddenly, right at the train station, felt a need to go and visit Father

Grigory, an impulse so strong that she knew it must be obeyed without further ado.

"There I was, Alix – my parents had already left for home, that's how close I was to getting on the train. I was so tired after seeing the lawyers and I was near fainting from hunger too, for Mama has a new cook and the luncheon was terrible – she is so stingy that my cutlet was next to invisible. Also there was no pudding afterward. And so –"

"Anya! Please tell me this instant what you were going to tell me without digressing onto the tiresome topic of food ... And may I remind you that you must address me as 'Your Majesty,' whether we are alone or not ... Now, you were saying that you felt the need to see Father Grigory urgently, and so I assume you did so or else you would hardly have burst in on me to discuss your mother's new cook, or at least one would hope that you would not have done so."

She looked affronted but, to my relief, managed to continue with her recital in a calmer frame of mind.

"Yes, that's right, I did. And you'll never ever guess what he told me, Your Majesty."

"No, I do not imagine that I shall, so please put us both out of our miseries – well, me out of mine, at least – by telling me what you have to say before I expire of old age."

"I am trying to, but you keep interrupting me, and you're always the one who says that is the rudest of things ... and now I can hardly remember what I needed to tell you, and it's very important and shocking too."

She made a pouting expression. I ignored it.

"Yes, I am almost certain it is, Anya, so do try."

So, with every puffy inch of flesh swelling and quivering with indignation, she began her ugly tale.

"I caught a cab to his apartment. It was terribly expensive, I must say." She paused and looked at me hopefully. When I did not respond, she went on. I was quickly losing interest and wondering if I could dismiss her before dinnertime so as not to have to put up with her then too, when her account suddenly drew me up to full alertness. "I found Father Grigory almost alone at his apartment, save for his daughters and his old servant and that strange Lokhtina woman who is always there. He was in a rather bad way. But, do you know, he wasn't even a bit surprised to see me. He said he had prayed that I would come and there I was. I think that's –"

"What do you mean 'in a bad way'? Do you mean he was ill?"

She waved her hands.

"No, not ill exactly, but, well … yes, maybe, but in a spiritual way." It was all I could do not to roll my eyes. Anya did so tend to overdramatize. I held my expression of interest, though, so as not to send her off on another futile discursion. "You see, while we were away, Father Grigory went to visit his little family in Pokrovskoe to see how his new house was coming along –"

Curious, for I had never considered such a thing, I asked, "New house …?"

She nodded enthusiastically.

"Oh yes, he told me all about it. You see, he had to have a larger house in order to have somewhere in Pokrovskoe to take pilgrims in to pray with him, and –"

"I wonder that he had the money for it. Nicky and I have not given him anything. Do you think –?"

102

"Oh, loads of people give him money for prayers and things," Anya replied airily, "but as I was saying –"

"Yes, but it is strange, is it not? I hope they do not give him money because they think –"

"I can't say a thing. You keep interrupting me!"

"Anya!" I began sternly. Then, realizing we would be here all day at this rate – or at least until dinnertime – I bowed my head, bit my lip, and said, "You are so right, Anya. Please go on. So, Father Grigory went to Pokrovskoe ..."

She nodded frantically.

"Yes, that's right, and he took some friends to pray for them, and that's when all the trouble started with the Montenegrins."

She looked at me intently.

"What was the trouble?"

"I'm fearfully hungry, Your Majesty. It seems like hours since lunchtime and that was awful anyway."

At times, and this was one of them, I felt that Anya had been sent by God to be my friend expressly to teach me patience. I had little enough of it, I knew, but I drew down on it now and said, "Yes, Anya, I am certain you are. We shall be dining in an hour and I hope you will join His Majesty and me."

She nodded eagerly. "Oh yes, I'd like to so much. I can tell him, too. I suppose I had better run home and change, though, because –"

"No, Anya, let me hear what you have to say first. I will decide whether or not you should bother His Majesty with it. He carries the weight of the whole world on his shoulders and I will not have him disturbed by small matters, of which this may well be an instance. In any case, I decide what to discuss with him as it pertains to our personal matters. Do you understand me?"

Anya shrugged in resignation.

"Yes, all right. Well, when Father Grigory arrived in Pokrovskoe with his friends, he was met by a group of priests from the Tobolsk Consistory. They, oh Your Majesty, they …" She broke off and I waited with growing agitation for her to go on. "They accused Father Grigory of the most terrible things. They said he was a Khlyst, and –"

"Do you even know what a Khlyst is, Anya?"

"Oh, I don't know, but it seems to be something bad. Shall I call Father Grigory and ask him? I was too shocked to think of asking him when I was there."

I shook my head and waved my hand to indicate that she should continue.

"They said he was a Khlyst and that he had been seen in Petersburg touching and kissing ladies."

She blushed, as did I.

"This is all quite horrid, Anya," I said. "Is there any more to your tale and what have the Montenegrin princesses got to do with any of this?"

"Because Father Grigory says that Mitsia was jealous and terribly angry about him seeing you without her permission, and –"

"*Her permission?* Why would he need her permission to accept an invitation to see me? Is anyone whom I, the Empress of Russia, wish to see to be required to obtain their permission – or anyone else's – to do so?"

Anya nodded heartily.

"Exactly, Your Majesty, and there is more … There are rumors that Father Grigory is using his new house in Pokrovskoe for prayer meetings upstairs, and –"

"As he should, being a man of God endowed with great wisdom."

"Well yes, that's just right, but it is being said that they weren't praying. I don't know exactly what else they were supposed to have been doing, but it is said that he took them to bathhouses and was intimate with them there, and now everybody in town is talking about him and saying that it is most abnormal for you to approve of his behavior, and so –"

"By everybody, Anya, whom do you mean?"

My voice chilled even me and Anya looked nervous.

"I don't know. I mean it's what Mama said. Father Grigory said it too. He said the Montenegrins told everybody all these filthy lies, and that they are the ones saying you aren't well, and that he is sure it has reached the Empress-Dowager. He is much more concerned for your well-being than for his own, and –"

I shook my head violently, causing her to stop. I could not bear it, I really couldn't. I squeezed my eyes shut. That Minnie would hear this … I could imagine what she would have to say about it – a great deal, the interfering old biddy. And that the Montenegrins, my friends, should be the ones to do this to me … What might everyone be saying by now? Any excuse … God help me!

I clawed my nails into my hands but even that pain did not help calm me, and the room began to tilt and sway sickeningly as if I were reliving our recent shipwreck.

"Anya – my heart! Please fetch Dr. Botkin immediately. And not a word to His Majesty, if you see him."

"But –"

"Anya, for the love of Jesus Christ Himself, I am having a heart attack. Go!"

As was my way, I chose to spare Nicky the reason for my attack, merely intimating to him later that I had been taken suddenly quite seriously ill and that I did not know why beyond the fact that at times I found things all too difficult to bear.

Concerned, he leaned closer.

"Did something happen, Sunny, to bring this on? I know you have been ill, but Botkin told me you had suffered a heart attack. Was it Anya, darling? Did she upset you? I think maybe she can be too much for you at times. If seeing her disturbs you to this extent, I think we should tell her to come less often, don't you?"

I moved closer to him in as natural a manner as I could manage, but my thoughts were hurried. I did not want Nicky to blame Anya, but I did not want him to hear the terrible lies being spread around about Father Grigory either. He had been slow to welcome him into our lives and he was not still fully there. However, I wanted the Montenegrin sisters to feel my anger. I wanted Stana's husband, that histrionic, over-mighty grand duke, to feel the chill of the withdrawal of Nicky's slavish devotion to him.

Playing for time, I sighed against Nicky's chest and shed a few tears that I knew he felt.

His hands twined in my hair.

"There is something, isn't there, Sunny? Please tell me. Don't you know I would give up anything – no, everything – to make you happy, to make you well again?"

I shifted my position. Not this again!

Trying to hold my voice even, I said, "Nicky, my happiness has nothing to do with my health. Whether I am the happiest of women or the saddest, my heart remains in peril. I do not like it when you suggest that it is related to my state of mind."

"Sunny, you know I didn't mean that. I know how terribly ill you are, dearest. All I meant to say, and I'm such a clumsy fool, was that I want you to be as happy as I can make you, especially in the face of all your suffering. Don't be angry, darling, don't. I am such a fool!"

Mollified, I tilted my face toward his for a kiss, trying not to wince. I adored Nicky, and there were times, even as ill as I was, that I burned for his caresses and the moments that followed, but I did not like to kiss him on the lips anymore. Owing to his silly fears of dentistry and his constant smoking, my poor Nicky's breath had become well-nigh unendurable. Obviously I couldn't say so, because, if I had, he would have been so ashamed and demoralized that he would have moved into the dressing room right away. As it was, the only times I could see him and talk to him were in our bed, so I couldn't let my distaste show.

"Ah, Sunny, I do wish you were feeling better," he said longingly as I gratefully tucked my head under his chin and let his breath wash over my skull.

I stroked his back.

"I do too, my hubby, my one and all. You know lady misses boysy."

He chuckled happily at my use of the names we had given our most private of parts and moved a bit uncomfortably. I smiled to myself. I could still make Nicky long for me without any effort.

I felt better now, here alone with him, less hurt and angry than before, so I was able to speak gently while tracing our initials against his back.

"Soon now, darling, I am sure I shall be better soon. But you were right earlier, my hubby, when you said that something had upset me badly. You know me too well and are far too clever for me to try to withhold secrets from you."

He nodded against my hair.

"I knew it, darling. I always know. Tell me, was it Anya?"

"Yes, that's right, darling, you always know, but it wasn't Anya. All Anya did was to tell me what she had heard when she was in town today, seeing her parents and her lawyers."

"What did she hear?" His voice was edged with caution.

I let tears come. They were always near for me and far too easy in this life I lived.

Nicky rocked me against him as I poured out the story of Stana and Mitsia's betrayal, leaving out the part about Father Grigory's supposed activities, telling him only that they were spreading rumors in town that I was mentally disturbed.

Nicky was shocked.

"I shall summon Nicholas Nikolaevich to see me tomorrow. I shall tell him in no uncertain terms, you may be sure, to silence his wife. I am certain he has no knowledge of this. My poor darling, you must be so hurt."

"I am, Nicky, but you must promise me that you will not bring this up with Nicholas Nikolaevich or anyone, especially not with your mama. I am shocked, naturally, and I was hurt, of course, but talking it out with you has made everything better. What I plan to do is to do nothing, save to avoid those treacherous Montenegrins as best I can in the future. Really, darling, don't worry about any of this. You have so many more important things to think of."

Nicky shuffled against me.

"But I have to worry about it, darling. Stana and Mitsia are married into our family, and worse, Russia has always looked to maintain a relationship with their father, the King of Montenegro. It is a strategic port, you see. Are you quite sure Anya is telling you the whole truth? I think the matter needs to be examined further. As for not telling Mama, Sunny ... If Anya's parents heard this, do you imagine for a moment that Mama has not?"

I shuddered at the thought of it. This imperiled Father Grigory, who was targeted for no other reason than his care for us. I also needed to protect Anya.

"I trust Anya completely, and I suppose if the Black Women are —"

"Is that what you are calling them now, Alix? How funny! You know Mama has always referred to those two as the 'Black Peril.' Did you know that?"

I nodded against him.

"I did in fact. It is ironic that your mama was right about them and that I defended them against her, isn't it?"

"It is true that she never liked them," he answered musingly, and then I felt him give a decisive nod. "Who knows, dearest, but that this might not prove to be a point of shared dislike for you and Mama to agree over. It is not what I would have chosen, but if it brings you two to an accord on anything, I must say that I shall be grateful."

I gave this remark all the attention it deserved, contenting myself to mutter that I was glad that he was pleased. After a few moments I even thought he had drifted off into sleep, when suddenly he said, his voice clear and anxious in the dark, "But truly, Sunny, what should we do? This sort of gossip is damaging to our family and I think I should speak to Nicholas, or at least that you should address it with Stana and Mitsia."

"Don't concern yourself with these silly women's quarrels." I said, cutting off anything further he had to say on the subject. "It will be boring old news by next week, and I don't know why, but I really feel quite strongly that people will not be discussing this much longer."

I could feel him beside me hoping I would say more, but when I didn't, he gave up and finally slept. I lay awake beside him until nearly dawn, thinking things over until I decided what was best to be done, and then I too fell asleep at last.

Chapter 9

What I did do in the end was to summon Bishop Hermogen, the Bishop of Sarov, who was a leading member of the Holy Synod, the body of men who supervised the Russian Orthodox Church, and demanded of him, and of several members of the Saint Petersburg Ecclesiastical Academy, that any and all investigations into the activities of Father Grigory be halted immediately and never be taken up again. The priests gaped at me and Anya, whom I kept with me for moral support, as if I were speaking in tongues.

Bishop Hermogen went so far as to attempt to disagree with me. Bowing so deeply that his beard reached the carpet of the Red Drawing Room where I had summoned them to meet with me, despite a Number Two day with my heart, he said ponderously, "With Your Majesty's pardon for my saying so –"

I cut him off with an interjection that I tried to make sound light. "There is no need to ask for my pardon, Bishop Hermogen, if you do not choose to say anything that will require it."

Anya gave an inelegant snort of laughter behind me and Bishop Hermogen stared at her in momentary distaste before answering me in the gravest priestly tones he could manage, clearly trying to impress me with the weight of his beard, robes and great religiosity. I could only listen impassively.

"As I was saying, Your Majesty, the man of whom you speak is not well known to the Synod, or, I believe, to the Ecclesiastical Academy." He looked to the younger priests for confirmation of his statement and, like sheep, they all shook their heads solemnly, disavowing knowledge of Father Grigory, who I happened to know many of them had claimed as a friend not so long ago.

I remained silent, letting the Bishop speak, but the look on my face alerted him to the fact that he was wasting both of our times.

"But there have been rumors, Your Majesty, that have reached even me. It is said that your Father Grigory–"

"*My* Father Grigory, Bishop? Is not every priest a member of your organization, therefore, in truth, is he not *your* Father Grigory?"

He remained unmoved and shook his great head dismissively.

"Since these rumors have reached me, I have made some inquiries into the man known as Grigory Yefimovich of the village of Pokrovskoe in Siberia. You see, Your Majesty, I could find no record of anyone in the Synod who had ever met him, or taught him, or studied with him, which might lead one to the conclusion that his priesthood is rather …" he spread his hands and smiled, "… suspect and more, shall we say, a matter of opinion – of his opinion, in fact."

I inclined my head and elbowed Anya who was beginning to make strange bleating noises in protest.

"So then, Bishop Hermogen, are you saying to me that despite the Church's long and valued belief in the holiness of those who wander in search of Our Lord – '*starets*' as they are known here in Russia – these are men not touched by God? Is that what you mean to say to me?"

He smiled thinly.

"No, Your Majesty. I, like many in the Church, have a great appreciation for the men who choose to become *starets*, holy pilgrims bent on promoting peace and embracing Christ's teachings to us. In fact, I consider them to be pure of heart and –"

"Then why," I exclaimed, losing all patience, "do you not speak out against those who denounce them, and instead permit them to … to … to be investigated and persecuted? Do you of all people not know that they are innocents, holy innocents?"

"And some are Khlysts too, Your Majesty, and those the Synod will not endorse."

"That word again – 'Khlyst!' " I said throwing up my hands in despair. "Please explain to me exactly what a Klyst is and why it is such a bad thing to be considered one. I have never heard Father Grigory claim to be a Klyst. Perhaps if you could define the word, I would know one way or another if he was one."

The Bishop shook his head, his dark eyes more sad than angry now.

"I am uncomfortable discussing such practices with Your Majesty. It seems to me that His Majesty should be the one to inform you on such matters, if he should so choose."

At this moment Anya could constrain herself no longer, jumping in and saying, "I know what Khlysts are. They are men, and women too, who think that all carnal things are good, and even holy. They have orgies in bathhouses, and maybe outside too. I imagine they don't do that, though, in the winter or everyone would freeze to death."

"Anya! I said shocked.

"Mrs. Vyroubova!" exclaimed Bishop Hermogen, even more shocked.

Anya stared at us before continuing "Well, it's true. Everybody knows about orgies. They're in the history books. Romans had them and they practically invented civilization. But, of course, I wouldn't have one – I don't like that sort of thing at all – and Father Grigory has never once asked me to participate in one, and I'm certain that if he did such things, I would be invited, for he and I are good friends."

This extraordinary speech caused the young priests and me much laughter, leaving only Bishop Hermogen to act outraged.

"There you see, Bishop," I said, "now you have irrefutable proof that Father Grigory is not steeped in sin after all. Madame Vyroubova has, I believe, assured us all on this point." Then, growing serious again, I added sternly, "I do not wish to hear of this matter again, not from gossip, not from a newspaper, and most assuredly not from any member of our Church, be they of the highest rank or the lowest. For you will find that my own power to reduce the former to the latter is considerable. Father Grigory is exactly as he appears to be, a humble man of Christ, and His Majesty will consider all slanders against him a personal affront to our right to consort with whomever we please. Do I make myself clear on this, Bishop Hermogen?"

Bishop Hermogen inclined his grand head to the point where I feared he might lose his balance and topple into me.

"Yes, Your Majesty, your wishes are heard and understood, and I shall do whatever there is in my power to see that there is no such talk in the Church. It is interesting, though …"

I waited but he did not continue speaking. Impatiently, I asked, "What is interesting, Bishop Hermogen?"

"… that until you summoned me, I had never heard the name Grigory Rasputin. The Tobolsk Consistory is a small organization. Naturally, when I received your summons, I asked others if they had heard of him, and they had vague and inconsistent things to say about him, none of which were of a particularly favorable nature. It was then that I made further inquiries into the man to see if he had in any way studied for the priesthood, or if it was known whether or not he had held prayer meetings or healing sessions. I found –"

I raised my hand for silence. He broke off but his face reddened.

"I realize that you are about to cite people's opinions of him to me, Bishop. I do not care for such opinions and nor does His Majesty. I am only interested in facts, and there are no facts, and therefore I wish to hear no opinions."

He bowed deeply.

"While I am here, summoned to your august palace, Your Majesty, might I request an audience with His Majesty?"

"You may not. I speak for both of us in all such matters, Bishop, and I have made my feelings sufficiently clear, I believe. Bishop, Fathers, I thank you for coming and now you are free to go."

I made the tiniest of nods and the Abyssinians sprang to life, bowing and throwing open the doors, obliging all of them to follow protocol by bowing and making their way toward the doors, stepping backward as they did so. However, while I may have felt vindicated by this show of power, I had the uneasy feeling that I had just made enemies where before there had been none, and I had so many enemies already.

My reverie was broken by Anya.

"I think you handled that just right, Your Majesty."

I looked at her gratefully.

"I have thought about it, Anya, and you may call me Alix when we are alone. We are friends, after all." I smiled at her. "I must say, Anya, that was an extraordinary speech you made about orgies. I am sure those priests have never heard the like of it. Imagine them accusing poor Father Grigory of –"

"Of course, it is all true," Anya declared.

Confused, I gasped out, "What is all true? What are you talking of now?"

"Oh, the Khlyst thing, the bathhouses ... I'm certain he does all of that and more."

"Anya, what in the world ...? I mean, how could such a thing be true, and even if it were true, how would you of all people know about it? Did you not just announce to a roomful of priests that –"

"I haven't participated in one, and I don't know for certain that they take place, but Lokhtina –"

"Who keeps house for him, I would assume. Father Grigory is, as you know, a married man, Anya," I said censoriously.

She shrugged.

"Maybe that is what she does, I don't know. His daughter Maria lives there too and she is the only one I have ever seen keeping house for him, although not very well, I must say. But Lokhtina is married to the general, and her husband made her leave their house and children because of Father Grigory. And now she seems to live at Father Grigory's apartment, and she's been to Tobolsk with him and other ladies, and she told me they all go to the bathhouses and no one wears any clothes, and Father Grigory purifies them all there, so I suppose that's like an orgy, don't you think?"

Did I think so? Oh dear God in Heaven, what did I think?

I chose not to answer Anya and instead pleaded a return of my migraine and an inability to think of anything at all until it cleared. I needed to lie down immediately.

That much was true enough, but no, there was no headache that day – heartache maybe. Lying in my darkened boudoir as afternoon turned to night long before teatime, I struggled with Anya's words and how they contradicted what I wanted to be true. I needed so badly for Father Grigory to be what he presented himself to me as being: A simple holy man; a man who heard the word of God; a man specially chosen by God to be able to intercede with Him, because if he could hear God, then God could surely hear him too.

I knew God did not hear me – my son's terrible affliction was proof of that – but Father Grigory could lay his hands on my boy and take his pain away with a single prayer, with a single word. He did not even need to be with Alexei each time to heal him.

One night a week before, Alexei had woken up screaming from a pain in his ear for no reason we could ascertain. There usually was no discernible reason for his attacks, but they came anyway. His tiny ear was bright red and I had to hold his arms away from it to keep him from clawing at it and trying to pull it off his little head to end his agony. Botkin was helpless and so we frantically summoned Federov from town.

When he arrived, a nightshirt tucked into his trousers, he said an abscess had formed in his ear. My baby's face was swelling, his screams of pain filled the palace corridors, and dawn was hours from us. I do not know what made me think of it, but suddenly I thought that I should telephone Father Grigory. I knew no one would approve of, or understand, what I planned to do, so I did not have a servant connect us but rather arranged this myself from my boudoir.

I almost replaced the receiver as the ringing started – for why was I doing this and what could he possibly do for my boy from so far away? – but he answered my call. My sobbing breath was all I could manage, but he knew … That is the thing, he knew.

"Mamushka, you are in distress. It is good that you have called me. How can I help you? It is the little one, is it not?"

Just the sound of his voice settled my shaking limbs and eased the sweat of fear that had soaked my nightdress.

I tried to speak and couldn't, yet this too he understood and had anticipated.

"Breathe deeply, Mamushka. Close your eyes and see the blue river in the spring when the ice has gone. See the golden grain on the hills. See the small white church. The bell is ringing to gather the faithful. Do you see it, Mamushka? Do you hear the chimes?"

I did as he said, and I did see the church and the waving golden stalks, and I heard the bells peacefully tolling in the light summer wind, and I managed to say without tears or hysteria, "Yes, Father Grigory, yes, I can hear the chimes, and I need your help, but how can you help me when you are there and we are here? It's Alexei's ear ... his ear ... and he is in so much pain, and..."

My composure began to slip away again, for Baby's screams were echoing all around me. It was like a knife was being thrust repeatedly through my heart.

"Mamushka, you must be calm yourself. I will help ... I can help. You say Alyoshka's ear is hurting him? Well then, bring him to me and I will talk to the pain and tell it to go away."

"You mean that I should bring him to town, Father Grigory? I cannot do that. It is late, and so cold, and he is so very sick. Could you come here? I could send a car to collect you ..."

"Hush, Mamushka, all is well. Bring him close to the telephonic receiver. I will talk to him."

"You can help him from where you are? Are you sure? Thank you. I shall go to the nursery. You wait right there."

"I shall, Mamushka. Go now. Fetch him."

"I shall be back very soon."

Carefully setting aside the speaking device, I was in such a hurry that I climbed the stairs, rather than take the elevator, and was utterly out of breath when I entered the nursery where I found Nicky, the two doctors, and both nursemaids clustered around Baby's bed. They did not hear me enter over the sound of his terrible screams, but I pushed my way past them and leaned over him.

His screams intensified at the sight of me, as was often the case, as, to my great sorrow, I knew he somehow believed in his innocent baby heart that Mama could help him and wondered why I did not do so. His small arms came up and in an instant I had his hot, tortured little body against mine and I was turning to rush toward the door.

Nicky and the doctors called out to me, but I ignored them as I hurried to get Baby to Father Grigory. I heard footsteps coming up behind me and moved all the more quickly before taking the elevator.

Alexei had begun to kick at me and was screaming directly into my ear. I feared I might be jostling him, making the pain worse, and in any case I knew I was frightening him, but I believed in what I was doing, and so I ran with my poor baby into my boudoir and slammed the door shut behind me and locked it.

Breathlessly, I picked up the receiver. "Father Grigory, are you still there?"

He laughed in my ear. "I am here, Mamushka. Put on the little one before he deafens us both."

I held the receiver up to Alexei's bright red ear. He gave one final scream and fell abruptly silent. He even smiled.

I stared at him in astonishment and he looked at me sleepily.

"Alexei is tired," he said and yawned widely.

Carefully, so carefully, I set him down on my chaise, and despite Nicky's pounding on the door and all that had happened, he rolled onto his side and closed his eyes.

Shaking, I picked up the receiver.

"Father Grigory?"

"Yes, Mamushka?"

"What did you do? How did you …?"

He chuckled.

"Ah, I simply said to him, 'Burning the midnight oil, are you, Alyoshka?' and told him he should go to sleep now. Is he asleep?"

"He is, Father Grigory. I –"

"No need, Mamushka, I know what is in your heart, as does God. Good night."

He was gone, leaving me with my peacefully sleeping baby and a husband whose consternation died when he saw our son.

I did not know what the world saw when they looked upon Father Grigory, and nor did I care, but, as you can surely understand, I was determined to keep him near me and Baby, and to defend him. Let others judge us both as they would.

121

Chapter 10

Winter was hard upon us that year and even the joy and relief brought about by anticipation of the season of Christmas was overshadowed by my dread of Minnie's visit to see me.

I knew it would be a trial; it only remained to be seen how much of one. To think that once I had hoped she and I would be as close as two women could be. What a fool she must have thought me, hoping that I could be as a daughter to her. "Call me 'Mother Dear'," she had said in the beginning and I believed she had meant it, trusting that she would see my lonely heart and my ache to have a mama again.

Having no mama of my own, I would truly have welcomed it, especially in those dark days after I lost Grandmamma as well, but she did not like me and she did not approve of me. She had early shown her distaste for me, and so, instead of our forging a mother-daughter relationship, she merely became one more critic of who I was, and the most vociferous one at that.

Once I had Baby, I even tried to understand her again. Was it possible that her dislike of me was not personal? Was it perhaps that she was merely jealous of Nicky, her beloved, treasured son? I hoped not, but to guard against any similar behavior on my part, I made a point of adding a wish to be spared any such thoughts in the future to my nightly prayers for Baby before my last kiss to his perfect tiny face.

Whatever the reason, Minnie and I inhabited warring lands, and having resigned myself to being obliged to spend a bad hour with her, I did all I could to lighten my mood. My maid Maria and I together consulted with Count Fredericks and ordered the children's trees, as well as the servants' ones, to be brought to the palace immediately, then Anya and I rather hurriedly oversaw their decoration.

I told Anya that she should not come by unannounced – or at all, preferably – when Minnie would be with me for tea, for Minnie was never one to appreciate another guest when she had a spot of lecturing, or hectoring, on her agenda. Still, I had no desire to be alone with her, and did not consider Nicky's presence to be sufficient to shield me, as he tended to remain totally silent in the face of his mother's criticisms of me and to sit like a chastened child, leaving me to defend our way of life. This not only encouraged his mama to attack me, but inevitably resulted in a bitter marital argument afterward.

Given these sad truths, I had arranged to have our tea served in the children's playroom, right beside the tree, and although the big girls would be having their lessons, I would have my little pair and Baby there to join us. In this setting, with such endearing, and yes noisy, company, I was hoping that we three grownups would hardly be able to manage a serious word between us, and that would make for a nice time for all of us.

What a silly woman I seem sometimes even to myself, for I better than anyone should know that if you wish to make God laugh, all you have to do is to make a plan.

Funnily, or sadly – for my life has been one long trail of shattered hopes – the event turned out to be another disaster; no one living can outwit Minnie.

I was resting in my boudoir, dressed ready to be advised when Minnie arrived. I was wearing, somewhat charmingly I thought, a beautiful pink satin and embroidered silk kimono that one of Nicky's generals had sent to me from Japan years ago. I had even had Maria stick a pair of chopsticks into my chignon as I thought it would amuse the children.

Maria and Baby's nurse had already been told to fetch my three small ones and take them down to the playroom, but Olga and Tatiana had been so devastated to learn about our nursery party and to have been excluded from it, that Nicky and I promised to replicate the fun, without Minnie this time, for our final evening tea when the small ones were in bed.

In this optimistic frame of mind it was all the more shocking when Maria appeared at my door, flushed and clearly distressed. My first thought was that something terrible had happened to Baby, so I half-rose, a hand to my throat.

"Maria, what …? Is it Alexei? Has something …?"

"No, Your Majesty, forgive me for frightening you. It's nothing like that. The Dowager-Empress has arrived."

"There is no need to look so startled, Maria. We were expecting her, were we not?. Here, fetch my chair and take me down to the playroom. My legs are in a state and I dare not try to walk all that way. The Dowager-Empress can think what she likes. Is His Majesty with her already?"

Maria moved to get my chair, and leaning heavily upon her, I reseated myself. Even this small action caused me to gasp and cough.

Maria waited until I had settled myself and said, "Yes, Your Majesty, His Majesty is with the Dowager-Empress, but they aren't in the playroom."

"That is all right, Maria. I truly do not need to be kept informed about everyone's movements at all times. I am sure that by the time we reach the playroom they will have arrived there, that is if you can manage to begin wheeling me down there someday soon. Honestly, Maria, after all these years in my service, one might think that you could manage these situations with rather less hysteria. It is not you who has to endure this visit. Might we go now?"

She didn't reply but began wordlessly wheeling me to my elevator.

"Would Your Majesty like to join His Majesty and the Dowager-Empress in the Maple Room or should I take you to the playroom to see the children?" she asked.

I struggled to turn around in my chair to face her. Failing to do so adequately, I ordered Maria to step out in front of me. She did so, her face impassive. "Yes, Your Majesty?"

I felt sweat trickling down my temples from my unaccustomed struggles and a growing anxiety and anger.

"I ordered tea to be served in the playroom. I ordered you, Maria, to give those orders to the other servants ..." Maria shook her head, her lips firmly pressed together. "I see, then why, if you could be so kind as to explain it to me, are His Majesty and the Dowager-Empress in the

Maple Room, when tea and my children are in the playroom? You do see my confusion, don't you, Maria?" She nodded. "Maria, explain this to me now, if you please!"

She shrugged as if all the idiocy of this situation rested with me and not her.

"The Dowager-Empress has changed everything about and ordered that tea be served in the Maple Room instead of the playroom. When I told her that the children had planned on joining you for tea, she told me to order tea for them in the playroom and to send His Majesty in to the Maple Room, and that was it."

I stiffened in shock and my heart began to beat so fiercely that it was some time before I could allow Maria to push me to the Maple Room.

When we did reach there, Nicky was cozily ensconced next to his mother on a settee, pouring her tea. They hadn't even waited for me, and someone – probably Minnie, who had taken over ordering my staff about – had arranged for a great fire to be lit so that the room was absolutely stifling and I was drenched in sweat in seconds.

Minnie looked away from Nicky and arched her eyebrows at the site of me. Reluctantly I had to admit that she looked magnificent. Clothes were designed solely for women like her – tiny, delicate, dark. She was wearing the simplest violet and black velvet gown, tucked to the arms and the waist, and flowing everywhere else.

I resolved to relieve any tension by complimenting her on her gown.

"Minnie, it is lovely to see you," I said, "and what an attractive dress!"

She inclined her small, proud head.

"Thank you, Alix. It is good to see you as well. You must have forgotten the time, though, for I see you are not yet dressed. Nicky and I will be happy to wait for you if you like. It is still early. One can get so rushed about, can't one?"

I glanced at Nicky for help, an old habit I couldn't suppress. He knew what the kimono was, and had seen me in it before and even complimented me lavishly on it, but naturally he was busily lighting a cigarette and acted as though nothing was happening.

I plucked at my kimono foolishly, stiffened my spine, and tried to answer Minnie calmly, but I fear that my voice sounded too loud and strained.

"I am already dressed, thank you, Minnie. This is a Japanese kimono. It was sent from –"

She waved my explanation away with her tiny hand.

"I am aware of what it is, Alix, it is just that I always thought of them as dressing gowns. But then, I suppose, an old woman like me has little time for fashion. Do please forgive my mistake. Such an interesting choice, isn't it, Nicky?"

Nicky flushed and glanced toward the corner of the room as if espying something of great interest there.

I answered her instead.

"An interesting choice, Minnie? No, not really. Like you, I hardly follow the fashions. Kimonos are most comfortable and I dressed for tea with the children." I noted that this most comfortable of garments was now clinging to my back and legs as a result of the heat in the room.

"I meant 'interesting' because we were so recently, and rather disastrously, at war with Japan. It is most magnanimous of you, Alix, to have elected to have worn such a costume, don't you think so, Nicky?"

"Oh … uhm … well yes, you know, Mama that is all over with now. We are trading with them again, I believe. I shall ask Stolypin, but I am almost sure we are."

Minnie gave a tinkling laugh and turned to address my maid Maria.

"Maria, surely you are not going to leave Her Majesty stranded there in the doorway. Wheel her over to us and then you may go. I shall pour the tea for Her Majesty and we shall ring for you should it be necessary."

Maria rushed me over to the tea table in a hurry to do Minnie's bidding and offered her up the deepest of curtsies as she backed toward the doors.

She was rewarded with one of Minnie's most charming of smiles.

Minnie reached over and gracefully poured a cup for me, then held the cup out for me to take from her. However, because of the way Maria had angled my chair, I was unable reach it, so Minnie handed it to Nicky instead.

"Here, Nicky darling, why do you not take this over to your poor wife?"

Nicky rose obediently and handed me my tea, avoiding my eyes as he did so.

"Nicky darling," I said, "could you be so kind as to ring and ask them for a cup of coffee for me."

Minnie smiled.

"You are so interesting, Alix. Kimonos for clothing, coffee instead of tea ... Why, anyone meeting you for the first time might never even guess you were actually the Empress of Russia. You are so very *Continental*. Don't you think so, Nicky?"

Nicky nodded placidly and lit a cigarette as though we were all just enjoying ourselves tremendously, and said helpfully, "Well, Mama, she is Continental if you think on it. I mean, we all are, being Danish, German, English, and who knows what else. I don't like to admit it, but I am not sure there is much Russian left in our family at all. It is what Peter began when he decided to drag Russia into European life, whether we liked it or not. I mean, just think, French, not Russian, is the language of our court."

He lapsed into silence after this as though better to contemplate these bewildering anomalies, yet despite my prayer that Minnie might wish to do the same, she merely gave him a disapproving *moue* and attacked me with her pleasant voice again.

"Well, that was a very interesting point my son made, don't you think so, Alix?" then, not giving me a moment to answer her – as if she cared what I thought anyway – she went on, "but I didn't ask to come and see you today to discuss history, Russian or otherwise. I have been struggling in silence about an issue, struggling, I should add, while having to listen to the most –"

I waved my hand and nodded at the servant who had just arrived with my coffee, and Minnie lapsed into a momentary silence as he poured it out, bowed to all of us, and exited.

Taking advantage of this impromptu hiatus, I smiled as widely as I could before addressing both Minnie and Nicky.

"Nicky and I don't listen to gossip, do we, darling? I am surprised to hear that you do, Mother Dear. There again, I suppose gossip could be said to be the lifeblood of this and any city."

Minnie's smile tightened.

"Do you really believe that, Alix, or are you merely trying to put me off my train of thought? I shall give you this much – you are doing exceedingly well in that regard."

I looked at her, perplexed, as Nicky lit what may have been his tenth cigarette of the half-hour.

"I am sorry, Mother Dear, but I really do not know what you are referring to. You mentioned that some gossip had upset you, or at least that is what I thought you were about to say, so I suggested that you should possibly not listen to it. It is all rather provoking, isn't it?"

I laughed and raised my shoulders to illustrate my confusion while Nicky made a choking sound that we both ignored.

"Stop it, Alix. The role of the ingénue hardly suits you." She said this while regarding me so critically that I saw myself as she no doubt saw me, as a large, pale woman dressed in a strange, unbecoming garment, sweating and sitting with my legs stuck out awkwardly in front of me in a wheeling chair that no one but myself believed I needed. This *apercu* led me to break out in hives and to begin panting while my heart thumped wildly.

I could barely gasp out the word 'Botkin' before losing consciousness …

Nicky and Minnie were both beside me when I came to, choking on the fumes of the *sal volatile* and laid out upon the large settee, an anxious-looking Dr. Botkin waving the foul-smelling salt bottle back and forth energetically under my nose.

The smell nauseated me and I began to choke, prompting Nicky and Dr. Botkin to prop me up and pound away on my back until I begged them to stop. All the while there was Minnie, sitting so composed, tiny hands crossed in her lap, tiny feet crossed at her ankles, an onlooker to this scene bearing an opaque expression that I had trouble puzzling out.

She waited until I had quietened down and then moved over toward me. Perching daintily against the edge of my couch and taking hold of my limp hand that I self-consciously feared was damp, she said, "Alix, please don't be so afraid of me that you work yourself into these fits. I did not come here wanting this. I did not want to come here at all. I make myself do so, but only after …"

She broke off for a moment and to my astonishment I saw tears in her eyes. Nicky noticed them too and patted her shoulder. "Mama?"

Her eyes cleared and she shrugged Nicky off impatiently. Then, addressing herself to Dr. Botkin, she said curtly, "You can go, Doctor. We shall call for you at the first sign of any repetition of the problem, I assure you."

Dr. Botkin gave me not a second glance before scurrying out, such was the power of Her Dowager-Majesty.

I tried to pull my hand away from Minnie but she held it fast in her smaller one.

"No, Alix, please let us finish this, then you can return to your bed for a decade and I shall go and see my grandchildren. I am more exhausted at this moment than you could be in a hundred lifetimes."

"Mama?" Nicky started again.

Even I could see that Minnie was growing a bit desperate by now and I decided to allow her the space to address whatever issue she had in mind head-on by asking Nicky to leave us to converse in private.

He looked both startled and utterly relieved.

When we were alone, despite feeling sicker than I ever had, and with a frightening pounding in my heart, I chose to be brave. To be brave is to ask those who do not like us to speak out against us freely and openly, and – Empress or peasant – most of us try to avoid this degree of unpleasantness assiduously.

"All right, Minnie, you say you are tired. I am both tired and ill. But here you still are, so please say what you feel you must."

She rose from my side and arranged herself on a nearby bergère chair.

"I will Alix, for all the good it will do either of us. And know that I have waited a long time to come to you, while hoping all the while that it would not be necessary to do so."

132

"In that case, Minnie, you have worried yourself needlessly and have come to upset me for no good reason." I gestured about me to illustrate both my frustration at her behavior and my resignation to its inevitability. "There are no crises here. Nicky and I remain as happy and as united as the day we were married, the children are all well, and our country is at peace. So where in this can you find a reason for disquiet?"

"You think the country is at peace, Alix?"

As she said this I realized that I had nothing to fear from Minnie and all my anxiety fell away. She was, I finally understood, an old woman, and this is what old women do: They gossip with other old women and they wring their hands, and they fervently hope to be the recipients of bad news so that they can feel alive and useful again in the lamenting of it.

However, poor Minnie, not realizing that I had at last unearthed what motivated her, kept talking.

"The country is being held together, Alix, by a thin string that starts and ends with Stolypin. The people in general despise him –"

"But they do not despise Nicky. They love him."

"The people do not love my son, Alix. They merely have a habit for tsardom, but habits can fall out of fashion and come to an end."

"You, Minnie – Dowager-Empress, former Empress, Mother of the Tsar, and Widow of a Tsar – call tsardom a habit? Well, if it be merely a habit, as you wish to assert, it has been an impressively long one, hasn't it?"

I laughed to lighten this pointless exchange.

133

"It is a habit, Alix," Minnie shot back, "albeit a long one, as you say, based mostly on repression. Even I acknowledge that. But it is also based on love and a sense of communion. The people see – or should I say, saw – the Tsar as their Little Father, and this –"

"That is what our friend Father Grigory calls Nicky, and he is certainly of the people, Minnie," I interjected, delighted to be able to prove her wrong.

"Good, I am glad you have brought up his name, Alix. I did not want to, although others are beginning to. Yet another soothsayer in the palace ... and this one is a giant, shaggy, smelly, uncouth peasant who would complement your specious favorite – the fat, ugly, empty-brained Anya – quite nicely as a bookend. These are your people, Alix, but they are not everyone's, and an Empress does not get to choose her friends and companions. Indeed, it would be for the better if we had no favorites at all, for where there is a favorite there is also jealousy, and from that the turning away begins. Let me say this as well," she raised a hand to cut off the objections she saw welling up inside me, "at least you have those two – sad creatures though they are – to comfort you, while my son has no one at all, does he?"

I was crushed and could only answer in a near-whisper, "He has me and our children, and I like to think–"

"Poor Alix, do you not realize that it is what you *like to think* that has led you both to the brink of this precipice?"

"We are not on a precipice, Minnie," I protested. "Everything you say is wrong, Nicky and I are the most united of couples. We and our family, and the happiness we have created, are an example to the country. We are just like my grandmamma and her Prince Albert."

At this Minnie actually let out a despairing groan.

"Alix, this isn't England, you are certainly not the late lamented Queen and Empress Victoria, and my son is not a long-dead Prince Consort, for all that you have done your best to turn him into one. Do you not understand that the Duma is a mouthpiece for every discontented man in our country? It has given them a taste for freedom, but no one is ever contented with merely a taste when the whole pie is on the table and one is very hungry? My son should be there, in his capital. His father would never have let a single session of the Duma take place without him. For that matter, if he were still the Tsar, there would have been no Duma at all. You and Nicky seem to think that a revolution has been averted, that the people now have their little platform from which to air their minor discontents, and that whether Nicky honors a single promise he has made or not, it doesn't matter. If they talk too much, have Stolypin disband the Duma – he will take care of it. So you make him Tsar in all but name, but the people know that he is not the Tsar, so they feel free to hate him and speak out against him, but when he goes – for all ministers come and go – whom then do you think they will hate? At that point you and my son will see finally that the revolution may not have been suppressed at all, but only postponed."

I swallowed.

"What I see, Minnie, is that Nicky was right. Forgive me for saying it out loud, but he has always believed that you favored Michael over him, and he said this was true

135

for both you and his papa. That is a great sin on your part. God made Nicky your surviving first-born and heir because He chose that he should be so. Yet you say these ridiculous things, these impious things, and you say them for no other reason than out of jealousy. That's right, Minnie, you are a very jealous woman. You want to be able to tell Nicky how to rule, just like you did his poor papa, but Nicky loves me best, he listens to me, and to God. And if God speaks to him through the voice of a humble, filthy peasant, as you think of him, then Nicky listens because he is not only your son, Minnie, your creation even, he is also the Emperor and the Tsar of all the Russias, and he has God guiding him, and he does not need you, and you hate that."

Minnie rose with that singular dignity that was all her own and gave me an ironic curtsy, whereupon I noted, with distanced amusement, that her curtsy was somewhat lacking in elegance for it had been so long since she had had to curtsy to anyone. I took this as a clear sign that, reluctantly or otherwise, she recognized finally it was I, and not her, who was the true Empress now. She was defeated at last.

"Alix, I have long hoped that you were merely willful and not becoming mad, but I see that my hopes were in vain. Please tell my son that I am visiting with my grandchildren in the playroom and that I will not be staying for dinner. If he wishes to see me, he can find me there over the next hour or so."

Naturally I did not pass this message on to Nicky, and when he laid down happily beside me in bed with a sigh of pleasure, and asked, rather idly, how the rest of my talk with his mama had gone, I answered casually that I thought we had achieved a mutual understanding of each other at long last.

"That is good, darling. Sleep well," he said with a tired kiss.

Chapter 11

All throughout the year of 1908 I tried very hard not to be seen to be doing a single thing that could incite criticism, or worse, another visit from Nicky's mama. This was made much easier by the state of my health which seemed to have reached its nadir.

I had spent the preceding Christmas in bed and missed the ringing in of the New Year, and I hadn't been able to travel with Nicky to town for either the reception for our ambassadors or the Blessing of the Waters. However, this did have one benefit in that I was able to send Olga and Tatiana to accompany him.

I felt that my big pair had reached an age where they could begin to be companions and helpmeets to their adored papa, and I hoped that the sight of my very pretty young girlies would ward off any comments about why "no one ever saw the Empress."

Nicky was doing his part as well to increase the affection of the public for us. He did not say, and I hadn't liked to ask, but I assumed that his mama had passed on to him her opinions regarding the public's disaffection with us, for he began to have formal photographs taken of our family to be made into postcards that were displayed in every store throughout Russia.

The girls and Baby loved seeing themselves on the postcards, although Baby and Anastasia were terribly difficult to keep still during the photographic sessions. I did not like anything about the idea of photographs or indeed the photographic sessions themselves, and I think my distaste toward the whole process tended to show in the outcomes, although Father Gregory was the only one brave enough to ask me why I looked so sad in all of them.

"It is not good, Mamushka. The people want to see a happy Empress. Why do you not smile for them? You have all your teeth, do you not?" He asked this with genuine curiosity and then proudly displayed his own strong white teeth in a grin. I had to smile back, and began to laugh outright when he gestured for me to smile more widely so that he could see for himself. "There, you see, Mamushka – beautiful. You must do this for the photographs to show the Russian people how beautifully you smile. This knowledge should not be reserved just for those who are here in the palace."

"No, Father Grigory, I disagree. I think that showing a grave face to the people is the most dignified thing I can do, not that dignity and postcards are necessarily synonymous."

"What is that word 'synominisis'?"

I smiled at him, my body's pain lifting at the pleasure of his company.

"It means things they are the same, I suppose, but when I use it in a sentence, as I just have, it is to illustrate a difference. For example, when I see you, I see a holy man, a man of God, but others might not. They might speak harshly of you and ask why such a simple peasant should be chosen to represent God on this earth. They might say that holiness and you are not synonymous, do you see?"

He nodded and drank from his tea.

"It is good to learn these things, Mamushka, and I see many synominisis things myself. God has made a lot of them. I will use that word now for myself. But I think you are wrong when you say it is not synominisis with your dignity to smile. You see, Mamushka, the Russian people are too busy trying to live to think whether this or that is the right thing to do. Only people in great palaces care about that. You tell Father Gregory that you love the Russian people, and maybe you say to me, too, that you do not care what the people in town think or say. Is that not right?"

I shook my head. Now even Father Grigory was making it ache, and with some impatience I responded, "That is indeed what I have said. I do not care what they think of me, because, no matter what I do, they despise me. I love the Russian people dearly and live only for my family and them."

"Then what you say and do isn't synominisis, Mamushka."

"Please stop using that word, Father Grigory. You are giving me a headache. And if you must use it, could you please try to pronounce it correctly. It is 'syn-on-y-mous,' and I have no idea what your point is and am beginning to wish you would either make your meaning clearer or change the subject."

He put down his cup and stared at me unblinking, as only he could or even dared to do. I looked away as he spoke.

"I am sorry that I am making you angry, Mamushka." He shrugged as though he were not sorry at all. "I am only a simple peasant, so I cannot always say things that are pleasing or in a pleasing way, and I do not care about that. But I will finish what I must say to you. If you care for the people, you will smile for them to try and make them happy. If you care what people in palaces think, you will frown and they will say, 'Ah, she is cold, that Empress of ours. She doesn't like us much.' But maybe you think that the people in the palaces will say this too: "Ah, she is cold, that Empress, but she is very dignified,' and the peasants in their huts will say this too, even if they do not know that word. But they will not. They will just know you are sad for them, and maybe they will become even sadder. You please no one and that does not seem to me to be synonymous with anything but misery, and that we peasants do understand, Mamushka."

"Father Grigory, I ..."

I fell silent, overwhelmed by his wisdom, my annoyance fading, but the pain in my temples was increasing. I winced and pressed my fingers to my skull.

He stood abruptly and shouted, "Headache be gone!" then remained standing, watching me.

Within seconds it was just as he had commanded – my headache was indeed gone. Grateful to him beyond words, I rewarded him in the only way I could think of, by smiling at him.

"Thank you, Father Grigory, and I do not wish to argue with you about these matters, or about any matters. It is just that I cannot help but feel that, despite your close relationship with God, you might be rather ... oh, I don't want to say the word 'unschooled' ... but maybe because you were born to a certain station in life, you tend to see things from that point of view, rather than –"

"Rather than through the lies that cloud the thoughts and words of people in palaces, Mamushka?"

Annoyed again, I merely pursed my lips. Honestly, at times he could be a perfect simpleton.

He rose without permission, seeing, if not grasping, my irritation.

"Mamushka, I must take my leave of you, for there are many poor people who come to my humble home and ask me to pray for them. And I see you are tired and out of sorts. So, I –"

Nothing was designed to irritate me more than to be told that I was out of sorts and I snapped at him, "I see. Well, if you have people waiting to see you, you must go. Tell me, Father Grigory, are your guests mostly women? You see, one hears things even through all the lies that cloud our palaces."

He threw back his shaggy head and roared with laughter.

"Do not be jealous, Mamushka. I live only to serve you and your family. These other people – all these ladies – they just come to see me because they like to hear me talk, and I like them to hear me talk too. In my village, the women have to work hard all day, but here a woman has nothing to do, so they come to see me. I do not mind and they smell good, so it is nice for me."

I was horrified that he had accused me of being jealous and outraged. I tried to stand but found that my legs were too weak. Falling back, I pointed shakily at the door.

"Go!"

He was already on his feet and happily exiting, but he had time to throw me an insolent grin nonetheless.

"Do not worry, Mamushka, all is well. I'll be here when you need me."

After that meeting I tried to imagine if I could forego his presence, but I knew that I could tell myself, and tell Nicky too – for I knew he still did not fully like or trust him – yes, I could tell us both that I would not summon Father Grigory again, but I knew also that this would be a lie. For if Alexei became ill – and God knew that he would, for God did not hear my prayers – I knew I would call for this man again, this man whose powers I still hoped were from God, although I knew forevermore that his every act and utterance I would have to defend to justify his presence by my side. The terrible irony of it all was not lost on me. People were noticing and speaking of Father Grigory because he had access to the Imperial Family they did not have. The more he saw of us, the more they would talk out against him, and that talk might damage us because of his friendship with us, which had caused the talk in the first place. It could only be a matter of time before Minnie was treated to more salacious stories and then she would be telling Nicky to end our relationship with him. It was only by some miracle that she had generally chosen to criticize my friendship with Anya more than my relationship with Father Grigory, but that miracle, I knew, could not last.

Knowing that I could not stem this particular tide, I decided to meet with Anya and ask her to receive Father Grigory at her house, and to go to town privately and explain to him that, when he wished to see Nicky and me, and when we wished to see him, no matter what the urgency, he must meet us at her humble home, not in our palace. I told her there was a danger of gossip in town, and Anya, who never missed an opportunity to pass it on to me, especially if it was unattractive and concerned me, nodded wisely at this plan. In fact I knew that it made her feel at the center of a conspiracy and she loved that sort of underhand excitement.

What I did not tell her – because her reaction to this would have taken days to calm down and repair – was that I needed to make at least some show of distancing myself from her too. At times I found Anya's self-absorption so tiring and I also found dealing with all of this, without Nicky's support, lonely, so I decided to tell him of my ideas for keeping our private friendships more private.

"I think you are quite right, darling," he said that evening over supper in our bedroom as I was simply not well enough that winter or spring to dress and go downstairs. Carefully examining his cutlet to see if it was well done enough for him, and then nodding in satisfaction and spearing a mouthful with his fork, he chewed ruminatively before shaking his head and adding with annoyance, "It is no one's business but ours whom we see and whom we don't. It is damned impertinent of them to even think of these things, let alone speak of them." He pounded the prongs of his fork against the china for emphasis.

At that I had to bite my lip to keep from either laughing or saying something we would both regret. I couldn't help but think of the tales of Nicky's papa bending spoons and tearing whole books in half with his outsized hands to show his anger. My own poor hubby looked as fearsome as Baby did as his fork tapped the

144

china, and I thought of how his uncles and his great Prime Minister – the tall, stern Stolypin – would laugh if they could see him now, the Mighty Tsar.

I hated it when I thought like that, and for a moment I despised him too, but I nodded and forced a tight smile.

"Yes, it is dreadful and the bane of my existence. I do think, though, that if you spoke harshly to your mama and your sisters – spoke harshly just once, darling – that they would understand the vital importance of stopping all this gossip as soon as they first heard it, then there would be so much less going about in relation to our personal lives."

He carefully laid down his fork and pushed away his plate so as to illustrate that I had upset him so very greatly that he could no longer continue to eat.

"So, Alix, you believe that gossip about you begins with my mother and my sisters, but what could they possibly say since they never see you, and why do you think they would speak ill of me, for whom I believe they still harbor some affection?"

"Nicky, please darling, let us not argue. You always do this, deliberately misunderstand me and then saying unkind things to me. But no, dearest, do let me finish speaking. Obviously, I was in no way implying that your mama and your sisters told tales about us, just that there are those who surround them who might repeat, or even originate, malicious rumors regarding us, and that instead of listening to these vile scandalmongers, they should rather tell them that they must cease their antics immediately or face censure, or even a harsh punishment, for to speak against God's anointed ones is both a great sin and, I am certain, treasonous as well."

Feeling somewhat pleased with myself, I reached across the small table to stroke his hand, but he pulled it away and lit a cigarette instead. I was therefore expecting him to aim another unpleasantness in my direction and bracing myself for the continuing onslaught when his next words caught me off guard.

"I received a nice letter from Georgie in England today. I was going to read it to you after dinner, but I think I shall just tell you about it instead. He has invited us, on behalf of his father, to bring The Standart to Cowes next summer – in August, I believe he said. They are planning a series of yacht races there. Old Uncle Bertie is going to race even, and Willy is coming. It sounds rather delightful, don't you think?" He barely paused before going on cheerfully, "I was quite excited to receive the news, I can tell you. I simply could not help myself, so I called Mama right away, but she had already heard all about it from Aunt Alix, and she and Xenia and Sandro are already planning to attend on The Polar Star. Naturally we shall take all the children and that young rascal Dmitri, although I imagine he will try to talk me into entering The Standart into the race, the mad boy. And do you know, darling, I have half a mind to do just that."

"Nicky, it is impossible. We cannot … I mean, *I* cannot. Have you forgotten that Ella and poor Maria are coming here in a few weeks, and that we will be hosting the wedding right here, not to mention that the entire Swedish royal family will be visiting us? And then, I suppose, they will all stay on forever. We shall be burdened with company all summer and I do not see how I will be able to cope as it is if I don't have a peaceful summer to look forward to next year. No, it is simply impossible, and you are the one who ruined it for all of us this year. After all, you did give permission for this ridiculous misalliance with Sweden, with someone Maria doesn't even know, and somehow you have let Ella talk you into our hosting their wedding, an affair which is certain to drive me to a complete state of collapse. I am already so ill and I cannot imagine what Dr. Botkin will say."

"I most certainly did give permission for it. How could I have done otherwise between your sister Ella's constant letters to me and your sister Irene telling me it was for the best? For you to term it a misalliance is a bit much at this late date, darling. As for the trip, Dr. Botkin will accompany us, as he does every summer cruise, and this one is over a year away, so it seems a bit silly to be arguing or worrying about it at this juncture. And Alix, surely you were planning to be taking a cruise with the children and me next summer anyway, weren't you?"

"Well, I ... I ... yes, of course, but Cowes is too much for me. I shall be ill worrying about it for a year, whether you think I am being silly or not. All those people ... You know I don't —"

"Yes, I know you don't," he finished quietly.

I felt my tears beginning to flow. Nicky looked away, smoking and silent. I swallowed and tried again.

"But if your mama is going to be there, I won't be able to bring Anya. She doesn't like her."

"No, and I don't suppose Anya should come. As a matter of fact, I would prefer that she not accompany us this year either, as you have broached the subject. As regards Cowes, I am somewhat confused, darling. I shall

147

be there, as will be our children, your family in England, and Dmitri, or would you rather that we go to Livadia first and drop you off there before continuing on to England. I suppose, if we were to do that, you could keep Anya with you next summer, and the children and I would only be away in England for a few weeks or so."

I stared at him aghast.

"Surely you don't think I'd ever let you take Baby to England without me?"

He shrugged and spread his hands.

"No, you are right as always, dearest. That wouldn't work, would it?"

I shook my head vehemently. Nicky was speaking like a madman.

"So, it is settled. The girls, Dmitri and I will continue on to Cowes, and you and Anya and Alexei can stay quietly at Livadia in our absence. And now we can cease arguing over an event far into the future." He then had the temerity to finish this piece of idiocy on his part by smiling hopefully at me.

"No, Nicky, no, you cannot leave me in Livadia, and especially all alone."

"*All alone?* You will have Anya, our son, and a few hundred servants with you, darling."

"You know what I mean, Nicky. We have hardly been apart from each other for a day since I became your own wify. Why would you … how could you even think of separating us? And to take the girls away from me and Baby, that would be too monstrous."

Overcome, I burst into noisy sobs and staggered from the chair to the bed, dropping facedown. I heard Nicky stand up and I felt the bed depress as he sat beside me,

148

but he didn't touch me. I heard his lighter click and smelled the smoke, and thought unkindly that it would be hard for him to hide from people who were searching for him with that telltale plume floating all around him, and then wondered why I had even thought about that. No one was ever going to approach him unless he permitted them to.

I let out a groan that was loud enough to remind him of what he had done and that this sort of upset was dangerous to my health.

"Alix, we cannot do this every time we disagree. And I must say, if the prospect of a delightful family visit to England, over a year from now, upsets you this much, I fear you will never get better. I do not know where we will be then, Sunny, I really don't."

I hated and despised him for trying to imply that my very real illness was something I could control if only I were not so emotional. I therefore made a consummate attempt to regain mastery over myself.

"Nicky, please. You cannot truly believe that your announcing that we will be spending weeks with your mama and surrounded by all those people we will have to entertain – not to say perform for – will do anything other than exhaust me beyond reason."

"I know, Sunny, I know that is how you see it, but I want to go and I shall go. The girls will enjoy it and so will Dmitri. I love my mother and my sisters, and I have nearly given them up for you, but I shall have this. I am not giving into you this time, no matter what you say or do, so maybe we shouldn't talk about it anymore tonight … or maybe at all."

"But I want …"

Suddenly I did not know what I wanted; I just wanted things to be better; for Nicky to do what he was supposed to do, to make them better, but I could never articulate this. Not once in our marriage did I manage that.

Lapsing into silence, I closed my eyes.

Nicky lay down beside me, still fully-clothed, and gathered me up against him. I let him because there is a funny thing about being hurt by the one you love the most: they are also the only ones who can truly comfort you.

He kissed me and I returned his kiss.

"Will you sleep now, Sunny? Things are always better in the morning."

I have never found that irritating platitude to contain a grain of truth, but how would it have helped for me to say that, so I simply closed my eyes and murmured what he no doubt took to be assent.

After I heard his breathing slow, I sat up and moved painfully toward the window. As was often the case in Russia during the winter, the nights seemed brighter than the days, and it was so tonight. The moon was out, shining on the bare black branches of the trees and making the snow glitter.

Could I remain by myself in Livadia, in that ugly old so-called palace with its awful death room still utterly as it was on the day Nicky's papa had died in it, the day Nicky became Tsar of our entire world and I became empress of nothing? I hated that place and I could not be there without Nicky. I couldn't be in Russia at all without him and I couldn't be anywhere else either.

England, oh how I longed to see it again, but with all of those others there, judging me, and no grandmamma to shield me, and my awful cousin Willy there too ...

Involuntarily, I smiled at the thought of my bombastic cousin. Willy felt as uncomfortable around his English family as I did, if not more so. It was surprising that that had not drawn us together. In fact we did our best to avoid any contact between us as though our being pariahs huddled together would make it even worse for both of us. However, this time Willy would be my saving grace, because no matter how much Minnie detested me, her awkward mess of a mad daughter-in-law, she hated Willy much more, as did her sister Aunt Alix, England's queen, although I could never think of her that way. England would only ever have one queen as far as I was concerned. Nonetheless, Aunt Alix would follow her more dominant sister's lead, and if they scorned Willy, then the rest would follow suit and I would become even somewhat popular by comparison.

On the basis of this pathetic insight, I made up my mind to accompany Nicky to Cowes the following year and damn the consequences. If I became even sicker, Nicky's remorse would ensure that he never thwarted my will again, and that would be some sort of consolation. Some sort of anything always seemed the best I could manage.

I made a mental note to myself to write to invite Ella to join us on our yearly cruise to Livadia in the summer following the wedding of her awkward little ward Maria to the Swedish prince. Why not? Ella's growing preoccupation with becoming a nun would entertain me, and the more I considered that, the more determined I was to ask her to join us the following summer at Cowes as well. Ella would draw curiosity away from me, and since the sight of her always reminded Willy that she had chosen someone else over him, which tended to make him more agitated than usual, it would also serve to further distract attention from me. At least she would be better company than none, in Anya's absence, and now that she was pretending to be a nun, she wouldn't be able to leave The Standart and join Nicky for swimming or tennis. Maybe a quieter, less showy, Ella could become a true companion to me. I could only hope.

Having so decided, I turned from my window and staggered back to bed and, cuddling close to Nicky's sleeping form, I prayed, as always, for better grace, and at last slept.

Chapter 12

April of 1908 began with just the sort of terrible bustle and confusion, and an endless stream of entertainments, that I had feared. We had relatives and guests crammed to the rafters.

Nicky's difficult Uncle Paul, who insisted on attending his daughter's wedding and on bringing his embarrassment of a wife with him, was staying at the Catherine Palace along with a group of the Swedish royal family. I say 'group of' because the pointy-faced Prince Wilhelm, whom my Nastinka habitually referred to as "big ears" (he had those too), was staying there, but his haughty mother, Queen Victoria, would not as she refused to sleep under the same roof as Grand Duke Paul and his morganatic wife, disregarding the fact that the roof in question risked being larger than her entire country of Sweden. That necessitated moving her and her husband, King Gustav, to Petersburg and opening up the Winter Palace solely for them. Xenia and Sandro had been summoned to Petersburg to host them, so that necessitated daily forays to town for tea with the Swedes who were there or having the lot of them to dinner at Tsarskoe Selo and having to put on two separate dinners so that the father of the bride and the mother of the groom were never obliged to meet.

Grand Duke Paul was a constant annoyance with his endless bleating about Ella having "sold" his daughter into marriage to "a perfect stranger," and how he had not been consulted at all about any of this. To be fair, he was mostly right on both counts. It had been largely at my request that Nicky had banished Paul and his silly and inappropriate wife six years earlier, but it had not been my idea to give his children to Sergei and Ella. Ella, I felt, had no maternal instincts, about which I had been proven right when she subsequently requested that we take in both Dmitri and Maria following Sergei's murder. Our having chosen only to give a home to Dmitri, I had hoped that Ella would, with only one young girl to care for, have at least managed that, although I suggested to Nicky at the time that Maria should be sent to live with her papa, as she had requested. Nicky said no, as he did not think it appropriate for a Russian grand duchess to be raised in exile, and besides he had pointed out that Dmitri and Maria were unusually close, and that if Maria stayed with Ella, they would have opportunities to see each other.

As with most of Nicky's edicts, this satisfied no one and angered everyone. Ella, deep into her dalliance with the religious life, felt put upon by the continued presence of a girl she had never wanted in the first place; I felt guilty for refusing to move her to Tsarskoe Selo; her papa Paul was enraged at yet another insult as regards his qualifications to raise his own children; and because Ella and I did not get on too well, Dmitri and Maria saw no more of each of other than they would have done if she had gone to live in France with her father.

Then Ella went behind everyone's back and arranged a meeting between poor unprepossessing Maria and the lamentable Swedish prince, young Wilhelm. Naturally the Swedish royal family proved all too anxious to marry their son into the all-powerful Romanov family and to gain the immense dowry that accompanied such a bride. That Maria was only sixteen, and a terribly young sixteen at that, did not deter Ella in the least.

So the young people had met – but only once – and a proposal was tended that very evening. Maria, young and foolish, and probably eager to escape Ella, had said yes, with much prodding from Ella. Prince Wilhelm and his family decamped back to Sweden, while Ella wrote to Nicky for his consent, which he promptly gave and only then informed his Uncle Paul about the affair. Grand Duke Paul ran somewhat predictably mad at this news and wrote to both Nicky and Ella a spate of letters that verged on the insulting, and so once again Nicky, destined to please nobody, declared that the marriage would indeed take place, but only once Maria was eighteen – in the first week of April of this year – and that the wedding was to take place the following week, Ella being rather anxious to get on with her religious life.

By this time, or perhaps much earlier, poor Maria had come to the realization that she was being sent far from her homeland to marry someone she had met only once, and she came to me, a near stranger to her, in tears the day before her wedding, begging me to intercede and stop it all.

"You see, Aunt Alix, when he asked – Wilhelm that is – I said yes and I understand that sort of thing is some kind of solemn, unbreakable vow. I know that because Aunt Ella keeps telling me so, but I've decided that, despite this, I can't marry him. I don't know him, and I don't want to know him, and what's best is for me to go be with Papa in France, unless I can stay here with you and Uncle Nicky and be with Dmitri again, whom I miss

155

so much. I'll do anything you say, but I won't marry Wilhelm. I don't even like him."

Thereupon she buried her face in her hands and I took this opportunity to study the poor girl curiously.

At eighteen she hadn't outgrown any of the large awkwardness that had made her such an unattractive contrast to her beautiful, finely made, younger brother, and yet this very thing made me like her. How hard it must be, I reflected, to be born plain and fat in a family known for producing great beauties, all of whom tended to unusual slenderness and mostly a graceful height. Even my poor Nicky, dwarfed as he was by members of his family, retained the classic even features that had blessed generations of Romanovs before and after him. Poor Maria, on the other hand, looked more like a relative of my clumsy Anya's than a Russian grand duchess.

It was this last which compelled me to reach out and stroke the girl's bent head with a mother's touch, and to speak to her as though she were my own, while at the same time sending up a prayer of thanks that none of my own graceful, pretty girls would ever have to hear me speak thus to them

"Maria dear, I am afraid that it has all gone too far for you to change your mind now." She trembled under my hand and I inwardly cursed Ella for her selfishness, while continuing to speak soothingly but sternly. "If you were to cancel everything, dear, it would cause a great scandal all over Europe and irrevocably damage our relations with Sweden." As I said this I wondered if we even had relations with Sweden and made a mental note to ask Nicky if we could catch a minute alone. Speaking

156

more firmly, I continued, "And Maria …" I waited until her red, tearful eyes met mine and took her hands. She clutched mine hard, as though I might yet find a way out for her, and I tried not to wince at the pressure she was putting on my fingers. Truly, what was happening to her might even be for the best. I pulled my hands away and said firmly, "Maria, what I say now to you, I say as your auntie who loves you and as a mama, since your own dear mama is in Heaven, looking down. I know she would say the same if she were here. You have to marry Wilhelm, for there is no other place for you if you don't. We couldn't have you here, given the scandal."

"But you can. I'll be as good as gold and I can help you with the little ones and take letters for you. My penmanship is very nice and Dmitri loves being here with you and Uncle Nicky. He says you are ever so much kinder than Aunt Ella." Horror-struck at her own words, she put her hands over her mouth. "I didn't mean that, I didn't. Aunt Ella has been so good to me, truly she has. It is just that I want to be with Dmitri or Papa, and I don't know Wilhelm at all, honestly I don't, and I can't get married anyway because I don't even have a trousseau. Aunt Alix, please help me. You will help me, won't you?"

On finishing this emotional speech she fell to her knees in front of me and buried her hot wet face in my lap.

Reluctantly, I patted her. This was all Ella's fault, I concluded, but I would have to deal with it, so I focused on the one thing I could fix.

"Maria, what do you mean you don't have a trousseau? The wedding has been planned for over a year. You do have a wedding gown, don't you? Good heavens, what are you saying?"

She raised her face and fell back to look at me.

"Oh yes, I have Mama's wedding dress. Aunt Ella had it made over for me. She said they had to add extra panels of fabric because I'm so much larger than she was." Swiping inelegantly at her streaming nose she searched my face for something, and not finding it, she rose with a strange dignity and returned to her chair. She took the handkerchief I held mutely out to her and scrubbed at her face, then crumpling it, she stared at me solemnly. "You don't want to help me, do you? I don't think anyone will. I see it might be best if I go through with it. Maybe there's a home for me in Sweden. Who knows?"

She shrugged and looked so alone, and so much older than her years, but she was right: I didn't want to be involved in this. I wasn't well enough and it would cause such a terrible rumpus if I even tried. I did want to be kind to her, though.

I smiled. "I think you are being very sensible, Maria, and you will see that marriage is what we women are made for by God. And there will be children."

She waved her hand, her face reddening.

"I'd rather not talk about that sort of thing. It makes me feel like I might start screaming. I think maybe I'll go to lie down for a bit now, Aunt Alix, if you'll excuse me."

"No, wait. I want to know about your trousseau. What did you mean by saying that you don't have one?"

She shrugged as if nothing could be less important.

"Aunt Ella isn't spending a bit of money on what she calls worldly things anymore, and she didn't want to write to Uncle Nicky and ask for control of my money, and I wouldn't have known how to or what to order anyway. Aunt Ella has always picked out my clothes for me and told the seamstresses what to make."

"Maria, do you mean to say that you are going to Sweden, as a Russian grand duchess and a Swedish princess, wearing dresses like that?" I pointed with horror at the rag, for want of a better word, that she was wearing.

"This?" she said, plucking at the rusty-looking black velvet gown she was wearing.

My girls had been the first to notice Maria's strange gowns, asking me why anyone would wear black velvet in the spring. I had informed them that Maria was clearly still in mourning for Uncle Sergei and was to be commended for it. Naturally it was my naughty Anastasia who then asked with seeming innocence, her little chin trembling with laughter, why Auntie Ella wasn't also wearing black. Then, bursting into full giggles, she asked if Maria was sadder than Aunt Ella about the death of Sergei.

I had to fight down my own laughter to admonish her strictly against saying such terrible things and then explain that Aunt Ella was wearing white, which was the color of mourning in France. I didn't add that it was the mourning color worn only by French queens.

Nastinka accepted this explanation with the further witty observation that Aunt Ella wasn't French as far as she knew, and at that point I told her she was giving me a headache and to go and find her sisters or her brother, or, failing that, to go and find something else to do besides plaguing me.

So now, seeing Maria in yet another awfully dated gown, and one too small for her as well, and hearing her say that Ella hadn't bothered to arrange for her trousseau after forcing her into what I was becoming increasingly certain was going to be an unhappy marriage, I felt my temper rise.

I stood up and hugged the girl, saying, "You do look tired, dear. Go and have a rest. I shall see you at dinner tonight, and as for your trousseau, there is not much time for me to help you there, but I will send for Madame Lamatov and ask her what can be done. We certainly cannot send you off to Sweden in mourning. It would not be appropriate and I think we can call mourning for your Uncle Sergei to an end. You are going to be a bride, and a bright and happy one at that."

As she left I had a sudden flash of memory of me as a bride wearing black velvet hours before donning my wedding gown, and returning to it again hours afterward as the funeral bride. I shivered superstitiously and rang for Maria, telling her to find Anya and Ella and to ask them to join me for an early tea. My body quivered with exhaustion but there was no time for rest just yet.

I had my hands far too full in the weeks leading up to our departure for our summer cruise and then fall visit to Livadia, but Ella, selfish as always, seemed to expect my full attention, despite my illness, despite the wedding, and most of all despite Anya, who was sulking about being left out of this summer's cruise and had clung to me like a limpet. In addition I had to field constant complaints from my big pair about being "saddled with

160

that fat wet noodle, Cousin Marie." I admonished the girls firmly for speaking that way about their unfortunate cousin, who, I reminded them, was nearly an orphan thrice over, having lost first her mama at Dmitri's birth, then her poor papa when he was banished for an unwise marriage, and then her dear Uncle Sergei, who had been as a second father to her and had been blown apart by assassins. Unsaid was that their Aunt Ella, who should have been a second mother to the girl, seemed to share their dim opinion of her.

It seemed to me that Sergei and Ella must have nearly raised the girl as a nun, which was not too surprising coming from Ella, considering that she nowadays rattled on and on about her hopes, nay "her calling," Both Nicky and I had hoped that Ella's desire to sell off all her worldly goods and take up a life of poverty and prayer had been driven by her great grief and shock at Sergei's murder, and that she would at least wait to further any of it until poor Marie came of age, or married, or we could figure out whether to let her go to her disgraced father or somehow manage to blend the awkward girl into our own family.

However, Ella, it seemed, was not going to change her mind.

Knowing that I was for once unassailably in the right, I was rather looking forward to confronting Ella about Maria's situation, but, as always, Ella managed to force me onto my back foot. I don't know quite how she always managed to do this, for I was, more than anyone else in Russia, a truly believing Christian woman who shunned and despised all forms of worldly glory and tried very hard to raise my girls the same way, despite their exalted birth, and yet Ella managed to make me look frivolous and silly somehow.

It all started with my completely innocuous suggestion that our court dressmaker should be called in to sew up some decent dresses for poor Marie, who I feared was going to look ridiculous in Sweden, drawing shame down on both herself and us. I pointed out that the girl only seemed to have two dresses, and if she had more, she had clearly outgrown them, and the two she did have were cast in heavy outdated velvets. I went on to say to Ella that every time I saw Marie she was drenched in unladylike perspiration, and moreover that both her dresses were black, and what must Wilhelm and his parents think of Maria and our family? Mourning for Sergei was long over, although Ella still chose to observe it, but the color white was terribly becoming to both her and Maria, as well as being the proper garment for the summer and for sea travel.

Dealing with Ella is always a trial, so I gave her that compliment that white was most becoming to her at the same time as I suggested new dresses for Marie. She carefully set down her teacup and looked obliquely out of the corner of her eye at Anya, who was fanning herself and panting a bit as I had ordered the tea to be served outside on my balcony, it being a beautiful and unseasonably warm spring day.

I had to purse my lips hard not to laugh aloud. Ella's covert examination of Anya's "spring getup" was no more than to be expected.

I had recently given in to Anya's complaints about her deep poverty and granted her a small monthly stipend, and it seemed she had spent the entire year's worth of it all on one garish dress, a ghastly purple and red satin ensemble, complete with a hat the size of a table, and having purchased it, felt that she should wear it as often as possible.

When Nicky had first seen it, he had spat out his tea in a coughing fit and Anya had helpfully clapped him on the back so hard that she had sent him tumbling into the tea table. I could see that the lace at her cuffs was still stained from that misadventure. It was too unkind of Ella to test my composure now.

Anya, who never had a sense of how ridiculous she was or of Ella's obvious distaste for her, helpfully pointed at her dance hall ensemble and said, "You should let the dressmaker come for your niece. She made this for me and I get ever so many compliments, and I fancy," she blushed brightly, "that I've drawn several looks from gentlemen when I go to town to visit Mama and Papa and Father Grigory."

Ella inclined her elegant head and smiled thinly.

"I am most grateful, Mrs. Vyroubova, to my dear sister for her offer to help me clothe my poor ward, and to you for displaying so perfectly what Maria is missing. Tell me, Mrs. Vrubovya, is it customary for a woman in your position in life," she made a small *moue* with her lips and then smiled more widely, "a woman who is divorced, or about to be – I cannot quite keep it straight in my mind – to wish to attract the attentions of passing gentlemen at train stations?" Without allowing poor Anya to respond, if indeed she could have done so, she turned to address herself to me. "Darling Alix, do you think we should put such fine feathers on young Maria and hope for an offer for her? Possibly a nice train conductor will wish to pay court to her."

I grimaced, annoyed.

"Ella, you know very well that Anya was only trying to be pleasant. There is no need to bite off her head or to cast nasty aspersions, and I do not know a thing about train conductors and their habits, nor what their preferences might be for young females, and nor do you. I am more concerned about what King Gustav and Queen Victoria must be thinking, let alone that silly boy Wilhelm you are marrying her off to. I suppose it really is not my concern, but I was just worried for you, dear Ella, for what will her new family think of you as her guardian when they see that poor young girl wearing her heavy funeral rags while the rest of us sit around, yourself included, in cool white cottons and linens? I am both sorry and surprised that you are so far gone in grief, or religiosity, or whatever this," I gestured at her own gown which was looking distinctly nun-like, "is, that you now neglect your sole ward's barest comfort or dignity."

Ella straightened herself, and glancing down at her lap, fidgeted with the folds of her severe white gown. When she raised her eyes she looked at me directly and smiled serenely.

"I imagine that they don't think of it at all, Alicky darling. They know, as does the world, that I am a woman who has suffered unimaginable tragedy, and that in my grief I have looked to God for solace and for a way to walk my weary path down here alone. Unlike you, I do not have the spiritual support of someone like your dear Father Grigory. Possibly if I had such succor, I would have remembered to concern myself about important things like new gowns."

"I don't know if that's true," Anya burst in. "Father Grigory doesn't seem to pay much attention to clothing. He never says a thing about mine and his own is often quite dirty. I don't think priests overall are a great –"

"Anya, please be quiet," I snapped, and Ella raised her brows and gave me a little smile, which I returned. For a tiny moment there we were sisters conspiring together.

Impulsively I leaned toward her and held out my hand. She met me halfway, and I smiled into her eyes and said, "Ellie, I am sorry you have been unhappy, and if this thing you are following is helping you, then I am glad for you. Let me order some dresses for the poor thing as a gift from Nicky and me. We would like it if you would let us do that."

Ella's eyes filled with tears and she squeezed my hand while I heard Anya make a snorting noise, which I ignored.

Ella replied, "Go ahead, then, Alicky, order her a hundred pretty dresses if you wish. I have been neglectful and I am sorry I haven't been more attentive to her and more gracious to you when you brought it up. I –"

"No, don't say another word, Ellie. Let us change the subject and talk of something pleasant, and agree to fight no more, shall we?"

She smiled widely at me and leaned closer to kiss my cheek. Blushing with pleasure, she let out a little giggle.

"Agreed, sweet sister, let us not argue, at least not for the rest of the afternoon."

At that we both collapsed into laughter while Anya stared at us in annoyance and confusion.

Chapter 13

That year's cruise on The Standart was actually a most enjoyable one, despite the absence of Anya – or maybe, as Nicky naughtily said, because of it – and it was true that without her I was able to spend more time just sitting quietly with my girls on the deck, teasing them gently about their atrocious crochet work.

All four of my daughters adored their Aunt Ella, and she them, and that did make a nice change from Anya's company, for Anya tended to be terribly jealous of any attention I paid to anyone besides herself, except Nicky, whose every word she clung onto, to the annoyance of both of us. I found her behavior toward Nicky cloying, and Nicky in his turn used to be driven half-mad when he visited nearby estates to use their tennis courts and Anya insisted on accompanying him, and even playing, an event that was nearly always capped off by her getting tangled up with the net amid great hysteria.

Indeed, rather to my surprise, I found that I was enjoying my sister's company that season, and it was in this mood of reconciliation that I was able to listen as Ella outlined her wishes for the future. She wanted to become a nun, yes, but more than that, she wished to behave as a sister of both Mary and Martha, as she explained it to me.

"For you see, Alicky, I wish to worship God at the deepest level, but in my heart I feel this can only be done through acts."

"Faith without acts being worthless," I intoned, for this was not only the teaching of our Orthodox faith but was also advocated robustly by Father Grigory, who lived according to this principle so beautifully, as I then told Ella.

Ella looked as though she wanted to say something about Father Grigory, which would have certainly ended our nice tête-à-tête, but then she smiled and said instead, "Yes, and if he says that, it must be so."

"He says it for certain. There is no 'if' about it. Really, Ella!"

Ella put her hand over mine in a placating gesture.

"I didn't mean to sound as if I were questioning what you said, Alicky. I only meant that your Father Grigory was right, and that is what I want to do, to underpin my faith with acts, lots of them." She laughed and I noted that, even out here in the sun with her face brightly lit, she still looked like a girl. I wondered how all of life's adversities had left her so untouched and then mused as to how many people, seeing us both together for the first time, would mistake me for being the older sister.

Chiding myself for dwelling on such vainglorious notions, I made an effort to appear more interested in her ideas.

"So what you want is to serve God with both prayer and works?"

"Yes, that is it exactly, and that is why I want to call my order 'Mary and Martha,' for you see we shall be both Marys and Marthas," she gushed.

While it was delightful to see Ella so eager and enthused, I too am extremely religious and I found my mind wandering back to home while she went on in infinite detail about her plans for the order, "once those rather hidebound men at the conclave finally listen.

168

Couldn't you say a few words to Nicky for me to ask for his support?"

This last appeal shook me back to the present. I shook my head apologetically. "I couldn't really, Ellie. I don't like to involve myself in matters of State or Church. Nicky carries the weight of the entire empire upon his shoulders, so when we are alone, and as you can imagine," I waved around the deck of The Standart to illustrate the many sailors about us, "that is all too rare, I try to keep our conversation light and comfortable for him. You have been widowed now for quite a while, so it must be hard to remember the way it was with your Sergei, but I imagine it was much the same for you at the time. I am sure you avoided discussing politics with him when he was at leisure. What is it, Ella, why are you looking at me like that?"

Ella was positively goggling at me, looking as though she had swallowed a frog. I couldn't help but begin to giggle, and strangely so did she, and then rising gracefully, she enveloped me in a hug, which was truly odd considering that my sister rarely hugged anyone. In fact, I could never remember her ever having done so before.

I looked up at her questioningly. "Ellie?"

"I just felt the need to hug you, funny little sister. I am going to go to try to find my nieces now and see if I cannot organize a picnic. Who can know, but maybe my imperial brother-in-law will even join us." She gave a tinkling laugh at my alarmed expression. "Don't worry, Alicky, I won't make even a whispered reference to State or Church business to him. As you said, it has been so long now since I was a wife that I have clearly forgotten how not to be so pushing. We can all learn from your example. I wish you a restful afternoon, my dear."

With that she departed, leaving me to wonder why I felt once again wrong-footed by her, someone who was clearly impossible to deal with. I missed Anya, and I wanted to hear Father Grigory speak to me of God and life, and say reassuring things. I felt irritable and my legs began to ache. I therefore asked Maria to summon Dr. Botkin.

Chapter 14

As I had feared, all that entertaining and traveling in the spring, summer and fall had a most deleterious effect on my health, for I spent the entire winter of 1908-9 nearly completely incapacitated by pain with an overtired heart. Nicky and the girls hovered about me anxiously and Dr. Botkin was nearly beside himself with worry, exhorting me at every morning's visit to, "Please, Your Majesty, try not to exert yourself today. Stay in bed, I beg of you."

Poor Dr. Botkin little understood the duties of a wife and of a mother, and even less so if that same wife and mother happened also to be the Empress of one sixth of the world's people. Nevertheless, I did try to rest because I so wished to be better again, more for Nicky's sake than for my own. He was looking haggard with fear for my health and told me that he would rather go to prison or to a Siberian exile than to see me suffer so. I felt so moved by this declaration that I vowed to him that I would be well for our trip to Cowes in the coming summer, without having the slightest idea of how to make good on my promise.

I think the worst thing about that winter was how hard it was for me to arrange to see Father Grigory. My loyal Anya continued to invite him to her small house nearby, but I was mostly too ill to manage even that short trip, and I didn't see him at all over the holidays except for one short visit after he had come to bless the children for Christmas and to collect the gifts that our family had made for him.

171

I had sewn him three satin shirts, adding heavy floral embroidery around their sleeves and hemlines, this despite the headaches and neuralgia that plagued me whenever I tried to do close work, and my girls had all contributed to making him a pair of beautiful black velvet trousers to go with them. Baby, who was yet to receive an allowance, was 'loaned' money by me to purchase a pair of fine riding boots in the Don Cossack style to present him with.

Much as I had hoped to be able to join Nicky and the children around the Christmas tree in the nursery to present Father Grigory with his gifts, I was forbidden from making such an effort by all the fussing over me of Dr. Botkin that morning, who had stated that he was certain my heart was Number Two. I could have told him that myself, as I think I had, but I was too disappointed by his pronouncements to argue with him.

As often happened between us, though, Father Grigory felt my despair and loneliness, and sent Maria down from the nursery to ask if he might be allowed see me alone for a few minutes as he had a Christmas gift for me that he wished to present to me in person. I was beyond moved by this request, for where could a humble *starets* find a gift for an empress? I was also in a quandary, for despite Father Grigory being a man of God, I could not possibly receive him in my bedroom.

Having made up my mind to receive him regardless, I sternly ordered Maria and Anya, who was naturally with me, not to say a word to either Nicky or Dr. Botkin about my getting up, and with a great deal of puffing and huffing, and a most unattractive bout of sweating on the part of Anya, they were able to carry me bodily from my

172

bed to the chaise in my boudoir, where I was arranged clumsily to meet Father Grigory. The entire experience, which lasted all of five minutes or so, left me completely exhausted, and when Father Grigory arrived he looked at me with grave concern.

"You are still not well, poor Mamushka," he said, making the sign of the cross over my head before bending down and kissing me somewhat loudly three times on my cheek. "There you are, that has given your pretty face some nice color. Happy Christmas to you, Mamushka."

I had long ago become accustomed to not flinching when accosted by a man's malodorous breath and I fancy that I did not show my shock now either when I smelled the strong alcohol fumes emanating from Father Grigory as he kissed me, but I was a bit taken aback to be detecting them at that time of day, it not yet being noon on Christmas morning.

He knew what I was thinking, though, he always knew.

"Do not blame poor Grigory, Mamushka. When the Tsar of all the Russias says, 'Have a glass of champagne with me to toast Christmas,' what can a humble peasant do but say yes?"

I smiled in understanding. Poor Father Grigory had clearly not understood that when Nicky offered him champagne, he was expected to take just a taste. This was the reason that Nicky had once suggested to the Holy Synod that only water be served during communion, as the poor peasants tended to gulp down the entire cup, leaving nothing for the person standing behind them.

Thinking of this, I smiled warmly at Father Grigory and gestured to the sack he was carrying.

"You look like Father Christmas yourself today, Father Grigory. Might I know what is in your sack?"

My statement made him smile, which delighted me.

"Mamushka, I did not know about presents until I came here. In my village of Pokrovskoe, Christmas is just a day, a day we do not have to work on but go to church, if there is a priest who is not too drunk."

"Father Grigory, what a terrible thing to say. A drunken priest indeed!"

He shrugged, unperturbed.

"Don't judge the poor fellows too harshly, Mamushka. It is very cold in Siberia and the winters are very long."

"That is hardly an excuse, Father Grigory. I am going to have Nicky find someone to look into this."

He waved his hand to silence me.

"Mamushka, I wasn't telling you about this to ruin the lives of poor village priests."

Annoyed, I cocked my head and pressed my lips together.

"Do forgive me, Father, I was foolishly thinking about God as it is Christmas."

His laugh boomed out, shaking the walls of my boudoir and making the lilacs tremble in their vases.

"You aren't thinking about God at all when you talk that way, Mamushka, you are thinking that you are better than someone else. That's not your fault." He shrugged into my outraged face. "You're the Empress, and pride comes as a terrible temptation for you, much like wine is for us poor peasants. But I'll tell you, Mamushka, if I can love you and Papa, and I do, despite your positions in life, you can love the drunken peasant, whether he is a priest or a farmer. That is a good way to be, don't you think?"

As often with Father Grigory, I found myself torn between admiration at his simple, if not to say simple-minded, view of life and irritation at his lack of understanding, but it was Christmas and I did not wish to argue with him. Besides, his presence had made me feel happy, a somewhat alien feeling to me at that time, so I smiled at him.

"Yes, Father Grigory, thank you for your wisdom and also for reminding me that pride goeth before a fall. I will try to –"

"Not make a fuss in the villages with the poor priests either, Mamushka?"

I waved my hand.

"No, I shall not bother myself or the Emperor with that, but tell me, Father Grigory –"

"Yes, that is what I came to tell you, Mamushka, and to give you something, too. Well, this is really for Papa." He reached into his bulging bag and rummaged about it until, flushed and triumphant, he produced a broken comb which he pressed into my reluctant hands.

Startled, I forgot what I was going to ask him and instead examined the pathetic object, as I suppose was his wish.

The comb was an old wooden one with two teeth missing and, somewhat horribly, a long hank of what I could only presume was Father Grigory's hair still stuck inside of the remaining teeth. I shuddered involuntarily

175

and lifted my hand from it, causing it to fall to the floor where we both stared at it.

I looked up at him inquiringly. "Father Grigory?"

He frowned mightily and bent over to pick it up, whereupon I clasped my hands together firmly to prevent him handing it back to me. To my disgust, he sat it down on the tray alongside my tea.

"Mamushka, why did you throw my present onto the floor?"

"Father Grigory, you know very well that I did not throw it."

"It looked like you did, Alix," interjected Anya, who up until now had been silent, a merciful effect that Father Grigory seemed to create in her.

I shook my head at her in annoyance, but Father Grigory was pleased.

"Annushka speaks, and yes you did throw it, Mamushka. We both saw you do it, didn't we, Annushka?"

For a moment – albeit a short one, but it happened all the same – I wondered why the only people that I ever saw were of this sort, a fat idiot and a strange, dirty peasant who brought filthy items into my home and expected me to applaud them for it. I shook off this unkind thought and resolved to accept the comb from Father Grigory, this time trying to look appreciative.

"Anya, I certainly did not throw it. I was simply caught unawares. And tell me, Father Grigory, what is the comb's significance, for His Majesty and I are not short of such items?" I tried to laugh and appear grateful, but in truth I could not shake the feeling that I was surrounded by oddities and my head had begun to ache again. "What is it for, Father Grigory?" I asked tiredly.

"Why, I use it for combing my hair, Mamushka. That is what a comb is for, is it not?"

I prayed silently for the patience of the Mother of Heaven, sorely needed by me on this day of her son's birth, drew in a deep breath, and tried again.

"So we have established. What I meant is why are you giving it to us – for what purpose, beyond the combing of my or His Majesty's hair? Forgive me if I was unclear."

He laughed again.

"Ah, you are cross with poor Father Grigory and you do not like my present. But I will tell you this, and something else too, Mamushka. You shall like it and so will Batushka. For if ever a question is hard and you are thinking what it is best to do, then you or Papa must comb your hair and the answer will come, poof, like that."

He snapped his fingers for emphasis.

I rubbed my forehead and actually considered using the comb to resolve my problem of how to excuse myself and reappear, poof, back in the darkened serenity of my bedroom, but instead I mustered what I hoped was a grateful smile.

"Thank you, Father Grigory. I am sure your comb will be used a great deal, maybe by Anya as well."

I tried to end my statement with a light laugh, but even to me it sounded brittle and Father Grigory's face clouded.

"The comb is not for Annushka. She has her own gifts from me. "

Anya nodded emphatically but for once did not blurt out an answer. I wasn't all that curious as to what he might have given her, and anyway I knew that I would hear of them later, whether I wished to or not, so, planning to end this ludicrous visit, I raised my eyebrows at Anya and pointed at my bell pull, wishing her to summon Maria.

She half-rose from her chair, but was stopped abruptly by Father Grigory's bellow.

"Sit, Annushka. I have more to tell Mamushka."

Anya was so startled that in trying to sit again she caught the heel of her shoe on her hem and fell backward, knocking over the chair and landing on her back.

She shrieked and I let out a sound of protest, but Father Grigory said loudly, "No, Mama, leave her, and you stay there, Annushka. One can hear the truth while on one's back as well as when one is seated. You listen, both of you ... you especially, Mamushka."

I nearly got up myself to pull the bell and even for a panicked moment considered calling out for the Abyssinians outside the door, but he fell to his knees at my feet and stared into my own doubtlessly frightened eyes with his burning gaze.

"Mamushka, I don't come to you for myself. If it were not for the need you and Batushka have of me, I would go home to Pokrovskoe. What am I?" He patted his chest and his eyes softened. I relaxed and let him take my hands. "I am nothing – a peasant, a *muzhik*, a no one, the sorriest of all God's creatures – and yet He speaks to me and you know this to be true." Mesmerized, I nodded and noted distantly that Anya had

178

clambered to her knees and was beside my chair nodding as well. "I am here only to serve God by serving Russia, and you and Papa are Russia. As long as I am near you, no harm will befall you or Russia's treasure in the form of your son. If you do not desert me, if you believe in me, then you are faithful to God and you will never lose anything that truly matters to you. If, however, you desert me, Mamushka, I can no longer intercede on your behalf. Look every day for miracles and you will see them. Do you understand, Mama?"

Numbly I let my head fall to my chest, unable even to nod, and felt the dampness of tears on my cheeks that I was unaware I had even shed. He left then, and Anya rang for Maria, and I was returned to my bed.

That night I slept more deeply than I had in months. Nor did any dreams of pain – my own or my son's – shake me from my slumbers, as nearly always happened at that time.

The next day Nicky was so pleased with my cheerful mood and my – at least to him – surprising request that he take me for a carriage ride after tea, that he teasingly made a show out of using Father Grigory's comb at his toilette, hardly even flinching as he handed it to his valet Volkov to be cleaned first.

"I say, Sunny, it gives years to my life to see you looking so well."

I held up a cautioning finger, but smiled to remove the sting from my words.

"Thank you, dearest, but remember not to get too excited. My heart attacks can leave me and then return just as suddenly. Dr. Botkin has said that –"

He moved to embrace me, interrupting my speech.

"I know, darling, I know, but just allow me to enjoy you now while nothing untoward is happening."

I frowned.

"Nicky, are you saying that I am a burden and no enjoyment ... no wife to you, because I am ill so much?"

I couldn't help the tears in my voice and eyes as I waited for his reassurance.

I think when Nicky put his arms around me and assured me that all he could ever ask for, or dream of, in this life was daily true because of me, that was the first miracle. Yes, I had heard it before, but now I was more aware of the miraculous nature of things, and each day that winter, it seemed, I saw something else with renewed eyes, as did Anya. When the inevitable accident occurred with Baby and he screamed in pain at his swollen ankle, Father Grigory came and prayed over him, and my son was well all within hours. When on an icy day in February of 1909 I came upon Father Grigory during a sleigh ride with Anya and Tatiana, I saw him just as I was thinking of him.

That day I wanted to show my faith in him, and assisted by my friend and my daughter, I climbed from my carriage. He knew my intent and his hand was already held out for me to kiss in veneration, and that too was a miracle. That someone saw me do this and told others about the scandal of what they had seen, thereby raising a storm of gossip about me in town, that wasn't a miracle, but because I knew Father Grigory had many enemies, I held up my head and ignored the growing voices against him.

Chapter 15

I must say that never have I been more annoyed by a member of Nicky's family than I was that day, and by Nicky's sister Xenia of all people. She was once a very dear friend of mine and I had made a determined effort to remain pleasant to her, despite my growing dislike for her husband Sandro and the deplorable behavior of that crew of ill-mannered, rough boys she had produced.

Xenia's only daughter Irinia had always been an object of some worry for me. She was Minnie's favorite grandchild and the undisputed darling of both of her parents. In fact, the entire family had made a truly ridiculous fuss over that child since her birth as she was the first grandchild to be born, although only by a very few days before Olga who would have been first if she hadn't come so late, allowing Irinia to steal her thunder. Still, Irinia was only the daughter of a tsar's daughter rather than the daughter of the reigning Tsar, as my girl was.

Ella didn't help much in that regard. One might have thought that my own sister, and my daughter Olga's own auntie, would naturally have favored her niece, but in her endless desire to curry favor with Minnie, she had immediately agreed that Irinia was the most beautiful baby girl she had ever seen.

All of this fuss and attention had, at least to my mind, created in Irinia a rather precocious child who was far too sophisticated and forward for one of her tender years. Neither of my big pair liked her much, but my sweet little Maria followed her about adoringly whenever she saw her and would bother me to death for days afterward, asking plaintively why she didn't have lots of "cousin friends" like Iriny and get to go to dress-up parties all the time.

I also found Xenia's choices as a mother quite questionable. She and Sandro spent whole months in France, Italy and England traveling about and they took their children with them. In addition, living in town during the season as they did, their children were always off to parties and dance classes, and romping with other Romanov offspring, all of whom I considered both spoiled and frivolous. Nicky and I were in firm agreement that our girls were to be kept both innocent and modest, and that allowing them such liberties would lead to their attaining premature adulthood and therefore, no doubt, dissipation. They had each other and we felt that was more than enough.

I did understand that Olga and Tatiana were a little country unto themselves, and that Nastinka was both terribly independent and also closer to Baby's age – so they tended to be companions – which left Maria at a loose end sometimes, but I still did not like Maria's fascination with Irinia, and that was one of the reasons I had tried to keep Xenia at arms-length over recent years, not that Xenia minded my keeping my distance from her all that much. Xenia was very close to her mother and it must have been difficult for her to try to remain friends with me in the face of Minnie's relentless disapproval of me.

Then there was her husband Sandro. In their youth, Nicky and Sandro had been the very closest of friends. This continued into young adulthood, and when Sandro and Xenia fell in love, no one was more delighted than Nicky. Minnie, on the other hand, begrudged Sandro almost as much as she despised me, regarding him as a usurper who would steal her daughter's attention and affection away from her, the most important person in the world, although I doubt she found him personally objectionable. He was at least a Romanov and Xenia's marriage to him would assure her of keeping her daughter in Russia – no easy feat in a reigning family – and Sandro, who was tall, dark and handsome, must have at least seemed presentable to her.

Not so me, of course, for not only had I "stolen" Nicky away from her maternal embrace, I was also deemed hopelessly inadequate. Furthermore, unlike Sandro, I did not bring sons into the family, at least not until Alexei was born, and look what I had done there. I heard from Anya that Minnie had virtually accused me of "poisoning the blood of the Romanovs."

I hadn't passed that particular piece of gossip on to Nicky because I didn't think he would believe me when I claimed that his mother was referring to Alexei's condition, and moreover I didn't want to remind him that I had done exactly that, whoever it was who had said it. Anyway, Nicky had plenty of new gossip to listen to that day because Xenia had seen something that I knew she would be unable to remain silent about.

It was the day before our entire clan was to embark upon our yachts and sail off to Cowes. The Alexander Palace was in a state of semi-madness as the servants were running about aimlessly, much confused by the conflicting orders given out by Count Fredericks. All these preparations for our departure were further

183

complicated by it being the day following poor Maria's sad little wedding.

I suppose it was silly of me to ask Anya to accompany me outside as there was so much to command my attention elsewhere, but I was beyond exhausted and the girls were driving me mad, running in and out of my boudoir every moment with silly questions about clothes, and Baby was as over-excited as I had ever seen him amid all the unusual bustle, while Nicky was closeted in last-minute meetings with his ministers.

During all of this, Anya was refusing to leave my side for even a moment as she was simply falling apart at the prospect of being away from me for the summer, so I impulsively asked her to find two footmen, if she could manage to do so in all the confusion, and ask them to take a mattress outside for me to lay on, and she could join me for the day before returning to her lonely little house to begin waiting for our return.

It was so innocent and we had done it many times before, often with Baby. I simply could not bear to sit up outside for very long as my back and legs would ache in my chair, and it was just more comfortable to have a mattress carried outside and placed under a tree. Nor was it surprising for Anya and me to fall asleep in such comfortable conditions. I never thought of it as a strange thing, but that day I did, for I saw it in Xenia's expression.

Her entire family, along with Minnie, had been staying at the big palace, Empress Catherine's old palace, with the Swedish royals and had decided to accompany our family in cars to Peterhof where they

would board Minnie's Polar Star as we embarked upon
The Standart – quite the cozy affair – so maybe I
shouldn't have been surprised to wake up to find her and
a few of her ladies standing around my mattress,
gawping at Anya and me, but I was.

"Alix …?"

"Oh Xenia, you startled me. I was napping. I was …
I, well, what are you doing out here?"

Horribly then, and I know she only did it to make
everything all the more embarrassing for us, she
curtsied. It was not the custom in our family to curtsy to
each other. Nicky had made no ruling on it, but in the
light of Minnie insisting on her precedence to me, and in
the light of my illness, which forced me to be bed- or
chair- bound and therefore unable, as well as unwilling,
to curtsy to her, the whole practice had mostly been
abandoned except on formal and public occasions.
Xenia's curtsying to me at this moment was therefore
deliberately designed to place me at a disadvantage.
Still, I inclined my head toward her with as much dignity
as I could muster.

Xenia smiled and said, "We were just out strolling. It
is such a lovely day and we thought maybe we would
stop by the little palace and see you and Nicky and the
children. But what luck, here you are."

She finished by giving Anya, who was just rousing
herself, a pointed look.

Anya, who was still largely asleep and mostly
blinded by a large hat that she had pulled down over her
face as a sort of sunshade, tried to rise to curtsy to Xenia
in response, but lost her balance and toppled onto my

185

sore legs, causing me to shriek out in pain, which in turn drew a squeal from Anya.

"Ach, ach, ach," she said, and in distress tried to crawl off me as I pushed at her weakly and continued to cry out. The pain was terrible and it felt as though a building had fallen upon me.

Xenia gestured to her ladies to help pull Anya off me, which they did by dragging her face-down into the grass, whereupon Anya scrambled up, panting, while still attempting to curtsy to Xenia, but only managing to fall again in an ungainly mess, this time at Xenia's feet, while I fell back prone, unable to speak or to be of assistance because of the pain, although I did whisper weakly to Xenia to send for help.

Afterward, Nicky informed me that Dr. Botkin had said that he felt I would still be able to continue with our trip provided that I did not exert myself unduly. Then he added, "Quite a carry on today, wasn't it, darling, but no real harm done. Dr. Botkin said there wasn't even any bruising, so I suppose –"

"He couldn't be more wrong, Nicky. My legs feel awful and even the opium hasn't helped. I don't see how I can possibly travel after this. I think Anya and your sister between them have nearly killed me."

He turned around to face me and I saw his lips twitching. He thought this was *amusing?* I scowled at him to show that I knew what he was thinking.

He tried not to chuckle but failed, saying, "Well, darling, I would be the last one to contest that having Anya collapse on top of one would be painful in the extreme, and she seems to fall on top of objects with great regularity if the shattered state of several of your

186

tea tables is to be taken as any indication of her weight and inherent powers of destruction. I suppose we should both be grateful not to have been permanently crippled by some of our encounters with her clumsiness. But I really cannot see how Xenia was in any way at fault."

"You weren't there, Nicky. You didn't see how she just crept up on us. And then she made this stupid curtsy. You know she never does that and it made poor Anya feel as though she had to curtsy to her."

"Which is as it should be, Alix. Anya may be our friend, but it should not be forgotten that she is still a commoner, while Xenia is the daughter of one tsar, the sister of another, and the wife of a grand duke. Naturally Anya has to bow to Xenia."

I thought Nicky was being rather pompous and was ready to argue the point with him, all night if necessary, but he clearly wasn't interested in a further discussion of the issue. Instead, he moved over to me, leaned down, kissed me on the head, and started toward the door.

"Where are you going?"

"It is late and we have an early start in the morning and a busy day ahead of us. You need your rest and so do I, darling, so I shall sleep in my dressing room tonight."

I tried to sleep but I was at a loss, for Nicky had never before retired to his dressing room save during my confinements. I vowed then to remain so silent and circumspect during our trip to Cowes that not a soul, and especially not my husband, would find a word to say against me. For how could they if I didn't say a word?

I smiled, pleased with my plan, but still couldn't find the sleep I so sorely needed. It was my legs: they were aching terribly, and I just could not get comfortable. Pausing to consider the hour, I sighed and forced myself to ring for Maria, who took an unconscionably long time to arrive and looked quite the mess when she did so. Indeed, I could see the hem of her nightgown hanging below her black skirt.

"Maria, you took forever to come," I said fretfully, hoping for an apology as I was simply desperate for someone to act as though I was in the right on at least something. However, Maria was a poor prospect for such comfort as she pursed her lips, raised an eyebrow, and made a halfhearted curtsy.

"What is it, Your Majesty?"

I gestured to my legs.

"My knees are paining me and I want you to help me roll to my side and place a pillow between them."

She started to help me to roll over but somewhat roughly, I thought, and then, to make matters worse, she retrieved one of the stacked pillows from Nicky's side of the bed and pushed it between my knees with unnecessary force, causing me to cry out in pain and annoyance, "Good heavens, Maria, you clumsy idiot…"

I snatched the pillow out from between my knees and tossed it irritably across the room, whereupon I could have sworn that I heard Maria make a snorting sound.

"What are you doing, Maria? Why are you laughing?"

Maria bent down to recover the pillow and when she arose her face was solemn.

"I was not laughing, Your Majesty. If I made a noise, I apologize. I think I was surprised by Your Majesty's treatment of the pillow." She held out the pillow in front of her. "Does this mean that you do not wish me to place a pillow between your knees after all, Your Majesty?"

"Of course I do. I am in terrible pain."

"Would you like me to send for Dr. Botkin?" she asked, failing to stifle a yawn.

"Maria, how dare you?"

Maria's voice when she replied was tear-choked.

"Your Majesty, forgive me, I'm so … I'm so very tired. I've been up since dawn overseeing the packing and it'll be dawn again in a few hours. I … I'm just so very tired that I –"

"Stop it, Maria. I too am exhausted and need to sleep, so cease your hysterics and find me a small, flat pillow that is comfortable for my legs. The sooner you do this, the sooner we can all sleep. It really isn't that difficult."

Maria stood there awkwardly, then, still holding the fat pillow, she began to bow her way out of the room.

Left there sprawling uncomfortably on my side, I considered calling out to Nicky and rejected the idea, but by the time Maria finally returned with a selection of pillows that were smaller and more comfortable, I had twisted about so badly that she had to call two footmen to carry me to my chaise while she summoned maids from their beds to strip and replace the sheets and pillow cases before I could rest. Finally I slept, but it seemed like only moments later when Maria was again in my room with my morning coffee to wake me for our departure.

Given all this commotion, I was hardly in a state to face traveling, let alone to chatter mindlessly in a car with either Nicky's gossipy sister or his ghastly mother, and so I demanded that the children ride with Ella as

189

they were over-excited, especially Baby, and I would travel in another car alone with Nicky.

In the car I remained silent beside a concerned Nicky, and by the time I was carried onto The Standart, I was in a state of near-collapse. Dr. Botkin then proceeded to cluck about me and to dose me up with Veronal, while a gray-faced Maria settled me at long last into my cabin where I finally, finally fell asleep again to the sounds of the anchor being weighed and a brass band playing a nerve-jarring rendition of 'God Save The Tsar' as we set out for Cowes.

Chapter 16

I do not think it could come as much of a surprise to anyone if I were to say that I did not greatly enjoy our visit to Cowes. It was an episode I would very much prefer to forget although that trip sadly remains the high point of my girlies' young lives. For in the confusion of the to-and-fro of daily visiting between the yachts, and the equal number of shore trips made to attend a ceaseless series of regatta parties, they managed to slip away from their ladies-in-waiting, and nurses, and guards – all of whom thought they were under the care of one of the others – for two entire hours and conduct a shopping excursion of their own in the small village of Cowes.

I didn't even find out about it until the next morning when Olga joined me for breakfast, her face shining with delight.

"Mama, you'll never guess, the most wonderful thing happened yesterday." She hugged herself and leaned over to kiss my cheek.

I studied the sweet face of my biggest girl and realized how seldom I saw her look this happy.

So, smiling and wanting to share in her little pleasures, I obligingly asked her in a teasing voice, "Oh yes? And does this have to do with one of our young sailors with whom you have danced, or," I rolled my eyes in mock shock, "is it about that handsome young rascal David, Georgie's boy?"

Both Nicky and I had been very impressed with young David, the eldest of May and Georgie's many sons, a young man who we felt would one day make a fine and very handsome King of England. That he and Olga were of an age was lost on no one in Cowes and their every interaction, no matter how small, was met with great interest and clandestine smiles and gossip.

Olga shook her head, blushing.

"No, it's not a boy, Mama, and speaking of boys, you and Papa and everybody can just stop expecting anything to happen between David and me. He's far too short for me, and besides, when I get married, I'm going to marry a Russian sailor so I can stay at home."

I smiled at my adamant little one and inwardly wished that could be true as I did not enjoy even thinking about Olga's future marriage prospects and her inevitable departure from our home. Nor did I bother to suggest to her that David still had time to grow taller. Instead, I smiled widely at her and said, "Then darling, I am all curiosity. What wonderful thing happened to my girly yesterday?"

Olga was nearly bouncing up and down with excitement as she answered.

"Well, it happened to all your girlies, Mama! We were on Uncle Bertie's yacht ... You remember, Grandmamma made us go with her to tea there with Aunt Alix?" I winced. Yes, of course I knew what she was talking about. Minnie, whom I hated to hear spoken of as Grandmamma – that title in my mind being reserved to my dear lost one – had come over from The Polar Star far too early for visiting the previous day and had bustled into my cabin, but only after looking for, and failing to find, Nicky, who had gone off at first light to visit Cousin Willy on his yacht. Discovering me still in bed at nine in the morning, she immediately feigned shock – or was it disappointment, distaste, outrage, or despair, the usual range of emotions she displayed toward me?

"Alix, are you ill again?"

I rose up and rung for Maria, whom I planned to toss overboard for letting Minnie in, and said, "I am not ill *again*, as you put it, Minnie. I am *still* ill."

She cocked her small head. "Is there a difference?" Before I could answer, she went on as if my health was the least of her concerns, which I suspect it was. "Never mind, Alix, I haven't come to discuss your ailments. I have come to take my granddaughters off with me for the day. We shall take my dinghy to Alix and Albie's yacht for an early luncheon, and then go into Cowes for a bit of sightseeing. Willy is organizing a tea dance on The Hohenzollern for later today and the girls will of course be attending. Shall I instruct their maids to pack tea dresses for the day as well so that we will not have to come back for them and disturb your ..." she paused before saying the final word, eyebrows lifted, "... rest?"

"Thank you, Minnie, that would be so kind of you. I am sure the girls will enjoy the tea dance a great deal. I shall send Nicky for them this evening, then, shall I?"

She shook her head.

"That will not be necessary – sending him over, I mean – as he will already be there."

She smiled at me again, point won, and I tried not to let my hurt and surprise show. Nicky had not said a word to me about a tea dance. Much as I tried to conceal my reactions to her news, Minnie saw them anyway, she always did, with her bright black bird eyes, watching,

193

pecking, peck-peck-peck, watching, peck-peck. That was all she ever did, the horrible old crow, and somehow she intercepted that thought too, for her expression hardened.

"I am sorry if I am annoying you, Alix. I will just collect the girls and go, shall I? I am certain that if my son did not mention the dance to you, it was because he simply assumed, as we all did, that you would not be attending yourself. After all," she shrugged lightly, "as far as I know, you haven't left this boat once since you arrived in Cowes."

"Mama, Mama, are you listening to me?" Olga's voice broke in on my bitter thoughts. I rubbed at my forehead and shook myself back to the moment and to my excited child.

Instantly she was all concern.

"Oh Mama dearest, are you getting a headache? Am I giving you a headache? I'm so terribly selfish to chatter on like this when you're not feeling well."

Her loving concern brought me fully back and I smiled into her sweet eyes.

"No, darling. Well, it is just a little one and it doesn't matter anyway. Now, do tell Mama what was so wonderful."

She grinned mischievously.

"Well, after that terribly dull time with Grandmamma and Great Aunt Alix, Grandmamma kept her promise and took us into Cowes. Aunt Alix came too. But when we got there, they were so terribly slow, Mama, and you know how Nastinka can never bear to wait for anything…"

I nodded. I did indeed. Anastasia had the patience of a fly, as did Baby. They were always in a hurry. It made me grin right back at my girl to think of my youngest girlie pulling her grandmother down the streets of Cowes, but I tried to appear concerned about how Anastasia might have behaved. Misbehavior on her part would, after all, be but one more stick to beat me with.

"Oh, was she very naughty with Grandmamma and Aunt Alix?"

Olga nodded fervently.

"She was. In fact, as soon as the tender docked at the jetty and she saw that Grandmamma and Great Aunt Alix were going to dither forever about where we should go, just like that she took off running down the street. We didn't have anyone else with us because we'd come with Grandmamma and Aunt Alix, and Aunt Alix doesn't use a police escort. It's so strange and wonderful, isn't it, Mama, that she can walk around so freely!"

I nodded wordlessly. Yes, it would be quite wonderful not to be surrounded by police or Cossacks shadowing one's every step. At least, unlike my children, I had once experienced such freedom.

Olga, unaware of such things, was describing it all as though the day had been somehow miraculous.

"Grandmamma told Tatiana to go get Nastinka. I said I'd help and started running after them, and then Maria came too, and we did find Nastinka, but …" She looked down blushing and I tilted up her chin, smiling.

"But?"

She giggled.

"But we found her inside a little shop and we all had so much money, Mama, that it seemed –"

"*Money?* Where would you have got any money, darling? Do you mean *English* money?"

I was quite startled, for no one in our family ever carried money. A lady-in-waiting or one of the suite always carried money for us on the rare occasions that we required it, which, now that I considered it, had happened only once, when I had wished to drop a coin into the collection box of a small church I had entered.

"Grandmamma gave each of us a five pound note at teatime. She said they were keepsakes for our trip, but that if we wanted, we could buy something in Cowes, so we thought it might be all right. It was, wasn't it, Mama? And look, I bought you a present with some of it."

"My goodness, darling, give it to me right away, then."

Olga grinned and pulled the present out from her skirt pocket.

I examined it and exclaimed with delight, "Why, it is a booklet of stamps. I haven't had cause to use a postage stamp in years. Thank you, darling!"

Her face fell.

"What is it, Olga?"

"I thought I'd have to tell you what they were. I didn't think you'd ever seen stamps like this before. Where did you see them, anyway?"

I laughed at her disappointed face.

"Oh darling, once upon a time I used to stamp my own letters instead of having someone do it for me. The stamps I used came in sheets. I haven't seen them in these beautiful little booklets before. You see here," I

196

pointed to the little pad "you moisten it with water and put the –"

"Oh, I know that. The lady in the shop showed us and I thought it was the most cunning little thing and that you'd like it so much, but you already –"

"It *is* a cunning little thing, and I do like it, and these booklets are quite new to me, so stop pouting and tell me what else you naughty ones got up to and what other strange treasures you bought with Grandmamma's money."

She was smiling again, but shook her head.

"I will later, but the others have them all in their rooms. Well, maybe Nastinka has found Papa by now and given him her present."

I laughed.

"You must tell me what she got Papa. It is quite likely he has never possessed whatever it was that she found for him."

Olga looked at me seriously.

"Oh I don't think he has. She bought him a boar bristle tooth brush and Tatiana used part of her money for some tooth powder to go with it."

I had to look down and bite my lip, but I couldn't keep the giggles from erupting.

"Darling, I think Papa does have toothbrushes and powders."

She nodded.

"Yes, I said that too, but Nastinka said they must not be very good ones because his breath always smells so terribly. Tati agreed with her and said that no one else had breath like him, and they thought that with English people being so clever and all ..." Her voice trailed off.

There was really nothing I could say, or at least nothing I should have said, so I asked brightly what Maria had bought.

Olga's eyes lit up.

"Maria's things are the best of all, and we can all have fun with them all the time, but some of them are for Anya and Father Grigory too, and Baby."

I was so touched to think of my little Maria buying gifts for so many people.

"How very dear of her. What did she buy, darling?"

"Postcards, Mama, lots of them. They cost only a penny each, you see, and it seems that five pounds is a very great deal of money when it comes to postcards, but not so much for other things we found." Her forehead wrinkled in puzzlement.

"How, darling? Postcards of what?"

"Of Cowes, Mama," she answered, as though the answer should have been obvious.

"Darling, all of you have cameras so that you can take your very own pictures of Cowes, or anywhere else. Why would you pay for postcards?"

She shrugged.

"You couldn't understand how lovely it all was, going into the shops, wandering about before Grandmamma's ladies found us and dragged us back, buying little things, like ordinary people do. Maybe Maria liked the postcards better because anyone can have them. Free people can have them."

She then burst into such tears that her thin shoulders convulsed.

I was nonplussed and held out my arms to her as she stumbled from her chair and buried her wet little face in my skirts as I stroked her hair.

"Dearest girly, there is nothing to cry about. You had your lovely outing. Is my silly little one really crying over this? You were so happy a minute ago, sweetheart, and yes I suppose free people can buy postcards, but don't you think they would much rather have a camera to take pictures with and a yacht to take them from? Is being a little grand duchess really so upsetting, my girly?"

To my dismay her little head nodded.

"It is, Mama, although I suppose I don't know anything else," She sniffled and I tried not to laugh. "But yesterday, oh it was so wonderful, you can't imagine. I think it was the best day of my whole life, of all of our lives. We were just ordinary people for once." She shook her head in frustration and then looked at me with great blue, tear-filled eyes. "But you can't know any of this, can you? All you know is this ..." She gestured around the cabin and The Standart with a dismissive air. "How could you understand?"

"It is the greatest position there is," I said emphatically.

"What?"

I stroked my daughter's hot face. "That is what my grandmamma always used to say to me. It is the greatest position there is."

"What was she talking about?"

I gestured to myself.

"This, I suppose, but in particular she meant being Queen of England. That is what she hoped for me. She didn't think much of Russia, but still, to become the empress of a mighty empire, that was better than nothing, far better. She was very pragmatic was my grandmamma."

"Yes, Mama, I know." Olga sighed and leaned back on her heels, preparing to rise. "Being the Queen of England is what you and Papa would like to see happen to me, or if not to me, to one of us at least. And out there in the world," she gestured to the sea beyond my cabin, "is some baby girl, or maybe one not yet even born, who will marry Alexei and become the Empress of Russia one day, and be like you and Grandmamma Minnie. Of course it's all very grand, but I had such a good time yesterday. I liked just being a girl and that's what you can never understand. I think I'll go and see my sisters now. I'm sure I've made you very tired."

I reached for her wrist and pulled her back. Caught by surprise, she sprawled back to the floor, then laughing a little, she rubbed her wrist.

"You're much stronger than I would have guessed, Mama. What is it?"

"I do understand, I do. It is you who doesn't understand, Olga." She eyed me warily. I was so impatient – no, so eager for her to understand me – that I spoke all in a rush. "You don't understand me, none of my children understand how it was when I was a girl. You have been to see Uncle Ernie at Wolfsgarten, but we have never stayed at the new palace where I grew up. We can't, you see, for reasons of security. It is right in the very center of my lovely little Darmstadt. When I was a girl, I went in and out of the palace freely. I bought little notions if I had the money to spend on them. I talked to anyone I pleased and they gave me little gifts. And it was no different when I would go to England to see Granny. There was a little shop in Windsor where I bought sweets, and yes, postcards too, for I didn't have a camera."

Olga moved back onto her knees and held her hand out. I took it. Her eyes were clear and I had her interest again.

"I didn't know that … that you were so free when you were a girl. Were you happy, then, Mama? Do you miss it? Why did your papa and Grandmamma let you run free, and why can't you do that for us? I mean, if you liked it. Did you like it?"

I grinned at her barrage of questions.

"Yes, I was quite free because I wasn't a bit important, except to my own family. And I do miss it, darling. I hate all the police and soldiers being around us constantly as much as you girlies do, although of course now Mama is too sick to do anything much. I know it is harder on my young ones," I stroked her face, "but you see, dearest, I was not the daughter of a reigning emperor or king, so it has to be different for you."

Her eyes narrowed.

"Auntie Xenia is the daughter of an emperor, isn't she?"

"Of course she is, Olga, you know that."

"And Auntie Olga is also a tsar's daughter," she said, referring to her favorite aunt, Nicky's youngest sister.

I sighed and sat back.

"Yes, Olga, and are you going to keep asking me these silly questions to which you already know the answers all day or do you have something you wish to say to me?"

"Yes, Mama. You see, if I'm going to get married one day, I want to be able to choose my husband and I don't think I want to be an empress as I don't like being locked up. Maybe Auntie Xenia and Auntie Olga were when they were little, like us sisters, but they aren't now, even though I don't think Auntie Olga is a bit happy with Uncle Peter. But Aunt Xenia is happy and she does whatever she likes with Uncle Sandro."

"And ...?"

"And I don't want you and Papa to pick my husband for me. I want you to promise me you won't. I want to be like Aunt Xenia and Aunt Olga ... but not like Aunt Olga really, because Grandmamma made her marry Uncle Peter and he doesn't even like girls."

Olga was looking triumphant at having made a powerful argument; I was horrified. It was true, it certainly was, that Minnie had, following her own selfish agenda, forced her youngest daughter into marriage with a known sodomite, and done so to ensure that Olga remained near her – a sodomite, I might add, who had no money of his own and was, on top of everything else, a drunkard and a gambler. What horrified me was that my innocent thirteen-year-old daughter already knew this.

"Olga Nikolaevna, where on earth did you hear such a ridiculous story about your Aunt Olga's husband?"

"I heard Papa and Dmitri discussing it when they were playing billiards. Why, is it a lie? If it's a lie, why were they saying it?"

Having no possible answer to give her, I resorted to a partial lie.

"Darling, Mama's heart is beginning to tire. Could you run and find Dr. Botkin for me? These are all very important questions and soon Papa and I will tell you all about everything, but for now, I think …" I made a faint gesture of exhaustion.

Olga nodded wordlessly and rose to leave, leaning over to kiss my cheek.

"I'm sorry, Mama, I shouldn't have tired you so."

I gave her a half-hearted shake of my head to indicate that, yes, she should not have tired me and, no, I didn't mind too much that she had.

She gave me an odd smile and said, "I'll just send Dr. Botkin over to you, then."

Chapter 17

Later that night, when Nicky and I were finally alone, I patiently listened to his recitation of the differences in seaworthiness, agility, speed and ease of maneuvering of the various royal yachts, claiming, for instance, that Willy's The Hohenzollern was a great big, top-heavy boat which would be undone by England's graceful The Victoria and Albert. Yet I knew this laborious tale to be just one of Nicky's ruses to wear me down into going along with his notion of joining in the fun by racing our own graceful The Standart against the others.

Naturally I did not, by so much as a sympathetic word, let him believe for a moment that I would ever agree to this. Not only did I consider this splendid array of yachts at Cowes to be merely a part of a silly game of one-upmanship played by men who were still boys at heart, but also – and more importantly – I was not going to be bundled off The Standart to find myself on The Polar Star in the company of Minnie and my sister-in-law, while Nicky showed off his favorite toy in front of his fellow crowned heads and the world in general.

I didn't say that, though, since I had already made my feelings on this quite clear. Instead, I nodded pleasantly as if nothing could be of more interest to me than how displaced tonnage could make such a miniscule difference in speed on water, and then, when he had paused for breath and to light a new cigarette, I leaned in closer to him and said, "Nicky darling, I have had the most curious chat today with Olga."

He looked distressed to see our conversation moving on to another topic when he had not yet reached his goal of getting me to capitulate with regard to the racing, but his innate sense of fairness and courtesy compelled him to allow me to discuss a subject that interested me in my turn.

"Oh yes, and what did our eldest have to say? Did she tell you about her visit to The Victoria and Albert today with Mama?" he asked, hopeful that he might be able to lead our conversation back to the discussion of yachts and racing.

"No, she was telling me all about her adventures of yesterday. Did you know that all four of our girlies managed to slip off and wander about Cowes unattended and even spent time shopping for some quite extraordinary items?"

Nicky smiled without appearing particularly engaged.

"Oh yes. Nastinka bought me a funny thing, a moustache brush, I think it was." He fingered his perfectly barbered mustache and said thoughtfully, "I must remember to hide it somewhere. Old Volkov would be most hurt if he thought the girls felt that I wasn't up to snuff. I cannot for the life of me think why they would purchase such an item, can you, darling?"

"It wasn't a moustache brush, as you know very well, Nicky."

He waved his hand dismissively. Nicky could not bear me addressing the state of his teeth or his fears of the dentist.

I was a bit torn for I did indeed wish to speak of his lack of dental care which was causing me no small amount of unpleasantness, but I knew it would sour his mood if I were to do so, so I swallowed my words and merely smiled.

"What I was truly wondering was what you thought about their being able to escape their nurses and their guards, and to saunter off on their own around Cowes?"

Nicky continued to smoke serenely without the slightest sense of concern over the matter.

"It seems to have been a harmless enough adventure, if you ask me, although Mama is simply fit to be tied about their having got away from her unchaperoned, which she considers most unseemly."

He pulled a comical expression and I laughed appreciatively.

"I know, but I suppose the only important thing is that no harm came to them. But the willfulness behind it all ... Worse, having spoken at length to Olga, it seems to have been done out of a feeling of desperation, and that is worrying, is it not?"

Nicky arched an eyebrow.

"Desperation? That seems a bit strong, Alicky. They are just little girls wanting an adventure and now they have had one. And I have my curious brush to prove it. Say, did I tell you that Uncle Bertie is taking wagers on the race tomorrow?"

I dismissed his attempt to change the subject back to his preoccupation with being allowed to race.

"No, Nicky, desperation is precisely the right word. Olga became quite overwrought when speaking to me of her feelings of being trapped – jailed, I believe she said. She also mentioned that she understood that her Aunt Olga was married to a sodomite."

It was my turn to raise an eyebrow as Nicky blushed a beet red and dropped burning ashes into his lap in surprise.

While he frantically brushed at himself, I continued in a deliberately casual voice. "Yes, it seems that while I have been ill, trying very hard to get better, our girls have been getting restive and been following you and Dmitri around to learn about things best never spoken of."

Nicky straightened himself up and glared at me. He hated criticism and at times could become quite nasty if I dared to reproach him over anything. This, I saw wearily, was going to be just such an occasion.

"As you say, Alix, you have been ill for years now, it seems, and I do apologize, darling, if my tedious hours spent ruling Russia have made of me a less than exemplary parent, but as I recall, it was your decision not to engage another governess for our daughters."

I put on my most determined face.

"I do not want Dmitri to live with us anymore," I blurted out, and even to me it sounded as if I were spitting.

My declaration certainly threw Nicky off his guard.

"What? What?"

"You heard me, Nicky. He is almost grown and Ella has made the Belosselsky Belozersky Palace, one of the nicest palaces in town, over to him. He will hardly be out on the streets. Meanwhile, he is becoming positively rakish and a poor influence on our girlies. And he will be a worse one on Baby when Alexei is old enough to understand him. I simply despise his lazy manner of speaking and his use of slang."

Now it was Nicky's turn to catch me by surprise.

"What have I done now, Alicky?"

I looked at him, puzzled.

"I didn't say you had done anything, Nicky, don't be silly. I was speaking about Dmitri and our children. Why you feel attacked I cannot imagine."

"You are only raising the issue of Dmitri to punish me for something. You know how much I enjoy having Dmitri with us."

Nicky could be as difficult and childish as any of our children when he wanted to be, and I was just about to tell him so when he forestalled my comment by getting up and leaving the cabin without a word, still dressed in his robe and nightclothes.

I was shocked, for I knew that any behavior by my family that was considered out of the ordinary was gossiped about and then laid at my door during the interminable tea parties and concerts, luncheons and dinners that had been put on in Cowes since our arrival. Of course, I hadn't actually attended any of these, but how could I? My legs had never been so bad; I was plagued by neuralgia in my face; and my heart had never been better than a Number Two since we had departed from Peterhof. All of this and yet I knew I was being judged and spoken of by Nicky's family, by Willy's family, and by my own former English family.

We only stayed at Cowes for four days, the foreshortened duration of which, I suppose, was blamed on me as well. It was Nicky who offered our regrets but our early departure had been agreed upon mutually after I had conceded that Dmitri could see the year out with our family if Nicky would send a telegram to Anya to invite her to come to us in Livadia.

It was the first time Anya had ever been to Livadia and I can see her so clearly right at this moment if I close my eyes. I was resting on the balcony in my wheeling chair, for I had sent Dmitri in the carriage to pick her up as a bit of mischief, knowing Anya's steadfast designs upon him, and as I watched their arrival, I noted that Anya was uncharacteristically silent, nodding only briefly at Dmitri as he helped her bulky little figure out of the carriage. Then, instead of issuing her usual stream of "Ach, ach," exclaimed either in surprise or distress depending on her mood, she simply stood and gazed about her, not even rushing to me as I had anticipated.

I smiled, pleased.

Livadia could do that to anyone. It was a place apart, an island away from the rest of the world. We were, in fact, nearly an island, as the Crimea was surrounded on the west and south by the Black Sea, and on the east by the Sea of Asov, with very high hills, virtually mountains, protecting our estates from the icy northern winds of the north, lending the area almost a tropical climate, with the imperial estates the loveliest of them all.

Indeed, our estates occupy almost half of the Crimea, or at least they did – things could be terribly changed now – but then, oh then, they covered a vast area, shielded from any encroachment by Nicky and the tsars who came before him who loved them as much as we did. Nicky's dear papa had allowed but one small railroad track to be laid in the entirety of the Crimea – from Sevastopol to Moscow – but our palace could only be reached by carriage, on horseback, or, if you possessed one, by motorcar, the journey lasting several hours, thus enabling one to savor the magic of the place. It was the most un-Russian sort of Russia one could imagine, that is if one viewed Russia as a place apart from the world, an endless unpopulated expanse of ice and snow.

Yet to me the Crimea was the real Russia.

It was populated sparsely, despite its beauty, and the natives here were Tartars, a handsome race of tall, black-bearded men from whom our family drew our loyal Don Cossacks, and their wives – tall, flashing-eyed beauties who dyed their hair a bright red and gave white-toothed smiles to all they encountered. These people were the Russians I loved and understood, the true people of our land, for oddly, despite their inability to speak or read English or even much Russian, and although their religion was of the Pagan Muslim sort, they alone of all the millions of those living in Russia seemed truly to venerate and adore our family and our throne, and because of this Nicky and I considered them to be true Christian subjects, only kept from worshipping in our own churches by their differences in language.

As Nicky had once explained earnestly to me, "The Tartars, darling, do worship God in their own way. It is simply all tied up with other things, and we must remember that it wasn't they but the filthy Jews who spilled Our Lord's precious blood."

I knew that he was right about the role of the Jews in the death of Our Savior, but I never really lost my feeling that Hesse-Darmstadt and England were, if not more civilized, more enlightened when it came to the

210

Jews. However, I never said so, for it was my daily wish to be Russian in every way and I greatly enjoyed the wild and free people of the Crimea, and was glad that their loyalty to us was never tested by pogroms.

Of course, a person such as Anya, a simple person, could not know any of this, and even to consider such weighty concerns would be beyond her, yet the fact of the Crimea itself was almost more than she could take in and I was glad of it, glad of her shining eyes and loud exclamations of pleasure as she finally made her way to my rooms at the old wooden palace.

I had been feeling particularly ill, having suffered a recent series of heart attacks brought on by the stresses and strains of our visit to Cowes, and her joy at seeing all of this for the first time elated my sickened heart.

"Ach, Alix, there is so, so much here. Why, the vineyards and the sea and the flowers, and it's ... well, it's as though summer has just been returned to us. It's like a miracle." She giggled. "Do you know I brought my furs?"

I laughed indulgently.

"Your furs, Anya? Whatever possessed you to do that?"

"Well, it has been already freezing at night and there's ice forming on the Neva ... but look here," she gestured outside and gave a little hop of emphasis, "it's all perfect and warm, and this must be just what heaven is like. Do you know something, Alix?"

"No, Anya, tell me."

"I think God must love the Crimea and hate Petersburg."

I smiled indulgently.

"I see, Anya, and why do you think that?"

She narrowed her eyes and spoke in a hushed tone.

"It's quite obvious, isn't it? Everything here is alive and everything elsewhere is already dead, so it makes perfect sense, although," she tilted her head as if the weight of her own thoughts were too much for her, "then that wouldn't explain those terrible places where heathen yellow people live, would it?"

When Nicky came in to welcome Anya to Livadia, he found us both hooting like owls with laughter. Naturally he asked to hear the joke and joined us in our merriment after Anya explained everything to him.

It took him a moment to stop laughing and to wipe his eyes before he could say, "Anya you are such a tonic and as such most heartily welcome in the Crimea. I cannot think why we haven't had you here before," then, to forestall any protest from me, he added, "but I must show you my new tennis courts. Her Majesty tells me that you have been practicing your game and I look forward to taking you on."

Anya blushed wildly and simpered and wiggled in such a fashion that her entire bulk shook with it, and I looked away in distaste, only murmuring in agreement when Nicky asked if we could all have tea together in my boudoir later.

"Boudoir indeed," I thought, looking around me in distaste. The Maly Palace, as it was called, hardly lived up to the grandeur that its name suggested, being but a glorified peasant hut where Nicky's papa had created, in his enthusiasm to extol all things Russian, a level of discomfort that was almost unimaginable outside his

212

hunting lodge at Spala, another unimpressive 'imperial residence.'

Despite its magnificent location and sweeping sea views in every direction, the rooms were small, dark, low-ceilinged and reeking of mildew. The roofs leaked on the rare rainy days, and as in our ghastly hunting lodge in Poland, all the lights were kept burning during the daytime because the corridors were so dark that one risked falling down a flight of stairs at every turn. For all that I loved the surrounding environment, I detested the palace itself, and, to make things all the more ridiculous, the only room with a balcony that directly overlooked the sea was the room in which Nicky's sainted papa had died, so naturally we couldn't have it to sleep in, and nor could it become my sitting room. Instead, it had to remain exactly the way it was on the day he died, down to the last grotesque detail of his blood-spattered handkerchief and the empty oxygen tank lying by his chair. For me that room was haunted by his death and by my own terrible memories of that appalling week, the beginning of my time in Russia.

How different was Anya's arrival to mine, but she too would soon know the horror of this place, for it was nearly late October and on the 20th, without fail, our family and suite would crowd into the old death chamber and hold a service of remembrance, as if any of us could ever forget what had happened here or escape attendance, however ill we were feeling ourselves. Worse, to add to the misery of the occasion, my mother-in-law would then insist on reenacting the entire earlier proceedings, upon completion of the which she would collapse in a faint. What would Anya's reaction be to that? I wondered.

As it turned out, Anya not only did not mind it at all but was positively fascinated by it, jockeying as though she were a peasant at a fair for the position of being the nearest to Minnie in preparation for catching her as she folded, much to Minnie's disgust. Indeed, the prospect of Anya being the one to catch her so alarmed her that she broke with tradition and managed to stay conscious until the very end.

After the ceremony, all the rest of the party processed outside to picnic on the beach, and when they returned later that afternoon it was Nicky who caused me to be the one to faint.

Chapter 18

"What do you mean that you are going to Italy, Nicky? I don't want you going there, or anywhere else for that matter. I will not be left alone. Now, please, dearest, let us hear no more about it."

"But I am going, Alicky, I have to. It is a state visit, and it is important, and I did mention it to you months ago when Stolypin was arranging it. It is all settled. You are most welcome to accompany me, darling, I would love that, and I am certain His Majesty Victor Emmanuel would consider it a singular honor if you were to do so, but are you up to it? How is your heart today?"

He was shooting questions and ideas at me left and right in an obvious bid to confuse me, but I managed to seize on his last question.

"My heart is not famous today. Before you informed me of this ridiculous idea, it was Number Two. Now I fear a very bad attack. And why would we care what the King of Italy thinks? We have cities bigger than his whole country, although I do like its art," I conceded, trying to soften my statement.

Nicky arched an eyebrow, lit a cigarette, and gave me a smile I didn't much like the look of. He was, I could see, in one of his, thankfully rare but always upsetting, obstinate moods.

"Alix, I do not involve you in politics much for I know you aren't interested in them, and I know what you are going to say, that you would be if I spoke of them, but I don't wish to speak of them, God knows." He rubbed his forehead. "They are an endless and miserable part of my existence, but, like Papa, I must do my duty."

"Nicky, what in the world are you talking about? *Politics?* I am asking why you think you need to go to Italy. Can you please try to remain on point and not wander off into some silly philosophical discussion regarding your duties. I know them all too well, thank you."

He shook his head emphatically.

"No, you don't, and I strive to keep you from additional worry, but you are forcing me to explain this visit. We must maintain an excellent relationship with Italy so that our ships can continue to access the Mediterranean. Further, I wish the Slav people of the Balkans to remain free from Ottoman rule, free from the Ottomans and friendly with us. Surely you can see that, Alix? I have been discussing this with Stolypin for years."

"No, I don't see that and I don't care. The Balkans!" I rolled my eyes. "Why does everybody get so excited about the blessed Balkans? They are nothing but trouble."

Nicky's eyes looked cold.

"Well, in the end we must care, Alix, for not only am I the traditional protector of the Slavic peoples of the blessed Balkans, as you call them, but Russia must have access to a trade route that leads into the Mediterranean." I pulled a face which drew an exasperated expression from Nicky. My, he was so irritable today. "Whatever you choose to believe personally, Alix, please just accept that my visit to Italy is of the greatest diplomatic importance in maintaining good relations there because Italy has a great influence over what happens in that part of the Mediterranean. You absolutely must trust me on this. A state visit is of the utmost, utmost necessity. Now, my dear, since the question of whether or not I shall go is settled, for I am going, it only remains for me to ask you if you wish to accompany me."

I fell back and clutched at my chest. The expected attack had indeed come and the pain was beyond bearing. Through a reddened haze of agony and tears I watched him stand up, not quickly, and open the door to speak to a waiting attendant, then he stepped out and a moment later in bustled Dr. Botkin. Nicky did not join him, not while I was being ministered to, nor while Anya came to me to make bleats of distress.

It took an hour before I could sleep, and when I did awaken, it was to find only my faithful Maria by my side.

Maria smiled when she saw me looking at her. It was night, that soft-scented night that I have never experienced anywhere but Livadia. Forgetting for a moment my fight with Nicky and the attack it had caused, I stretched luxuriantly in the perfumed air and looked with pleasure at the starlight over the corner of the sea which was just visible in this cramped room.

Then I remembered.

"Where is His Majesty, Maria? No, never mind where. Just please fetch him here."

Maria didn't meet my eyes. Instead, looking down, she said, "It is very late, Your Majesty – after midnight. The Emperor retired a few hours ago, Dr. Botkin didn't think you should be disturbed and His Majesty is leaving at dawn, which will be here soon. He slept aboard The Standart."

"Maria, you go down there right this instant and tell His Majesty that if he does not return to our rooms I fear he will not see me alive again." Maria didn't move. "Maria, I gave you an order."

She rose reluctantly and left the room. I waited, and in the stillness I fancied I could hear the sounds of people – sailors probably – moving about below me on the water.

The Standart was docked nearly directly below my rooms. I could simply rise and walk to the balcony, but of course I would never do such a thing as to call out for Nicky in front of others. But was that the sound of the anchor being weighed?

Maria re-entered the room and I looked behind her expectantly, but it was Dr. Botkin she had brought and not Nicky. Dr. Botkin moved in front of Maria and produced a syringe. I leaned back into my pillows as far as I could and held up my hand in protest. To my dismay, I had begun to sob again. I tried to stop but I couldn't.

Dr. Botkin bowed his head.

"Dearest Majesty, be calm. You mustn't allow yourself to become so upset. Everything is fine. You just need to rest."

"No, no, I don't want sleep. I want Nicky. No, no, no. Maria, where is he? I told you ... No, get away from me."

Maria fell to her knees beside me.

"Please, Your Majesty, I couldn't take him that message. You aren't going to die –"

"Die?" interjected Dr. Botkin. "Of course Her Majesty is not going to die. Here now ..." and with that he touched me without my permission and plunged the needle into me. I shrieked. It was a madwoman's sound – even I noted that.

Five days he was gone ... five days ... and not once during that time did I leave my room. I refused all visitors, even my children, and even Anya. I also refused all food, so the opium sulfates that Dr. Botkin nearly forced upon me left me half-conscious at best.

However, on the day Nicky finally returned, I had to rouse myself, much as I didn't wish to, because Baby had fallen again and I could hear his screams in my darkened room.

Chapter 19

All was mad confusion, and grief, and suffering, when Nicky arrived back from his little jaunt, for Baby had tripped over a jumping rope that Anastasia had carelessly left lying on the portico and hit his knee, not too hard, but a fall never had to be that hard for him to be plunged into unimaginable suffering.

It went as it always did: a fall – or maybe simply a minor collision – followed by a brief period of hope – nearly always dashed – that this time the blood would not begin to flow freely beneath his skin and become trapped at the joint and around the nerves, bringing him pain, terrible endless pain. Then the screaming would begin and he would want only me and I would be left with the shattering, terrifying uncertainty of whether this was it – of whether I would lose him this time.

Having been in bed when Baby fell, I was still in my night wrapper when Nicky found us all in the makeshift room that passed for Baby's nursery. In he came, tanned and smelling of wind and sea salt, but beneath his ruddy skin I watched him pale as he looked at our treasure writhing in agony upon his small bed.

"What happened? What happened, Alix?"

I barely glanced at him.

"He fell, Nicky, he fell and hit his knee. You weren't here."

"The doctors …? Have you summoned Ostrovsky from town yet?"

I turned back to my son and stroked his crumpled face.

"Botkin summoned him hours ago, not that he will be of any use."

Alexei's eyes opened, his great gray-blue eyes, surrounded by black circles.

"Won't anyone help me, Mama? It hurts. I am hurting so much. Please help me."

I closed my own eyes in an agony that matched his own. If I could have drained every drop of my blood into him to save him an hour of this, I would have done so, but then it was my blood that had done this to him in the first place.

I felt Nicky come up to us. His legs trembled against my back and I heard him sob low in his throat, but he was easy for me to ignore in the face of our boy's suffering. Why did I feel it was Nicky's fault this time? I cannot say, but my back straightened so that his legs were no longer touching me.

"Of course we'll help you, darling," I said. "See, Papa is here to help too now."

That was so unkind of me, so wrong, but I took a savage enjoyment from Nicky's gasp.

Sure as anything, Alexei's beautiful tragic eyes looked above me to Nicky.

"Papa, Papa, can you help me?"

Nicky moved around me and knelt by Baby, saying brokenly, "The doctors will help you, Alexei, and God too."

With a strength that surprised both of us Alexei screamed aloud, "He won't. He never does. The doctors hurt me. You, Papa, you help me. You have to. Help me, help me!" He gave a nerve-rattling wail.

Nicky gasped again and held out a hand to me. I took it and my anger fell away in our shared horror. I tried to speak, but my throat was so dry I only emitted a strange clicking sound.

In tears, Nicky said, "I can't, Alexei, I can't help you. We would die for you but we can't stop the pain."

He broke off when Alexei closed his eyes to him and whispered, "Father Grigory, I want him."

I rose suddenly, nearly knocking Nicky aside.

"Yes, of course, I shall send for him. I shall send him a telegram. I shall do it now."

Baby moaned. "No, Mama, Papa can do that. You stay. It hurts. I want Mama."

Nicky scrambled to his feet.

"Yes, I'll do that, Alicky, I'll do that. I'll go now, shall I?"

Nicky's relief at being given an excuse to escape from the room was so palpable that I feared even Alexei would notice it, not that it would matter as Nicky would do what our son had asked of him and help would be on its way, which is exactly what happened. Father Grigory received the telegram and placed a call through to Livadia, and that was all it took, just his voice over the telephone.

"Mamushka, I am here. Let me speak to him."

The telephone had already been moved into the nursery in anticipation of Father Grigory's call, so it was easy for me, even with shaking hands, to hold the receiver to Baby's ear. Baby had been drifting in and out of consciousness for the last hour but his eyes cleared at the sound of that beloved voice. A few words later, words that I couldn't catch, and then I saw my son's face

222

relax. Nicky saw the change come over Baby too, as did Dr. Botkin. All I wanted then was to be home in Tsarskoe Selo to see Father Grigory for myself and to rest in the reassuring embrace of his faith, but Botkin said I was too weak to travel for weeks and the much over-rated Ostrovsky, when he finally arrived from Petersburg, said that Baby must not be moved, so I was made to understand that we would not be home until Christmas, and then only if we were fortunate.

Instead, there I was stranded in a poky, depressing palace, and all I wanted was him – not Nicky, but him – the one who could erase all pain. Being unable to see him or speak to him, my longing for him grew such that the sole way I could relieve it even a little was for me to write to him and tell him my feelings, and that was the day I wrote the letter that would damn me for all time in the eyes of those people who meant me the most ill.

This was what I wrote:

> *My Beloved, unforgettable teacher, redeemer and mentor: How tiresome it is without you. My soul is quiet and I relax only when you my teacher are sitting beside me. I kiss your hands and lean my head on your blessed shoulders. Oh how light do I feel then! I only wish one thing, to fall asleep forever on your shoulders and in your arms. What happiness to feel your presence near me. Where are you? Where have you gone? Oh am I so sad and my heart is longing ... Will you soon be again close to me?*

Come quickly. I am waiting for you and I am tormenting myself for you. I am asking for your Holy Blessing and I am kissing your blessed hands. I love forever.

Yours,
Mama

Chapter 20

We barely made it home in time for Christmas, and given the weakness that Baby and I were still suffering from, I considered it something of a Christmas miracle that I was still able to organize the trees for our family and the servants, but somehow I managed it. In the end that Christmas turned out to be a uniquely wonderful one, for we had much to be grateful for in our sweet old home, although I could now see growing restlessness in the girls. Olga and Tatiana were pestering me for their own bedrooms and using Maria as their spokesperson, which served only to put me out at all three of them so that I decided to keep things as they were for another year or so.

However, this fraught episode did also bring to my attention the fact that they had reached the ages when they could be included in some court events, and so it was that both our big pair joined Nicky and me in late January 1911 at the Marinsky Theater for a performance of 'Boris Godunov.'

It was the first time I had been to town in years, but I had been having a rare period of heart health and at Christmas Nicky had presented me with such a stunning set of rubies and diamonds that I confess I succumbed to a womanish desire to dress up and show myself off a little. Naturally, as soon as Nicky mentioned to his mama that we would be attending the theater, she cheerfully announced that she would in turn graciously deign to join us there, but on that one lovely night I did not really mind as, for privacy's sake, I sat, as I always did on my rare visits to the theater, in the far back of the imperial box, an arrangement that suited both Minnie and me perfectly as it gave her the opportunity to sit next to her son without the annoyance of having to deal with me, and I did not have to deal with her either. I think that in her aging, bitter mind such moments allowed her to feel that she was the reigning Empress again. Would that I could have let her be one, for I found my ceremonial duties to be most onerous and unwelcome. Still, God had put me where I was, as Father Grigory often reminded me, so I did try to fulfil my appointed role whenever my health allowed me to do so.

So, that evening I think God decided to answer both Minnie and my prayers at the same time, an occurrence that was unusual enough to make me smile secretly to myself as the magnificent music played below us, although I fancy our two beautiful girlies were the ones drawing most of the admiring glances. Those sweet little ones did not seem to mind, as I did, the fact that it was our family who tended to attract the audience's attention at such times and not the performers themselves.

Maybe it was the sight of the girls that prompted what happened next, for suddenly the chorus appeared on stage with the wonderful lead tenor and they all fell to their knees and burst into a beautiful and beautifully spontaneous rendition of 'God Save the Tsar,' our national anthem, and, as Nicky had once slyly confessed to me, his very favorite piece of music. I saw Nicky stand first, and then Minnie, and then the girls. In a nearby box Xenia and Sandro and Irinia also stood up, and then I saw Nicky's hand stretched out behind him toward me and I rose and went to his side.

The whole of the audience below had turned to us and was clapping. The tears of joy in my own eyes were reflected in those of my husband. We were beloved and no one could ever tell us otherwise, for here was all the proof of devotion any ruler could ever ask for.

The month of January continued to be a fine one, despite all the children and Xenia being struck down by the chicken pox.

Alexei was the least affected as it brought on no fever or bleeding for him. It was Anastasia who got the brunt of it, not for the disease itself but because her siblings claimed that she had kissed a chicken and thereby introduced it to the entire family. Anastasia responded in her usual good-natured way by kicking each of them soundly, save Alexei whom she merely punished by wandering after him clucking loudly whenever she saw him.

To enhance our pleasure in this time, we were able to see Father Grigory two or three times a week. He would go to Anya's little house and we would meet him there, and shiver wildly over tea and cakes, all of us with our feet tucked up underneath us, for her house had no insulation and to put your feet on the ground there was to risk frostbite. Father Grigory said it reminded him of peasant huts in Pokrovskoe and Anya blushed with pleasure as though she had been complimented. During this time Father Grigory and Nicky grew much closer and there were afternoons when Father Grigory did not go to Anya's but visited Nicky directly.

Father Grigory was so irregular. Failing to understand – or rather, disdaining – all rules of imperial protocol, he would just come to the palace unannounced, breeze through the room where the ministers sat clutching their briefcases and tap one of our Abyssinians on the arm.

"I'm here to see Papa."

That was all and in he went. If Nicky was surprised by his visits, I think he was also intrigued and comforted by them. I wasn't even a bit jealous, for I knew that as long as both Nicky and I listened to this man of God, we and our son would remain safe. Nicky didn't often tell me what they discussed, although he did mention that Father Grigory had told him that one day we would see his village of Pokrovskoe for ourselves.

"Oddest thing, Sunny. He said we would see it one day, either willingly or unwillingly. I cannot think what he meant. Why ever would we go anywhere unwillingly?"

I smiled at him and held out my hand for his which was always there.

"I don't know, dearest. Father Grigory has dreams."

"Yes, but do you think he is referring to our Tercentenary journey?" Nicky mused worriedly.

"Our Tercentenary journey? Why?"

Nicky looked at me, puzzled.

"Yes, it is less than two years away now and we will have to do much traveling. Stolypin and his staff have been working on it for years already. The celebrations will take the entire year, although I confess that I have been somewhat reluctant to broach that subject with you. I think all we have to do is show up and wave, and I cannot say I am looking forward to it, but then again, as Mama says, it is a triumph of time if nothing else."

Of course, I was aware of the significance of the year 1913 for the family, but Nicky and I had never discussed in any detail what we would be doing to celebrate the three hundred years of Romanov rule. A whole year of ceremonial duties – what a ghastly thought! Still, it did suggest that what Father Grigory had foretold might well be correct, including the fact that we might be there unwillingly, or at least I might be.

I turned to Nicky triumphantly.

"You see, Nicky, somehow Father Grigory knew we would be touring the country and that we will be going to his village."

"I don't know that we will be going to Pokrovskoe, darling. The whole point of our imperial progress will be to show ourselves to the people, so it might be best for us to go where there are some people, if you see what I mean."

He chuckled at his witticism and I smiled too, but half-heartedly, because I saw he did not yet understand.

"I'll tell you who is going to see Father Grigory's village, Nicky – Anya. She and two of her friends from town are off to see his house and meet his family. I am paying their expenses. You don't mind, do you, darling?"

He shook his head.

"No, of course I don't mind, but I have to wonder what they'll find to do in Pokrovskoe. Was it your idea?"

I waved my hand to suggest it wasn't worth discussing.

"I thought a trip would be nice for her."

"To Siberia?" he exclaimed incredulously.

I giggled.

"Well, Anya doesn't mind the cold – you have been in her house – and anyway, I got a telegram from Sister Ella, or Mother Ella as she is now, and she is coming to see me from Moscow soon. To have to put up with her and Anya in the same rooms would be too much for me."

"Ella's coming? When?" Nicky asked with obvious pleasure.

I wrinkled my face.

"I suppose she could be here by tomorrow morning. Funny, isn't it, a nun traveling about. It is all a bit confusing. I mean, Ella is my sister, but she is also a Sister of Mercy, and she is still a grand duchess, but she has taken a vow of poverty, or I think she has. I shall ask her about it when she arrives."

Nicky shrugged.

"I am certain she has, actually. She made over her Belosselsky Belozersky Palace to Dmitri. He is moving in soon, he tells me. And Xenia bought some of her jewels. She sold them all, you know."

I pursed my lips; that was a rather sore subject with me. Ella had indeed put up her fabulous jewelry collection for sale last winter to fund her Mary and Martha Convent, and I had felt that certain pieces should have been presented to our girls as gifts, but she had explained that she would need all the available monies from them for her good works. It all seemed a tad martyrish and showy to me, and I knew from Anya's stories that many in Petersburg eyed her new religious zealotry with distaste. Still …

"I am glad about Dmitri's news. He is too old now to be hanging about the nursery and I don't like his friend, the young Yusupov boy, Felix. The thing is, how can I not admire Ellie for what she has done and yet I don't find her changed all that much. I mean ... well, Nicky, I think ..." I trailed off, reluctant to speak of it to him of all people, and yet it was Nicky, and if I couldn't tell him my worries, that left only Anya and she tended not to understand much.

So when he said, "You think what, darling?" I felt relieved and spoke in a rush.

"Oh, Nicky, I think she is coming to talk to me about Father Grigory, and it is none of her business and I positively don't want to hear any of it. It is all such terrible gossip and nonsense. They hate him because we love him, you see that, don't you?"

Nicky couldn't quite meet my eyes, taking his time lighting a cigarette instead.

"Yes and no, darling, but I am glad you brought the subject up. You see, it is more than idle gossip. Stolypin has been to see me."

"*Stolypin?* What has that interfering old man got to do with this?"

Nicky shrugged.

"To begin with, darling, he is hardly an interfering old man. He is probably one of the greatest ministers Russia has ever had. And anyway, it is not just him. I have had letters from Guchkov too."

"Oh him! He is just a member of the Duma. Who cares what he says or thinks? They are all mad revolutionaries despite their cheap suits, Nicky. We cannot care about them or their opinions. They merely wish to make trouble."

231

"And I have received a letter from Bishop Hermogen."

"Why would he write to you?" I asked, trying to keep my question from sounding querulous and not succeeding too well, for I spotted Nicky's back flinching.

He sighed as though it was all too much for him to deal with – and that I was all too much for him to deal with too – and turned to sit in the chair by the window, wisely keeping as much distance between us as he could, for he knew I would be angry.

"He says there have been improprieties, reports. Iliodor –"

"Iliodor? That is Father Grigory's friend. He brought him to Anya's once, don't you remember? And what improprieties? Oh never mind, I don't want to know. Saints are always subjected to vicious calumnies in their own time, Nicky, you know that – even the Apostles."

"I don't think the Apostles did what Father Grigory is being accused of, consorting with women, that sort of thing," he commented sardonically.

"Consorting with women? We know how ridiculous that charge is. It was even leveled at me, as you well know. And what does it matter to us? It's just idle tittle-tattle spread around by people who have too much time on their hands. You have seen what Father Grigory can do for Baby. If we cut him off, then our son ..." My voice broke. I couldn't say it out loud. God help me, I couldn't even say it in my prayers.

Nicky understood and looked at me with compassion.

"I know that, Sunny. It is why I haven't said anything to you about it when so much has been said to me about him. There have been rumors for over a year now. And don't tell me to pound my fists at people," he looked ruefully down at the hand holding a cigarette, "it's no use, it's not my style. I am not Papa and I cannot rip a book in half either to put people in their places, or bend spoons as he did. I can and I do speak coldly, and say that our private lives are no one's concern but our own."

"Well then?" I shrugged. "What else can anyone say to you? For it is true, it is none of their business, and that includes your mama who I imagine has had quite a bit to say. Am I right?"

He smiled.

"Yes, she has, but I told her the same thing as I have told everyone else, and I shall keep saying it, Alicky. But you need to understand that it isn't a private matter anymore. People know that he comes to see us, and they hear what he does, and his behavior reflects poorly on us. The more the people hear, the less they understand. It is the way it has always been. It is why royalty has to live in a sort of …" He hesitated, trying to find the right words.

I helpfully supplied him with them.

"A sort of distant perfection, is that what you mean, Nicky?"

He nodded eagerly and I mocked him.

"You think I, raised by the greatest Queen that Christendom has ever known, do not understand how rulers must be seen. My grandmother –"

"I am not going to get into a prolonged discussion about the virtues of your grandmother, Alix, beyond saying that she was an extraordinarily lucky ruler. I don't find that I have her luck, so we may need goodwill, or so Stolypin and Mama constantly tell me."

"Nicky you are being ridiculous, but I will ask Father Grigory to come to see me today to clear up this nonsense before he and Anya leave in the morning. There has always been gossip, but it is only a fool who listens to it."

He gave me a half-bow.

"Your Majesty's court fool at your service, M'am."

I smiled back at him but I wasn't as relieved as I appeared. I was worried, and I rang for Maria and tersely ordered her to call Father Grigory in town and to arrange to send a car for him. He would be joining me for tea and I hoped he would understand that this was less an invitation than a summons.

I studied him carefully as he bustled into my boudoir. He had on a full-length black bear coat and his beard was frosted. He looked so sweet, like a great shaggy bear, and, as always, he was ebullient.

"Mamushka! What a surprise! There was old Father Grigory sitting alone in his apartment in the filthy town, and the telephone rings, and it is Maria. 'Mama wants you to tea, Father Grigory,' she says. 'A car is coming for you in a few minutes.' I was so glad to hear this, for I did not think I would be able to see you before we set off on our trip to my home village."

He shrugged off his coat and I saw that he was dressed in black velvet trousers, a silk shirt that I had embroidered for him, and a pair of boots that looked as fine as anything Nicky had ever worn. Where, apart from the shirt, did such things come from? We never gave him

234

any money. I liked to make shirts for him, but I handed him no money. Oh well, it was probably best simply to ask him about what was puzzling me, so I did.

He grinned happily, looking much as Baby did when he had stolen an extra piece of cake from my tea table.

"Presents from ladies in town, Mama. They come to see me. They say, 'Will you pray for me, Father Grigory,' and I do. Then they come back with presents for me. It is very nice." He smiled, satisfied, and popped a piece of bread and butter into his mouth.

"And is that all they want from you, Father Grigory – prayers?"

His shaggy eyebrows raised in surprise.

"Why are you asking me this, Mamushka? Have you been hearing bad stories and listening to them?"

"You have not answered my question, Father Grigory."

He scowled.

"What does it matter, Mamushka, what they want, what I do?"

"That is for me to decide, so you will answer me, please." I felt my patience slipping and my sense of unease growing.

Father Grigory stood up and tried to pace about, but my boudoir is a small room and poorly set up for pacing. After a moment he sat back down and fussed with the samovar, not looking at me nor answering me.

I made a sound of disapproval and he looked startled, and yes, furtive, which unsettled me further. With that expression upon his face, he looked more like a shifty-eyed peasant than a holy man.

235

After a time he decided to be honest with me and sat down heavily in the chair by me, pulling apart a piece of bread while speaking.

"Yes, Mamushka, some of what they say about me is true. The ladies come, ladies such as I had never imagined, silken sorts of ladies. They smell very fine and have white teeth. They come and they bring me treats and they look at me and look at me, and I think maybe they want Father Grigory to bless them in a new way, so I –"

"Stop," I said, horrified, and feeling my face becoming puce with embarrassment and outrage.

He met my eyes. His were calm, maybe curious.

"But you asked me, you demanded me to –"

"I wanted you to deny these accusations, for Heaven's sake."

He filled his cup, took a gulp and laughed into my outraged face.

"Oh, I don't suppose Heaven wants me to lie for its sake, Mamushka, I think you do, though, yes?"

My body was twitching with anticipation and fear. I certainly was not jealous, but I was short on words as my brain worked feverishly to find an argument that would make him sorry for his behavior. He knew that too and was watching me with amusement.

I wanted to strike out at him, and then I did, triumphantly saying, "You are violating every law of our Holy Church, Father Grigory if you, if you … if you kiss these women," I finished somewhat lamely.

"I'm not a priest, Mamushka. If I were, it would be a great surprise to my wife and children. I'm a simple man who is sometimes blessed to speak with God. I violate no church doctrines as far as I know." He nodded, satisfied, and then said, "Is this all you wanted from me today, Mamushka?"

A red mist formed in front of my eyes.

"All I want is for you to be worthy of the special love God shows you. No, you are not a priest, but as you have just observed, you are married, and it is a deep sin if you have ..."

I couldn't say what I wished to say and he laughed again.

"If I have ... and I have said I have."

He stretched luxuriously and scratched at himself, finishing off this discomfiting display by standing up without permission.

"God loves the sinner best, Mamushka. The sinner gives Him a chance to forgive us. But I will promise you this," he smiled, "if God comes to me and says, 'Grigory, you have sinned too much and now you must stop sinning,' I will do what He asks. Until then I will try to be better, but temptation is a cross that all us humans, even God's son, have borne."

"Jesus did not kiss strange women, Father Grigory. How dare you!"

"It is hard to know, isn't it, Mamushka? Now, Mamushka, you are making us both very unhappy being like this. And here is Father Grigory leaving in the morning. I do not like to argue and I do not want you to be sad, so why don't we pray and ask for forgiveness together?"

"How dare you suggest I pray for forgiveness? What is it you think I have done?"

237

He shrugged again and had the astounding effrontery to look bored.

"Who can know that either? I do not know, I am not your priest. You have a priest and he does know … or maybe he doesn't. Sometimes we do not say everything that is in our hearts to priests, isn't that so, Mamushka? Maybe that is what you need to ask forgiveness for, or maybe it is for judging me and doubting me. I do not like this life, it is bad for me, but I stay here for you and Papa, Mamushka, and then you are angry and treat me like a pet who has messed on your fancy rugs, and you want me to be good. But I am a man, Mamushka, and neither good nor bad, and yet God speaks to me and helps me to help you. If this is not what you want, I will leave you alone, and you can talk to Him yourself."

I felt myself blanch and my heart drop like a stone. I gasped and clutched at my chest, but he made no move, neither to aid me nor to leave. He simply waited until I choked out, "Are you threatening me, Father Grigory?"

He arched an eyebrow.

"Me, a peasant, the lowest of your husband's creatures, and you, the Empress of all the Russias, Mother of the Russian land? Do you think I would dare to threaten you, Your Majesty?" I couldn't really think clearly anymore. He was confusing me; he was upsetting me; he was threatening me. "You summoned me, Your Majesty. You act like an Empress and so I will happily pay you your due. I ask you now, Your Majesty, to be allowed take leave of you. I am setting out in the morning for my village. Maybe it would be best if I did not return."

Not return? No, this wasn't what I had meant, or was it? Then, as if he was in the room with us, I saw Baby, not as he had been that morning when he came in for a kiss – already tall, so beautiful, the bright shining pride of Nicky's and my life – no, not like that, but as he was when he was sick and screaming. If it happened ... when it happened ... again, only this terrible – or was he great? – man ... What was he, the one standing before me, tormenting me?

"My son, Alexei, you could never leave him. You wouldn't!"

My voice broke and he smiled at me and fell to his knees in front of me. Bending his head over my hands, he kissed them passionately.

"Never would I want to do that, Mamushka. I do believe God chose me to help you, but if you do not believe it too, then what good am I to you?"

My hands gripped his and, terrified, I raised them to my lips and kissed them. His expression didn't alter.

"I do believe in you, Father Grigory, I do. I just ..."

He disengaged his hands and stood smiling down at me.

"... You just want to listen to those who try to come between you and what matters most to you."

I drew myself up straighter, rigid, totally shocked by what he had just said. 'This man thinks he matters most to me? He thinks he has power over me?' I thought.

"... Those who try to come between you and the health of your son and heir," he added.

Chastened, I bowed my head in acknowledgment of the truth of what he had said, and with a half-wave and a wish that I should have a peace-filled month, he left me in readiness for his trip to Siberia.

Chapter 21

Trouble, once it comes, is, I find, nearly impossible to banish. You cannot even send it to Siberia. Strangely, though, many of my troubles did indeed come from, and in, that frozen wasteland that encompassed much of my husband's empire.

They also say that trouble comes in threes, but early in 1911 it was more like three-times-three-times-three. So often did it come that I lost count after a while.

This made me ponder Jesus' admonition to us that we should forgive those who trespass against us seventy-times-seven, but what if you can't? What if all the things that must be forgiven go on and on forever, and one simply does not have time or energy to bring oneself to forgive others? What then?

Ella arrived on the same early train that carried Anya off to Petersburg to meet up with her friends and Father Grigory before starting out on their journey north. Because of this, I was at the station to greet her, having wished to see Anya off. However, Ella took my presence there as a sign of my eagerness to be with her, exclaiming happily after kissing me, "How did you know, Alicky? Why, I didn't even know myself that I would be able to arrive so early. I got in quite late last night from Moscow and chose to stay with the Yusupovs. I must say Zenaida was noticeably put out, but I told her, 'Darling, I simply have to get to Tsarskoe Selo to see my sister, and she said –'"

"Ellie, it's nice that you are here, but I don't care what that scatter-brained Princess Yusupov has to say about anything. You haven't even asked me yet how Nicky and the children are. Don't you care?" I shook my head in annoyance. "I simply cannot get used to you like this, Ellie, your playing the role of Sister Elizabeth." I smiled to soften my words, but truly I thought she looked a bit theatrical, maybe even ridiculous, and I wondered what the very fashionable Zenaida Yusupov had thought of her get-up.

"I am so sorry, Alix, that the robes of our religion are upsetting to you with their centuries of tradition, but I hear that you favor a more *modern* approach to those who have given, or possibly not wholly given over, their lives to our faith. Would that be fair to say?" Continuing on to the carriage she also continued on speaking. "It is why I have come, in fact. I need to talk to you, Alix. It is not easy for me to leave so many poor and sick people behind because those who come to our convent —"

"Ellie, if you could manage a few moments of silence until we arrive back at the palace, I will be forever grateful as I am not convinced our coachmen or guards need, or even wish, to overhear our private discussions."

Ella shot me a glare over her shoulder as she ignored protocol and climbed into the carriage ahead of me, not even allowing the door to be closed before she shot out with, "Oh certainly, Alicky. I shall stay quiet. I imagine they prefer to read about all that sort of thing in the newspapers in any case."

"The newspapers? What in Heaven's name are talking about?" I blurted out before I could stop myself.

Ella's perfectly tended eyebrows shot up and she smiled more widely, then she made a locking motion over her lips. I noted that her hands, her nun's hands,

242

were clad in the softest gray leather gloves which almost distracted me from her silly, provocative gesture. I wanted to say something else about her apparel, but more I wanted to know what she had meant by what she had just said. However, she chose to keep silent, which was of course what I had asked of her. Sometimes I felt something more resembling hatred than anger toward my beautiful older sister, the woman who, it might be said, had helped me to be all that I had become.

More exasperatingly still, once we arrived at the palace, Ella seemed unhurried in her desire to speak privately. First she insisted on going to her room to freshen up and change into an identical habit, but without the gloves, then she wanted to see the children. After that it was lunchtime, whereupon she announced that while she would simply adore eating just the two of us, she couldn't wait to see Nicky, so I took my lunch alone without even my faithful Anya for company as she was somewhere on a train heading to Siberia with Father Grigory.

Normally I liked to, indeed needed to, rest alone for several hours in the afternoon, but I was not going to postpone my meeting with Ella, no matter how much I might dread it, as, if I didn't see her, she was likely to go to Nicky with her tales. He had a soft spot for Ella and lingering doubts about Father Grigory, and I could not give Ella an opportunity to reinforce those doubts, so I was waiting for her in my boudoir with tea and cakes and a badly palpitating heart when she finally made her way upstairs.

She shunned the cakes, saying ruefully that she had given up delicacies whenever possible, "for if the poor cannot have even gruel, why should I have cakes?" This immediately wrong-footed me, as had been her intention, and left me wondering whether I was obliged to defend our policies in Moscow – which had been her own late husband's policies – or would be better advised to stay silent and let her say her piece to bring this interview to an end as quickly as possible.

Ella made the decision for me by saying, "Alicky, I have waited a great deal of time before coming to you and I have heard from very many people before doing so."

"The poor, you mean?" I suggested helpfully.

She ignored me.

"Alix, your Father Grigory, he has to go."

I half-rose but she waved me down, producing a letter from her sleeve.

"Alix, he goes into your daughters' bedchambers when they are in their nightgowns to hear their prayers."

My face reddened and I felt my hands begin to swell. I could barely speak for outrage.

"Who told you such filthy lies? You will surrender their names to me or leave now."

She pursed her lips.

"Can it be that you are more upset about who said it, Alix, than by whether or not it is true? Is it true, Alix? Have you been aware of this?" She looked at me hard. "Then it is true?"

"Who told you?"

Ella shook her head. I repeated myself. She mumbled something I couldn't hear.

"You will tell me, Ella, or you will leave. I do not say this in jest."

"Fine. It was Mitsia," she revealed reluctantly.

I laughed in relief.

"Oh, Mitsia. She would say anything. She is a terrible liar and terribly jealous of our seeing Father Grigory. You see, Ella —"

"But is it true, Alix? Does he come into their bedchambers when they are in their nightclothes?"

I ignored her and proceeded to explain that Mitsia and Stana had once befriended and commended Father Grigory, but that when he had begun to be a dear friend to Nicky and me, they had behaved in a thoroughly nasty and spiteful manner, not only toward Father Gregory but toward us as well.

"Their nursemaid, Tyutcheva, wrote to them Alix, and then Mitsia wrote to me and also to Minnie."

I could barely see for the red mist before my eyes and all I could hear was Minnie declaiming, "She's unfit, she's mad." It was as though she were in the room with us.

"Tyutcheva said this?" I choked out.

Ella nodded, but then she shook herself, straightened her posture, and began to speak in a monotone to the effect that whatever might come of any investigation was of no consequence to her.

"Oh Alix, it is true isn't it? Never mind, I know that it is. Tyutcheva risked everything to expose his abominable behavior, but even if she hadn't done so, people know, Alix. They talk about his escapades and they are vile. Worse, they are beginning to be reported in the newspapers. He drinks, he carouses, he takes bribes."

I could not let this last accusation pass unchallenged.

"He does not take bribes, Ella. That is a scandalous lie," I shouted at her. "People go to see him. They want help. He helps them and they bring him gifts. They get well. That is not bribery. It is simply not, Ella. Take back what you have just said!"

Ella leaned her head back and looked at me with seeming amusement.

"It won't work, you know, not on me."

"What won't work? What are you talking about?" I demanded.

She pointed at me.

"This, your shouting and screaming and crying, and maybe in a few minutes pretending to have a heart fit or some such thing. I have known you since you were born, Alicky. You have always done this. It won't work with me." She smiled at me, her eyes gleaming. "Say, do you have any of those French cigarettes of yours handy?"

"What? I ..."

I had to stop and gather myself. This new tack was unexpected.

Trying to decide whether to shout some more or laugh, I said rather lamely, "I don't smoke cigarettes. How ridiculous!"

Ella began to giggle and then so did I when I saw that her amusement was making her veil flap like rabbits' ears.

"No, of course you don't, Alicky. Ladies such as ourselves do not smoke. But do you remember when Minnie set her dress on fire trying to hide her cigarette from the Austrian ambassador?"

I hadn't been there but everyone knew the tale, and shaking my head at my sister's malicious gossiping, I gestured behind her.

"That screen. If you get up and look, there is a small escritoire with cigarettes in the drawer and a Fabergé lighter that Nicky gave me to celebrate me not smoking."

I grinned and continued to do so as she brought the forbidden things back with her. We lit them and exhaled, giggling at our naughtiness. Ella looked particularly dreadful smoking in her habit but wonderfully human, and I told her so. She stood up and moved to kiss me. I also got to my feet and put my arms around her. We stayed locked together like that, swaying, for a few moments, lost in the memories of love from an older time.

I was the first to break away and sitting down again I put out my cigarette, reflecting that it was an obnoxious habit, if occasionally enjoyable. Ella sat down too, and hands in laps we looked at each other. I could almost feel all the walls we had built between us trembling around us. Would we ever manage to tear them down or would we remain separated forever?

I chose which I would do, because in the end I had no choice at all.

"So is that the only reason you have come, Ellie, to warn me, or rather to tell me, to distance myself and my family from Father Grigory, or is there anything else you wished to say?"

Ella's own expression was as cool as mine. She shook her head.

"No, I wished to accomplish nothing else beyond saying that if you continue along this course you will bring condemnation down upon the entire family, and that the path between condemnation, disrespect and revulsion is but a short one."

I shrugged.

"And so, Ella? What do I care if some ignorant and ill-meaning people in society do not like our talking to Father Gregory. It is none of their business. They have always hated and disapproved of me anyway, so your fabled path isn't a path at all, it is merely a swamp, which is entirely appropriate for Petersburg. None of this matters to me or to us in the slightest. It is of no consequence."

Ella looked at me curiously.

"Do you really believe that, Alix, after the events of 1905? You insist that what people think of our family doesn't matter?"

"Ella, if I desert Father Gregory, I run the risk of losing my son. My son, Ella, Russia's heir!"

"And if you don't, such considerations might not matter anymore anyway," she answered me with deathly calm, a calm that she had deprived me of since her arrival.

"You do not know anything about Russia or our people, Ella. You and your little convent, who do you see, who do you talk to – the wounded, the sick, the desperate?"

"Yes, Alix, all of them. And how do you think they became that way? Do you think they do not wonder that themselves, that they, even in their gratitude to me, do not show hatred at times?"

248

I shrugged.

"Every country has malcontents and the poor are forever with us, as they say, even in England I might remind you."

"England?" she said, her own voice rising. "You sound like Sergei, God rest his soul." She piously crossed herself before continuing. "He used to say that, that the poor of England were even allowed to say angry and disrespectful things in the newspapers, which of course they are here too with the encouragement of our darling Duma. He didn't think it mattered in England. He said that England's royal family was entirely safe from the threat of revolution, but the situation here is a little different, isn't it, Alix, from the England of dear old Grandmamma," we both crossed ourselves at the mention of her name, "where the poor do not lay their sufferings entirely at the feet of their sovereign. Here there is just Nicky."

"And here the people, the real people, see Nicky as a god, Ella. This is not England and we don't need to pander to the people."

"Damn your stubborn heart, Alix. You do need to do just that because, should a time come when Nicky is not seen as being a god anymore, if he should ever only be seen as a man who gives in to his wife and lets a filthy madman trample dirt on the floors of his palaces and allows this same man to see his daughters in their nightclothes, then as a mere man he can make mistakes, and be judged, and be blamed. When that happens, Alix – should that happen – he might end up being blamed for everything."

She finished softly, out of breath and clearly shaken. I wasn't.

Getting to my feet, I said, "You will be leaving us now, Ella. I believe that there is a train this afternoon. Please see to it that you are on it."

That night in bed, after he had kissed me and settled himself comfortably, Nicky inquired idly after Ella. I told him that, regrettably, Ella's duties had suddenly called her back to Moscow.

Nicky nodded in acknowledgement.

"Yes, I imagine she will find her duties all the more onerous as the years go by. Strange choice, wasn't it, darling, after being a contented wife for so many years?"

Chapter 22

The next round of troubles came from the Church itself, a body of people one might have hoped would spend its time dedicating its lives to God and peaceful pursuits, but as events showed, it was no less troublesome than Sister Elizabeth was proving to be.

First it was Bishop Feofan.

Bishop Feofan was my own dear priest and confessor, and no one, not even my husband or Father Grigory, had heard more of my private torments and prayers than this man, a man whom I had considered completely holy and above earthly temptations; but he was not.

He asked to address me in the privacy of my chapel following confession.

"Your Majesty, might we speak?"

I was surprised but not alarmed. Over the years Father, then Bishop, Feofan had occasionally made this request, usually to express concern over how short the prayers of my children tended to be, or sometimes to ask a boon for a monastery or school. I was always more than willing to listen and to assist, if I could, so I agreed to an audience on this day too, our last as priest and penitent as it happened.

"Of course, Bishop."

I moved from the small booth to a little settee I had placed there years before for Anya and the children to sit on while they awaited their turns with Bishop Feofan, who was also their confessor. Indeed, Anya was already sitting there as I emerged from the confessional.

"Anya," I said, "Bishop Feofan wishes to speak to me in private. I will call you when we have finished." Anya did not move. "Anya!"

"I don't see why he cannot hear my confession and then have his private meeting with you," she replied. "I have been sitting here waiting for an hour."

I couldn't be bothered to argue the matter out with Anya, who could be as mulishly stubborn as Nicky sometimes, so I told Bishop Feofan that I would receive him in the Red Drawing Room when he had heard Anya's confession. I cannot say he was pleased with this change in our arrangements, but he acquiesced.

He was even less pleased when Anya accompanied him to the Red Drawing Room and sat herself down.

"All right, Anya," I said. "But you must remain silent," and, astonishingly, she did throughout the ensuing interview.

Bishop Feofan bowed to me and I gestured to him to take a seat.

"What is it, Bishop?"

He sighed.

"Grievous words have come to me, Your Majesty. Worrying events."

It is odd that I still had no suspicions as to what he was planning to say, even after my recent conversation with Ella, so his next words were all the more shocking and treacherous when they came.

"What, Bishop? Tell me."

"Your Majesty, I wish to address the improprieties of the man who calls himself Father Grigory Yefimovich Rasputin, although in point of fact, Your Majesty, he is not a priest or recognized by Our Holy Mother Church, and the sorry fact that he calls himself 'Father' makes his activities, which I personally consider to be offensive to both God and man, all that much more heinous."

He finished by ponderously stroking his beard, but if he was awaiting shocked exclamations of horror to come from me, or Anya, he must have been disappointed.

"You have been speaking to the Black Women, haven't you, Bishop?" I inquired politely. At his puzzled expression, I smiled and clarified to whom I was referring. "The Montengrin sisters, Grand Duchesses Mitsia and Anastasia." His high color was as good as an affirmation, so before he could say anything further, I went on. "I cannot tell you, Bishop Feofan, how sad this makes me, that you, a supposed man of God, would sit in judgment on another such man of God. Do you forget so quickly Christ's exhortation to us about not casting stones unless we are without sin ourselves?"

Bishop Feofan's old face, one that I had found endearing as recently as a minute beforehand, quivered with outraged hurt.

"You quote scripture to me, Your Majesty?"

I shrugged.

"It seems you need to be reminded of a few things, Bishop, including that I do not discuss my private life outside of the confessional with anybody, neither priest nor prince. His Majesty and I do not tolerate those who judge, or worse comment upon, our private choices. We are going to leave you now, Father, and I shall pray for you."

He appeared stunned by my coolness and the calmness of my reaction.

"Your Majesty, I only ..." he twisted his old hands together, "... I only spoke to you of these matter because of the tales I have heard of his indiscrete behavior with the young Grand Duchesses, such wonderful girls, and to think of that ... that man ..." he said these words with as much disdain as if Father Grigory had been a rodent who had climbed onto the beds of my daughters, "... coming into their private chambers and –"

I rose sharply, which startled him so that he involuntarily stepped back, and Anya struggled to her feet too. Then I glared at him fiercely and he stepped back again.

"You go too far, Bishop, too far. You must promise me now that you will never speak about me or about my family again ... or about Father Grigory. I will not be held responsible for what happens to you if you continue to do so."

Shaking and white with fear, he replied, "Are you menacing me, Your Majesty?"

I lifted my shoulders.

"No, Bishop Feofan, I am making more of an imperial promise," and with that Anya and I swept from the room.

I felt strong and triumphant, verily a Valkyrie in my resolve. Any mother would have felt the same, for what is stronger than the sacred bond between a mother and her son, and whether the good Bishop saw it that way or not, he was attacking the safety of – the life of – my child.

It was in this militant mood that I left Anya and made my way, unaided by either chair or servant, to Nicky's study and motioned the surprised Abyssinians to open the doors to me.

Nicky was deep into a solitary game of dominoes, something that he enjoyed greatly and which he claimed relieved his stress every bit as much as a long walk, and my entrance surprised him to such an extent that he dropped the domino he was holding, causing it to scatter several others.

He looked up in annoyance to see who had dared to disturb him unannounced, and upon espying me his face went through a kaleidoscope of contortions from annoyance, to puzzlement, to surprise, and finally to pleasure at seeing me up and about.

"Sunny, what are you doing here, darling?

"Are you not happy to see me, Nicky. I wanted to surprise you with the idea that we might have an early lunch together."

His forehead creased with confusion, and after an awkward moment of staring at me and then sneaking a regretful look at his disrupted game of dominoes, he pulled out his watch and looked at it carefully.

"But it is only ten in the morning, darling. We don't eat lunch until one. Why would we eat lunch now?"

Momentarily halted by his irrefutable, if somewhat simple-minded logic, I paused. Nicky had to be handled right or he could easily stick his heels in and become an immovable object. I should have waited until the proper time, but I was here now.

"There is something I need to speak to you about that I felt could not wait – if you are not too busy, that is."

From his expression it was clear that he badly wanted to say that he was very busy and I could almost see his mind turning over his excuses, but there were the tell-tale dominoes laid out in front of him and he knew that I knew that he could do what he wanted, so rising with a stifled sigh he came over to kiss my cheek.

I stopped him with my hand against his face and placed my mouth against his. He nearly melted into me, and when he did step back, I noted his glazed eyes and his skin flushed with pleasure.

Keeping his arm about me, he guided us to the chairs facing his desk. I sank gratefully into mine and turned to smile at him.

"Look, darling, it seems we are awaiting an audience with His Majesty, but where can he be?"

"I am right here with my beautiful Empress," he replied, delighted to see me all playful. "What a lucky fellow I am. So, my Sunny, what did you want to tell me?"

I looked down and spoke in a hesitant near-whisper both to show my upset and to make him lean in closer.

"Bishop Feofan, he ..." as I had wished, his face creased in concern, "... he, I ... after confession he asked to speak to me, and ... oh, Nicky, it was terrible. He simply came out and attacked Father Grigory ..."

Nicky stood up. I fell silent and waited while he skirted his desk, opened his cigarette box and lit one. Finally, after he had stopped fussing and gratefully inhaled his first puff of smoke, he gave me his full attention.

"Father Grigory again? It is a bit endless, isn't it, Sunny?"

I was immediately suspicious that Ella had gone behind my back and stupidly exclaimed, "I knew it! Ella approached you and –"

"Ah," he said, "so that is why Ella came to see us so suddenly, and it is also why she left just as quickly. I did wonder. Was it about Tyutecheva?" He came over to me to place his hand on my shoulder as my high spirits sagged. "Sunny, darling, were you trying to keep that from me? Why?"

I looked away and pulled at my skirt.

"Because I know how much you like Ella."

He laughed.

"I imagine you also know how much I love Sunny, though."

I smiled up at him, ashamed, relieved and glad, so glad of him and of his sweetness to me and to our children.

I reached up and clasped his hand.

"I am a silly old wify, Nicky darling, a silly old woman, am I not?"

He gazed at me, his blue eyes becoming serious.

"Sometimes yes, darling, but you are always my one great joy and love." I couldn't talk for the lump in my throat and he continued, his voice soft. "It is no use either of us trying to keep secrets from the other, Sunny." He gestured to his desk and laughed a little ruefully. "Under my silly game of dominoes there are a thousand telegrams and letters, all urgent according to their writers. Sometimes I think there isn't a secret in Russia I do not know. I almost wish I didn't. But there should never be secrets between us, my girly."

I nodded and removed my hand from his as I played with my fingers.

"I admit I was wrong, but so was Ella, and Bishop Feofan, and whoever it was who told you such lies too. I want you to silence them. It upsets me a great deal and there is nothing we can do about it anyway, you know that."

"What in the world do you mean, Sunny? Nothing I can do about it? I think I can do almost anything I want. And as for Father Grigory, well ..."

He broke off and returned to his cigarette, gazing off into the corner of the room.

"There is no 'well' about it, Nicky. If we desert Father Grigory, Alexei will die. If my baby dies, I will die, and you will have killed us both. So please tell whoever wrote to you, or any tattle-tale who comes to you bearing malicious gossip, that they must hold their tongues now and forever, or they will be sent to Siberia. You can start by sending away Bishop Feofan."

"You know, the Metropolitan came to see me last week ..."

"Yes, well that explains how you heard Tyutecheva's nonsense," I snapped back.

"You would have been proud of me, I think, Alix. I told him that the affairs of our family were no business of his or of anyone else, and sent him on his way quite coldly."

I nodded, pleased.

"Good! Well then, I suppose that we can –"

"He said something before he left, though, that I cannot help thinking about ..."

I wanted to return to my boudoir; I was no longer hungry and did not feel like conversing with other people. I felt I had achieved my ends and I hated talking critically about Father Grigory.

"I don't care what he said. I don't want to hear any of it," I finished, childishly placing my hands over my ears, which just made Nicky laugh.

"But I am going to tell you anyway."

"Why? I just told you that –"

"I am going to tell you because, if you truly believe that our son will die without that man, we have to recognize that this interference, or however you want to look at it, is unlikely to come to an end and I don't see why I should be the only one who has to endure it. As you know, Alix, I am very sorry to have to say this to you, but I do not believe in your holy man any more than his so-called enemies do. That is why I am going to tell you."

I looked away in despair.

"Go ahead. It will not matter to me but go ahead."

"Daily I am receiving letters from priests and ordinary people alike who want to know why we keep Rasputin near us. What do you think I should tell them? What do you wish me to say to Stolypin, for example, Sunny?"

"Tell them what you said to the Metropolitan, that this is our private business."

"Oh yes, the good Metropolitan … I am glad you brought him up again. Do you know what he said? It is rather interesting."

I shook my head. "I do not know and I do not care to know."

"I thought you would say that. What he said was that the situation with Rasputin was not merely a family affair, rather that it was an affair that affected the whole of Russia, that Alexei was not only our son but the future ruler of Russia. Naturally I dismissed such talk as nonsense, despite its being true. Unfortunately it seems that my Prime Minister concurs and that the newspapers are printing story after story about Rasputin as well. I said to Stolypin that he should fine them, shut them down. He said to me, 'Sire, you granted them freedom of the press when the Duma was formed.' I said that he should fine them anyway, that he should find a reason to do so. He said, 'We have and we do, Sire, and they just print the same stories all over again, for the people are so very interested in the activities of Rasputin that they sell enough newspapers to pay their fines a dozen times over.' Isn't that interesting, Sunny?"

I stood up and rearranged my skirt. I had worn pink for Nicky, his favorite color on me, that day and he hadn't even noticed.

"No, it's not interesting Nicky, and I don't like Stolypin, and neither does Father Grigory. He is a bad servant to you."

"He is a great Prime Minister."

"He is a man whose power has gone to his head and blinded him to the needs and rights of anyone but himself, that is what he is. Shut him up, Nicky, or we will be sorry, I know it."

"You won't listen to me or talk to me, will you, Alicky, not if I question a word that your Father Grigory says."

I approached him and kissed his cheek.

"Now we do understand each other, Nicky."

Nonetheless, Nicky sent Father Grigory to Jerusalem for an extended holiday that we paid for, while, in his absence, I suffered several heart attacks and remained in full seclusion.

Chapter 23

After March, things accelerated quickly, and Nicky took to walking about with a troubled expression and muttering dark things about how we were, yet again, in a time of troubles and what could he expect but this sort of thing having been born on the Day of Job?

This sort of 'thing,' as he referred to it, was, I believe, the disloyalty of Peter Stolypin, a man Nicky had much admired – why, I do not know. I suppose it was in my husband's nature to be attracted to tall men with booming voices which made even their most foolish utterance sound important. Maybe they reminded him of his father. Naturally, my awful mother-in-law simply adored Stolypin, and I believe it was her aiding and abetting him that made the odious man forget his place and where his loyalties and services were meant to be directed, for without any permission from my husband, the Emperor of Russia, Stolypin took it upon himself to banish Father Grigory from the capital upon his return from Jerusalem.

I was enraged by this and railed at Nicky, who just sat with his head down, although I found out from Anya that Minnie had been meeting privately with him, doubtless to speak of what a madwoman I was. I demanded that Nicky rescind the order, which he did. Then Stolypin threatened to resign and Nicky told him he would not accept his resignation, and to my horror he also said other things that he insensitively chose to repeat to me.

"I told him, darling, that I knew that he loved me and was loyal to me. I even said that what he had said to me might even be true, but that it did not matter either way because I was not going to have you upset by the removal of Rasputin. You see, I do think of you all the time."

"Oh, dear Lord, Nicky, what have you done to me?"

He looked confused.

"Done to you? Darling, I did what you wanted. Don't you see, by telling Stolypin that your feelings mattered to me more than even my Government, I have –"

"Have confirmed every sordid bit of gossip that calls you henpecked and me a madwoman who is under the thrall of a madman. Nicky, how could you?"

He stood and clenched his fists, scowling down at me where I lay prostrate in bed.

"What do you want from me, Alix? I ask myself that every day … no, God help me, every minute. *What would she want me to do?* If they call me henpecked, isn't that the simple truth? I need you, I need you to love me – that is another truth – but I do not like to say it, not to Mama, not even to you, as I am doing now."

What could I have said to him but that the idea that he was henpecked was a lie? Nicky never did anything he didn't want to do. Nevertheless, I later solicited Anya's opinion on the subject.

"Anya, I'm feeling distressed and I know you speak to a great many people when you visit town. Have any of them ever suggested that Nicky was … oh, that dreadful word …?"

"Short, do you mean? People ask me that all the time in town, but I always tell them that he is almost as tall as you."

I laughed at that but quickly sobered up.

"No, Anya, I want to know if people tell you, or if you have heard anyone quoted as saying, that I henpeck Nicky or dominate him in some way."

Her forehead creased and she stared at me as if I had run mad, but she did not answer me. This went on for so long that I had to snap her out of her silence by saying her name sharply. "Anya!"

She flinched.

"Well, everybody thinks that. I mean, it's true, isn't it? He does everything you want. We all do, don't we? Isn't that what you want? Why are you asking me this? I don't like it at all and now you are looking at me in a funny way."

"Of course I am, Anya, because it is not at all true, is it? You take back what you have just said, and when other people ask you, you are to say that it is not true, do you understand me?"

I had spoken calmly and reasonably, but she still looked at me resentfully. I would have let the subject drop at that moment because the conversation hadn't gone the way I had expected and I was thus more than willing to change the subject, but Anya was always Anya and she muttered audibly to herself, "It is too true!" forcing me to be angry with her, which I hated to do.

"Anya, I am very sorry that you think I henpeck His Majesty, but I will not take this nonsense to heart as I realize that you know nothing about marriage, despite

264

having once been married yourself for a short while. His Majesty and I are the happiest and most united of couples. I suppose it is easier for those whose own marriages are lacking in both happiness and unity to throw stones rather than look to themselves. Now, let us talk about how many new dresses I need to order for the girlies for our nice trip to Kiev, shall we?"

I was referring to a special trip that our family would be making during our next annual spring-to-winter travels. Normally we would depart first for Peterhof (as we would this year as well), and then go on to Livadia, before taking our beloved cruise around the Finnish Skerries. We would follow that by visiting gloomy old Poland and that ugly hunting palace, after which we would travel back to Livadia and usually return home to Tsarskoe Selo in late November.

However, this year was to be different as Nicky was finally keeping an old promise to me. Once, a long time ago, a young prince had promised the princess he was going to marry that he would build her as many palaces as she liked, one for every day of the year if she so wished. Of course I had never needed, or wanted, a new palace a day, and we had palaces we would never see in places we were unlikely even to want to go, but that hideous, dank old wreck of a shack in Livadia had long made me unhappy, and so, unbeknown to me, Nicky had, back in 1909, decided to commission a real palace much more to my liking. The naughty boy hadn't even told me until the Christmas of that year, and to my endless delight he had given some old sketches I had done years before of Italian villas to the great architect

Nikolay Krasnov, asking him to build me one just like these, only even better.

Thereafter, many a wonderful, cozy evening had been spent by Nicky and me while we pored over the plans, and now it seemed that Mr. Krasnov had somehow managed the miracle and raised it from two-dimensional paper to three-dimensional marble, and it was almost ready for us. So this year we would not be going to Poland, but, because our new palace would not be fully completed until the September, Nicky asked me if we might instead go to Kiev and attend the unveiling of a statue of his papa that was being raised there.

Normally I would have pleaded the truthful excuse of ill health to avoid such a thing, as the excursion would involve ceremonies and teas and a special opera, but I had never been to Kiev and I had heard that it was quite a lovely part of our realm. In addition, I had decided that if I could, that I would try to make an effort to appear to our people and be more a part of things, but not in Petersburg which I considered rotten to the core.

Besides, as Nicky had said, we really did have to find something to do before going to Livadia in September. Surely I wouldn't want to stay in Peterhof until then, for, sadly, we could never have a cruise that lasted longer than two weeks as Nicky felt that two weeks was the longest period of time that he could be completely out of touch with his Government, not that the ministers didn't still complain about having to "track him down" to Livadia or Poland, the word 'track' being an excellent choice of words, I thought.

Now Anya was staring at me in confusion as her mind was not of the sort to respond quickly to any change of conversation. I found it most amusing to observe Anya as she tried to gather her thoughts almost as though she was doing so literally, wandering around her brain picking up and discarding objects.

Foolishly I said so out loud. She stared at me.

"I am not sure how I could walk around my brain, Alix. I doubt that there would be room."

Anya, how I loved her and needed her – better not to mentioned that bit. I smiled affectionately at her.

"Nor would there be, dear. I was only having some fun with you. Now, enough of this silliness – what do you think of pink for a new ball gown for Olga, or should it simply be white, as most befits a young girl?"

Anya was clearly still lost in the room of her thoughts, but she enjoyed speaking of clothing enough to manage to focus on my question with all the serious attention that one might give to an emergency. In fact she looked distinctly alarmed when she said, "A ball dress? You didn't say that there would be a ball in Kiev. I only have the one dress and it's not very nice. I was planning to wear it to the ball you and His Majesty are giving for Olga at Livadia, but I'll look silly wearing it twice ..." Her voice trailed off. "Oh, you're speaking of the ball in Livadia, aren't you?" she said, almost annoyed.

I nodded. Anya scowled.

"I am having trouble keeping up with you." She held up her plump fingers and began counting off things as she spoke. "First you said you wanted to talk about what to get the girls for Kiev." She folded a finger. "Then you made me tell you what I thought about you and His Majesty, which was horrid." Her lower lip stuck out as she folded a second finger. "Then you said you could see me wandering around my brain, which was very worrying to me because I didn't know that." Waggling her fourth finger in the air as a warning, she continued. "Then, while I'm still upset about your comment about my brain, and before I can even start to think about anything else, you begin talking about Olga's ball, but you never said that was what you were talking about, and I must say," she curled her finger down, "I'm getting a headache too." She glanced down at her little finger as if wondering what it should do. Finally, shaking her head, she partially uncurled her fist and placed it in her lap with the air of one who had been most hard done by. "I think that is all."

I could only acknowledge that it was.

Anya seemed mollified by this and decided to ring for cakes.

"Anya dearest, you certainly have your thinking cap on today, and I am glad of it, for, as you have shown me, I am all at sixes and sevens. But truly, dear, what do you think about pink for my big girly Olga? It is a lovely color on her and the other girlies will have new gowns as well and," and seeing that Anya still looked a bit irritable, I cleverly added, "and you will too. You look so fine in white."

Anya clapped her hands loudly in delight. It was as well that the cakes had not yet arrived, for surely she would have crushed one or dropped it on the floor, or both, if she had been holding it in her hand, such was her excitement.

"Maybe my new ball gown should be pink too," she mused enthusiastically.

When Anya had left me, I stretched back against my pillows and closed my eyes, picturing how it all would look.

Once, so long ago, my dearest papa had seen my funny childish jealousy at my beautiful older sister Ella's coming out ball, and that night he had surprised me in my lonely nursery by bringing me up a wee bouquet. It was all tiny white roses, save for one pale pink one in the middle. I had never seen a prettier thing and I kept it for years, long dried up but still magical to me.

My big Olga's ball would be like that. Our new white marble palace would be gleaming from the light of a thousand white candles and I would order a thousand white lilacs from our greenhouses to match them. The lights would spill over onto the balcony and reflect in the sea. Inside, all the women and girls would be wearing white to complement it all, and my Olga would be the sole pink rose in the very middle of it all as we celebrated her sixteenth birthday.

Chapter 24

Kiev was a city I had not previously visited nor known much about beyond Minnie's strong affection for it, which seemed a good enough reason in itself for me to have formed a vague disliking of it, not that I had given it much thought at all.

It was Minnie's love for the place that had driven her to persuade Nicky to have a statue of his papa erected there, even though his papa had had no connection with Kiev whatsoever as far as I knew. Anyway, our trip to Kiev marked the beginning of the end of all happiness for our family, now I come to think on it. After Kiev, the true horrors began for us, but maybe I only see things this way in hindsight.

At the time, what I initially saw was a very large and beautiful city that seemed to boast the same fine weather we were spoiled by in Livadia. Nicky, who had made many trips here with his mama in his youth, was pleased by my initial delight of the place.

"You see, darling," he burbled earnestly, "it is the capital of the Ukraine and it is one of the oldest cities on earth. It was settled by the Slavs in the eighth century – although some people claim it goes back to the fifth century – and it was a trading post for the Greeks. Why, Saint Andrew himself once passed through here and they built a magnificent church for him. I'll show it to you, shall I?"

I laughed pleasurably at his schoolboy enthusiasm while fanning myself frantically, for Kiev was decidedly hot and sunny that day. I was enjoying the sun but the elevated temperature was more than I could bear, although worse for poor Anya who had been sweating and panting like some heat-maddened farm animal since our arrival two days previously, her decision to wear her tomato velvet gown so as to be "festive" having proved to be a rather disastrous one.

"Dearest, I would love you to take me to see the dear old church. I think, though, it might be best to wait until the evening as it is suffocatingly warm during the day, isn't it?"

I fanned myself for effect and waited for his inevitable concern about my health to surface, which, to my irritation, it did not, for Nicky loved sweltering heat as much as I detested it. In fact he had been out on deck so frequently since our arrival that his face had acquired a ruddy color already, one which suited him beautifully, I thought, but did not say so.

Ignoring my comment on the weather, he stretched out his arms in happiness.

"It is wonderful here, isn't it, my Sunny. Will you be able to join Mama and me in the parade today, do you think?"

I squinted doubtfully at the glare of the sun on the water, which was making my head ache already, and rubbed my forehead to indicate how I was suffering in the hope that Nicky would be the one to suggest I miss the event. However, he simply wasn't his usual self that day and just stood there looking at me with a hopeful expression that tested my patience.

"Mama is going to be in her carriage with Xenia and Sandro," he said and added cunningly, "so you and I could ride together," implying, I thought, that for once

Minnie would not be taking precedence over me and the crowd would have occasion to cheer both of us together rather than to cheer him and ignore me, as was usually the case. "We could take Alexei along in our carriage as well and the four girls could ride behind us."

I narrowed my eyes.

"Where would your mother's carriage be, then — behind that of the girls?"

Seeing my flushed face, he put his arms around me and kissed me soundly, not to say resolutely.

"You know it won't be, my silly darling girly. Mama's carriage will take precedence over the girls', but you and I will be together in the first carriage."

I capitulated because I could not resist the opportunity of riding in our carriage in front of Minnie and pretending that maybe some of the joy directed at our carriage was for me. Also, although I was suffering from the heat, I was enjoying the sun, and Baby had been so well that year that I wanted to show him off to the people. The girls would enjoy the event too. Kiev was such a strange and marvelous city.

The cheering proved indeed to be deafening and Nicky looked so handsome and was clearly almost beside himself at the nearly overwhelming display of love and devotion from the crowds. It seemed that they could not scream 'God Save the Tsar' loudly enough, nor restrain themselves from extolling the virtues of the Tsarevich, and hundreds of them knelt down or prostrated themselves fully to kiss the shadow our carriage cast. If the acclamations were not necessarily for me personally, at least there I saw no frowns nor heard any condemnations of my presence. Yes, they shouted for Minnie's carriage, but they loved, nay worshipped, my husband and my children, which made the smile I was able to give from our carriage all the more sincere.

Because we were in the front of the procession and the noise of the crowd drowned out any possibility of hearing anything else, we did not know about the drama occurring further back in the parade, not until after we had unveiled the statue to Nicky's papa and Nicky had given a short, but I thought well-judged, speech. It was Minnie who relayed to us the sordid story of what we had missed that day when we joined her back at the palace she kept in Kiev.

I had never been there because I had never been to Kiev before. As far as I was concerned it technically belonged to Nicky and me, and the children wanted to go there as they enjoyed any sort of novelty, so I agreed to pay a visit despite my rule of trying to avoid any contact with my mother-in-law wherever possible. Besides, I was feeling uncharacteristically healthy and optimistic; it was so good to see and hear from our devoted subjects. I remember, and this is painful to think of now, how overjoyed and buoyed I felt by the people who shouted and waved as we passed them, and for once I was not at all dismayed by the slow progress the crowds imposed upon us. It was a joyous noise, the silence coming only as we drove at last through the gates of the Mariyinsky Palace, which could have been built for Minnie, given its name, but was evidently much older than that according to its style.

I had never thought about it one way or the other, beyond being grateful that it was far away from Tsarskoe

Selo and that Minnie liked to spend great swaths of time there. However, I felt differently when I saw it. It was magnificent, a perfect miniature replica of the wondrous Catherine Palace at Tsarskoe Selo, although the word 'miniature' might be a misleading description of its size.

Involuntarily, I made a little noise of admiration and Nicky smiled at my response.

"Beautiful, isn't it, darling? Now you can see why dearest Mama spends so much time here."

I nodded curtly.

"Yes, I can, although she must at times be hard pressed to decide how to apportion her time, don't you think?"

Nicky looked back at me, confused.

"What do you mean Sunny?"

"Oh nothing, darling, only that she has two oversized fortresses in Petersburg, the Anichikov and Gatchina, and now I see this ... She seems somewhat spoiled for choice, wouldn't you say?"

Nicky looked away and told the coachmen to stop, whereupon Alexei, who had been getting quite restless and bored by the long carriage ride, nearly leapt over the side. It was only my sharp exclamation that made Nagorny catch him by his shirt tail before he could fall.

Nicky looked over his shoulder at the girls' carriage that had been forced into an abrupt stop by ours and said, "Nagorny, take Alexei for a bit of a run around the grounds and let him burn off his energy before lunch, will you?"

Nagorny nodded and lifted a protesting Alexei onto the emerald-colored grass of the palace park, hastening after him when he broke free and dashed up to his sisters' carriage.

I watched him, charmed, as he opened the carriage door and held out his hand to Anastasia.

We couldn't hear him but we could gather from his excited gesturing at us that he was telling his sisters that they had some free time before lunch, and Nicky and I both laughed as we saw the girls clamber out of their carriage in a most unladylike fashion, nearly falling upon each other in their haste to be out and about and exploring.

I adored their little animal high spirits and I know that Nicky did too, and we exchanged a look of warm complicity seen only between parents who are proud and happy with their offspring.

Gazing at me lovingly, Nicky motioned with one hand for the coachmen to put down the steps and held the other out to me.

"Would Your Majesty fancy a brief stroll around the gardens? We can keep to the shadier paths and then you will be fully prepared to compliment Mama on her design or alternatively to evict her from the premises, as you please."

He grinned at me and I giggled in response

"I will say yes, you naughty boy, but only if we truly can keep to the shade. The weather is somewhat stifling for my taste. And don't tease me anymore about your mama."

He leaned in and kissed me right in front of the embarrassed servants, hoisting me into his arms in order to swing me boyishly onto the grass.

"Your wish is my command, darling."

After a minute's walk he guided me to a small bench in a delightful little Chinese summer house surrounded by lush gardens that swept out as far as I could see.

Seating himself beside me, he lit a cigarette and surveyed the scene with admiration.

"It is beautiful here, isn't it? I had almost forgotten how beautiful it was."

I leaned against him, contented just to be there with him.

"How did all of this come to be established way out here," I asked idly, "and why does it look so much like the Catherine Palace?"

He stroked my arm with his free hand to show his appreciation of my interest and told me the funny tale behind the building of the palace, which turned out to be yet another tale of enormous sums of money spent by previous Romanov rulers to reflect their own glory, whether they ever bestirred themselves to see that reflection or not.

"The Mariyinsky Palace was commissioned by my rather feckless ancestor, Empress Elizabeth, Peter the Great's daughter and Russia's first empress to rule in her own right. She was, by all accounts, vain to the point of madness, and when she got old, you know, Sunny, she ordered all the women of her court to shave their heads and wear trousers to balls, and all the men to dress themselves in wigs and ball gowns."

I gawped at him.

"That is indeed mad, Nicky. Why would she do that?"

He shrugged.

"I cannot know for certain. No one left any written record about the why of it, but Mama always thought it was so that she would still be the prettiest woman at the ball, no matter how old and fat she was, or at least the only woman at the ball who was still recognizably a woman."

I leaned against him, collapsing into laughter.

"Was that why all this was built, in case she came to Kiev and wanted to throw a ball?"

"I don't know. I don't even know if she ever did come to Kiev. I do know she liked Rastrelli who designed the Catherine Palace. Well, many people did. He is considered Russia's greatest architect, as you know.

"You think she never even came here?"

Nicky nodded.

"Well, she might have come to Kiev once for all I know, but she never came to this palace. It wasn't even completed until after her death. Then I think it just sat empty for years and years until Empress Catherine came to visit it, and she liked it so much that she stayed here for three entire months."

"I see, but she has been dead for over a hundred years, darling. Did it just sit here empty after that? It seems a terrible waste, doesn't it?"

My husband, a man who insisted that his boots and gloves be ruined completely beyond repair before allowing his valet to order new ones, stared at me blankly as if the very idea that an empty palace might be considered wasteful was a notion bordering on the seditious. He finished by muttering to no one in particular that he supposed some might see it that way.

I nudged him playfully to bring him back to me and he grinned. Nicky was always easy to rescue from a sulk; I often wished Anya were as accommodating.

He turned back to me and said, "You are right, darling, no one has lived here since forever. Then, as luck would have it," his eyes gleamed with mischief, "it caught fire and burned to the ground."

I threw an involuntary glance around me to reassure myself that all of it, the fairytale palace and the fountains and the sweeping emerald lawns, were still there and hadn't suddenly vanished, as they did in the books I had read as a little girl.

"But Nicky, it seems to be all here now."

He laughed enthusiastically and kissed me.

"That is the wonder of it, Sunny. You see, Papa had seen some excellent watercolors depicting it, some painted by Empress Catherine herself, so he hired another very fine architect, Konstantin Mayevsky," he paused to see if I would humor him by asking about the architect, which I didn't, so he continued only a bit abashed, "and gave him all the drawings and pictures he could find of it, and asked him to rebuild it exactly as it was before. However, this time he had it named after Mama and presented it to her, much as I will be doing to you with our new palace in Livadia next week, my own little wify."

"But there is a palace by that same name in Petersburg, isn't there?"

"Yes, but the spelling is slightly different. Papa had that one built right before this one as a gift for Mama as well, but they never lived there. I don't think she liked it very much. She does like this one, however, and I suppose she will be inside awaiting us for lunch as we speak, so we should go." He looked about. "I hope the children have already presented themselves for lunch. You know how she detests people being late." He held out his hand. "Shall we, darling?"

Silently I rose to my feet and gave him my arm, allowing him to guide me slowly toward the great entrance. I didn't speak for I was girding myself for luncheon with the lioness in her pretty den, one that I had hoped, before hearing Nicky's story, truly belonged to us.

Minnie was waiting for us in the Palladian foyer, pacing back and forth with two bright spots of color on her cheeks and, uncharacteristically, a cigarette visibly clutched in one tiny hand. Xenia and Sandro were with her. Xenia came up and kissed Nicky and me, but Sandro remained where he was, a curious expression on his face.

It was Minnie who broke the strange tableau by speaking.

"Nicky and Alix my dears, I am so glad you have arrived early. Stolypin is joining us in a few minutes. I invited him to take luncheon with us. Well, I had to, hadn't I?"

She seemed to be assuming that we knew what she meant, which we most assuredly didn't.

Nicky said, "Mama?" but then Sandro came over to us and began speaking rapidly.

"They don't know yet, Minnie. Nicky and Alix, there was an incident during the parade. Rasputin was there and –"

279

My knees buckled and Nicky caught me up in his arms before suggesting, "Let us all go into the sitting room. The heat has been hard on Alix. It is my fault. I kept her out in the sun."

I buried my head against Nicky's shoulder as he carried me into a nearby grand room I did not wish to enter to avoid whatever storm was heading toward me. If only I could have got to my feet and escaped to our carriage and thence back to The Standart, but I was helpless.

Nicky laid me down on a divan. Minnie was at his side, speaking over Sandro's attempts to tell Nicky all about it before he had even had a chance to turn around and face them.

Minnie continued, "As Sandro wished to say, that rascal of Alix's was there, Nicky, running after Peter Stolypin's carriage ... running after it, I tell you ... and flinging his hands about, shouting out for everyone to hear that death was chasing him. To be blunt, the only thing chasing your Prime Minister was that madman you keep as a pet. Everyone saw and heard him, Nicky, and poor Mr. Stolypin was so upset that naturally I invited him to lunch."

Nicky rose and glanced at Sandro for confirmation of Minnie's triumphant recital. Sandro nodded.

Xenia came over to sit beside me and picked up my limp hand to stroke it reassuringly. I wanted to pull it away from her but instead I just closed my eyes against all of them and lay there prone.

Then I heard an excited rustling from the doorway and Baby's voice asking where I was. The children had come in for lunch.

280

I made a small grunting sound and kindly Xenia rose to her feet, saying, "Nicky, Mama, I think I'll just go and take the children in to lunch, shall I? The poor things are probably famished. Join me when you can, Alicky. Can I send for something for you, maybe tea?"

I shook my head wordlessly. I refused to open my eyes but I knew I was going to have to listen to the ramifications of this incident being chewed over at great length and with much exultation at my expense. I couldn't even place my hands over my ears this time around without risking Minnie slapping them away.

I wanted to rise and follow Xenia but I couldn't trust my legs to support me, so, my eyes still squeezed shut, I lay there helpless as Sandro and Minnie gleefully told Nicky that "our pet peasant" was out of control, beyond tolerating, and must be exiled permanently out of Russia, or at least out of our part of Russia. Maybe we could risk sending him back to Siberia, but their preference was that he should be kept out of harm's or the Romanovs' way by being safely and traditionally incarcerated in the Peter and Paul Fortress.

To my surprise it was Nicky who took charge of the conversation, and I smelled his tobacco smoke and felt my body begin to relax as he replied in a lightly amused tone.

"So, if I understand you correctly, you wish me to arrest a poor peasant, a man of God, for saying aloud what might yet prove to be true?" This drew a squawk of outrage from Minnie, but he continued. "Mama, I do agree that his expression of his belief wasn't particularly tactful, but any member of our Government will endorse the notion that death stalks us all. We have all seen

281

ministers and government officials by the tens, even by the hundreds, being brutally assassinated over recent times. Father Grigory has visions, and whether those of us raised with different manners like it or not, he is determined to put voice to these visions. I will certainly agree that poor Stolypin must have been somewhat shaken by this pronouncement and I shall speak to him about it. And yes, before you give yourself a fit, Mama, do not fear – I shall also speak to Father Grigory and ask him in future to communicate his visions privately to Alix and me, or at least to confine them to a less public setting."

I heard Sandro clear his throat and murmur something I couldn't catch to Minnie before he said, "But Nicky, can't you see that this man is damaging the prestige of the Imperial Family itself, that people see and hear him, and might attribute his actions and words to you and Alix? If they should do so, God help us, God help us all, because –"

I never got to find out what miserable fate Sandro was planning to detail out for us next, as at that moment it was announced that Prime Minister Stolypin and his wife had arrived for luncheon.

Chapter 25

Stolypin indeed died the very next evening, or better I should say that he was shot the very next evening, as, sadly, he lingered on amid the agonies of this world for three days before expiring.

It happened like this ...

On Dr. Botkin's very strict orders, I had been put to bed on The Standart, as had Baby alongside me, for he had got a touch of sunburn the day before and was running a small fever. There was a gala performance of Rimsky-Korsakov's 'The Tale of Tsar Saltan' scheduled that night at the Kiev Opera House, and so Nicky decided to go and to take Olga and Tatiana with him.

The little girlies, Baby and I had a quiet supper in my cabin with Anya, who had not been asked to the opera out of deference to the sensibilities of Nicky's mama and had sulked all evening long. Anastasia, my naughty one, who was a veritable terror of a girly, teased her, saying, "Isn't it horrible, Anya that you couldn't go to the opera? Why, I bet there are at least some people here in Kiev who haven't ever seen your red dress. It's nothing like Petersburg."

I didn't intervene in spats between Anya and the girls, for it seemed to me that if she was going to behave like one of my daughters, including my youngest one, in terms of words and temper, she would have to handle these situations herself, which she did in this case by sticking her tongue out at Nastinka, who promptly pinched her, which caused Anya to cuff her ear, and then they both burst into tears, which made Baby, Maria and me laugh uproariously at their antics.

We had a fine evening, just us ladies and Baby, the girlies showing off – for they were unaccustomed to being near me without their sisters – and it made what came later all the more terrible as it is much more alarming to receive unpleasant news when one is relaxed and happy than if one is expecting something of the sort.

I sensed something was wrong before I knew what it was, because when I heard the tender pulling up alongside The Standart, it struck me as strange that they should have been back so soon. The opera was scheduled to last until ten, and Nicky had said that he might let the girlies spectate at the ball that was to follow on from the opera for an hour or so after that, and they had been terribly excited about that part.

I glanced at my small Fabergé traveling clock in confusion. It wasn't even half-past-nine.

Baby, who was half asleep beside me, sat up and said happily, "Oh good, Papa and the girls are back. I'll tell them all about Anya and Nastinka. Won't they think they missed the best of fun, Mama?"

I squeezed him to me and then I heard the sobs that seemed to be coming from Tatiana, the calmest of my daughters. My heart seized but I kept my face and voice calm for Baby's sake as I told him that it was very late and that I now wanted him to go to his own cabin for bed. He began to argue with me, saying that he wanted at least to see Nicky before he went, but for once I held firm and, pouting at me horribly, he reluctantly obeyed my orders.

Tatiana ran into my cabin a moment later, crying hysterically, and fell into my arms. Peering over her head, I waited for the seconds it took Nicky to follow her in, and terrified beyond measure, I could only whisper out, "Where is Olga? Where is my daughter?"

Nicky stood in the doorway, his face gray.

"She went straight to her cabin. She is quite shaken."

I looked at him steadily, my arms protectively around Tatiana.

"What happened tonight, Nicky?"

Remaining where he was, Nicky said haltingly, "Some filthy revolutionist shot Stolypin right there in the middle of the opera house. We all saw it happen, including the girls."

"Oh Mama, there was so much blood, and poor Mr. Stolypin, he ..." Tatiana could not continue for her sobs.

I needed to hear everything, but first I had to attend to my wounded child, so I said to Nicky over her trembling head, "Nicky, you look terrible. All in. Why don't you go to the lounge and find Dmitri or Volkov. Have a large brandy. I am going to see to Tati, and in a little while you can come back and tell me all about this. You can bring me a large brandy too."

Nicky nodded, seemingly relieved to be sent away, for it was clear he could not help our child at that moment.

When he was gone I gently eased Tatiana off my chest and rolled her to her side. Then I curled around her and murmured the ancient endearments known only to mothers.

"My sweetest one, my beautiful little girly, it is all over now. You are safe. Mama is here. We are all here safe and together. Everything will be all right, my darling."

I gradually soothed Tatiana's sobs into exhausted hiccups and then silence, to the accompaniment of soft kisses and stroking, and sat up gently so as not to wake her in case she had finally fallen to sleep, which she hadn't.

Abruptly rolling onto her back, she stared at me with great wounded gray eyes and asked, "Why? Why, Mama? Why did they shoot Mr. Stolypin?"

I could see she was about to become hysterical again, so I grabbed her hand and smothered it with kisses.

"Ssssh, darling. You mustn't think of such things now. You need to sleep. You are very tired. In the morning Papa and I will explain it all to you. Rest now and know that Mr. Stolypin is with the angels."

Her eyes widened yet more.

"Is he dead, then?" she asked and her sobs began anew.

Inwardly I cursed myself for not having asked Nicky that much at least before I sent him away. I leaned over and nuzzled my face against hers which I found to be hot and wet.

"Darling, I'm sorry. Silly old Mama is tired too. I only meant to say that if Mr. Stolypin should die from his wounds, then he will go to a better place, the home we will all return to one day."

"Will they shoot Papa one day, too, Mama?" she asked, her voice growing shrill.

I reached over her and rung for Maria, who must have been standing in the corridor outside, given the speed with which she arrived.

"Maria! Good, there you are. I want you to help Tati back to her and Olga's cabin, and please send for Dr. Botkin. Stay with her until the sedative works and then you can go to bed. Is that clear?"

Maria nodded wordlessly and came over to help Tatiana up, who in turn threw her arms around my waist and wailed as though she were a much younger child.

"No, Mama, I don't want to go to my cabin. I don't want anything. I'll have nightmares. Please, please let me just stay here with you tonight."

Gently I untangled her and forced her to her feet while Maria aided me by coming and putting her arm around Tati's waist.

"No, dearest little one, not tonight. You will feel much better in your own little bed, I promise you, and that is why Dr. Botkin is coming, to make sure my girly doesn't have any dreams at all." She began to protest, so I said much more firmly, "Tatiana, Mama needs to speak to Papa, and you need to do what I tell you. Please go now," and then to Maria, "When you fetch Dr. Botkin, please see that you find the Tsar. He should be in the lounge. Tell him I am waiting for him, will you?"

She nodded and then carefully maneuvered the still-crying Tatiana out of the door and after a moment I heard her sobs fade into the distance. I moved over to my wardrobe and searched impatiently for a warm wrap, thinking that Maria should have seen to such things while she was in my cabin. I did not know where she or my wardrobe maids stored such items when we were at sea, and I couldn't find it, so I nearly rung for her, but fairness stayed my hand. I had loaded Maria down with instructions and I did not need to distract her. Frustrated,

I snatched up a folded shawl from the top shelf and wrapped it around me, and then went to look out of the portholes at the strangely peaceful night while I waited for Nicky to come to me and tell me what had happened.

It took him quite a long while to do so, and when he came he seemed rather intoxicated. His face was no longer pale but terribly flushed, and he gave me a witless smile as he staggered into the cabin and fell onto his back, dropping his lit cigarette onto the sheets in the process. I watched him as he flailed about for a moment in an attempt to find it before we all went up in smoke. Then, having done so and extinguished it, he held a hand out to me pleadingly.

"Sunny, won't you come and sit by me, let me hold you?"

I shook my head and pointed at the bed.

"No, Nicky, I need to ring for the maids now, despite the lateness of the hour, and have them come to change the sheets. Look, you have spilled ash all over them and I am sure they have been burned somewhere."

He nodded sadly and sat up on the edge of the bed, looking down at his feet.

"Yes, you are right as always, darling. I have made quite a mess of things, haven't I?" When I didn't answer he went on in a broken voice. "How is Tatiana? She seemed so upset. I'm sorry, I couldn't comfort her. It was all so dreadful."

I started to ring for Maria to send in the maids to change the bed, but I thought I had better wait for a moment. Instead, I rose and poured Nicky a draught from a wine decanter that we kept in our cabin as he had forgotten my brandy.

"Nicky darling, please, I must hear it all. You will feel better when you tell me."

He looked at me blankly. With a shaking hand, he raised the glass I had poured him and drained it in one gulp, gesturing weakly for more. Wordlessly I poured him another glass. I was beginning to wish that I hadn't sent for him at all. I had never seen him like this. He looked for all the world as though it were he, and not poor Mr. Stolypin, who had been shot. He was dead white and his eyes had sunk back into his face, and it appeared as if a hundred new wrinkles had scored themselves into his flesh.

I shook myself – superstition, dim light, that was all it was. No one could age overnight.

Trying to speak both briskly and calmly, I asked him again, "Just tell me from the beginning what happened tonight, will you?"

He lit another cigarette off the embers of the last.

"Yes, of course, Alix, although there isn't much to say. We were in our box. The band began to play 'God Save the Tsar.' There was a small scuffle below us in the main theatre, but I didn't notice what it was because people had begun to stand up and look up at our box, as they always do when the anthem is played ..." He stopped and stared at his hands.

I prompted him. "Nicky, is he dead?"

He shook his head.

"No, not yet, but he is suffering terribly his doctors tell me. I am sure he will be soon. The scum, those miserable revolutionist scum, Alicky."

He buried his head against my shoulder as our daughter had done earlier. I clasped him to me. Through his muffled sobs I made out that at first no one had understood that Mr. Stolypin had been shot through the mass confusion. When they had realized what had happened, the girls had become hysterical and Nicky had had them wait with Minnie, Xenia and Sandro while he tried to follow Stolypin and the doctors, but they had stopped him.

That detail arrested me.

"They stopped you, darling? Who would dare to stop you?"

He looked away as though ashamed to meet my eyes.

"Madame Stolypin, Alicky. She said terrible things. I know she didn't mean them, the poor woman, she was so distressed. They have been a very happy couple, a happy family. That is why she said what she said."

His voice broke again. I felt most awfully for the Stolypins, of course I did, and yet …

"What exactly did she say, Nicky?"

He shrugged.

"You are right as always, darling. I have made quite a mess of things, haven't I?" When I didn't answer, he added, "How is Tatiana? She seemed so upset. I'm sorry I couldn't comfort her, but it was all so dreadful."

"Tell me."

He sighed grievously and without emotion described what Mrs. Stolypin had said. "She was upset, Alix. She was screaming and crying – terribly, terribly upset. Anyone could see it was a fatal wound. She didn't want me near him because she blamed me, blamed us for what had happened. She said that we had sent Father Grigory after him yesterday. She said –"

"How dared she?"

"… She said that it was his service to us that had wounded her children in 1905. That we'd nearly killed him in our service then and that now at last we had succeeded."

"No more!" I commanded him. "I don't want to hear another word of whatever she said. She must have run mad with grief."

Implacably, he finished.

"She said you in particular hated him, hated him because your Father Grigory hated him. She said … she said you would be glad that he was going to die. Are you, Alicky? Are you glad? Was she right?"

I was so stunned by his question I could only gape at him.

He whispered it again. *"Is it true?"*

"Why would you…?" I started. "How could you even say that? How could you ask me that?"

He stood up and paced around the cabin, irritated by its small confines, and I felt a moment of violent dislike for him as I watched. At one moment I even wished I could toss him bodily into the sea, but I bit my lip and drew a deep calming breath. He was upset, we all were, I was … but he and the girls had seen a man being mortally wounded in front of their eyes and I needed to be the one to remain in control of myself.

Chapter 26

The assassination of Stolypin had indeed been a tragedy, but not one that needed to have a damaging effect on our family or on our dynasty. However, Nicky was so shattered by events that the messenger who came to inform him that Stolypin had finally died from his wounds found his Emperor barely able even to raise his eyes to receive him.

I felt that it was better for all of us if we carried on as we had planned, and so without even consulting Nicky, which would have been useless in his present condition, I summoned the captain and gave him orders for our immediate departure to Livadia.

Minnie and Xenia and Sandro were caught unawares by my decision. In fact, Minnie was closeted onboard with Nicky, discussing Stolypin's death, when the anchors were weighed, and she came flying out onto the deck looking like a mad crow in her black gown, nearly knocking us all over as we stood there.

"Alix, what in the name of Heaven do you think you are about?"

I looked down at her calmly. For once she seemed to me to be a silly woman, small and insignificant. I was in control here.

"We are leaving for Livadia as planned, Minnie," I replied with a small laugh, "and if you don't hurry, you may find yourself sailing off with us. Xenia and Sandro will be wondering where you are."

Her face grew purple.

"Alix, the Prime Minister of Russia has been murdered. Our family will follow the fleet to Saint Petersburg to attend his funeral and to show our proper grief and respect."

I shook my head.

"No, Minnie, that we shall not do. It would be far too dangerous for us to return to Petersburg now. Who knows what those beasts have in store for Nicky, or for any of us for that matter? We are proceeding, as planned, to Livadia, where we will celebrate your granddaughter's birthday. I am deeply sorry for the plight of Madame Stolypin and her children, but putting our own family at risk will not lessen her grief or that of the nation. Now, are you planning to accompany us or do you prefer to follow us on The Polar Star, for it seems we are nearly underway."

It was quite a comical scene. Minnie was so seldom lost for words and here she was almost entirely at sea, if I may make a pun, for what she should do next. Would she push past me and try to raise Nicky from his apathetic shock in order to convince him to countermand my orders, or should she return to her own yacht?

With most unregal haste and a last spiteful look at me, she moved toward the waiting tender, which in retrospect was a shame. In my fantasies she could have accompanied Nicky over the side. She would barely have made a splash.

"I will see you again in Livadia, Alix. I see all too clearly that your wish to see Nicky's gift for you supersedes all else in this world. Let us all pray, Alix, that this choice of yours doesn't end all that you take for granted."

I didn't bother to answer her, but waited until she was safely in the tender and being rowed away before waving gaily at her and wishing her a safe journey.

Then we were off, and it was a bright and beautifully blue day. Nicky never even commented on my decision, but I could see from his happy demeanor at luncheon that I had indeed chosen wisely. His color was back and he ate heartily. He didn't say a word about Stolypin or his mama, and seemed so successfully to have put the entire sordid mess behind him that he was genuinely taken aback at the solemn demeanor of Olga and Tatiana. He even laughed heartily when Anastasia said that she thought that, now that Olga was going to turn sixteen, we should marry her, Tatiana and Maria off as quickly as possible so that she could have more space for herself.

"Mama and Papa, Alexei and I have been talking and we have decided we are the best of the whole lot of us, and I have decided to stay at home forever to keep house for him when he's Tsar. My piggish sisters have to go, and they'll need to do so soon before their intendeds find out what they're really like. All Olga does is read books and mope about. She practically never bathes. And Tati's so bossy that you'll have to find a deaf prince for her. And if Mashka gets any fatter," she blew a raspberry at Maria," "you'll have to marry her off to a very rich king who can afford to give her a thousand pastries a day. In all seriousness, you two must listen to me."

In the middle of our jollity, Olga interrupted our fun.

"Papa, Mr. Stolypin did die, didn't he?"

Her words fell like a stone into our merriment and my three youngest children stared at her in shock

Baby was the first to break the silence.

"What does Olga mean, Mama? What happened to Mr. Stolypin?"

I looked to Nicky for help, but as always received none. He was staring into his borscht as if he was hoping to find some answers there and wouldn't meet my eyes even as I kicked his ankle under the table. Anya stared at me, horrified, obviously eager to say something, but my warning glance silenced her.

Looking at Alexei, Anastasia and Maria who were seated across from me, but weighing my words for Olga and Tati, I said, "A few nights ago, darlings, at the theater where Papa took Olga and Tatiana, Mr. Stolypin met with a terrible accident, and although the doctors tried very hard to –"

"*An accident?* He was shot, Mama, shot right in front of us," Olga interjected, causing Tatiana to burst into sobs

Maria yelped, "Shot, Mama? Who would shoot Mr. Stolypin? Oh no!" whereupon Nicky stood up abruptly and left the room.

I watched him leave and turned to Maria.

"Darling, in this old world of ours there are many people – good people mostly, but some bad."

Anastasia took this opportunity to push poor Maria and announce, "Something you might have already noticed, Mashka, as we are followed around by dozens of soldiers and policemen everywhere we go, not that we go to many places beyond Tsarskoe Selo." She giggled at her wit and pushed at her sister again before turning to me. "The trouble with Mashka, Mama, is that whenever she sees a soldier, all she thinks about is marrying him and producing fifty babies as soon as she is as old as Olga. She probably doesn't realize that those soldiers are there to guard us."

Maria turned a violent shade of red, and knocking her chair over backwards as she stormed to her feet, she hastily followed her father out of the room.

I shook my head in disapproval at Nastinka for her naughtiness, but in truth I was quite relieved. She had managed to irritate her sisters, set her baby brother giggling, and seemingly put to rest the topic of poor dead Mr. Stolypin, or so I was hoping before Tatiana said quietly, "Please go on, Mama. What were you saying about bad people?"

I shrugged, wanting the topic to be behind all of us, so maybe I was less reassuring than I meant to be when I replied.

"Yes, Tati, exactly. There are some very bad people, always angry about this or that. It is no use worrying about them, for as your terrible little sister said, we are surrounded and protected at all times and nothing will ever happen to any of us."

"But, Mama," Olga protested, "it happened to Mr. Stolypin right in front of us. It could so easily have been Papa who was killed instead, if the man with the gun had only pointed it in Papa's direction."

I saw that Olga was scaring Alexei, and that even my fearless Nastinka was looking decidedly nervous, so I became rather irritable I regret to say.

"Enough, my big pair. You are scaring the little ones and there is no reason for that. We are protected both here on earth by our brave soldiers and policeman, and by Him," I pointed above our heads, "by God Himself

296

who chose your papa to be the Tsar. He will not let any harm befall his anointed one, which is Papa now and will be Alexei after him."

Then Anastasia made us all laugh by rolling her eyes and observing, "You should tell that to all those policemen who follow us around, Mama. Tell them to go home and leave us to do what we want. God will look after us. There is nothing for them to do but get in the way."

I was pleased to see that my big pair was laughing just as heartily as Baby was at Nastinka's little joke and I sighed in pretend exasperation.

"You, little monkey, go off this minute and tell all our sailors outside what you have just said. See where it gets you."

At that, Nastinka scrambled off her chair, closely followed at a run by Alexei who needed to slow down. I raised an eyebrow in warning at Derevenko, his sailor, who was behind his chair, and didn't let out my breath until he nodded back and scooped Baby up under his arm, laughing, as he said, "Here, Alyoshka, I'll give you a ride and we'll overtake your sister on her way to the sailors."

Alexei shot him an angry look but didn't struggle, and as soon as they had gone I looked at my two oldest daughters and said seriously, "Darlings, before you go, I do want to say that Mama is so sorry that you had to see such a sad thing, but that is sometimes the lot of a woman, and both my girlies are going to be all grown up quite soon now. We women will know and see things in our lives that will break our hearts. We will live through them and we will get on with our lives holding our heads up high and our backs straight, for we are made of sterner things than men, although they believe otherwise. After all, we are the ones who bring life into the world despite all the pain we suffer and all the blood we shed doing it, and when it is all over we merely smile as though it were all quite easy."

"Is that why Papa left the room, Mama?" Olga asked, her blue eyes clear and direct. "Is that why he hasn't said anything to us about what happened, because he isn't as strong as you?"

I hesitated. Olga worshipped Nicky – all my girls did – although maybe in Tatiana's case there was sometimes a hesitation in her dealings with him, so I didn't know how honest I should be.

I looked at my big pair with all the pride any mother has for her children and knew that I sometimes saw all my babies as just that, babies. Yet Olga and Tatiana were nearly grown, and both tall and graceful, and gazing at them now I saw that they were also intelligent and sensitive observers of our family life and of the world around them. Maybe it was time to give them at least some partial truths instead of treating them the same way as my younger ones, as I was wont to do.

"Darlings, what I say to you about men, and about your papa in particular, is only something that I as your old mama think."

"What does that mean, Mama?" Tatiana asked.

I shook my head.

"I suppose it means that I don't know much about men. I knew my dear papa and he avoided trouble if he could, and your Uncle Ernie grew up but still remained a boy at heart, and then I married your darling papa, and Papa is –"

"… Is weak, is that what you are trying to say, Mama?" Olga's voice had begun to rise and her eyes were growing stormy. Tatiana, I noted, merely looked curious.

"No, Olga, that is not what I was going to say or ever would say. Your papa carries the whole of Russia on his shoulders, as did his papa before him, and as Alexei will after his time. That is a burden that no weak man could undertake and Papa is not weak. All I am saying is that he is a man and that I haven't known many men, but the ones that I have known all seem to me to be very much the same in one way, and that is that they … Well, you see, they have stronger backs than ours – you know how Papa is physically very strong – but their hearts … their hearts …" I could not think how to tell my girlies about the hearts of men, about their terrible fears, about their desire not to see what is so clear to us women. My voice trailed off in confusion.

"Mama, are you all right?" Tatiana, my sweet girl, asked. She was always thinking of me. Olga, on the other hand, simply stared at me with arched brows, waiting for me to reassure her of Nicky's invincibility.

I straightened my shoulders and smiled with what I hoped was a renewed air of confidence.

"Yes, Tati darling, Mama is fine. I am a bit tired from all the excitement and my heart is –"

"… Stronger than Papa's?" Olga interjected rudely.

I scowled at her.

"Interrupting isn't pretty, Olga, and nor is sarcasm. The sooner you learn these things, the happier you will be." I held her gaze until she lowered her eyes and offered me a mumbled apology. I nodded, satisfied. "As I was saying, my heart is a bit enlarged today, Number Two, I believe, but I shall be fine, I think … And now back to what I was trying to tell you girls …" I shook my head again. "I cannot quite remember what I wanted to say, but my point is this: A man, any man, is set above us by God's law, by man's law, and by their own physical strength. This sometimes leads them to feel that they are more invincible than they really are. That is where we ladies come in …" I glanced at the girls. Their faces were rapt, even Olga's. I continued. "No woman or girl wants to be the one to let a man know that he isn't quite as strong and as smart as he thinks he is, so we must play along a bit with how he sees himself, nod and look pleased at whatever he says, pretend not to notice when he is tired and upset. And always," I raised a finger, "this is the most important thing girls, so listen closely," their pretty heads nodded in unison. "always be as gay and happy as you can be when men are around, no matter how heavy your heart or thoughts are, for they rely on us in every way to bring sunshine to the darkness they carry within them on account of their God-given responsibilities. Whether you are married to an emperor or to a farmer, this is a true thing. If you do that, you will have a happy home and that is our God-given responsibility as women. Do you understand what Mama is trying to say, darlings?"

They nodded as if their little heads were on strings and Olga abruptly rose and came over and kissed my cheek heartily.

"It is why Papa always calls you Sunny. I understand now, Mama, and I'll try to be sunnier too."

I looked up at my pretty girly in gratitude.

"Thank you, my darling. I know it isn't always easy, but we do have to try, and remember there are rewards. I have been so lucky myself as a wife and mama, and one day, not too far away now and far too soon for me, my own girlies will be wives and mamas, and all that matters to me and your papa is that you be happy ones."

Tatiana came over and knelt beside me, wiping tears from her eyes.

"Mama, we love you so much. I never want to leave you."

I stroked her soft cheek and clasped Olga's hand with my other hand. I felt so blessed with their sweetness and faith in me, and surrounded by all that was best.

Wiping a sentimental tear of my own away, I gestured that they should help me rise, which they did. With a girly on each arm, I smiled brilliantly at them and said gaily, "Well, let us not worry about the future quite yet. It is a beautiful day and there is so much to look forward to right here and now, so let us go and spread some sunshine of our own onto your papa, shall we?"

They nodded enthusiastically and out we went to join Nicky and the little ones.

Nicky, seeing our beaming faces, came to us right away and my big Olga laughed at his enquiring look.

"Papa, Mama has just been explaining to us that you will open my birthday ball next week with a dance and that your partner will be me. I am terrified. If I misstep, what will everyone say, Grandmamma especially? She'll say you and Mama are raising savages instead of grand

301

duchesses!" She finished off her thought with a look of comic distress that made Nicky laugh aloud.

"We certainly cannot have that, can we?" He bowed at the waist and extended his hand to Olga, who grinned in delight and dropped to a curtsy.

Nicky shot me a grateful and loving look over her head, and grasping Olga's hands, pulled her up and half-dragged, half-danced her the length of the deck to shouts of delight from the other four.

Our morning's entertainment was completed when Maria grabbed one of our poor sailors and dragged him into an attempted waltz, being immediately joined by Baby and Anastasia. They all looked like happy savages indeed and my joy in the moment was completed when Tatiana sank down beside me into a deck chair and leaned over and whispered in my ear, "You are our miracle mama."

Chapter 27

That was a good year, a good fall, and a good winter as we stayed on at Livadia until nearly Christmas, so impossible was it to pull ourselves away from the miraculous dream palace that the architects and builders had wrought for us, that white palace shining on the hills overlooking the sea, the loggias and flowers, and the heavenly scents in every room.

Nicky had kept his old promise and built me a fairytale palace where I felt like a young princess again, and our love flowered with the vines that I had ordered to be twined around the columns so that it looked as though it had always been there, that it had grown up from the ground. Similarly, that summer and fall, our love, old and weather-tested as it was, felt refreshed and new again, like we had built ourselves a new palace in our hearts.

Olga, young and fair and flushed, and the first of our girls to be presented with the pearl and diamond necklaces that Nicky and I had commissioned for each of them, surely looked touched with the magic of it all at her sweet little ball. The night began with my feeling quite the old wife and mama as I watched my firstborn twirling about the floor in the arms of young officers, but ended in my own hubby's arms wherein I felt as young and beloved as if I were only a few years older than my own girly.

I think that Nicky and I shared the unspoken belief that if the summer and fall at Livadia could only continue, so would our happiness, but neither of us wanted to voice this sentiment out loud. Thus our return to Tsarskoe Selo was an unwelcome proposition for both of us, for there awaited the ministers and the crushing responsibilities we always lived under.

Olga merrily captured our unaired thoughts one day when she said, "In town we work, but here we live."

She was right, and of course for my little ones that feeling was underlined by Nicky and my more relaxed attitude toward lessons. We had brought the dear Monsieur Gillard and our English tutor Sidney Gibbs with us, but only smiled indulgently when those good men complained that the girls, and Baby in particular, wouldn't sit for their lessons for more than a moment without running off to engage themselves in some more rewarding pursuit.

That year, oh that year, was the first time that I felt that my son might be well forever. Naturally, he still had to be followed around closely by Derevenko and his assistant Nagorny, and I had spoken to them harshly, and many times, about their great responsibility of seeing to it that my son was always protected from the slightest injury, and yet also kept constantly amused, because when he wasn't he would tend to take mad chances and ended up getting hurt. Therefore I cannot know for certain whether it was their renewed dedication to their sacred responsibilities, or simply a result of good fortune, or maybe because at last my prayers were being heard the way Father Grigory's always had been, but he was well that year, healthier than he had been at any time since his birth. This wasn't a question of my deceiving myself with false hope; everyone who saw him commented on it. He couldn't play tennis, but he retrieved the balls at every game; he teased his sisters and the suite relentlessly; he became as brown as a berry; and he displayed the worst table manners any child not raised outside of a cave could have done, getting into the habit, of all things, of licking his plate after he had finished eating.

Nicky and I were appalled by this, but on the bright side he was eating so heartily that in the end we ignored his madcap ways, Nicky only commenting ruefully that, "I tremble for the Russian people under the coming reign of Alexei the Terrible," not that he mean it. We didn't care, because, for the first time in our precious one's little life, we were beginning to believe that he would indeed grow up to reach a healthy manhood and one day rule Russia.

There was one incident that fall that seemed quite funny to us. The newly appointed Prime Minister, Mr. Kokovstov, came to Livadia to see Nicky to present his first formal report. We both had great hopes for our new Prime Minister and I even roused myself to be up early on the morning of his arrival in order to greet him personally. He struck me initially as quite charming and I believe Nicky felt the same way about him.

Anyway, we were awaiting Nicky in the reception room, and he was chatting pleasantly with me about his journey, when Alexei came wandering in. He always liked to know where I was, and ignoring Mr. Kokovstov, for really he was quite shy, he came straight into my outstretched arms.

Mr. Kokovstov smiled at him and I returned his look with a proud smile of my own, for truly Alexei was the most beautiful of boys – tall, auburn-haired and straight-backed – so what mama would not have been proud of such a son?

Mr. Kokovstov said, "Ah, Your Majesty, what a treat for me – the heir," and to Alexei, who had turned his head at the sound of a new voice, he smiled widely and addressed himself to him with his hand held out. "Alexei Nikolaevich, I presume. I am Mr. Kokovstov, your father's new Prime Minister, and it is a great pleasure to make your acquaintance."

Alexei pulled back from my arms and moved in front of Mr. Kokovstov.

"When the heir to the Russian throne comes into the room, you must stand and bow," he said, sounding like his grandfather.

I stifled a laugh and said, "Alexei, don't be ridiculous. Mr. Kokovstov is a –"

"Do it now!" Alexei said fiercely, and before I could intervene again, Mr. Kokovstov stood up and did just as Alexei had ordered him while carrying an indecipherable expression on his face.

I felt a bit embarrassed but realized that our new Prime Minister had not been put out – rather he had gained an amusing story to tell others on his return to Petersburg – and I made a note to tell Nicky about it later because I knew he would laugh uproariously at our boy's high-handed antics.

Following this performance, Baby grinned happily and ran out of the room without another word, leaving us to shake our heads in wonderment. I considered apologizing to Mr. Kokovstov, but realized that Baby had in fact been correct, if not polite, in his actions. Nicky and I tried very hard to raise all of our children with excellent manners, and our suite and staff were always instructed to address the children by their names and not by their titles, but Baby knew he was different and no amount of shielding him could keep this fact from him. He was destined to lead a life surrounded by almost absurd levels of obsequiousness coming from everyone he encountered, so what was the point of teaching him to behave otherwise.

Mr. Kokovstov glanced furtively at his watch and at Nicky's closed door.

I said, "I am sure he will only be a moment or so more, Mr. Kokovstov. He is quite prompt with his appointments and I do apologize that you have been stuck here with me. I know you must have a great deal of business to conduct with His Majesty."

"Oh no, Your Majesty, it has been a great honor to have had the opportunity to speak to you. I must confess I feel rather nervous about seeing His Majesty this morning."

I cocked my head.

"Why is that, Mr. Kokovstov? Surely as Deputy Prime Minister you will have had many occasions to speak to him."

"Oh yes, I have met His Majesty, but always as an attaché to Mr. Stolypin." His voice caught a bit. "I know that I can never fill the shoes of a man like Peter Stolypin and I am sadly aware that His Majesty must think as much too. That is why I –"

Agitated, I interrupted him.

"Mr. Kokovstov, you mustn't speak that way or even think it. You need to understand that if God takes someone from us it is because their time here has ended in order for them to make way for new people to serve Him, which is what you do by serving my husband. For the Tsar is God's anointed here on this earth and by helping him you help God."

He stared at me with the same opaque expression he had given Baby while being ordered about by him, one that I could not exactly make out and was not sure that I liked. However, before I could inquire as to what his thoughts might be, Jim, the Abyssinian who was accompanying us this summer, opened Nicky's study doors with a silent bow, at which Mr. Kokovstov leapt to his feet, bowed to me and vanished into Nicky's study.

I considered waiting for him to finish with Nicky because I wished to discuss Father Grigory with him. Stolypin had been unkind in word and deed to Father Grigory, which is probably why he was no longer with us, and I had hoped to let Mr. Kokovstov know that, to retain the confidence and faith of our family, he needed to understand that protecting Father Grigory was of paramount importance to us all. There again, maybe it was for the best that I did not do so, as it was Nicky's place to speak of it with him.

As I rose to return to my boudoir, which was pink here in Livadia instead of mauve, I wondered if Nicky would speak of it, for Nicky's true feelings for Father Grigory were also, to my distress, somewhat opaque themselves.

All good times must end, and usually sooner rather than later, but I fancy that year our return trip to Tsarskoe Selo was more silent and subdued than in previous times.

There was an early deep snow to greet us as the children sullenly scratched pictures of our new palace at Livadia into the frost on their bedroom windows. Only Anya seemed truly glad to be home, immediately taking up her accustomed busy social life again, running into town to see her parents, and meeting up with Father Grigory both there and at her home, where I was sometimes able to converse with him in the evenings.

I could see that something was troubling him, but he didn't say what it was, and nothing about Father Grigory's manner encouraged prying. Nicky accompanied me once or twice to Anya's house and I remember that one evening he went there with a terrible headache. These headaches were a recurring problem for him. Although he did not suffer from constant neuralgia and head pain as I did, he did get fearsome aches in the front of his head as a result of his being attacked with a sword during a long ago trip to Japan. Nicky wasn't one to complain but I always knew when he was having these incidents as his face would abruptly become gray and drawn and he would fall silent. This is what had happened that night at Anya's just as we were heating ourselves around her samovar.

I glanced curiously at Father Grigory who, as always, was watching Nicky carefully when he was present, and no sooner had Nicky rubbed his head than Father Grigory said quietly, "You are in pain tonight, Batushka. Your head hurts, doesn't it?"

Nicky looked at him tiredly.

"Yes, it does rather, Father Grigory," adding lightly, "I find that the weight of my crown is heavier on some days than others."

Father Grigory and Anya chortled loudly at this pronouncement as if it were the wittiest comment they had ever heard, while I merely smiled tightly, for it was an oft-repeated joke in our family, much like Nicky's birthday being the same as Job's. In point of fact I found it a bit self-pitying as I tried always to make a point of never complaining about the near-constant agony I suffered across my entire body.

Father Grigory, who rarely addressed my own illnesses with me – that night being no exception – then leapt suddenly to his feet, stared at the ceiling, closed his eyes, and made fists with his hands. Although the room was dimly lit and Anya's stove smoked abominably, I could see beads of sweat forming on his face.

We all remained silent and tense until his eyes shot open again to stare intently at Nicky as he shouted, "Headache begone!"

There was a moment of stunned silence and then Nicky said wonderingly, "Why, it is gone, Father. Alix, my headache is gone. How did you do that?"

"Not me, Batushka, never me. It is God who does these things."

In bed later that evening, Nicky was still puzzled as to how Father Grigory "managed such tricks."

Indignantly I responded, "They are hardly tricks, darling. Do you think a trick, as you say, could end Baby's bleeding or vanquish your headache just like that? It is that God works through him. Whatever His reason or purpose, that is the simple truth. And Nicky, if we fail to believe in him and his powers, then I fear that _"

310

Curiously, he asked me, "What, Sunny, what do you fear? That Alexei will die? Because, my darling, he might. We cannot live in denial of medical facts. We cannot lie to ourselves about that. It will be difficult —"

"Difficult? Is that all you can say about the death of my baby, that it will be difficult, that if I do not accept its inevitability, it will be all the worse for me?" I rose up on my knees and started speaking wildly, and yet I meant every word I screamed into his shocked face. "Let me tell you this, Nicky. If Alexei dies, I die. If he dies, it is because I have lost – or you have caused me to lose – Father Grigory who was sent by God to save our boy and our dynasty. If he dies, you will have killed him, and me, with your lack of faith."

He grabbed my flailing hands.

"Alix, no, stop it. Stop it! You don't know what you are saying. Here, I am going to ring for Dr. Boktkin," which he did. Then, clutching my hands again, he said, "You have said your piece and now I shall say mine. You do not love and value our boy one iota less than I do. You do not grieve or fear for him more than I do, for all your hysterical utterances."

"*Hysterical?* How dare you? Let go of me, Nicky. I'm warning you, I will have a heart attack right this instant if you don't let go of me and apologize to me for your cruel words."

I watched, astonished, as his whole body shook with rage. Nor did he let go of my hands and he was hurting me.

"You *are* hysterical and you will never hear me apologize to you for saying so. You want," he continued, anger flashing in his eyes, "to make it so that if

311

something happens to my son, my only son, Alix, it will be my fault because I didn't … oh, I don't know…" his face twisted with fury, "because I didn't kiss your crazy Father Grigory in a sufficiently reverential manner, or didn't use that filthy comb he gave you on my hair, or failed to walk backwards while reciting my constitutional oath. Or maybe it will be because one time I didn't enter my bath left foot first."

"He never said that," I spat back at him.

He actually laughed right into my face.

"Oh no, of course not – he is the very soul of reason, isn't he? But never mind, Alix, I'm not speaking of him, I am speaking of us and our son. And know this, if Alexei dies of his disease, the disease *you* gave him, I will not have been the one who killed him, but I will have to carry on with my life, and, yes, with loving you too, for I know of no other way to live. Can you say the same of yourself?"

"Er hum … Your Majesties, you called for me?" came the hushed and horrified question from poor Dr. Botkin who was standing in the doorway, the Abyssinians having let him in.

Nicky dropped my hands, stood up and brushed past Dr. Botkin without a word, adding over his shoulder, "I shall sleep in my dressing room tonight."

Poor Dr. Botkin couldn't seem to gather himself together to more than murmur a few words I could not understand, but at least his hands didn't shake as he filled and then emptied the needle into my arm with that blessed antidote to wakefulness.

Chapter 28

As if to underscore the horror of Nicky's ugly words to me, right after Christmas, during the earliest days of the year 1912, Father Grigory and I faced an attack the like of which nearly killed me and nearly put an end to my close friendship with him.

It seems that during the preceding year, poor Father Grigory was the victim of rank jealousy, not just in the filthy gossip-laden drawing rooms of Saint Petersburg, but also yet again within the one place that should have held him in reverence, the Church he so beautifully represented.

His one-time dear friend and admirer, a young monk named Iliodor, had inexplicably decided that Father Grigory was not a holy man, a *starets*, but instead a low, vile intriguer and opportunist. He had accompanied Father Grigory on a journey to Siberia and during that time something turned his love and admiration into hatred and envy.

I never found out exactly what occurred there, for events overtook us, but during the visit somehow Iliodor became aware of our family's letters and gifts to Father Grigory, which he stole from him, including a few items of clothing that I had embroidered for Father Grigory myself. Most of these objects were of little consequence, and Nicky and I could have defended him from it all, but the letters were a different matter.

He had taken my letters, and one in particular – a letter of faith and love to him, the one where I had written that I wanted to fall asleep forever in his arms.

Oh God help me, I could have died for the shame of it, and very nearly did.

That Father Grigory had kept this letter as though it were a trophy was bad enough, but that he had shown it to that little monster Iliodor and allowed it to be taken from him and given to a low, revolting publisher of a filthy rag of a newspaper – that I found hard to forgive.

It also damaged any hope we may have had for a good relationship with our new Prime Minister, Mr. Kokovstov, who requested an audience with Nicky right before the letters were published. Somehow, through his secret police, or through the offering of a bribe, or in whatever sordid manner ministers do their business, he had received one of the many copies of my letter that Iliodor had put into circulation, and, according to Nicky, he had begun his audience by wordlessly handing this letter over to Nicky for his inspection, whereupon Nicky uttered, "This is no forgery."

At this, Mr. Kokovstov had the sheer effrontery to launch himself into some sort of pompous diatribe about Father Grigory and the "danger" he represented for the prestige of the crown.

Nicky, still reeling from our last encounter with regard to Father Grigory, told me that he was most curt in his response to Kokovstov.

"I completely cut him off, Sunny. You would have been proud of me. I told him in no uncertain terms that the business of our family was not Russia's business, or his either for that matter, and I ordered him to hunt down every last copy of your letters and to see to it that they were not published."

I was pleased by his firmness, but completely unnerved by the prospect of their being seen by anyone with the means to buy a newspaper. Worse, all I could think of was Minnie's reaction. Still, Nicky had told Kokovstov to stop them being published and what else was this nondescript Prime Minister good for if he could not even do that?

I felt too ill that day from heart trouble – it was certainly a Number Three day for me – to do more than nod at Nicky's reassurances, which inevitably proved to be worthless, for the very next day my letters were published in a dozen newspapers stretching from Petersburg to Moscow.

The uproar was immediate and savage. First came Minnie, huffing heavily as though she had run all the way from town to see us instead of riding to us in her private train car.

"My God, what have you two done to all of us?"

Nicky, who always became utterly calm to the point of apathy in any crisis, smoked and looked at his mother inquiringly.

"Mama dear, don't you think you are exaggerating this a bit? Yes, it is a crime and a sin that my poor Alicky's private letters should have been exposed to the few hundred Russians who can actually read, and naturally I am sorry you have been upset by it all, but –"

"Nicky, you sound so foolish that I am ashamed to call you my son today. A few hundred Russians? Between a million and ten million of them would be more accurate."

"Mama, general education has hardly reached that many."

"Nicky, no one needs an education to speak to one another, and I assure you, my son, there is little else being discussed between your people today beyond the contents of that letter."

Nicky licked his lips nervously and lit another cigarette from the last, and one glance at his pale face showed me that I could expect little further help from him, as ever, during this interview.

Minnie shot him a sideways look and appeared to come to the same conclusion. Shoulders and head held high, she turned on me.

"Alix, tell me," she began with serpentine composure, "why would you, a married woman, reputedly a happily married woman," she looked at Nicky with one eyebrow raised, "write such squalid endearments to another man? *'To fall asleep forever in your arms'?"* She gave one of her charming, tinkling insincere laughs. "You must admit it creates a certain impression. It would all be strange and distasteful enough – the endearments, the clear physical longing that comes across in your little missive – but you are not simply some lovesick housewife pining the lonely hours away, are you, Alix? No, you are not indeed." She gestured around my beloved boudoir with a look of distaste. "All these so charming little cozy corners and, oh look, even a darning basket … Is that in case Nicky's socks need mending, Alix? Never mind, I have no interest in why you choose to behave as though you were an English housewife or a German *hausfrau* with your little hobbies and economies, for, whatever you tell yourself, and however much my son wishes it were otherwise, you are the Empress of one sixth of the world

316

and what you do, and now what you say, is of interest and of consequence to everyone, everywhere. You even were so indiscreet as to put your idiotic gushings into writing, lest there be any doubt as to their provenance. Why neither of you can understand the import of all this is frankly beyond me and indeed everyone else in Russian society and beyond. They will be behaving in no time like a pack of hyenas in London, Berlin and Paris, I do assure you, and sadly for me in Copenhagen too. You were not raised for this in your postage stamp-sized grand duchy, Alix, but you were, Nicky ..."

Nicky roused himself a bit.

"Mama, please, you know why. Can't you extend any kindness to us, to Alix?"

Minnie smiled thinly.

"When you say 'I know why,' I assume you are referring to my grandson's inherited illness, his so called 'English disease'. You mean why can't I believe that this filthy peasant charlatan is a healer of extraordinary powers, as you choose to do? Do you really, Nicky, do you really believe that?"

Nicky wouldn't meet my eyes or his mother's, and shrugging and puffing on his cigarette ceaselessly, he muttered, "If it makes Alix happy, Mama, I don't see why I should mind, or why anyone else should mind, for that matter."

"Happy?" I shrieked, feeling my mastery over myself beginning to slip. "Nicky, you know very well, and you should know, Minnie, that this is not a matter of my comfort, some little fad I have indulged myself in merely to exasperate you and to cause a scandal. This concerns my baby's life, our son's life – our son, your

grandson – who is heir to all of Russia. My God, what would you have me do, Minnie, you who are such the perfect mother yourself?"

Her eyes narrowed and she nearly hissed her next words at me.

"What does that mean, Alix?"

It was my turn to shrug and look away. Then, feeling a savage power suddenly arise within me, I turned to face her.

"Oh, nothing, I suppose, but you know even here in my little – how did you put it? – English housewife's life, my *hausfrau* existence, one hears things."

She glared at me.

"Oh yes, I can certainly believe that, from that fat, gossiping, creature Mrs. Vrouybova's little trips to town, I would assume. And what do you hear, Alix? I am all agog."

I had never thought to attack Minnie directly. I had spent seventeen years trying to hide from her or to recover from her onslaughts when my avoidance of her could not be sustained. Now I found I wanted to speak out at her and so I did.

First, though, in order to be as provocative toward her as possible, I yawned.

"I suppose poor Anya does get lonely and likes to take tea with lots of people, Minnie, but it is surely wrong of you to blame her for any of the gossip she passes back to me. She doesn't start any of it, after all. She merely takes it in and, being a confiding soul, tells me what she hears. And you can imagine that a little country mouse like me can hardly resist listening to it."

"Alix!" Nicky tried to interject, but I just smiled at him and continued speaking right into Minnie's reddening face.

"It is odd that you and I, Minnie, both have had exactly five children who have survived infancy, isn't it, Minnie? And as mamas, we always worry about our youngest ones the most, don't we?" I smiled angelically. "You say that I endanger the autocracy by my appreciation of the man who allows my son to live, but have you ever considered calling Father Grigory to visit you, Minnie, for maybe he could aid you in working out how to rid yourself of some of those who threaten your younger children."

Minnie drew herself up as high as she could in her chair, which wasn't exactly very high at all, while Nicky, conversely, was doing everything he could to shrink into his.

"One hears the most unfortunate stories from town about darling Misha and that terrible woman Natalia Wulfert. Twice divorced, I believe." I nodded. "Yes, that would be right. They say that Michael actually wants to marry the perfidious creature, and this of course," I sighed heavily, "isn't just gossip from my sad, fat friend, as you call her, Minnie, because Nicky has received a letter from his poor deluded brother asking for his permission to do just that. Naturally, Nicky turned down his request, didn't you, darling?"

Shocked, Minnie sat even more bolt upright in her chair.

"Is this true, Nicky? Did you receive such a letter from Misha and fail to tell me about it?" she barked.

319

Nicky twitched in his seat and appeared to be attempting to smoke two cigarettes simultaneously.

He muttered, "I was going to, Mama. I mean, it is true and I was planning to tell you about it."

"I am quite sure Nicky was planning to tell you all about it, Minnie, but your arrival caught us unawares, you see, so now I am telling you. This must be *such* a difficult time for you, what with the terrible tales of Sandro cavorting with some officer's wife in France, breaking poor Xenia's heart, and the scandal of dear Olga's marriage, and now this … your last son caught in the sleazy web of an adventuress."

Minnie stood up.

"I shall hear no more of your filth, Alix. It is quite evident to me that your sole defense of the wreckage that you are wreaking around our Imperial Family is to throw spadefuls of dirt at those whose actions you presume to judge but without understanding. I will concede that my children have made unfortunate marriages." Her voice hesitated a little as she continued. "In fact, there are days, during my prayers, when I thank Our Father for His wisdom in taking my darling George away from me while he was still young and unsullied by choices that might have destroyed all his happiness here on earth. Apparently none of my other children have been so lucky." Turning from my undoubtedly shocked face, she went over to Nicky and laid her hand on his shoulder. "Get up, my dear, and give your mother a kiss goodbye."

Nicky obeyed her with evident reluctance.

"Mama, I —"

Minnie put her hand to his cheek and smiled lovingly at him.

"It is all right, my son. Here ..." She touched her heart then his, and both their eyes filled with tears. "We are always one and always shall be. Don't believe for a moment that your mother doesn't understand everything, and I know that your father watches over us all."

Nicky pulled her into his arms and stared at me with resentment.

"Don't, Mama. Let us not talk about Papa now. I cannot bear it."

Nor could I bear to watch this vaudeville melodrama play out for another second, so rising heavily onto my aching legs I tottered painfully out of my own boudoir, my haven, and left them to put their final touches to their moving scene.

Chapter 29

The immediate aftermath of the publication of my letter to Father Grigory was that relations between the new Prime Minister Kokovstov and me were over. They also worsened between Nicky and him as well.

That did not immediately affect me, but Nicky's decision to send Father Grigory away did. I blame myself for this almost as much as I blamed Nicky. Father Grigory had called and sent notes to Tsarskoe Selo begging me for an audience, but I was angry, deeply so, at his carelessness and my subsequent humiliation, and I refused his calls and sent his letters back to him unopened. He pleaded with Anya when she went to see him in town and she in turn begged me to forgive him and to see him.

"Ach, Alix, if you could only see the state of him. Poor Father Grigory! He says he must speak to you and His Majesty to explain himself in person so that you will–"

I cut her off.

"Anya, it is of no use your discussing this with me and I forbid you to bring it up in front of His Majesty. Father Grigory has caused us no end of trouble, as you well know."

"He said you'd say that. He also said to tell you that your anger does not affect his devotion to you and His Majesty, and that when you need him, and you soon shall, he will be available to you."

Her words chilled me, but I didn't let that show, and I tried very hard not to become afraid for the future during that time. Baby's excellent health and high spirits continued and I hoped that maybe God had finally heard my prayers. Besides, Nicky was adamant on the subject of Father Grigory. Usually he was amenable to me and what was best for our children, Baby in particular, but there was also an immutable core of stubbornness in my usually sweet husband, and once he had hardened his heart toward something, it was difficult – not impossible, but difficult – to change his mind.

So Father Grigory made a very bad choice on the day he decided simply to show up at Tsarskoe Selo without our prior permission. I did not even find out that he had been here until Nicky told me later that he had come and been sent away, away from me, away even from Petersburg.

Before I could even begin to gather my wits together in the face of this momentously high-handed decision, Nicky shook his head at me and said, "There isn't a thing you can say to change my mind, Sunny. He has crossed the line and if I receive one more ministerial report about that man, I'll go mad, I tell you. I am in the middle of dealing with a rather disastrous mining strike in Lena, and we have to prepare to celebrate the Battle of Borodino, and I will not have it, I tell you. He has been sent back home and there he will stay."

"For how long, Nicky?" He shrugged and looked away. "For how long, Nicky?" I repeated. He met my eyes squarely this time, his beautiful blue eyes looking as cold as I imagine my own gray ones did.

"Until I say otherwise, Alix, and I shall say no more on the matter." Stunned, I began to gasp and clutched at my chest, but instead of rushing to my side or ringing for

Dr. Botkin, he lit a cigarette and said in a conversational tone, "My, my, Nicky, how worrying that strike sounds. Do tell me all about it, darling."

I was so surprised by this sardonic remark that I had to laugh, albeit reluctantly, and deciding to address the issue of Father Grigory later when Nicky was in a less aggressive mood, I obligingly lowered my hands from my chest and asked, with as much interest as I could muster, "All right, Nicky, since I ventured to asked," he returned my smile with gratitude, "please do tell me all about the Lena mining strike, whatever it is."

Rushing to my side, he covered my face with kisses before straightening, lighting another chain cigarette, and beginning to pace nervously around the room.

I resigned myself to listening to what would no doubt be a long and boring recitation of some tedious storm in a teacup, but he surprised me.

"Lena, my darling ignorama, is a town in Siberia along the Lena River, which is important as it is virtually made of gold."

I raised my eyebrows. "That sounds romantic, darling."

He laughed.

"Not so much romantic as financial, but the gold taken out of the ground there rivals that of any other mine in the world and it has attracted several important investors over time, old Witte being one of them," I frowned at his look of distaste, for I had never shared his hatred of the old statesman, "and Mama being another."

I winced.

"And so this river of gold makes even your very rich mama richer ... What is the problem then, Nicky, besides doubtlessly the greed that such an enterprise will inevitably attract?"

"Your remark about Mama aside, dearest, you must see that my position is difficult, for the miners are my subjects and, in addition, there are some important British investors. But now the two sides on this issue have fallen into grave disagreement and I may be forced to send in our soldiers to resolve their differences, because, in flagrant disobedience of their employers and of our stockholders, the miners have gone on strike and shut down production."

"Why?"

He shook his head in irritation.

"The usual nonsense. They want more money and a damned eight hour workday, the same as we were hearing from the factory workers back in 1905. Oh, and there is a scandalous rumor some of the filthy reds have begun about the food they eat. It has even been taken up in the Duma by some young loudmouth named Kerensky."

I frowned in sympathy but was curious about one thing.

"What scandal could there have been about the food?"

He blushed.

"I'm sure it is not true, darling, so I don't like to mention it."

"Well, now you have to say it because I am dying of curiosity."

He shuffled his feet and looked down.

"They say that they are being starved and that the little bit of food they are given is made from horse appendages."

I felt my own face redden with shock.

"What?"

He waved his hand.

"I am quite sure it is all nonsense and that some damned agitator has got to them and roused them all up into a frenzy. And, of course, the Duma, that nest of traitorous revolutionaries in the making, has taken up the cry. But the real problem is that they won't go back to work and a great deal of money is being lost."

I felt a sudden pang at the absence of Father Grigory with whom I would have liked to discuss this matter, guessing that his views might have been rather different.

"But Nicky, what if ... what if it were true that they were being forced to eat these ghastly things? Wouldn't that be just awful? And I suppose everyone always wants to be paid a bit more ..."

"They are asking for thirty percent more, Alix!"

"How much are they being paid now, then?"

He stared at me so aghast that he even forgot to smoke for a second.

"How in the world would I know that? The point is, Sunny, that I am certain they are being paid a very fair wage, and if they cannot manage their finances, their situation will hardly be improved by their not working and therefore by their not being paid at all, will it?" Before I could answer he continued. "If you think of it, by the very nature of this action, it shows they are probably being overpaid, for if they weren't, how could they afford to stop working. I certainly don't have the time or the money to take unscheduled holidays."

There was no answer I could give to that, as it was true that Nicky took his duties most seriously, even when we were aboard The Standart or at Livadia. Still, it seemed to me that he might be being a trifle unfair in his views toward the unfortunate miners and I tried to be tactful.

"What you say is true, darling, you do work very hard, but maybe the miners are sad because they have families too, and if they really are eating those things …" I blushed again. "Or maybe the food is just so terrible they just think that is what they are. Couldn't they be given a little bit more money, Nicky, for their wives' and their children's sakes."

Nicky waved his hand dismissively.

"I shouldn't discuss political matters with you, darling. There is far too much you do not understand."

"I understand that you sent away Father Grigory without so much as a by-your-leave, and you will say that that was a political matter too. Maybe it is," I went on quickly before he could interrupt. "So, you see, Nicky, as I am Empress and our baby is the Tsarevich, it might at times be difficult for me to separate the personal and the political. Nor should I have to."

He came over and planted a kiss on the top of my head.

"Sunny, you seem a bit overwrought. I had better leave you to rest. I will send up old Botkin, shall I?"

I looked at him in horror but he was already leaving, and so it was that by the time Dr. Botkin did arrive, my heart was indeed Number Three and I was fighting for breath. He, as always, clucked about me like a tiresome hen, but I did swallow the Veronal drops he had brought me.

Over the next few days it seemed that I was almost always swallowing Veronal drops as I read the newspapers that Maria brought to me at my request. I needed to read them despite the awfulness, for I wasn't speaking to Nicky.

The negotiations with the poor miners had broken down badly and the soldiers had been sent in to fire upon them when they refused to go back to work. The Russian newspapers did not mention a word of it, but the dreadful British rags were all over the matter. They said two hundred unarmed "starving and disheartened" miners had been shot during a peaceful demonstration. They went on to quote Nicky's Minister of the Interior, Makarov, who rather unwisely said, "It has always been this way in Russia and it always shall be."

I detested seeing my husband's government being criticized and I found their words hypocritical as well, since I knew from Nicky that some of the Lena shareholders were British, but I also thought that the use of bullets on unarmed men was a sin against God and remembered what had occurred during so-called "Bloody Sunday" back in 1905, leading me to shudder with superstitious dread.

However, there was one bright spot for me personally and for my son. All of this drama made Nicky come to his senses and allow Father Grigory back to remain by my side to comfort me during it all, as well as to pray to God to give me renewed strength to face the tedious and exhausting ceremonies scheduled for the celebration of the Battle of Borodino in the spring and summer.

Chapter 30

The Battle of Borodino was an incident from Russia and the Romanovs' glorious past, celebrated as a Russian victory that ended Napoleon's dominance in Europe. Long ago, as a wee girlie at dear Grandmamma's feet, I had been told all about it as it greatly amused her.

"You see, Alicky dear, the Russians have always claimed that they were the ones who stopped that dreadful man Napoleon Bonaparte in his tracks and saved all the rest of the world from being enslaved by him, which is quite wrong in fact and somewhat vainglorious of them to say so. It was not any special military genius on their part that defeated Napoleon, it was their great general, General Winter, who accomplished the deed!"

I hadn't been particularly interested in the story, but I had liked the name "General Winter," and so had asked Grandmamma if he had been as smart and brave a general as such a noble name implied.

She laughed and pinched my cheek.

"Darling Alicky, General Winter has always been a fine general indeed, the only decent general the Russians have ever had. We had Admiral Nelson and General Lord Wellington, of course ..."

I took the liberty of interrupting her as I had already heard far too much from her about the Great Admiral and the Great General and how they had soundly defeated England's traditional enemies, the French.

"Yes, Grandmama I know that Admiral Nelson and General Lord Wellington were the best of men and true heroes, but who was General Winter?"

She frowned at my comment, but unable to resist speaking of her other favorite subject, the general awfulness of Russia, she told me about General Winter.

"You are a caution, you are, my little one. You see, my Alicky, General Winter is not a person but a name they have given to their impossible weather. They had lost to Napoleon again and again – the Russian Tsar of the time, Alexander I, was a useless general but he did so insist on trying his hand at it – and Napoleon had made it all the way to Moscow and would, I suppose, have turned the whole of Russia into France, although why he would have wanted to do that escapes me. But once he had won everything and had Russia at his mercy, the terrible, dark, freezing cold of Russia defeated him and he had to lead his troops back home in a ruinous retreat that killed most of them, which, of course, was surely God's judgment upon him. And so, you see, to this very day, the Russians celebrate the Battle of Borodino in which, in their own minds, they defeated Europe's great enemy, and yet they did no such thing. But, I suppose, if one has to live in such a frozen wasteland, then one must seize what opportunities one can to find the good in it."

How her old voice rang out in my head now as I stared out of the windows of the small boudoir carriage on our private train. We would be in Moscow in a few hours to attend the ceremonies. Following up behind us in her own train was Minnie and her inevitable traveling companions, Sandro, Xenia and their seven children. More striking than their attendance, which was expected at the celebration of this glorious Romanov triumph, was the absence of Nicky's brother, Grand Duke Michael, and his little sister, Olga and her strange husband, for whether Minnie wanted to acknowledge it or not, her children were in great disarray.

The favorite couple of the nation, sweet Xenia and dashing Sandro, were, behind their public façade of unity, completely estranged. Sandro was keeping a mistress with whom he was madly in love in France, and, if the worst of the gossip Anya brought to me was to be believed, Xenia had become involved with the woman's husband. It was quite a sickening situation. I wondered if they would divorce and if so how Minnie would feel, especially after her words to me years previously when my poor brother had been divorced by the dreadful Ducky, that it was far preferable to die than to face the scandal of divorce.

Then there was Michael, the heir to the Russian throne after Alexei, who had a stubborn and even obsessive love for the twice-divorced Natalia Wulfert, who had gone so far as to bear him a son. Now Michael, the mildest-tempered and weakest member of our family, was so determined to marry her and to legitimize his bastard child that he had demanded Nicky's permission to do so, a demand that Nicky had refused out of hand. Michael had then taken himself and his fancy woman off on a tour of Europe in the hope that Nicky would eventually relent. So no, Michael was not to be with us at the Borodino celebrations and I couldn't say a word about it, for Nicky, who adored his younger brother, was nearly as desperate in his grief over the whole tragic affair as Minnie was.

I was actually quite sorry that Olga would not be joining us. I loved that sweet-natured, sturdy young woman almost as though she was my own daughter, and all of my children adored her as well. However, Olga had also got herself into a fight with Minnie, and Nicky had naturally taken his mama's side. Olga had been married at eighteen, against her wishes, to the drunken – and rumor had it, sodomite – Peter of Oldenburg, Minnie having forced this grim alliance onto the defenseless Olga so as to keep her close to her, and, to my mind, in a state of unrelenting unhappiness. Olga had been stuck in this distasteful marriage for over a decade now and had no children, and it seemed she had finally found her true love but with an ordinary officer. Hoping to end her sham of a marriage, she had approached Nicky for permission to divorce her useless husband and to marry her lieutenant.

I had urged Nicky to accede to her request. What could it matter? I said. She could never inherit the throne, no female could, unless every male Romanov was dead, and there were dozens of them. Why not? I asked. Yes, divorce was a sin, but there were greater ones, I argued, like selling innocent young girls into distasteful unions and depriving them of any chance at happiness.

I think Nicky would have given way because he loved Olga so much and did sympathize with her plight, and because I wanted it too, but then Minnie got to him and, as always, Nicky bowed before his mama's wishes. So Olga, in despair, and being a young woman of integrity, had in her turn refused to attend the ceremonies and to show unity where none existed.

Speaking of the which, as we drew into the station, I had already had to exhort a pouting Anya not to whisper even a word of our family scandals to anyone she might encounter during our stay there and to try her best not to let Ella upset her.

"If I can bear the trial of having to deal with my sister, you certainly can," I said.

Anya, sporting a ghastly purple taffeta ensemble that she had unwisely purchased for the occasion, grudgingly promised to do as I asked, "But only if she doesn't say anything nasty first."

Inwardly steeling myself for the tedious days ahead, I managed a smile as Nicky appeared in my compartment looking wonderfully handsome in his dress Colonel's uniform and offering me his arm with a smile and a bow.

"Your Majesty, my Sunny, are you ready to face the hordes?"

With a last worried glance in the mirror at my platter-sized new hat, I slowly rose and held out my hand to him.

"Into the breach, darling."

The station was a hot crowded mess of something like a hundred overdressed men and women, military and nobles, gathered to greet us and to stare at us. Ella was there too, accompanied by her great friend Zenaida Yusupov. Additionally, there were seemingly thousands of ordinary people standing behind the barricades to gawp at Nicky and me, but I never minded real Russians, and despite the jostling on the platform and the odious and disingenuous professions of loyalty and joy at our family's appearance, I heard only the comments and shouts of the nice Moscow residents over the mindless chatter of their betters.

"Look at the heir. Isn't he a beautiful boy? God bless his sweet face," I heard one say and I threw a look of loving pride at my son and managed to tilt my head around some princess' feathered hat and wave at those pinned behind the barricades. This gesture was greeted with a great shout of approval which turned my forced smile into a genuine one as I completed the ordeal of confronting the sycophancy and judgment our arrival had engendered from those assembled on the platform.

Later, back in our rooms at the Kremlin, I lay exhausted on the chaise in my boudoir, examining it with distaste. Long, long ago, when I had been a young uncertain bride, new to Russia and overwhelmed with all the novel sensations and responsibilities thrust upon me, I had allowed Ella, then a grand duchess, now a nun, to choose all the decorations and furnishings for Nicky and my apartments here. It was not a good decision on my part.

Ella must have consulted Minnie's book of bad taste when she chose the décor. It was all dark, heavy wood and tapestries. She even had my chaise reupholstered in a somber red with a gold stripe. That she had done this knowing that I liked only white wood, and light pink and mauve in a floral pattern, only went to show that she had retained her old feelings about me, that my wishes and opinions were not to be taken into account, that I was merely her silly younger sister and that she, Ella, knew best.

Now, eyeing her sitting across from me, I thought that it certainly wasn't I who was looking silly.

With many reservations about doing so, I had invited Ella and her peacock of a friend, Zenaida Yusupov, to take a small tea with Anya and me at the Kremlin, this despite my utter exhaustion after enduring the endless welcoming ceremony at the station. So there they sat, Zenaida Yusupov, a woman of preternatural beauty, with her raven hair and sapphire eyes, clad in a dress of silk so fine that it might have been spun by fairies, and beside her the oddity that was now my sister, Sister Ella.

Before Ella became a nun, she had rivaled Zenaida for grace and beauty, and one never noticed in those days how tall she was or how wide her shoulders were, not when she had been so slender and drooping in her elegant gowns, but now she resembled nothing so much as a large, gray bird of prey, and it was all I could do not to laugh.

I did laugh inwardly a bit as she and Anya exchanged barbed pleasantries. Ella inquired politely whether or not Anya had purchased her gown at an upholstery shop that she, Ella, had once frequented in Petersburg, and Anya returned the compliment by sweetly asking Ella if she walked into objects or got hit by them as, "you must not be able to see at all to either side of you in that enormous wimple you are obliged to wear."

The normally serene Zenaida appeared quite uncomfortable at the tone of their conversation, or maybe it was just that she felt that they were drawing attention away her, for she was clearly used to a great deal of attention, and unlike me, was the equal to it.

Feeling I was being somewhat lacking as a hostess, I inquired politely about her son Felix whom I had briefly seen on the station platform earlier.

"Tell me, Zenaida," I said, "what are your son's plans now that he has finished his studies at Oxford?"

Ella raised her eyebrows and Anya started in her seat, blushing terribly, for during our train journey to Moscow, Anya, inveterate gossip that she was, had shocked and entertained Nicky and me with scandalous and salacious tales of Zenaida's only living son who Anna claimed was a sodomite, while Nicky and I decided to withhold judgment on the matter as it was unfortunate, but true nonetheless, that Anya was rather obsessed with the existence of sodomites and the threat to common decency they posed, not least her former husband who had subsequently remarried and produced two sons.

Felix, who had inherited all of his mother's beauty and who would one day inherit all of her vast wealth, was a hard boy to get to the bottom of, one might say maliciously in this context. He was charming, terribly charming, and his manners were impeccable, but I saw a darkness in him. He had become great friends with Dmitri and had led him into all sorts of drunken scandals in Petersburg and even as far away as Paris. Indeed, he seemed to have no other purpose that I could see beyond the hedonistic pursuit of pleasure, but maybe I was being unfair to him as I had only met the boy on a few occasions, and seeing his mother's lovely face light up with pleasure at my question, I felt a stab of guilt. I was becoming as bad as Anya.

"Well, Your Majesty, Felix is taking a great deal of interest in the management of our estates, as is only natural and appropriate." She then sighed languidly as though she risked breathing her last at any moment,

337

which was a bit over-dramatic, I thought, considering that she was only Ella's age. Thereafter she roused herself a bit and threw a small smile in Ella's direction. "I suppose he might be thinking of marrying soon," she said and stopped, this despite my clearly interested expression and Anya's excited rustling in her chair which drew irritated glances from both of my guests.

I threw Anya a warning look and she subsided, but I wasn't really annoyed. She obviously had picked up more news about Felix while in Moscow and was struggling with the almost overwhelming temptation to spill some beans. For my part, I was hoping to keep the conversation focused on Felix for as long as possible to prevent Ella somehow raising the topic of Father Grigory. However, as Zenaida had clearly already said as much about Felix as she was ever going to, I decide to switch the conversation over to Ella's work in the convent. Better to bore us all silly than to be forced to defend my association with Father Grigory yet again.

Ella, unable to resist my bait, launched into a long diatribe about Moscow's poor and the hideous conditions they had to contend with until her friend grew pale and Anya seemed to be on the point of nodding off.

When, mercifully, Ella and Zenaida had departed, Anya informed me that the object of young Felix's interest was none other than Xenia and Sandro's beautiful only daughter Irinia. I passed this news on to Nicky as he yawned and climbed into bed beside me.

He frowned in disapproval.

"Yes, I had heard that. Sandro would be mad to let such an alliance move forward. Do you think we need to discuss this with him and Xenia?"

338

I giggled.

"No, sweet one, I think when they heard that we got the rumor from Anya, they would dismiss it as being another of Anya's little idiocies. I suspect that Anya is a taste that your sister has yet to acquire."

Nicky cuddled up to my side.

"I suppose not, but there have been many other stories about Felix and from much more reliable sources. Count Fredericks mentioned that Felix's escapades gained him quite a bit of attention in England. Did you hear the one involving Cousin Bertie?"

"No, tell me!"

Nicky lit a cigarette and grinned mischievously.

"Well, it seems that young Felix has an unfortunate tendency to dress up like a woman, which is possibly where Anya's stories got started, and that as a woman he is just as beautiful as he is as a man." He fluttered his eyelashes at me and stroked his beard. "I say, Sunny, do you think I would make a pretty woman too?"

I hit him with a pillow and held out my hands menacingly.

"Nicky if you don't tell me all about it right now, I will tickle it out of you and I'll hide all your cigarettes into the bargain."

He didn't look very alarmed but continued with his story anyway.

"Well, all right, I'll tell you, but it isn't a nice story, except for the part about Felix, I mean. Apparently Felix was looking particularly appealing in the role of a woman when he appeared at Whites one evening." He licked his lips in pretended lust and I glared at him until he resumed speaking. "So there was Felix, looking quite the thing, and in came the King, and we all know Bertie likes a beautiful woman. Of course, this is all a rumor and may not have happened at all, but what Fredericks told me is that Bertie asked that the attractive young stranger be brought to him for a dance, and dance they did, and then …" He stopped to gauge my interest, which was considerable, and laughingly finished his tale. "Then he tried to kiss him and Felix fled."

I was utterly shocked.

"Good Heavens, Nicky, do you think Bertie found out who it was? What a humiliation! And having heard that, I think you had better tell Sandro right away before this goes any further." I giggled. "I can hardly wait to tell Anya."

Nicky shook his head.

"I doubt anyone has plucked up the courage to explain what really happened to Bertie yet, and as for Sandro and Xenia, I think I shall leave them to find out for themselves. I do not wish to be the one to open up any of Pandora's boxes just at this minute. There is far too much scandal flying around this family as it is. But don't worry too much, darling. I promise that if this thing gets at all serious, and I cannot imagine it will – after all, Irinia is a sensible girl – naturally I shall speak up about it, and they will require my permission to marry in any case."

It was all yet another burden on Nicky, who was already so tired and with another dedication ceremony to get through in the morning before we were able to leave Moscow. Looking at the bags under his eyes, I was glad that I had agreed to a change in our annual travel schedule. While I longed to see Livadia and my beautiful new shining white palace, I had agreed to our paying a visit to Nicky's old palaces in Poland, which he adored and I hated, so that he could hunt aurochs and relax a bit. Poland was so remote, and to my mind so gloomy and so boring as well, that none of Nicky's ministers would be traveling there with us. I didn't blame them, I didn't want to go there either, but it had been years since our last visit. In fact, my last trip to Poland, to the lodge at Spala, had ended with the death of my dear little niece, Ernie's only daughter, Elizabeth, so it was only natural that I had insisted that we avoid it in the intervening years. However, I had received the lovely news that my dear sister, Irene of Prussia, would meet us there, and it was the prospect of seeing her that changed my mind.

I had not actually seen Irene in many years either, although we had stayed in very close touch through our frequent letters to each other, but even so I had been surprised when she had accepted my invitation. She had two sons who suffered from the English disease, like Baby, and was seldom in a position to travel. My anticipation of a fortnight or so of her dear company alleviated my dread of the dark forests and miserable palaces of Poland, and, after all, we would be in Livadia by mid-October and all good marriages are based on compromise.

Having thus reassured myself that all this was for the best, I kissed Nicky good night and quickly fell asleep myself.

Chapter 31

It began as so many ill-omened stories do – innocently.

We arrived in Poland by train and traveled to the imperial hunting lodge of Byelovyezh in pretty little carriages. The lodge was a fairly new one in that it had been built on the orders of Nicky's papa and was only finished in the late summer of that fateful year of 1894, the last year of his life. In fact, the poor Emperor was already suffering greatly from the disease that would eventually kill him and had been advised to travel to Corfu for a long, sunny rest, but that core of stubbornness that resided in my own Nicky was an iron one in the case of his papa, and so in the August he had arrived in Poland with his family to visit his new lodge there in total disregard of the urgent advice of his doctors.

The building he had ordered was to my mind an odd one, although to me all of Poland, and any enjoyment one would be likely to find there, was odd. All there seemed to be were endlessly depressing forests, a breed of noble animals called aurochs that were bred and born in those forests to be hunted down and killed as sport for the aristocracy, and bizarre-looking dwellings that the Romanovs referred to as palaces, presumably because they belonged to them.

Of the two palaces, I preferred Byelovyezh to Spala. At least Byelovyezh was relatively new and had a decent dining room, even if it was still impossibly murky due to the encroachment of the surrounding forest. Also, unlike Spala, I had never experienced any greater tragedy there than boredom. Nicky and the children loved it, though. To them, the forest was a mystical place with fairy rings of mushrooms, and for Nastinka it provided a thousand trees to climb, or to hide behind, or to jump out from at people. We had both M. Gilliard and Mr. Gibbes with us, and with their unquenchably sweet optimism they attempted to take advantage of the forest to interest the children in the natural sciences, and may have succeed in the case of Olga and Tatiana, while my pretty, and increasingly stout, Maria confined herself to wandering around the forest dreaming of the life of a fairytale princess that might one day come her way. The natural sciences were far too prosaic for her.

However, this place held the greatest joy for Nicky, for it was stocked, and had been from time out of mind, with the beautiful auroch, a proud, stately creature that resembled a large caribou. Nicky, who disliked most forms of hunting, and especially the hunting of grouse in England, for he was not much of a shot, if the truth be told, very much enjoyed hunting aurochs because it was virtually impossible to miss them. The procedure was that a decent marksman among his entourage would shoot the first one, a young auroch, knowing that the rest of the aurochs in the vicinity would, as was their custom, gather around the stricken one in order to grieve its loss, whereupon Nicky and his guests would pop up from out of the bushes and massacre the lot of them from point-blank range. Then, as evening fell, they would invite me to inspect by torchlight the carcasses of their tragic, sad-eyed prey and wait for me to voice my admiration for their skills in wiping out so many of them, something I could no longer bear to do as I found the whole scene utterly reprehensible.

The Byelovyezh Palace also housed "the bath," a huge, sunken swimming bath that Nicky's papa had ordered to be constructed in his new hunting lodge. It was somewhat out of keeping with his character that he should have done so, for nothing I had ever heard about him had ever indicated that he had a love of leisure or self-indulgence, but maybe I was wrong, for the swimming bath did exist and Nicky had told me that, from the first moment he had seen it here, he had been determined to have one just like it installed in every residence he lived in, with the result that we had replicas of it at the Winter Palace, in Tsarskoe Selo, at Peterhof and at Livadia, as well as the original one here at Byelovyezh.

At home in Tsarskoe Selo, Nicky's swimming bath was a thing of wonder and excitement for the children, who begged to use it as a special treat, but were seldom allowed to do so. Nicky was a profoundly jealous of his indoor swimming pool and kept a team of two servants with him at all times just to clean it after each use; others using it, even the children, upset him.

It was only natural, then, that Baby, while exploring the lodge, was delighted to come across one of these special baths all the way out here in the remote forests of Poland. His sailor, Derevenko, was with him at the time, so how this particular misfortune happened I really do not understand. Derevenko's explanation was that, on seeing his papa's swimming bath, and before Derevenko even knew what was happening, Baby said he wanted to show him how the sailors on The Standart jumped into the sea, and then, without warning, hurled himself into the empty bath, falling onto his side and twisting his foot.

Derevenko said he didn't cry out or admit that he was hurt. What Alexei did say was, "Please, Derevenko, don't tell Mama," then he fainted.

I knew from the moment I heard about this mishap that Alexei was going to be very ill, and it was made so much worse because both Baby and I had enjoyed only his good health and his high spirits for such a long time. Yet this brutal disease gives no hope and no quarter either, and within an hour his beautiful little face was a ghostly white and his large eyes were ringed by circles. He tried so hard to be brave, but the swelling began, and the blood became trapped in his groin, and his leg drew up, and then there was nothing left for him to do except scream out his agony.

I stayed with him for every moment of his sickness while Nicky came in and out of his room with the girls, Nicky's forehead creased with worry and the girlies' sweet faces taut with sympathy and love. Dr. Botkin could only wring his hands over the fact that he was unable to do anything for Baby – either to get him well or to relieve his pain – although he did caution me pointlessly not to overtire myself when I was already too exhausted and frightened to do more than wave him away.

Nothing, nothing, eased Baby's pain, but he wanted me, always me, just me, and there were moments there in which I hated myself so much and wished that my sore legs could carry me away from his bedside. I wanted to escape into the forest and see trees and sky and not his tiny twisted face and agonized eyes, eyes that I felt were not just pleading with me for help but were also accusing me of being responsible for what was happening to him. *Why, Mama, why did you subject me to all this?* It wasn't true, of course, but sometimes, as I explained to my sister Irene, I was possibly the only person alive who could truly understand what he was going through.

"Sometimes a thing is true even when it is not," I explained.

Irene stayed alongside us in that terrible room, neither flinching nor hiding, rising exhausted from this excruciating vigil each evening to get dressed and head downstairs to play hostess for Nicky's guests. She understood all and was as much a comfort to me as I hope I was to my agonized little boy.

On the third day he opened his eyes and only moaned slightly – no screams, no pleading.

"Mama, what day is it?" he asked.

Kissing his forehead, which I noted was cooler, I said, "Friday, my agoo wee one. Why?"

My brave boy tried to smile for me.

"I don't hear the music outside, so I thought it must be Sunday. Where is the music, Mama?"

The precious little one was asking about the concerts that Nicky's cavalry played day and night while he was in residence. I had ordered them stopped as my aching head could no longer take the sound of them and I feared they might disturb Baby from his sleep, should he ever achieve that state of grace.

I smiled at him.

"I made them be quiet, darling."

"But Mama, I like to hear them."

I kissed every inch of his wan face until I was rewarded with a giggle.

"Then I shall ask Papa to make them play again. You are a true soldier's son, my angel."

After that he recovered. He was weak but he did manage to eat a bit and his spirits got better. He liked to have M. Gilliard come in and read to him, and Nicky felt that this was a sign that he was getting stronger, although Anya opined that his recovery could not be sustained without the presence of Father Grigory.

The girls began to resume their daily wanderings again and two weeks after our arrival at Byelovyezh, Alexei was well enough to be carried out by a large Cossack to our train which was heading for our next stop at Spala.

Chapter 32

Spala seemed to be crouching there ominously at the edge of the great forest, waiting for us. How I hated that place.

The palace comprised two buildings, the moldering, old wooden one that housed our family, and a much newer building next to it that resembled a small European hotel, which is where our suite and upper servants would be quartered.

Once there, we were doomed to wander about its damp halls in such murkiness that the electric lights had to be kept burning all day and in every room for us to be able to see what we were doing.

Irene, Anya and I found ourselves huddled over tea, draped in shawls, despite Maria having ordered up fires for us in each of our rooms. Maria told me later that the language of the Polish servants was entirely incomprehensible to her and that they spoke very little Russian, so she was never confident that any of her orders would ever be obeyed.

Irene created a lighter moment by saying, "Alicky, just think how much dearest Grandmamma would have loved this place. It is impossibly damp and terribly cold, cold enough even for her, I think."

We laughed merrily as Anya smiled at us, puzzled, wanting to participate in the joke but not understanding it.

Irene, who was always kind, patiently explained to her Grandmamma's lifelong belief in the healthy benefits of being half-frozen and her face brightened as she exclaimed, "Oh, she would have liked my little house so much. Their Majesties and I are always so cold there that we have to sit on our feet!"

Irene and I laughed appreciatively and agreed that Grandmamma would indeed have enjoyed that. I am glad we had that moment; it is the only one I can remember fondly amid the literal and figurative darkness.

Baby was still pale from his ordeal at Byelovyezh and insufficiently well to join his sisters on their forest romps, and I found him sitting by the window of his bedroom, hunched like a little old man in his chair, staring sadly out at a world he could not join.

It broke my heart, and kissing his head, I said brightly, "Baby, would you like to go out on a little ride with your old mama and Auntie Irene and Anya, to see if we can spot any forest creatures? You wouldn't know it, but I think it is quite a nice day out there, once we escape the forest."

His small face lit up.

"Oh, Mama, I'd like it so much. Can we really go out?"

"Of course we can, my precious. I will just go tell them to bring round the pony and trap. Derevenko can help you get dressed. All right?"

He nodded happily.

As it happened, Irene said she didn't want to come as she was in the middle of "a monstrous pile of unanswered correspondence," but Anya was of course eager for anything, and so the three of us set off on our little journey.

It was indeed a glorious day once we were on the wide, sandy road that ran through the forest and around the estate. The sky was a deep blue and the scent of pine was heavenly. We three smiled at each other, well satisfied with our little escape, and I was just beginning to tell Anya how it appeared that we would be leaving for Livadia within the week and that I hoped Irene would be able to accompany us there, when Baby let out a small moan.

We both looked up in alarm. His face was gray and his head had fallen back against the cushions, and he seemed to be losing consciousness. I ordered the coachman to turn around and make haste back to Spala, but every tiny jolt caused Baby agony and his moans soon turned into screams.

Anya yelped that we needed to go slower but I was afraid of Baby losing all consciousness. If I close my eyes, I can believe that that ride lasted my whole lifetime.

When we at last reached the palace, Baby was carried up to his room, now very much awake and screaming horribly. Botkin was summoned but could only clutch his hands as Baby's screams mounted in intensity.

It had begun – my road to Calgary.

I could speak at length of this time, a period that lasted eleven days in total before, in complete desperation and without telling Nicky, I sent a telegram to Father Grigory. Until then, Baby only stopped screaming when he passed out. The others – the servants, Nicky, the girls, all of them – stuffed cotton batting into their ears so as not to have to hear those horrendous and interminable screams. Not me. I heard every scream, every moan and every whimper. He slept, if one can call it that, only intermittently. I bathed only twice during the whole of that time, when my dear Irene took my place, for only she could bear to watch it all up close as I did.

It is odd what happens to one when one is deprived of sleep. It creates a form of madness, they say, a fact to which I can attest. All that existed for me during that time were Baby and me, the smell of sweat – mine – the smell of urine and vomit – his – and at times I fancied I could smell blood, but I suppose that wasn't true. He would allow no one to touch him and we could only change his sheets when he was unconscious. His leg drew up to nearly under his knee. He never let go of my hand, and when he could speak at all, he begged me for help, help I couldn't give. We were both mad in that room. I wish it could have been burned to the ground and salted afterward. His fever reached terrifying heights, and even without the sad pronouncements of the Doctors Botkin and Derevenko (who had been drafted in from Petersburg), I knew my boy was dying.

He knew it too, for in a rare lucid moment, and looking far more tortured saint than nine year old boy, he said, "Mama, when I die it won't hurt anymore, will it?"

I shook my head unable to answer, unable to know what to pray for anymore. He took my nod as an assent and looked at me with an ancient's gaze.

"I know it won't. I dreamed it would stop. When you and Papa bury me, though, please put me somewhere where I can see the sun again, not in the forest, not here."

Nicky, who could barely bring himself to enter the room, and who left it sobbing each time, allowed himself to be persuaded to bring in a priest to give Baby his last rites. Baby seemed glad to see him, but I turned away. I do not mean to make it sound as though Nicky's cross was easier to bear than mine, and in many ways I think it might have been worse, for we had to hide it all; Baby's illness had to remain a secret. At least that was true up until the priest arrived, at which point a statement was issued in the bulletins announcing that the Tsarevich was gravely ill, and during that time Nicky had to preside over the hunts, and kill the aurochs, and watch their blood spill into the ground, wondering, I imagine, whether their blood represented the blood of his son, the very blood that was killing him slowly, the cursed blood of his mother, an expiation for our sullying the land with the innocent blood of the aurochs who, like our son, only wanted to live.

I do not know whether this is what he was thinking – no one does except Nicky, and God, and maybe Father Grigory, whose answer to my desperate cable came within the hour.

"The little one will not die. Do not let the doctors bother him too much," he said.

I told the doctors to leave Baby be, and when Nicky saw my radiant face, his burden must have become that much lighter, thinking that at least poor, exhausted, half-mad Alicky was enjoying a few moments of relief. Let her believe what she will, for tomorrow our son will die.

But Baby didn't die.

Father Grigory's telegram was all he needed and it was everything to me, for that night Baby slept, not in a faint but with the blessed healing sleep that Father Grigory had sent him from thousands of miles away.

From that night Baby began to recover, although I feared I might not. My heart was badly enlarged and my migraine had endured so long that, like my little boy, I had lost all memory of a world without pain. Yet I felt peace and, like Alexei, began to sleep again at night, and although our recovery took weeks and weeks, we were eventually brought home to Tsarskoe Selo for Christmas on a train that moved at less than ten miles per hour, sadder from the shock of it all but wiser too, for we understood, Baby and I, that the only source of our safety was Father Grigory. Yes, I think we were both purified and damaged by our shared ordeal, but we were also grateful, oh so grateful, to be together and securely away from that dark forest and the horrors it had brought down upon us.

Chapter 33

After that ordeal, nothing at Tsarskoe Selo was really the same, although it appeared unchanged. It was welcoming and beautiful as always, and masses of lilacs had been placed in my boudoir, as always, ordered by the trainload from our greenhouses at Livadia, the ones we had been unable to visit that year. The girls resumed their lessons, the servants' and the children's Christmas trees had been arranged by Count Fredericks, and Baby was back in his own rooms. Yet it was all somehow different.

Baby was so altered by Spala that I feared we would never get back our healthy, laughing boy. During his ordeal his leg had drawn up against his stomach and any attempt to straighten it, no matter how gentle, gave him terrible pain and made him scream out piteously, leading the doctors to fear that trying to straighten it would start the bleeding again.

Only Professor Fyoderov, a specialist who had joined us at Spala and accompanied us home on the train, was willing to give advice, his advice being that another specialist beside himself be brought in. I consulted with Father Grigory, who informed me that while his prayers had saved Baby's life and would continue to do so as long as we kept faith with him, fixing his leg was something he could not do.

"Mamushka, if God allowed a humble sinner like me to fix every broken branch on a tree or the wing of a sparrow, He would need many more like me and there aren't many like me to be found."

That was true enough and so I gave permission for Professor Wreden to be brought to Tsarskoe Selo. Baby liked him right away, which was a nice thing. The not-so-nice thing was that, unlike the previous "specialists," Professor Wreden suffered no doubts or fears about how to treat his illness and seemed to me to be positively reckless. He insisted that Baby's poor leg had to be placed in an atrocious metal brace straightaway, pompously addressing Nicky and me, while raising his voice constantly over Alexei's anguished sobs at the discomfort of the contraption, to declare that, "Your Majesties will forgive me, I hope, for speaking so frankly, but if the Tsarevich's leg is not corrected immediately – and this device, however unpleasant, will I assure you do that – then ..." He spread his hands out and trailed off.

It was Nicky who spoke next.

"Then what, Professor? Finish your speech. You have nothing to fear here from speaking frankly."

The Professor nodded and made a gesture toward Baby and then the hallway. We understood and followed him outside, where he continued in a grave tone.

"It is more than possible that if rigorous attention to the Tsarevich's leg is not applied, the child will be rendered permanently lame." I flinched and Nicky shuddered but he went on inexorably. "Given that he is your heir, I cannot in any conscience do less for him and for Your Majesties than to pursue this course of treatment to its completion."

He bowed his head and Nicky mumbled his appreciation and dismissed him.

Baby began to scream from his room behind us, "Take it off, take it off!"

That night I used all my remaining powers of persuasion to convince Nicky to send the good Professor away so that we could free Baby from that torturous device.

"I cannot bear it, Nicky, not one more day of it, not one more second of his begging. Can you bear it, after what he and I have been through? Will you be responsible if his crying starts a new round of bleeding or if I have another heart attack that kills me this time? If so, go ahead. I won't be here to see it."

After that I cried so terribly that Nicky summoned Dr. Botkin to tranquilize me. Meanwhile, he gave Professor Wreden an honorary position as a court physician and then dismissed him from serving our family. Nagorny, who was on duty with Baby that day, was instructed to remove the despised brace and maybe we could have all begun truly to recover after that but the Tercentenary ceremonies, with all their terrible duty and strain, bore down upon us, and, as always, there was to be no peace for me or mine.

The Tercentenary was to be a year-long celebration of the three hundred years of Romanov rule, from 1613 to 1913, and I had known about it for nearly as long as I had been in Russia. The approach of the glorious Tercentenary had been a common topic of conversation since the advent of the new century and was seen as an assurance of continuity – of the continuity of Nicky's rule and of Baby's thereafter, promising great good fortune for the country and furnishing undeniable proof of the might, power and endurance of the Romanov dynasty.

Years of planning, according to Count Fredericks and Nicky's loathsome ministers – particularly Father Grigory's enemy, the Prime Minister Kokovstov – had gone into preparing for the forthcoming celebrations. Hundreds of banners were to be erected throughout Petersburg and Moscow alone, displaying the Romanov double-eagle and the dates of the Romanov dynasty. There would be banquets and fêtes and balls, and accordingly all of Russia would enjoy itself so much that all discontent and grumbling would be banished for decades.

Nicky, though, had made some demands of his own. Instead of focusing solely on the cities, those hotbeds of discontent, he wished to reenact the journey of the first Romanov, Tsar Mikhail Romanov. We would, he decreed, make a pilgrimage to the towns of ancient Muscovite Russia to remind people of our long and glorious past and its mystical associations with the divine right of the tsars. The ministers were not pleased. What about the planned receptions in Petersburg and Moscow? His Majesty could not be seen to snub his own two greatest cities, could he?

Inevitably Nicky conceded. We would do both, he declared, and so, despite the state of my health, which had never been worse, and the horrible fact that Baby was still unable to straighten his leg, we would go on what, to my mind, was a never-ending parade to present ourselves to Russia as a model of the perfect family.

The goal of the jubilee was to revive the cult of the Tsar, to show our family's connection with the ancient past that must endure forever, to show that Russia belonged to Nicky and would belong to Baby after him, and that it must be so because the Tsar was the very embodiment of God on earth. The ceremonies would focus on reinforcing the feelings between the Father, the Batushka Tsar, and his worshipful Orthodox subjects, and everything was being done to make that possible. All symbols of the state were pushed into the background, and only Nicky, his forebears and his successor were to be seen and considered.

It did not begin well. The weather was dreadful, which came as no surprise, I suppose, for February in Russia, but how dispiriting were the soaked banners and overturned soggy food tables. Dignitaries from the entire empire, accompanied by high priests, were waiting to greet our family in Petersburg and hundreds of thousands of people came to see us, bringing the traffic to a standstill in a city decorated from top to bottom with ribbons and garlands and giant portraits of Nicky and of all his ancestors reaching back to Mikhail Romanov.

The ritual began at the Kazan Cathedral where a crowd holding icons stood in the icy rain for hours awaiting us for the solemn service of thanksgiving for our reign. The girls and I wore white despite the cold and tried not to shiver violently. The crowd, at first raucous, soon fell silent when it caught sight of Baby, pale and small and being carried into the cathedral in the arms of a giant Don Cossack.

I tried not to hear the whispers, but I could not avoid them.

"Why is the child being carried?"

"What is wrong with him?

"He looks so ill."

He had insisted on playing his part in it all and I had been too afraid of his reaction to say no. I should have said no, though, because the ripple of shock running through those who saw him was as palpable as the coldness that my appearance always engendered.

The Tercentenary dragged on and on. We traveled to Moscow, where the crowds were equally enormous, yet our reception was muted. However, in the small towns to which we traveled from the beginning of May, people's reactions were utterly different, showing innocent delight in our presence and great reverence toward Nicky as God's anointed on earth. It was so beautiful their love, their belief in us, and at times, as we sailed down rivers or rode by in our train, I saw them fall to their feet and kiss our very shadows.

I think we were all as cheered by the people's adoring response to us outside of the cities as we were by the arrival of the Russian springtime with its gloriously bright days. Then we made our way back to Moscow for the finale of the Tercentenary, where, after a resounding reception at the station, we stepped into carriages to head for the Kremlin, with the exception of Nicky who proceeded our carriages, riding sixty feet ahead of us and alone on his white horse. He looked magnificent and every inch the Tsar.

The crowds that day were even larger than they had been at our coronation and the decorations were superb, so much nicer than they had been in Petersburg six months earlier, but to be fair the weather was on our side, as everything else seemed to be as well. I had decided to ride in one carriage with my children so this time I heard only cheers, even more so than those that greeted Minnie's carriage, which, given her mean-spirited insistence on her rights as Dowager-Empress, preceded me.

The next day was the culmination of the Tercentenary. We rode in the same manner as the previous day to the Uspensky Cathedral. Baby had been resting and doing a bit better – he had even practiced putting a bit of weight on his bad leg – and I felt that the combination of my will and Father Grigory's prayers were at last proving to be more effective than the medications and solicitations of any doctor. At the Cathedral the plan was that Nicky would dismount from his horse at the start of the red carpet and the rest of us would leave our carriages and follow him for the hundred yards to the doors of the sacred space, but Alexei only made it a few yards before exclaiming in pain and starting to fall. A Cossack caught him up and carried him the rest of the way, but the crowd saw what had happened and made a collective exclamation of dismay. After that I had trouble keeping to my own feet, and indeed that night at the closing ball I fainted into Nicky's arms and had to be carried back to our rooms at the Kremlin.

Despite these humiliations, the Tercentenary celebrations had overall been a great success and we felt triumphant, bathed in the renewed love of our people and their belief in our God-given right to rein over them. Even the newspapers, those rags of discontent, were silenced and awed by the spectacle.

The spirit of Russia is incarnate in her Tsar. The Tsar stands to the people as their highest conception of the destiny and ideals of the nation.

"Darling, isn't that a nice thing to say?" Nicky trilled happily as he read this piece aloud to all of us in the train dining car as we returned to Tsarskoe Selo. I nodded and was about to profess my pride in him and my love for him, despite the presence of others, when Anya spoke first.

Grinning happily, she said, "It is all true and I saw and heard it all with my own eyes over and over again during our trip. Why, one young man who didn't know who I was," she made a comical face to illustrate how ridiculous that was while Nicky and I tried to stifle our mirth, "he said the best thing …"

"What was that, Anya," Nicky asked. "what was it he said, the best thing?"

Anya looked puzzled momentarily as though she had already forgotten what she had said, which with Anya was all too possible, then gathering herself, she spoke, her tone triumphant.

"He said three hundred years of Romanovs. Why not three hundred more? Then he started to cry, overcome with happiness. I felt the same."

Nicky's grin had died on his face and I looked at him curiously. Finally he smiled and raised his glass.

"Yes, that must have been it. Here's to him, then, and to us. Three hundred more years of Romanovs."

CPSIA information can be obtained
at www.ICGtesting.com
Printed in the USA
LVOW10s1435080817
544255LV00032B/552/P